The Distant Trees

Mary Ellen Wall

Printed in USA

ISBN: 1466495278
ISBN-13: 9781466495272

Library of Congress Control Number: 2012903659
CreateSpace Independent Publishing Platform
North Charleston, South Carolina

chapter 0

Going Away

Marta jerked herself conscious and nearly panicked when she banged her head on the rough-barked tree she leaned back on. In another second she began recognizing the swirling surroundings: the hardwoods, the starlings, the clovered grass, the Bursars' Office across the way with its heavy oaken door. Sticky with the thick Kentucky humidity and stifling early heat, her head refused to clear. This was no dream.

The Doberman. She'd practiced for weeks to get fast enough to shove her stolen knife into the dog's maw and *godverdomme*! In a single instant his fangs spattered her face with saliva as she scurried back backwards into the trash pile she'd been searching. He lunged, jaws wide - in went her boney arm but from the side not the front - only chance - thrust it in straight than angle straight up in one momentum-fraught motion - his teeth crunching her arm providing that last levered punch. He reared high and she couldn't let loose of the knife or unhook her flesh from his fangs so she stretched high on her toes, finally falling as he did.

Her gut roiled; the hurt was nothing compared with the punishment to come...

"Hey, you sick or something?"

1

The young man's concerned tenor pulled her back from the replay Not cold, bare ground. Warm grass and a hot breeze? *Fout*, school! She rolled to a sitting position on the grass and looked up though it hurt her eyes with the best smile she could manage. "Yeah, I shouldn't have eaten the left over pizza this morning. I'm okay, thanks."

A registration glitch for all the 2110 classes. She came up a day early to sort it out. The graduate scholarships and grants she depended on, right and truly flushed down the toilet.

Her head throbbed with the flashback residue and with reliving the humiliation of having 'unknown' pay codes, the memory of being escorting out making her nauseous again. Reaching for her pack, she tugged it closer by a strap and fished a drink out, didn't matter which since they all had mega-caffeine: brain cleaner.

Failure. Breathing as her Zen book recommended eased tensed muscles. She bet her snooty classmates hadn't had a glitch with their funding.

She imagined her Aunt Gretchen's reaction to the news, but Auntie didn't need to know all the details, never had.

"I couldn't find my advisor, I think they booted him out too, because his office was dark and his name was even off the door. Auntie, they said I had to clear out of the dorm by dinner and archived my meal card and student ID, everything! I thought they, well you know what I thought, that they were going to take me to prison or execute me in the quad or something."

"It sounds like they caught him in something dirty and some of the filth fell on you. Have you looked into the train schedules?"

Marta shook her head angrily, feeling more desperate by the moment. No call, no trusting the waves to reach her Auntie and no one else. She felt so heavy, so like a broken branch that lingered on the ground for years but never more to sway in the wind, never more to feel the tingle of photosynthesis in the sunlight. What she wouldn't give to be independent and not put up with this crap!

The old train would get her the hundred or so kilometers by midnight and she'd arrive smelling like goats. She stood shakily and brushed at her clothes.

Back at the farm, Auntie's sympathy would last two shakes and Marta would bear the derision for the failure in both subtle and overt ways until the end of time; she would never have any real authority. Even the grass stains on her jeans would acquire mythological status. The great work in the forest would be enough, though, wouldn't it? What of the inner whipping, her internal punishment for not living up to her mighty parent's expectations?

Marta paced between the oak and a nearby Acer Saccharum, sugar maple. The bottom line was money; she'd have to find a way to pay a full immigrant's tuition for the dozen required classes and fees. No way!

Papa would not have given up, she was not raised to give up, but here she was giving up! The vision of him sailing up to the little pier at her childhood home made her ache to get his advice. Now the fresh blood to her brain was working, yes, now she could find a quiet spot to work the problem like Papa had taught her.

Cutting across a green to get farther from foot traffic, she sat down beneath a shapely tulip poplar, her sentimental favorite, to make some plan to salvage herself a future, one that included independence and clout. Elbows at her side, she thrust her hands before her about half a meter apart like she was grasping a beach ball, with no ball, Papa's trick to help focus.

She envisioned a great knot of problems balled up together and labeled them, an immense root ball that seemed to be made of tensile steel and impossibly knotted. She gathered internal strength to force her hands together, her hands feeling the immense resistance of her problems between them and slowly, one by one, hidden ideas squirted out of the mass as if the pressure of her ordered will forced them up and out. She twisted strands and weeded out bogus elements; mental Reidemeister moves to simplify, to refine, to solve.

Holding her breath, she looked at the options. Only one had the power pay her way, and if it worked it would erase any stain from her advisor. She accepted the risk even as it dizzied her. Standing with effort, she decided it was time to put up or shut up.

Marta's DataMate student-economy grade tablet guided her to the humongous Patriot Office Building on Nashville Road, the largest structure in town, then further within to the Department of Defense offices, then finally the United States Expeditionary. Red-faced and drippy from the snail-slow overcrowded bus, her hand trembled as she thumbed the door pad. Walking in, she imagined a wave of calm descending through her from head to toe.

"Good afternoon," said the clean-cut young blond man behind the counter, "How can I help you today?" Large paddle fans suspended from the high ceiling stirred the air and played with the light filtering through the window shades, reminding her of the dappled shade of the forest, a good omen. Seeing there was no line to jostle her from behind, she smoothed the stray hair at her temples back and smiled the way she'd practiced for meeting important people, her calm holding so far.

Marta concentrated on flawless Midwestern American English cadence and intonation. No stray gutturals or odd conjunctions!

"Sir, I read that there are sometimes openings on Expeditionary voyages for civilians. I read on the school newsnet that there was perhaps an Expedition ship heading out to one of the candidate systems toward Cameleopardis; are any spots open now?" Spots! She felt moronic for saying that but refused to let it show.

They'd scanned the Immy chip in her shoulder as she walked into the building and were probably tracking her every move. Oh yes, there, the officer was glancing over to a display off to the side.

He reached for and twiddled a pencil, a real pencil with an eraser on the end. "The Giraffe trip is settled, but there was another slot that might be open that might not have shown up on the undergrad net. The colony supply ships, the Buses, right? Anyway, they don't normally go through Expeditionary Department; however I do happen to have an Exped request outstanding for some special deal on said Bus." He looked at her expectantly.

"That sounds very interesting. Can you look it up for me?" She smiled, he smiled, all good.

He laid the pencil aside and tapped his main screen a few more times. "This is it. It's a Scientific Aide spot for a week's work at an undisclosed destination prior to the colony stops. It's been active for 29 days and it looks like it's not going to be filled either. Not unless you have an advanced Life Science degree, have no criminal record and are willing to be the low person on the totem pole for at least fifteen months. Why would a scientist want to waste a year and a half like that?"

A stern looking stocky woman with severely pulled back black hair and an impeccably decorated uniform appeared behind him and stepped close to quietly look over his shoulder. Marta glanced at her nametag and chose to completely ignore Lieutenant Carvello. It occurred to her that she'd better answer his question. "Ah, does it entail an enlistment with the rights and credits?"

He nodded as if that was an acceptable response. "It says here that it's a limited Warrant slot; that's a four-year active reserve enlistment that gives you access to the Corps Stores, the FirstNet and pro-rated social duty credits for the duration of the transit, doubled for colony contact time." He tapped one spot decisively and the result seemed to genuinely surprise him. "Zow, you'd need to head out for orientation tonight too, this is almost closed out. The base pay is low, but the tour bonus is a nice bundle. Sound good?" He gave her a high school hero face and reached over the counter. "Let me scan it, please."

As expected, he officiously raised his eyebrows as he read 'Immigrant - Germany', tilting it so Carvello could see.

Marta pushed the memory of the towering Customs Official so many years ago farther back in her mind; the one whom she feared would order a strip search or some other disastrous invasion of her true self. That was before she got the chip as Marta. Now they thought they knew all about her and so didn't need any more invasive measures, no more rough tactics here in the pinnacle of civilization. There was no booth to the side here, anyway.

"I don't know if they'll take an Immy. Van Rijn is a Dutch name," he said suspiciously, saying 'van ridgin' instead of 'van rine'. Drowned Holland's refugees were on the long list of beggar peoples America refused, Soggies, but she was officially *not* Soggy.

Marta strived for a humble tone. "My great grandfather was from Holland, but we are from Mainz, Germany," she explained. "Father thought I should get the best education, so of course I have come to America with my Aunt as guardian. Father is of high rank in the NATO Enforcement Section and easily got the permissions."

She allowed the faintest, softest accent through, German-style, to convince him without being too different from her previous speech. "I am living with my Aunt here in Kentucky many years now as I attend school. I miss father and Germany, but I love America," she said, smiling more brightly.

Carvello strolled away. The reasoning held that Germany, a Eurussian powerhouse and a strong political ally against the Chinese bloc, might well want to foster her children in the US like the kings of old, strengthening loyalties. "It might already be filled but not updated, and they still might want that higher degree. Let me scan it anyway and waive the advanced degree part for the query."

She felt a bead of sweat run down the nape of her neck in the cool office. 'This will work!' she thought sternly, beating back the mental image of a dark angel with a sneer and a spear aimed at her, the same one that has been lurking in the dark places she passed all morning.

He flashed a toothy grin at her and said, "Miss Van Rijn, can you leave immediately?"

chapter 1

welcome Aboard

"*H*ola, *Senorita.* I am Bartolommeo Rogelio San Luis." The muscular, crag-faced Hispanic man, a hand width taller than her at least, spoke with a deep, rumbling voice. It reminded Marta of Bruno, the Alsatian, whenever he smelled a coyote. She blinked away the reminiscence to see him curl his lip on one side, a lopsided but endearing expression, seeming as if he could only manage half a smile but that it was better than none at all. Old man Jewel's phrase 'rode hard and put up wet' came to mind.

"I think you are Marta Amalie Van Rijn, from northern Germany. Your file says you came to the great empire of America to study, but the timing is for when Holland collapsed and *el Rio* Rhine flooded into Mainz. Maybe your *padre* sent you to not get the typhoid?"

She hung there alone with this foreign stranger on an access ladder in one of the USS Peck's passageways with her regulation duffle bag dangling from her left hand, dumbfounded. Queasy from the LEO light gravity at the geosync Topside Station, she had to concentrate on what he was saying, deciphering meaning from the lilting Spanish accent. The ladder was a misnomer as the walls had shiny metal parallel bars that served as broad ladders or at least grab bars the entire length and height of the passageway and across the overhead as well. Surely for grabbing when weightless!

She tried to shake off her excited confusion between the strange set-up, the light grav and him. Was he trying to be funny? Sympathetic? From orientation, she identified him as a Passenger, a security kind of guy. Perhaps a mole trying to trap her in her story? Should she correct him, that cholera was the killer they'd dreaded?

He mashed his lips together as if he regretted what he'd said. He reached over to her doorway and thumbed it open. They had to wait until the halves retracted fully into what seemed to be the ceiling and floor; the room itself was on gimbals but the door was part of the corridor wall, opening side-to-side relative to the room only under thrust grav.

"*Senorita* Van Rijn, this is your cabin. Let me help you." When she hesitated to let go, he added, "I did not mean to worry you, *Senorita*. Bad memories, *si?*" He gently took the bag from her and walked into her cabin. She shook off her surprise and suspicion so she could get from point A to point B and awkwardly followed him in.

"I thank you for your assistance Mr. San Luis."

"*Senorita*, I did not mean to be so ..." he said, searching for the right word.

"Personal?" she finished.

"*Si*, personal. I have read up an all *personas* on the ship. You are the last and I saw no crew to help you. I have been on ships with changing gravity and also through floods, so I know how hard it can be. I though you might like some help making this place *su casa*."

"I'll get used to the grav, and the floods were a long time ago. I mean, it's been years and I hardly remember it," she lied. Marta reconsidered her first impression and determined that she appreciated his presence and his apparent sympathy; it was a good sign for her first person she met to be a strong, dark, bright eyed and generally rough-handsome kind of guy. After all, she was a foreigner. She smiled back, more genuinely than her studied version, quickly discarding the preposterous notion that he could be attracted to her homely self.

"I got the rapid-fire Orientation on the way to Ecuador. Aren't you the great Protector of the Pantanal, the famed Paraguayan Policeman? Do you make it your business to know all about each person aboard?" As she spoke, she noticed he too stood straighter and became more formal.

"Like you say, that was a long time ago. I keep the habit of *securidad*, though. What your bio does not say is why you would want to travel so close to all these Patriot people, these *Norte Americanos*. I think they do not care too much for people like you or me. Immigrants, *si*?" He lowered his voice further still, theatrically, "You are not here to cause trouble? There is no room in America for troublemakers!" Grinning, he added, "Not you, no, but they will suspect you anyway. People like us get the pointed finger at us."

"Like you?" she asked, puzzled. "You haven't immigrated? You're still Paraguayan?"

When he did not respond she started getting nervous again so she added, "I guess we immigrants aren't quite American enough, but I am used to it. I spent my high school and college years here. I needed the money and social duty credits for more school and have learned to appreciate the marvel of America, so here I am in the Patriot service as an aide to Dr. Alain Cartier." She felt queasy. "I have sponged off my Aunt much too long, you see, I have to find my own way." She regretted saying 'sponged' as soon as it was uttered; his limited vocabulary might not include her slang and she did not want to embarrass this super-friendly guy.

Did he see through her lies, as pat and practiced as her story was? He seemed to look into her soul with those deep brown eyes. She shoved her belongings into niches, her mind racing. 'Is his imperfect English a ploy to put me at ease for some sinister purpose? Paranoia!' she thought, 'Don't panic!' Part of her mind drifted as it would, considering the meanings of 'sinister' while she tidied up and returned to face the man.

He abruptly crossed his arms and squinted one eye, staring at her with the other. The study tickled Marta's armpits uncomfortably.

He finally looked away to survey the little room. "Some of these persons will be very mean to you, little sister. These Patriot persons think they are the kings of the planet with all *Norte* America and all the way through Brazil in their greedy hands. They act like some of us are lucky to be their *campaisanos.* Immy or Soggy or Sicky, all are poor labels for living persons, no?"

"I have to admit Mr. San Luis I think that kind of talk counter-productive." She said that in a dutiful, monitor pleasing way, hoping to signal to him that she said it because she felt it necessary. Unless that's what he was waiting for? "I wouldn't want either of us to get in trouble before we even started." She really did not want to make an enemy right off the get-go no matter what his aim.

"*Senorita*, somebody come and say 'San Luis, you in trouble' I kick their ass." With that quirky one-side dimple grin again, he added, "I do try to not let things go so far."

"I figure I'm tough enough to get by," she said in what she hoped was a confident tone. "One day at a time."

"You are maybe tough like my sister. *Si,* maybe I will help you some, and then you can help me."

With a twinge of bald apprehension she blurted, "I won't spy for anyone."

"No, no *Senorita*," he said with humor. "I need better English, and maybe you will not make fun at me. You speak *Aleman*, ah, German first, and learn very good English. I think you know how hard is the difference between speaking English and speaking it very good."

In a snap, she released her last reservation and counted him her firm ally. She truly suffered through the shame and ridicule of speaking imperfect idiomatic American English. "Mr. San Luis, I would be pleased to help you on one condition. May we take turns? I would really like to *habla mas Espanol.*" She hoped she pronounced that right, it was about all of the Spanish she knew besides the names for everything at home, like *pollo, perro, gato, leche.* And the days of the week, the colors, numbers. Simple conversations and training classes only, stuff she picked up on the farm.

"Okay, deal." He nodded once sharply as if he'd completed a good bargain. "I must go and check in with the Bridge." He moved into the open doorway, but turned back to whisper, "When I go in person it makes the Commander pull herself together like a wet *arafia*." He winked and left.

She tried to relax and rubbed her forehead and tops of her eyes to stop the incipient headache. 'He bought it,' she thought, 'and so will everyone else including his spider-woman. I am Marta Van Rijn from Mainz and have been for over seven years. Why lose it now, stupid?' It also occurred to her that she'd blown her resolution to trust no one and to keep to herself. She sat too low on the totem poll to spy on, right?

Of course, there were the others he'd spoken of; the image in her head of circling turkey vultures, one with a black shroud and a spear, didn't help any. There was little room to pace, two steps to the door and two back to the closet. She practiced walking until she got the knack of how to set her feet; she'd hop and maybe hit her head on the low ceiling despite the magnetic cleats on her shoes if she wasn't careful. Pace. Vultures. Pace. She knew she looked young for her supposed age, but it was a little late to worry about that now. Maybe they'd think she had the pampered life of some of these Patriots. She felt she had aged hundreds of years.

She pressed her temples between her palms hard. What lunacy! Now she insisted on perpetuating her lies into space! All this worry about spies and lies revived unwelcome memories of the past that were much better left buried deep.

Suddenly the visitor light blinked its blue alert.

"Why is he back?" she wondered aloud, moving to actuate the door.

"Oh, hi! I wanted to meet my new neighbor!" The shapely, slightly shorter, curly haired brunette stood with her hand extended, hanging herself from the outer wall into the doorway with élan. "Naomi Bloom!" she announced as if it explained everything.

Marta shook her hand politely and after a beat asked the woman (about 30? 35?) to come in. Naomi slung in smoothly, athletically. Marta instantly yearned to learn how to do that even though departure was only about three hours away. There would be docking at the sling and at each colony stop, and then the return trip, anytime the gravity-imitating thrust stopped. She studied the woman's movements and decided she might practice in – out – in – out for an hour or so. More elbow flexion than wrist, sure, use the heftier joints.

Marta realized she had drifted off in her own little world again while her visitor stood impatiently and it jolted her; couldn't she maintain a straight task like this without her brain haring off? She smile apologetically and waved her hand to usher the woman further inside. The small cabins allowed only one flip-chair, so Marta folded the chair down for her guest and sat on the narrow bed. Naomi slid her hand on the seat to keep it level until she settled on it with a wiggle of her hips.

"I'm so glad you've come aboard. I was so afraid I'd have nobody to talk to." Naomi went on in a friendly but somehow nervous manner, a Deep South twang very evident. "I just hate these little in-system cabins; everything sacrificed for the sake of thrust. I've been to Mars three times and once all the way to Callisto, checking out how zingers from the magnetosphere slam a fleeting atmosphere into being. This your first time?" Unless she was smiling, her slight overbite and very plump lips made her appear awkward, kind of horse faced according to Marta's limited field of experience. Marta felt obligated to make her welcome, but wasn't sure how, knowing herself to be a few degrees lower than merely socially inept.

"Yes, ma'am." There a nanosec of panic, she almost said 'm'vrouw' instead of ma'am, she almost screwed up! Auntie used to slap her silly when she defiantly uttered Dutch. Calm down! Don't stray! What was the advice in the manual she got before heading off the college? 'Maintain casual eye contact, but don't stare! Use casual gesticulation when appropriate!' She realized seconds still ticked away, so said, "I suppose I'll get used to this soon enough." She flopped her hand over to end palm up. "You are onboard for the Expeditionary part of the journey Dr. Bloom?" As she casually laid her hand back on her lap, she reran the orientation segment in her head: 'Bloom, Naomi Bloom the Atmospheric Scientist. Right, a boss.'

Bloom flashed an incredibly sad expression so fast, Marta wasn't sure she'd actually seen it; now she showed bright-eyes and an even and brilliantly white upper row of teeth.

"Oh, nix it with the Doctor and absolutely never again ma'am. Please call me Naomi. Can I call you Marta? Van Rijn is a fine name, but it's not general conversation material, is it? At least not for our little chitty-chats. We can wait on the other when we get into the lab; they'd better have every bit of my equipment onboard!"

The woman specialized in a kissy-grin, at least Marta thought it looked like that, puckered up in a cutesy way, emphasizing her voluminous lips. Marta noticed some version of it punctuated her every phrase; natural or contrived? Bloom continued, "We'll see about that later. For now just plain ol' Naomi, okay?" She waited with exaggerated expectation for a response.

"N-Naomi," Marta stuttered. "Of course." Her guts churned with the strong desire to pull out her etiquette book.

"Good, good." That settled, Naomi went on. "I take it you've met Barto? Big man of steel? Bartolommeo San Luis? Is he not handsome on the hoof put a bridle on him and giddy up?"

Abashed, Marta couldn't help but picture the scene of Naomi on the back of a silvery robot horse with San Luis' face, bit clamped between steel jaws. With that quirky grin.

"Oh, honey I didn't mean to embarrass you. I just rattle on sometimes. Still, Barto is a fine addition to the ensemble don't you think? And so close to my own vintage so as not to notice. I would also offer my professional observation that his shape and mine would complement each other quite well, in the jigsaw manner."

Marta tried to quell her growing agitation. "Mr. San Luis does seem like a solid, dependable sort."

"Solid? My dear could you not feel the feral heat emanating at his proximity? Doesn't it make you want to cozy up and purr?"

"Naomi, please..." Marta's brain was busy enough without these jangling, graphic metaphors!

"Oh my, look at that pretty blush. I'm a bit darker than you and it just doesn't show well on me. Sephardic Jew, you know. Not that I embarrass easily anyway, not for stuff like that. Of course, I can generate three distinct levels of dimples, a handy skill I assure you. Still, but nothing screams innocence like a pretty blush, does it?"

"Naomi, would you like some tea? I believe there is a dispenser in the cabin somewhere according to the briefing."

"Nonsense. An Alabaman does not do dispenser tea. Let's go to the galley and make some fresh as soon as thrust grav settles out. I can hold out stoically until then, although that kind of effort is a bit rusty from disuse. And goodness, who knows who else might be there? The available men are few but at least that one is a gem."

Aside from the fact that they all had access to the published Crew and Passenger complement, the thought of confronting the dreaded Patriots San Luis warned her about made her uneasy. She remembered the very recent ordeal when she had to squeeze into the last rope car going Topside before the Peck left, one full of black-uniformed military officers that jabbered amongst themselves and answered her prayers by ignoring her and her newly issued, uniform and two-ton duffle bag.

"I thought I might stay in my cabin most of the time, at least until we rendezvous with the sling past the asteroid belt." Auntie'd always told her to keep to herself, to not get caught up in socializing, that strangers would be sure to get her in trouble. Marta now concluded being trapped on this ship was insane and that her Aunt was older and wiser and gave good advice.

"No! No! In-system is the long leg, a negligible distance relatively speaking but half the trip time. Then we accelerate though the outer system at a fast clip-clop that is much farther in a bit less time, like putting our cart and horsy in a slingshot. Once we get to Kuiper and catch the interstellar Bus away we're almost there."

"That's all it takes to get to the stars," Marta murmured weakly. "I feel I will need time here alone to adjust to all this." Here, alone and bar the door.

"Honey, I tell you it is best to be always out among them, watching. Know thy enemy!" She added, "And we might find an ally, really, dear, who knows? Might be one anywhere," she said, peeking under the corner of her seat cushion.

"Enemies? Allies?" Were the walls thin? Bugged? "Wait," she said hurriedly and worriedly, reviewing her past conversations, trying to separate what she'd said from what she'd thought about saying. "I don't remember talking about allies or enemies at all."

Naomi tilted her head with an appraising look, noting the way she phrased that. "I have not offended you by joking about our imminently Patriotic friends, have I? No harm?"

"No, I mean," Marta said, flustered, "I mean I understand you were joking."

"Right." Naomi was getting more serious now, perhaps reconsidering friendship? Marta instantly hoped not, though Naomi didn't give her the warm fuzzies like San Luis did. Was it because she's as American as they come and Marta had never been very close to a real American before? She reasoned if she was assigned only to the Agronomist, Naomi may be trying to get on her good side to siphon off some of her time. Or maybe she's a naturally friendly person? Or maybe she was practicing her 'know thy enemy' tenet? Marta wanted to tease it apart, but glanced up to notice Naomi looking in expectation again.

"I'm sorry Naomi. I just got here and I feel like a little yellow chick in the yard with hawks racin' to the scene." Seeing a moue starting on Naomi's face, she quickly continued, "And it's like you and Mr. San Luis are the hens trying to get me into the chicken house. Ah, to safety." She bit down on her urge to apologize for that *lame* comment.

"Marta, honey, I will be content to be characterized as an old hen if you promise to have lunch with me, okay?"

Marta had to agree.

chapter 2

Rerouted

The Exec turned a sour look toward the main Bridge hatchway. "Captain, I'm glad you made it aboard before lift off."

Olivia O'Reilly swiveled part way from her Nav post to watch the exchange; these two were always sparring and Olivia liked to keep score.

"You need not try so hard to hide your disappointment Commander Umana-Jones." Captain Fajar struck his aristocratic pose and held his gaze toward her hairline. Olivia thought he did that well, nearly two meters tall with aquiline features and a bald pate, all packaged in a black dress uniform with full insignia and his decorations for valor in a Martian uprising a few years ago, crisp and polished to his pointed boots.

Olivia knew he liked adding the 'Umana' because that acknowledged her Ghanaian mother's side of the family, the family she'd abandoned. Ghana was a country devastated by a tight quarantine led by the Americans with rampant alcanthra, aids and a mutant malaria, a land of suffering starvation, of flooding and death; a country he knew she hated reminders of. She suspected he also despised her for disowning her family in order to become a registered Patriot since his culture venerated ancestors and could recount centuries of lineage. From his perspective, Jones was the poster child for the arrogant and self-seeking Patriot autocracy, a model new-style Pat-Brat.

Charenne Jones stood straighter and rolled her shoulders. "Yes sir" she said, "We are green to dock with Farragut station, sling out to Kuiper 1 and take the Franklin Bus on to Tenembras and points beyond."

"There is a change in plans, Commander, we have a side trip. Astro Command wants us to co-op with Exped to use the expertise on board to check out an anomaly on the way, before Tenembras. I have released the orders if you'd care to download them."

"We are not a research ship! We have a schedule to supply Tenembras, Chanx, Solomon, Marguay, Lutz and Roundabout then come back after bare little home leave and do it again. We do not explore. This trip is to follow the program and back by next Christmas!"

"When you are finished with your emotional outburst, I will tell you what we are going to do this time. We will meet up with the Cerberus sling for a boost 1.2 times faster through the system, slip with the Franklin at Kuiper 3, thereafter to include an opening stop at the Lyra 9976 system to check out an anomalous life indication Astro's been monitoring. Lyra 9976 is 335.26 light years away, in the habitable zone, 1.37 times the size of Earth with larger, slightly redder sun, ample water and may have been visited by an earlier European ship that was lost twenty years ago, one of the pioneers. We are to check to see if they have indeed visited, landed and survived or not as an important political point. If they left behind contamination, we're stocked to clean up. You may have noticed the Passengers that are allowed up here to prepare for the assessment?"

Olivia could have laughed at Jones' look of barely suppressed anger, but she preferred discretion. Certainly, the Commander was accustomed to the colony bus stops the Frankie invariably made before returning to Kuiper - it was programmed with the AI, you were locked down, simple to remember. The side trip could not be a true surprise to her, though. It cost a ransom to reprogram it for a one-off side trip and that alone rated the internal news. Why was the new girl, Marta, brought up unless the change was not only known but advertised? And this curious hybrid mix of Passenger-exiles?

Olivia decided the XO must mad about not getting the official orders released until the last bloody minute. She might also be fishing for some tidbit about the Exped target, an old EU foul up they'd known about for years. All that was clear was her acute anger over the invasion of the so-called Passengers into the cohabited parts of the Peck and later, the Franklin. Olivia thought it all emotive as a grammar school play, Char presumably thought the overt consternation reasonable.

"Cerberus," Char fumed. "We haven't used Cerberus since the Farragut replaced it, or have you forgotten that Cerberus is considered too hot a shot for a ship this size? Speed kills?"

The Navigator tried to watch every nuance of the exchange without a telltale twitch of the lip, difficult as it was. In her opinion, the XO was absolutely playing bit much too far. The more Olivia considered it, the more unimaginable it was that she didn't know all about it, at least as much as some of the Passengers and probably more and sooner than the Captain because of her secure political connections.

Meanwhile the Captain made it sound like they decided on this over a coffee last night, writing the itinerary on napkins. He had to have planned his entrance and lines to the last detail. At least they were doing something other than staring coldly at each other; this way was more fun to watch. This could turn out to be an intriguing trip in more ways than one.

Oh no! She almost missed her cue! Olivia piped up sprightly, "Nav for Cerberus sling through the system to Kuiper Station 3 and slip confirmation to Lyra 9976 loaded and verified, 124 days transit to Lyra destination, sir!" 'That certainly was fast,' she thought, 'were they trying to beat someone else, say Eurussians, there? After all this neglect, was the ambiguous, non-human life indication really worth the expenditure?' "Relays confirm the Franklin will be outfitted and ready for our transfer 26.4 days early. Our tether is checked green for Cerberus docking and the program to boost to Kuiper 3 is standing by."

"Lieutenant Commander O'Reilly," Jones ordered, "Please report when the additional stores needed for this jaunt are actually aboard, whenever that occurs." She glanced at the Nav display. "We still have an ETA to reach Cerberus, irregardless of the further stellar direction."

Olivia was disappointed to see the Captain flinch at the grammar. She had heard too many times that Char considered him a prissy foreigner and didn't like to see her win points off him.

The Captain took a deep breath and addressed the Navigator very politely, "We have another crewmember, a Marta Van Rijn. She came up the Rope with me and is here specifically to assist Doctor Cartier and perhaps Bloom with the analysis of Lyra 9976. I've assigned her as a Warrant Ensign and believe you'll find her on the manifest as such."

Looking back to Jones he added more gruffly, "Commander Umana-Jones you have the next 2.7 hours to perform your administrative magic with regard to interfacing the Peck with our new orders. We depart on time because the Franklin will not wait. If there is any issue, notify me immediately. That's all."

chapter 3

spread the word

When the Captain went aft, Charenne Jones slumped her shoulders as if deflated and looked over to Olivia, vexed. "The Cerberus is so ratty one of these days it'll fall apart mid-sling. I like my bright and shiny American-made Farragut."

O'Reilly kept her eyes on her panel. "The Argentine-made Cerberus is a hard-working sling and after extensive re-engineering it is the best ever. It's vital to be able to use either system as a back-up, unless you want to beg the Chinese for a boost on one of their slings?"

"Don't lecture me. What good is a redundant relay point if one is junk, upgraded or not? Who did the upgrade? Cluck-Cluck out of Costa Rica? 'Best ever' bullshit!"

With a warmer tone, the Navigator added, "My partner Tatiana is now head of the Cerberus gyro department. She assures me it will not fall apart on her watch."

Char shook her head slowly, disgusted at the blatant reminder of Olivia's predilections. Shrugging, she slouched at her console to do her validations. She verified the last of the data perfunctorily; they had never found AI off by a jot and she couldn't be all that worried about the transit detail. If something failed, none of them would have time to realize it.

* * *

At the sound of footsteps, the Exec swung around in her chair to see San Luis, a damned Passenger, wandering about her ship freely. She automatically rose and re-inflated to see him eye-to-eye.

"Mr. San Luis, what brings you to the Bridge unbidden?" The first time she'd met him, she'd called him by name and then looked pointedly at his nametag; she still chastised herself, she should have checked his tag first to preserve the illusion that she didn't know his every secret. Now she could forget his tag, but he still irritated her.

"Commander Jones," Barto reported, "I have checked the Crew and Passengers and all is in order. I remind you that if I may be of any service in this voyage, please let me know."

"Very well Mr. San Luis." Why was he acting as if there was an actual security position onboard? Why couldn't he make his reports via Comm if he felt so anachronistically compelled? Foreign idiocy, everywhere she turned. "I doubt there will be any need to thwart guerilla activity aboard my ship. We do have automated security and surveillance, but be sure to let O'Reilly know of any trouble right away."

Dismissed, he nodded and stepped away smartly.

Sour about the preponderance of aliens on her ship, Char noticed her arms tightly crossed and shook them out to restore circulation. She headed out to apprise the glorified Passengers and her Crew of the schedule changes, holding her head high. Her ship, yes, soon this would be her ship.

She spotted Naomi in the corridor with several cookies and a bulb of real milk, a treat while it lasted. That the Passengers had access to the main cafeteria rankled her and that tensed her up again.

"Dr. Bloom? Are you prepared to do extra duty on Lyra 9976?" The Commander spoke tersely with tightly crossed arms and knees pushed together as she stood before the daintier woman, making an effort to look down on her rather than across to her.

"Oh yes, Commander Jones. I have all I need, assuming it was actually loaded."

"You heard about it when," Charenne asked coolly.

"About five weeks ago, I guess. A Captain Shaltos from Exped rescued me from oblivion and suggested I bone up. Then Alain, I mean Dr. Cartier, called and we discussed what additional equipment we might need and had it sent to the Rope. Our labs on board should be stuffed full."

"Alain Cartier?" Another one to watch, a do-goody Canadian. She would make it a point to remind him it was all America now, Bucko. "Fine. Remember those labs are at the convenience of the service as requested by Exped for your *diligent* preparations. I will expect regular written reports onboard and on-planet. Carry on." She did not like having dissidents onboard and was looking forward to dumping them at the colonies. She smiled at the idea.

Char went down the corridor to Ensign Lee Bodine's cabin. As she pressed the call panel, she consoled herself that with her expert guidance, Lee was good Patriot material. He was due a promotion, but she had to get it by Fajar if she wanted to push it through this trip.

"Ensign Bodine, you are prepared for the side trip to Lyra 9976?"

He was shirtless and glistening with sweat, biceps reflecting a glint of the overhead lights. Instead of responding correctly, he rubbed his face with a towel.

"Ensign, please verify the programmed off-loading of the menus and services for the six day trip on the planet in two shuttles, the Passengers get the outside rations. As long as the local stats match what we have now, they'll spend the whole time out there." That gave away a little information, but the boy wouldn't have a clue what it meant.

"Yes, ma'am, I will get right on it." He smoothed his short platinum blond hair back with his fingers, flexing his pecs casually and put on what she thought of as his Boy Scout face.

She smiled to indicate he had pleased her. She raised an eyebrow as if looking over Lee's shoulder into the room and added, "If you see Barbara, let her know too, okay?" She approved of his liaison and his feigned embarrassment.

He ducked his head, saying, "I sure will ma'am."

Satisfied, Char proceeded on her mission. She saw the enigmatic Tomlinson had 'Do Not Disturb' posted on his door panel in what looked like blue marker on a wide piece of chartreuse adhesive tape and that suited her fine. The less she had to deal with these Passengers the better and she had no interest in talking to the little mutant freak. Next! Hmm, did she really have an obligation to inform her newest Ensign of anything? Who was she? Some refugee Immy the Captain had foisted upon her, Van Ruin or something?

Bypassing both of those and also that incredibly annoying San Luis's place, Char's next stop was at the Scot's cabin. He answered his call very quickly; she deduced he must have been ready to go out.

"Mr. Crannog, we haven't had a chance to talk much yet. How are you this fine day?" Usually the 'volunteers' were half a step from arrest, but she hadn't uncovered any dirt on this one yet.

"Well."

"Um, you know we are making a side trip for a look-see at the added garden spot? Lyra 9976?"

"Yes."

"Fine," she said, thinking what a brilliant conversationalist this one was. Damned foreigners.

"You'll be staying on Tenembras, I understand." She did not understand; how could anybody choose to abandon everything for Tembo? Unless he expected to be shipped off soon anyway, that had to be it. "Have you skills to contribute for the journey or the Lyra 9976 landing?"

"Ma'am I did mark on the roster that I could perform any engineering work needed, including the drawing of plans to troubleshooting. I can perform some repairs with a wee bit of a study."

His light brogue did not impress her and she decided did not like his ambiguous status as a volunteer Passenger among the others. Still, Great Britain was a good political ally much to the ongoing dismay of the Eurussians who saw American inroads and influences at every corner. "I have discovered we have a Van Ruin for inciden- tal repair duties. I could use someone capable at the Nav Comm console when Lieutenant Commander O'Reilly is off duty if you want to keep busy." Maybe that way she could observe him without having to spend excess time among 'them'.

Cedric replied, "Yes."

chapter 4
Nau watch

When Char went on her way, Cedric revised his planned recon-noitering of the ship to get his bearings while the Peck was still attached to Quito's Topside Station to include Bridge introductions. He was not going to let his unsteady balance keep him from looking about.

Upon eventually reaching the Bridge with only a few minor contusions, he found the Navigator by herself reading something in a stranger script than his usual technical reading materials. He clutched at a rail obviously installed for that purpose and settled his demeanor and stomach.

"Lieutenant Commander O'Reilly?" The woman would be quite tall if she stood, he thought, nearly his own 1.974 meter height. The sable pixie cut suited her softly angular face although she was porcelain-pale.

"Char Jones warned me you'd be up soon. I'm Olivia, please, and I shall call you Cedric."

She said it sed-rik, which always scraped his ears. "If you insist, Olivia, and the correct pronunciation is ket-rik if you don't mind. I am here in response to a request to look in on the secrets of Nav Comm and hope this is not a bad time."

"Oh, this," she said, waving a hand in the direction of the display. "I was studying the *Bhavagad Gita* in the original Sanskrit. *The Song of God* has endured thousands of years and will not be diminished by waiting a few more minutes for my humble self. Oh, and apologies for the mispronunciation; my father was Irish but I went to school during my late teen years in Boston."

He had not been farther than western Eurussia and was disinterested in her obscure geographical references. "I would not disturb your studies, but Commander Jones seemed imperative."

Olivia's face hardened. "Did you get special instructions, sir?"

Unsure what happened, he replied, "Yes, she said she'd like to have someone at the console when you're off duty? That's all."

To his surprise, she twined her arms together, reaching up and inhaling, then twining the other way while exhaling, then reaching up again. After three repetitions she seemed more relaxed. Glancing back to him, she said, "Yes, that bit about how the ship needs human oversight and so forth. Fine I'll show you the bells and whistles. Do you have questions to start?"

"They will demonstrate my ignorance." He sat at the next console chair down from Olivia and strapped in; it appeared the rest of his exploratory walk would have to wait until they got underway. "Why a Navigator in the first place? The Boris Peck is as modern an in-system ship as exists, with the latest AI Nav." He would be fascinated to be there when the bridge changed orientation for thrust and the viewports lined up.

"We can't neglect to maintain the façade that we are in charge, sir. We shall have a Captain, an Executive and a Navigator all capable of doing nearly everything manually on the Peck even though we never will have to do more than jockey ourselves to and from the ship, also with AI guidance. I assure you that not one beating heart is required on the interstellar Franklin, great wheel and pinnacle of human ingenuity that it is. However, arrowing through the Solar System on the mighty Peck we do have the bracing duty of concurring with the AI plans at certain decision points. Also Nav includes communications and administration of all the various ships systems." She sighed wistfully. "It's all courtesy of AI, so the hard won glory of my esoteric education is largely wasted."

As an engineer, Cedric felt an upwelling of sympathy. He knew about the rigors of becoming expert in a complex technical area and frequently feared obsolescence in favor of AI. He knew the interstellars had full human crews for the first decade, dwindling over the next; now the only crew was relegated to the sections they operated planetary missions from.

"I noted on my cabin monitor before coming up here that our sling is to be Cerberus. I thought that was only for trips inward from Saturn, at least that's what it was built for."

"No, no, the old Cerb' was the granddaddy that got us to the outer iceballs within a lifetime. You're thinking about the repurposing for supporting the Mars actions, but it's been reassigned. It has plenty of punch to get us to Kuiper Station on the far side of the belt. First time up, isn't it? Worried about getting slung into an asteroid or moon, or even Neptune or something?"

"The last big ship to sling from Cerberus to Kuiper didn't make it, it came in faster than the deceleration program could handle and interacted unfavorably with certain Kuiper Belt Objects."

"Unfortunate that." Olivia pause with bowed head for a second, then continued subdued. "In the ensuing two years we have gutted and remade Cerby. We have a new generation of AI to control the sling sequence. I would not defy the proverbial gods, but will say I believe the new Cerb, new AI and the new crew in synergy make it as safe or safer than the Farragut or either of the Kuiper slings."

His face remained blank. "And we try it first."

Without a hint of concern, she held his eye and said, "Yes."

He took a deep breath to close the matter. "In that case, if you will show me enough to monitor our progress and keep the Commander appeased I will be content."

chapter 5
well underway

"The Topside sendoff went well and grav has nearly plateau'd," the Captain told Olivia needlessly. Comfortable now in a regulation tan jumpsuit, he brought tea in two insulated cups. Peering dramatically around the Bridge to emphasize their being alone, he handed Olivia one, settled into the plush Command chair and nodded toward her. "Darjeeling, my dear, my personal stash."

"Captain, I know you don't believe in standing watch on these ships." She sipped the hot amber infusion and then slowly inhaled the enticing aroma.

"Olivia, I just thought I'd see how you were doing this trip. Jones taxes your patience, but otherwise how are you? Shore leave agreeable?"

"I'm looking forward to resuming philosophical conversations with Ronnie Sue. And there is an interesting Scotsman aboard this time. Otherwise it's the same old thing." She did appreciate the soothing Darjeeling, the subtle bouquet with its association in her brain back to simpler, happier times.

Longingly, he said, "The old doctor nor the Scot has my charms, dear."

That broke her forming reverie. "Captain, how's your wife and sons?" The man never gave up! She was simply not interested no matter how lonely the trip got. "How tall are those boys? Getting up there, I bet. Alessandra doesn't seem old enough to have teenagers. My Tatiana was enchanted by your wife's landscapes; she looked them up on the net and swooned. I had no idea they went for so much." Ah, the fictional Tatiana; when *would* she have time for a satisfying relationship?

He sipped his cooling tea, his eyebrows bunching as if telegraphing to her that she was wasting her womanhood. She made a show of indifference.

After a couple minutes of silence, he leaned forward, elbows on knees, pensive. He spoke softly as if he did not want his words echoing back to him, "Olivia, I trust I can share this with you, and you may be the only person I can confide in about this." He gazed intently and whispered, "Raoul, my first born pride, joy and wonder to my heart has told me, Olivia I can only say this with great pain, he told me he is gay."

Olivia stifled mirth at his mournful expression, barely containing herself. He was the product of what must have been a really straight-laced background in an era of increasing class stratification; decreased international and intra-national travel allowed feudal tendencies to surface.

"Captain, there has been a range of sexual preferences since there have been humans. My advice is to mentally equate this to a calling, like to the priesthood or something. Unless you force him to rebel, he'll probably continue as a perfectly acceptable son in every way, with his choice of his intimate relationships the only difference. Without pressure from you, I imagine his relationships will be within the same social class and as discrete as you would have otherwise expected."

"Olivia, he's my eldest, the heir! How could Alessandra and I have let something like this happen?"

"It's not because you let him wear a pink shirt once, or any other thing you or Alessandra did. Is he hunchbacked or have goggle eyes or something?"

"Certainly not! He is the image of his great grandfather Ambrosio Gregorio Fajar. No, he *looks* like he should."

"So he doesn't dress in filmy pastels with stiletto heels yet?"

The Captain did not respond, clearly horrified by the picture she painted.

"Captain, I advise you to treat him special."

"How, please?"

"Treat him like he's your heir and beloved son and that you agree his choices are his right because he's a responsible man now." There, she had helped him vent his worry and that's probably all he wanted anyway since Alessandra led the family with a velvet fist. "Sir, now that we're at grav it's about time for the adaptation check-ups and I'd like to get mine out of the way." She finished her tea and handed him back the cup. He absently nested it under his own, staring into a mid-distance.

She leaned over and said softly near his ear, "That really was exceptionally good, sir, and I thank you very much."

* * *

As the Captain drained his own cup, the wraith-thin Scot came in.

"Good Afternoon, Sir. I've come to sit in for Olivia, Lieutenant Commander O'Reilly, while she's getting her check-up. I passed her in the corridor."

The Captain tossed the cups into the recycle bin. "You know Nav Comm? I though your field was power generation."

Cedric sat stiffly at the Nav console, facing the Captain. "I've committed to be rather a student for when she's off duty, Commander Jones requested it. I have a manual the Lieutenant Commander downloaded for me." He held his tablet at an angle the Captain could see.

Fajar nodded. "Ahhh. I think the systems aboard require no actual persons; we simply do it to make ourselves feel needed. Ms. Jones likes to maintain a veneer of command and disapproves of me for not doing the same."

Relaxing slightly, Cedric ventured, "Perhaps then, I will feel less subversive by also bringing my power tables with me to study. I've concentrated in turbines and geothermal systems lately and my nuclear is rusty."

"I see no problem with that at all, Crannog. It is good to have another European aboard, I must say. It's not all that common on an American ship, for all the ballyhooed cooperation. I'm from Spain, Andalusia, long story there. Have you traveled on the Continent?"

Cedric smiled and crossed his legs, elbows on the chair arms and an eager expression on his face. "Yes sir, and I found Spain exceedingly beautiful and the language intriguing; I picked up quite a bit although I wouldn't consider myself fluent by any means."

"*Muy bueno*! (continuing in Spanish) *I miss the mother tongue very much on these long voyages and despaired of any live conversations with it although most of the new territory American claims is the home of Spanish speakers.*"

Cedric happily replied in Spanish, "*That San Luis is South American, si?*"

"*Oh, si, but he's so coarse; it would be best for him to not be underfoot.*"

Cedric blinked at what sounded like racism, but who was he to judge the Captain? "*Regarding my time in Spain, my particular love was for the music of the old guitar masters, grand memories. My family went to a concert in Granada where my father was working and I have prized the guitar since.*"

"*You play?*"

"*Si, and I brought my guitar with me. I fancy I shall get much practice in on this trip.*"

"*Muy bueno indeed. If you'll excuse me, I have correspondence to attend to now. Buenos dias, senor.*"

Cedric rose and stood straight until the Captain left, then sat stiffly and without expression to study his chapter on the chemical and thermal properties of the fuel rod/moderator interface during a departure from nucleate boiling state in a pressurized water reactor during a transient, the Petersen NG3 Mark 4 PWR being the type built for Tenembras, his destination.

chapter 6

check up time

Barbara, the Corpsman, knew she should already be in Sickbay by now, but was behind the sauntering Navigator and wanted to give her plenty of room.

Olivia stopped at Naomi's open door to watch the woman standing on the fold down chair seat trying to stuff something in the upper cubby.

"Hey, you're Naomi Bloom, hot shot Atmo diva! I'm Olivia O'Reilly, navigation and comm."

Startled, Naomi stepped back into thin air and fell on her backside with her shoulders against the wall. "Oooof!"

Barb stepped closer to see the klutz.

"Oops! What happened?" O'Reilly seemed contrite. "I didn't mean to scare you." Hanging onto a passageway rung, she reached over to help Naomi, but Naomi rolled and pushed herself up.

"I'm sorry, just fell, no harm," she told Olivia with chagrin. "I've been out enough to know better." She rubbed her right buttock gently, looking vaguely toward her hip. "Did you need something?"

"No, heading back to sickbay for my med check. You sure you're okay?"

Barbara waited impatiently for Olivia to get out of the way. She squeezed past her in the narrow corridor carefully, as if afraid of touching her.

Barb walked quickly, almost at a trot. When she got to Sickbay, Doc Trogden was there arranging the supplies she'd hauled out herself.

"Doctor T what is up with that Bloom's stumbling around? She just fell in her cabin. Jeez! The spastic ones go in the padded room."

* * *

Letting the girl's remark pass, Dr. Ronnie Sue Trogden responded, "Hello Barbara, it's good to have you on board again. I was worried not seeing you 'til now. How are you, then?"

"I went home to see Mother in Terre Haute and my sisters were fine. Jenni got accepted into the Hotel Management program at IU and Lila is doing okay at the chime design place."

"What about you, honey. Any news?"

"Oh Doc," she said like a grade schooler bringing home A's, "I passed the written quals for the DynaStar series and the molecular regens, the Foxxes and Refrebeners too. I almost blew it on the Refrebener TachStick annealing temp but remembered you saying it was a good ten degrees higher than the Foxx for no good reason. I passed!"

"Here honey, let's have a hug. You did so well. Did you try the TruTech 2nd Level Chromatography exam?"

"I flunked that one," Barb replied, face falling.

"Honey that was a lot to take on at once. You did well, and this time out we'll go over the modulators and review that TruTech equipment again. Let me guess, manual peak integration?"

"Yeah. You really think I did okay?"

"Better than okay. How many other people didn't even try? Now, settle down and tell me why your arm is hurting? Yes, it was obvious."

"Well, I spent the time from boarding until now with Lee, and these cabins have awful skinny bunks."

Doc saw the girl's self-satisfied grin and also looked over her arms and saw finger-spaced bruising. "Honey, Lee is not the last man on Earth. If he's not good to you, move on. Life's too short for abusive bastards."

"Doc, Lee's not your business," she said coolly, like flipping a vid channel. "We like what we have. I'll take care of me." The vid flipped back. "Is there anything I can help you with? I might as well work since I'm here and the parade will begin shortly, I passed the Navigator on the way here."

Doc decided not to reprimand her for being over an hour late, too mentally tired for it.

Just then, Barto stuck his head in the open door. "Are you open for business yet, ladies?"

"Sure," Doc said, patting the examining table's sanitary film. "Park it right here."

Indeed, it was going to be a parade of one after another, same spiel each time. The boring routine was initially a tonic to Doc; the South Carolina Displacement Camp had taken its toll; the misery in her hospital had ground at her soul. When the Philippines begged for mercy they were Soggies, when Savannah to Charleston was flooded out they were 'displaced'. In Ronnie Sue Trogden's mind, they all were the Lord's children. What did the good Lord think of the thousands of his children either waiting at Kuiper or being shuttled there right now?

Barto cleared his throat, bringing Doc back to the present.

"Okay," she started, relying on routine, "How are you feeling, San Luis? Any headaches?"

"I am fine." He said somewhat nervously. "I did training for my new job on Mars' Ticonderoga Station so there are no problems."

So what bothered him that wasn't adequately covered at Ticonderoga? Doc didn't want to admit she hadn't even glanced at anyone's med files yet, a task she meant to do instead of setting the room and supplies up. She let him evade if he wanted to. "Okay, you can go."

Olivia let the big man pass before she came in.

Doc laughed good-naturedly. "Livy, it's good to see you again! I haven't had a chance to come up yet and you never slum around down here. Anything exciting I need to know about?"

"The Captain's still making passes and Jones is still trying to lock in some kind of elusive personal power. That Engineer, Crannog, he's coming up to the bridge for the trip out."

"What on earth for? Surely he's not making passes?"

"Oh, no. He's a cold fish, that one, all proper and professional. Charenne wanted him to study up on the Nav in case I had a heart attack or something."

"He said that?"

"No, no. He says very little, like a jinn stuck in his bottle."

Barbara added, "He's just looking for some little thing to rub his bottle, don't you think?"

"Oh, really," Olivia said with a quelling look. She took a step back toward the door. "Ronnie Sue, I'm fine. Okay to chill out in my cabin? I want to review the recorded profile of Earth's magnetic field dissipation as we passed through. I watched it real-time, but can play with it now."

"Sure, Livy." Doc wished the Navigator hadn't shut Barb down so fast. Sure, the girl's remark was risqué, but she knew Livy was no prude. Besides, there was a slim choice of positive examples for the little tramp. Unfair. Whatever.

"Livy," she called out, "send in the next one if you please."

Marta pressed her back against the waiting room wall involuntarily as Olivia came toward her. "Good afternoon, ma'am."

"You must be Marta Van Rijn, the new Warrant Ensign. Impressive resume so far, with all you've done at the Sequestering unit at home and great grades. This trip should certainly help with your future endeavors." She gave Marta a closer look and smiled. "Doc's ready for you, go on in."

The doctor didn't look up as Marta came in, trying to find the stylus she'd dropped. Retrieving it, she rose and asked, "All right Ms. Van Rijn, how are you feeling today?" She patted the table and tucked the stylus in her breast pocket, poking at the pocket to verify there weren't any holes.

Marta compliantly hopped onto the table.

"Any headaches? Disorientation?"

"No ma'am, nothing,"

Doc's professional eye and the diagnostic AI noticed the girl seemed anxious about something, and furthermore anxious to not let it show. "Anything I need to know about? This is your first shot into the great abyss and it's all right for you to be a little uncomfortable about it. I'm a licensed shrink ya know."

"No ma'am, nothing."

"Fine. I'm always here, so come on by if you change your mind. This kind of work can get to folks and I can soften the sharp edges if needed, keep *that* in mind. Send in the next victim on your way out."

A chunky and stern looking Southeast Asian man stood in the doorway, loose arms and slightly bent knees as if prepared to strike out.

"Thao Tomlinson, that right? Sit up here if you please." Doc pulled a step up to the table with her toe in a fluid motion, not wanting to embarrass the short statured Thao.

Doc noted the body temp redline on the monitor right away, elevated enough for concern. "You have a very high body temp, sir. You have a fever?" She reached for thermometer tabs for a more accurate reading.

"No. I have a modified metabolism. Other than my room being much too cool, there is no problem."

She dropped the tab back into the bin. "Is this modified metabolism something I need to know about? It was not specified as a risk on the manifest."

"My records are classified. May I go?"

"Sure," she sighed. She'd guessed right about his records before he said it. The tiny blip of interest faded. "Next!"

The reluctant Scotsman came in to sit primly on the table where she indicated.

"How you feeling Crannog? Any headaches?"

"I am fine, thank you."

"Tough guy, huh? The first time away from the bosom of Mother Earth can unbuckle tough guys. Varying gravity bounces the belly." Could he be even paler than when he came aboard?

"I am fine."

"I'm a bona fide Psychiatrist." Why is he so stiff and intent to betray no emotions? She wondered what poorly concealed trauma might drive such a man to leave Mother Earth.

"I am fine."

"I could recommend you a strict diet and exercise regimen to shed some of that flab."

Cedric gave her a chin-up look of disdain. "I am fine. Thank you."

"Got it, kiddo." At least she got a rise out of the walking skeleton.

Naomi, waiting at the door, exchanged places with him.

"Dr. Bloom, I understand you fell earlier today. How about a scan to be on the safe side, hmm?"

"No, really, no Doctor. I mean, I fall all the time. Not all the time mind you, but sometimes, and it's okay, no harm. Sometimes I feel I'm playing a game with gravity and only by falling can I know where in the system I am, if that makes any sense."

"If you say so, that's fine, but I don't bite. How about headaches, dizziness? You fell because you got lightheaded?"

"No, I was startled. Nothing, really. Is that all? I'd like to go."

"Look whatever's bothering you, you can come here any time in confidence." She felt like it was the 10,000th time saying that to someone; the displaced non-persons, the political exiles, the Passengers. No one trusted her, or maybe closer to the mark, no one trusted the medical establishment anymore since everybody knew a court of law could and would use med results against you. She watched Dr. Bloom, once with unlimited prospects, walk away dejected. Leaving Earth for good would be enough to shake anyone.

Next was the agronomist, Dr. Cartier. "Have a seat." She felt too drained too early in the afternoon these days. She droned, "How do you feel? Headaches?"

"Come now, that's no way to treat your elders!"

"Elders? Let me see," she said, sloughing off the creeping depression. Checking the screen for his chart she said, "You certainly don't look ninety plus. Congrats!" She was surprised at how pleased she was to have someone older than herself on the ship, and by twenty years at that!

His indignant posture faded. "I certainly don't feel ninety-four, either. Of course I attribute much of that to working outdoors and exemplary genes."

"Sure. Not much of dear old Sol for a while, though, I hope it doesn't cramp your style." She bit her lower lip hard, wishing she hadn't said that. He didn't act as if he heard her. She maneuvered a stethoscope pick-up over his rock steady heart to compare it against what AI reported on screen and heard it start to thump harder.

"I see here you have a calcium multipatch. We may have to adjust that if you're going to spend extended time on Lyra 99 whatever. I hear it's a bit more gravity, the air isn't poisonous but it's sure to have slim to little oxygen, so you'll have to supplement. Between the two, we need to, um, let me confirm, dit-dit-dit, ah, yes. We have to ease back about 11%." Should she ask him if he brought a supply? This kind of patch only lasted about ninety days and Lord knew what the medical situation at Tembo was.

"Dear Doctor, I do not allow myself to dwell on dear old Sol. I do wonder about your comments about Lyra; you must be aware that Lyra 9976 is not cleared yet so even if the air was perfect we'd still be totally protected from it by suits and canned air." He crossed his arms and gave her a disapproving look, perhaps the same look given to a student for over-watering the beets. "Wait a minute that calcium patch is supposed to combat osteo, and you're reducing it for a place where I'm more likely to fall and fall hard?"

She was puzzled, farmers and Ag scientists had hung on this man's words for over six decades, he's an icon! And now an exile! She calmly explained, "One, the actual amount delivered in about six days of exposure to that gravity will end up being very close to your upper recommended intake. Too much of this delivered in a short time could increase the chance of the dreaded side effects, like stroke. The bone-building process is a slow one so it is much safer to err on the low side. We're reducing the chance of a bad spike, so relax."

"Sorry, Doc, you're the expert." He began describing the glories of the sunny Saskatchewan cornfields and how he won a wager that he could judge the protein level in standing wheat to the tenth of a percent.

Before he got past dawn on the day of the bet, the Commander knocked a staccato on the wall. "That's all for now, Cartier. Beat it."

Alain smiled aggressively at the interruption and curt dismissal on the way out. Char noticed and sniffed.

"You think he'll last the whole trip?" Char asked Doc, within earshot of Alain, twisting around to make sure.

"Char, he's in better shape than either of us after a century of open air and sunshine. Everybody's checked in except Lee and survived the departure intact. How long to 99 whatever orbit?"

"We're on the tail end of the 9C loading window at Kuiper even at increased acceleration. Ronnie Sue, I need some help. I get sick to my stomach anticipating the interminable wind-up of that decrepit sling. I'd rather go the Chow Mien route than Cerberus. You know the history! I keep feeling the wind-up is happening and is starting vibrate, the rattle and, and see? Or we get thrown out like a ball of fire and slam into Quaoar? I get so jumped up I can't stand it." She looked away clutching her elbows as if ashamed of voicing fear, then turned back shyly. "Please say you brought more Nervana?"

Doc minded the slight pause between the explanation that was planned to evoke compassion and the plea that was orchestrated as a natural and reasonable consequence of the poor woman's angst. Doc had heard it many times before, including real professional-grade tearjerkers. "I brought some."

"That's really helpful," Char replied more happily. "You know I stay jangled because Captain Fajar won't *do* anything and you can't take a step without some malcontent lurking." She jumped up off the table and tapped her toes.

Doc went over to the only locked cabinet in the whole sickbay and counted out six little azure pills. "Not more that one in any eight hours, remember?"

"Oh, thanks, yes. I'll see you around." Char cradled the vial in cupped hands at her breast and walked away with a spring in her step.

Doc locked the cabinet back with a real mag-key, not an easily overridden thumb access. 'We do everything we can to keep from thinking, whilst the AI gets smarter and smarter.' She returned to the exam room unenthusiastically; there in the doorway was the delinquent.

"Lee, you're the last. Hop up here, I want to get finished."

"I don't have time for that, Doc. Where's Barb?"

"I sent her to the back to run a standard through the GC. She has to wait until it completes the cycle so she can verify the QC result and compare the chromo through AI and her own independent interpretation."

"I thought this was a modern lab? Let the computer verify it."

Yeah, give it all to the computers and forget how to even tie your shoes. "Son, you need to understand the process or you're no more that a Tech. Barb wants to be more than a Tech."

"Why? Tech pays pretty well and you don't have to sign a contract."

"Son, I won't argue it with you. Barb will be at least another hour."

"Tell her to hurry it up; I got a job for her." As Lee smirked and sauntered off, Doc made tracks toward clearing out of sickbay for a while, putting her supplies away and wiping down all the surfaces out of ingrained habit. She tossed the wipes and gloves in the disposal. Stretching toward the overhead on tiptoes then bending to touch those toes helped a little.

Now it was her time, her 100% manual projects, also known as handmade craft. She walked around to the linen storeroom and carefully opened a closet artfully arranged to accommodate her new and improved still. She was pleased that it survived the varying grav vectors so far. She reviewed the steps for firing it up tonight, definitely tonight while Olivia was still involved with her field study. All in place and ready!

She closed that door and opened the one below, the one that contained her special joy; the nut brown ale started a couple hours ago would be fermenting in earnest by this evening and would be ready to bottle in a week, nicely converting sugars to alcohol. The ale resided in two white 30 liter buckets with tight white lids featuring low-tech no-leak gas permeable airlocks, all under the still shelf. She looked forward to the bloop-bloop of the bubbles through the airlock; it meant the little yeasties were in 'go forth and prosper' mode, happily transforming the malt into alcoholic nectar in a millennia-old process.

She had enough blocks of hopped malt on hand for four more double batches, but only the two buckets, one case of bottles and limited kegging supplies. Her retirement stash rested among the common lab supplies and she didn't want to go and draw attention to it. Satisfied with the safety of her project, she camouflaged the brewing equipment again, latched the closet and fled the place for an evening with Weldon's spectacular percussive arts to pull her mind away from problems and then with Schumann to sooth away the last wrinkles.

chapter 7

Meetings

Doc Trogden was glad she'd started her exercise program earlier today for two good reasons. First, she gained too much jiggle and got too lazy on her shore leave. Excess thinking, excess drinking, she felt safer from herself in these confines. Secondly, the increased circulation got her anticipating a grand start to debate season. In general, she knew she needed to be in better physical and psychological shape to face the rigors ahead. 'Retirement later, it's a long way to Roundabout,' she thought as she threaded through the corridors to the Bridge. Around a corner, she saw the other southerner aboard.

"Naomi, hi, I was just going up to the Bridge to discuss the philosophical aspects of miracles with Olivia. Want to join?"

"No, Doc, but thanks for asking."

"Why not dear? Olivia doesn't get out much and it would do her good to have a little challenge. You might have an interesting cultural angle we haven't thought of, or maybe we could give her a double dose of Dixie." She saw the rejection in Bloom's face before she voiced it and assumed it was the crew/Passenger thing.

As if it were dead fact, Naomi looked Doc square in the eye and stated, "She can read minds." Then with a little less conviction, "Can't she?"

"What? A top ten grad talking about mind reading?"

Bloom showed classic anxiety mannerisms. "I mean, sorry, I, well I heard she can read minds," she mumbled miserably. "I'm a very private person."

Doc refused to let this incident drag her newly elevated morale down. "I see. No dear, no one can read minds, at least not to the satisfaction of modern science. She is shrewd and can draw pretty accurate inferences. It could seem uncanny I suppose, but she'd be appalled to hear you say it was telepathic; I'm the metaphysical apologist around here." The woman was so nervous she was trembling, for goodness sakes. Not wanting to push, she simply said, "Some other time then?"

"Okay, and thanks again." Bloom hurried into her cabin and shut the door.

All the way to the Bridge, Doc wondered about what was eating the scientist and where she's heard such a thing. You'd think she'd be resigned to being dumped at a rock far from civilized notice by now and she'd be pleased to have it far easier than most of the poor shmucks. She probably thought some of her more subversive activities were secret. Ha!

When she reached the Bridge, her mind shifted gears away from the dreariness of political machinations and underhanded surveillance. Olivia actually made her think of something besides wretchedness again!

Perceiving the bridge occupied only by Olivia, Doc entered the bridge casually. "Hello, Livy. I tried to get new meat, but Naomi Bloom turned us down." Phooey! There's Jones,' she groused inwardly. Jones would certainly disapprove of fraternization unless she personally sanctioned it. "Oh, hi, Char, I didn't see you at first huddled up in that chair."

The Exec swiveled around and uncurled to stand. "No matter. I think I'll leave you two to your palavering. I could use a little lie-down." She spoke liltingly, at ease. She pushed the chair in and executed a whole body yawn on her way out.

* * *

Char almost stumbled into Thao Tomlinson in the passageway.

"Commander Jones," he said in his incongruous fluting voice. "May I have a word with you?"

A gnome was lousing up her beautifully dreamy state. In her Commander's voice she asked, "Certainly, Dr. Tomlinson, what can I do for you?"

"My cabin is much too cool. The thermostat will adjust no further."

"The cabin temperature ranges are set by regulation. I'm sorry. Is there anything else?" It was like talking to a slant-eyed chimp! He was staring up at her like he wanted a banana! Well, she had no bananas. "Good day." She brushed by, already trying to recapture her mood.

chapter 8

out of Breath?

Cedric stopped by the galley for some real tea, hot, and saw Marta there just folding into booth with what looked like milk and oatmeal cookies, biting her lip as she maneuvered with an overfull glass. Completely against his habits, he lingered by her on the way out with his tea paraphernalia, maybe because of the hominess implied by the milk and cookies. He'd seen her twice now, but hadn't actually spoken to her yet. Wouldn't it be civil to do so now?

He sat opposite her, telling himself he wasn't afraid of women. He got along fine with Olivia as an example. He had decided some time past that he was simply unsociable and that caused him to avoid all persons, male or female. He had a direct reason to see Olivia, but no reason to stop here. All reasonable.

Before he knew what he was doing, he actually said words to the young lady with half a cookie in her hand. "So are you a Passenger, too? I didn't see you in orientation."

She covered her mouth self-consciously and replied, "No sir." She took a sip of milk to clear the crumbs out and continued normally to say, "I came on board in the last hours to be an assistant to Dr. Cartier on Lyra 9976, but I'm assigned to the ship since they're

staying and I'm coming back. I have been doing some odd maintenance. My orientation was via my tablet on the way to Ecuador."

He nodded. "I remember the Captain mentioning you now; you
needed the cash and credits? He said he saw you on the elevator."
He knew all about scrimping for school.

"Er, yes sir. I ran out of scholarship money for continuing my
education and can't take any more from my Aunt without giving
something in return."

He found himself thinking, 'Why was she treating me like some
old guy with the 'sir' routine? She can't be more than, hmm, I
wonder how old she is?' Aloud he simply asked the obvious next
question, "Studying what?"

"Horticulture and Botany, and I was going for a Tree Physiology
Master's. My aunt has 1100 acres in Kentucky with management
oversight of 17,000 more, all hardwood carbon sink with sustain-
able harvesting and watershed control. You would never think it to
look at her, but she's an organizational and technical genius having
deal with the city, county, state and federal rules and regs as well as
managing the health of the biota and the people living throughout,
with a farm the size of a town of her own."

"I take it you lived there and contributed to the work." He was
intrigued watching her trying to time a cookie bite with his questions, watching surreptitiously while he made his tea.

"You bet, as much as I could learn to do. The beetles and more
borers are moving up fast from the south, and the Tampa blight. If
you could skooch up all the ticks and mites you could find and fling
the wad into orbit you'd have a whole 'nuther moon! And then there
are the lack of real winter, the longer, hotter summers and ever
more floods and twisters. We're hoping I can come up with some
solutions to save the trees from at least the biological threats, maybe
a viral suite. Meanwhile, we've written several journal articles on
splicing techniques and grafting applications, as well as improved
general disease control methods."

"Horticulture," he said flatly, old demons crowding out his pleasant musing about relative ages and her singsong narrative. His personal demons flew in like carrion birds any time he got near a girl.

Before he could remedy his poor response, he saw her face fall and with it his own heart. He tried to beat back his demons and memories and attend to her but they kept flogging him with wooden canes. He saw her panicky expression and wanted to reach a hand to her but couldn't. It pained him to see the panicky lines drawn in her simple but lovely features, completely uncontrived.

"Yes, my Auntie isn't the only green thumb, either; it runs in the Leeuwenhoek family. Her sister, my mother, was a Booskoop habitat migration engineer. She tried to get the most out of each greenhouse since land has always been so precious. Even though every inch of every polder was taken by greenhouses with raised floors - saline encroachment you see - even if there seemed to be plenty square meters of growing trays, she said every grain of sand had a purpose."

His memories took a backseat to the dangerous confession she was making, to him, a stranger! "I thought you were German. Polders and greenhouses sound remarkably like Holland, or at least the Holland that was. I wouldn't think there'd be many Dutch refugees in America." She instantly looked so nauseated he wondered if he needed to grab a bag or a basket or something before she threw up right in his face.

"I'm sorry; I do tend to mix stuff up." She spoke rapidly as if while running. "I meant I heard about such a person, a great aunt, and was inspired. Yes, my grandmother talked about her and made her seem so real." She seemed to be aware her story was not very convincing. "My family did come from Holland a few generations back." Counter to her anxious eyes she smiled winningly, at least he thought that was her intent. She got a startled bird look and said, "Saline encroachment is a problem in Mainz, all of the lowlands. We have many greenhouses there and I worked there, imagining what Holland must have been like." Now she nodded once and leveled that more genuine, endearing smile out for him.

So she was a secret Soggy, a wet-footed illegal. How could he let her know her secret was safe with him? He deeply regretted never having time or willpower for women before; he was completely out of his depth and grieved that he was behaving absurdly when she needed someone to confide in so plainly. "You idolize the great Dutch dream, trading the sea for flowers even though it all drowned. That's a strong inspiration."

He shifted on the bench, changing from his comparatively petty personal anxiety to more of a shared melancholy of grand things lost forever. "That is admirable. I also considered a natural science path; my own mother loved flowers and considered herself an amateur horticulturalist. I assisted her, of course, but initially aimed for coastal studies at her urging. I eventually went with the more practical Energy Systems Engineering instead."

She seemed relieved that he was letting her off from her blunder. She replied, "That's quite the leapfrog, from one to the other to the other."

He watched her minutely and was quite aware she still guarded her relief, those tender-looking lips too thin. He didn't know what to think of the solidifying link between her inner turmoil and his, as if their souls could naturally synch.

'Chin up,' he told himself. "It's what Father wanted, a career on the priority list. Nature for nature's sake isn't even on the list in Scotland any more; Power Gen has been at the top for quite some time." He prayed she wouldn't ask about his parents, especially his mother and her wishes.

"It's not as high as you'd think in America either, but as an immigrant I was not expected to do anything vital."

"I see." He relaxed some, glad they'd veered away from touchy subjects. By chance his next glance, the same kind of glance one commonly does while conversing, loitered. Careless at first, his eyes met hers. He looked more closely into her eyes, those green and ebony flecked deep brown eyes, really seeing them for the first time. His tight jaw slackened somewhat. He floated, he felt so alive, and he was not alone in this, she was participating, the link was tangible. Then *snap* it was over and he pulled back, dazed.

"Mr. Crannog, it was so nice to meet you." Marta darted forward from the galley, away from him, as if chased by wolves, leaving a quarter of a cookie and a few swallows of milk.

Cedric finished her snack for her and gathered the plate and glass. He stood dumbly with thoughts drifting though his brain like 'what just happened' and 'who is she' and most disturbingly, 'how soon can I talk to her again?' Not even before college, never had he been jarred like that, never a connection with a person like that. He felt a strange euphoria like a comet might as it careened toward the sun, burning off the outer crusty bits in an ostentatious blaze.

The clacking demons swarmed around his ardor, quenching it with muck. His jaw clenched tighter, overcoming the simple, almost happy grin. He deposited the dishes and returned with his tea paraphernalia to his cabin, resolved by brute force to pull away from the sun and defend his icy core. All night he was a prisoner in his throbbing skull.

chapter 9

The Least Favored

Blue – blue – blue! Marta was distracted from her pollinator-series course by the door alert. Sighing at the intrusion, she flicked a finger to pause the lesson and found Naomi Bloom at the door. "Won't you come in?" She'd practiced saying that and thought it sounded rather natural.

"Huh-uh, buttercup, we're going to lunch. Barto is going to meet us there and I think we can talk him into showing us some of his tattoos. Come on!"

"Naomi, I'd rather stay in and finish this lesson. Now that I'm in the military, I have access to millions of courses and I have enough to keep me busy until we get back!"

"We talked about this before, why it was essential. What is this compelling lesson?"

Sheepishly, Marta told her, "The role of flies in wildflower migration."

"Right. I understand egghead honey, I are one. But we still need to mingle. We've been on the Pecker seven entire days already and I have yet to set you down for lunch. It's my mission!"

Soon Marta found herself in the presence of Cedric. He sat in the same booth in the same spot as disquieting encounter three days before, reading something titled 'Actinides' on his nice fold-out tablet, a new scientific model. Gosh, hadn't she drooled for one of those!

Marta steadied her breathing. Not seeing a hair of him since then, she thought maybe he was avoiding her and she agreed with that; her notion that he could be attracted to her in any way was a silly idea. Besides, she'd stayed holed up with her new-found courses as well.

He had to know she stood right there, but wouldn't deign to say hey or anything, therefore confirming her conclusions. What about that man made her spill her guts like she had? Here he was, the one guy on board she thought it would be possible to test her damaged emotions on, a reserved and proper kind of guy so unlike those who'd hurt her, not American at all, one who was definitely leaving her life forever on Tenembras in a few months. Not least, here was a man so smart and meltingly handsome with that satiny, dark chocolate ponytail that revealed contrariness and the slim figure that knew no indolence. Such a knight was not for her, though. She started to back away to perturb him less, to show she understood the rebuff, but Naomi wouldn't have it.

"Mind if we sit with you?" Naomi asked, already sliding in the seat across from Cedric. She pointed a beringed finger at Marta and then pointed to the bench by him.

Marta saw Naomi's intrusion bothered him and took another tiny step back, right into Barto.

"And where are you going, Hermana?" He nudged her closer to Cedric's bench, making her put her hand to the table to steady herself. He set a tray with chips, cups and a pitcher on the table and slid in next to Naomi leaving Marta standing idiotically neither here nor there.

Cedric switched his book off, folded the screen and stared at the table, not even glancing at Marta.

Naomi impatiently swatted a hand toward Marta, "Well sit down hon, I'm getting a twinge looking up at you." She invited herself to the crispy white chips while Barto reached over and poured the cold sweetened tea, three cups because Cedric already had hot tea.

Marta felt she was fading into another plane as she tried to sit without actually taking up any space, feeling like she and he were both cold south poles, the magnetic repulsion as strong now as the attraction was before. She tried to think something else, anything else. The table was too low to the bench, the corner of the table by Naomi was chipped and showed the laminated layers below; the temperature in the room was on the warm side but only middling humidity and getting stuffier by the minute. Her thoughts jinked from one idea to the next; she decided intuitively Cedric would not take any sweetener in his tea at all. She successfully avoided more troublesome thoughts with petty observations and thinking of all the English words of four letters or more she could make from the word 'actinides' until the seconds stretched to minutes.

She sat on the edge of the bench but that was near enough to feel the heat from his body, or if not heat, then, the energy of his presence, his aura. Her thoughts spiraled into the grav well he'd created. 'Why won't he speak or even peek this way?' Marta's mind raced, her electric encounter with his brilliant blue-violet eyes was now more real than the current awkward circumstances. 'Was it so bad? Didn't he feel the shock? Did I piss him off when I ran away like I did?' She struggled to come back to the here and now before she did something else lunatic. What would a normal person do and how would she know? She politely asked, "Mr. Crannog, do you mind if I share your seat?"

With an even tone and without looking anywhere but the table, he said, "Certainly not."

Naomi finished her first glass of tea and drummed her fingers on the table to get the attention of all. "We're getting Marta here acquainted with the cast of this drama. We'll start with you Cedric! Tell us where you're from."

Cedric nodded slightly toward Naomi, coolly relenting to the social pressure that Marta felt. "Inverness."

"Ooo, that's high up in Scotland. I'd love to go there. Wouldn't you Marta?"

Marta did not mistake his response as Naomi apparently did as if it were a glad recollection of family and pets. She was so fretful he'd turn a glaring rebuff her way that she spoke from a distance, without her accustomed forethought. "I heard Inverness to be a failed industrial city whose sole purpose is to administer and supply the Orkney/Shetland Displacement area."

No one spoke at all for a minute; Marta heard the chow signal beep and saw Barto get up and return with a stack of sandwiches, then top off his and Naomi's tea. They attended to their drinks but no one touched the little off-white rectangles. She vaguely noted they had something orange in the middle. She knew she should have kept her damn mouth shut and felt sick about it.

Naomi broke a chip in half with a loud snap to break the mood, announcing, "I'm from Concordia, Alabama, home of the Enviro-Optimization Research Complex. It is a veritable jungle with kudzu, wild yam, wild grape and honeysuckles battling it out. Oh the bugs!"

Barto asked in a low, contemplative tone, "How many of the bugs you have to eat?"

Marta, surprised by this rudeness, pulled her mind nearer and looked over to see Naomi blush deeply enough for notice and drop the chip pieces. Marta instinctively wanted to escape and tested excuses in her mind for returning to her cabin, but she didn't want to abandon Naomi; at least she didn't think she should.

Barto shook his head briskly as if coming out of an unwelcome memory. "*Lo ciento*, I speak before my head. Is only that *refugios* are places of *mucho* sadness. *Senor* Crannog, you have not been to Inverness in a long time. Where since?"

Marta had little attention to spare for Barto's lapses into Spanish. She had to will herself to keep her mind in the present time and place, to keep it reeled in. She knew exactly what a *refugio* was and implored the sweet angels on high that the talk would not go there.

"Edinburg, I spent the last ten years or so there in school and working. No bugs intentionally eaten."

Remotely, Marta noticed that Naomi was close to tears for this not going according to her notion of etiquette; after all, she considered herself the hostess. She saw Barto look over to Naomi regretfully, but then he turned to her. She saw him through an increasingly thick fog.

Talking softly, only to her, Barto said, "Look, I know you're from where there were terrible floods. There had to be bad memories. Come back to here, little one. Look at me."

Marta did look more directly at him, her lifeline. How did that insipid fading out happen so fast? It was only talk! That and the unmistakable taste of grasshoppers in her mouth, the feel of serrated legs in her teeth rubbing sores inside her lips. Her physical vision was already shaded and she found it tough to see anything or anyone distinctly, but the picture in her brain comparing the size of a German cockroach to a gargantuan American cockroach was crystal clear.

Marta was ashamed at her weakness and, exacerbating the tense effects. She considered, 'Maybe if I crammed a few chips in my mouth?' It would get rid of that taste, but no, nobody was eating now and she reconsidered the effect of the crunching. Too bad all there was to drink was that syrupy sweet tea, yechhh. She'd made plenty of it for the fridge at home, but always made some of the plain stuff for herself.

Feeling a little better, she glanced back across the table but Barto had faded into obscurity. This was not a good sign, probably indicating restricted blood flow. She sat quietly and tried to loosen up her muscles inconspicuously. They didn't respond well. Okay, apples. She tried very hard to remember all the sensory delights of eating an apple. That ruse worked at school and should here, too. Apple, only. Apple! Good! She could see the others again, and hear them, too.

Naomi whispered, "San Luis, I know you were fighting in the Pantanal since you were a kid and lived through some gruesome times. I just wanted for us to break the ice." She looked down her open hands. "I don't have the right to ask you guys anything."

"Again I say 'Lo ciento', senorita. I know you also were arrested for demanding to know about the Hollands people, when most of the country drowned."

That hit Marta like a ton of compost. The Granny Smith apple tree she'd imagined vanished. She was an instant block of granite, shot through with tiny sharp crystal points. She vaguely felt someone reach over to touch her cold thigh in response to her obvious distress; Cedric? It had to be and it was so welcome. She tried to imagine Cedric giving her an apple.

She heard noises that were most likely continuing conversation and after a minute or two with his reassuring touch, she started coming back to the present company. When she willed herself to open her eyes, she was disturbed to see Barbara the Corpsman with arms crossed over belly, belligerently pushing her breasts out, barging in most unwelcome.

"Cedric, I missed you at lunch in the wardroom. I know Olivia invited you."

Marta retained the feeling of the compassionate pressure of his hand on her leg even though he'd retracted it to his lap; she felt the lingering warm impression. He wouldn't want a pretty girl like Barbara to see him being sweet to her. She breathed slowly, deeply, trying to reach some kind of equanimity all by herself, grateful to him for the cheery green apple regardless of his fidelity.

She dialed her fractured mind in to the frequency of the crisp teeth-into-the-apple sound. The delightful, juicy-tart taste that went with it brought her back closer. She peeked over to see him looking down at his cup as if to conjure the tealeaves. She felt so sorry for him that moment.

"Apologies Barbara," Naomi rushed to explain. "We ate down here, thinking about what's ahead and getting to know each other."

In Marta's opinion, Barbara got a look on her face as if something stank; she'd seen it before on many of her classmates.

In a snotty voice, Barb said, "What's to know? Soggies!"

Barto visibly braced but said nothing.

Marta wanted to stuff the apple core into the bitch's throat and jam it in tight.

"Wait a minute, Barbie; you're out of line throwing out slurs like that. Beside, we're not Soggies! He's from Scotland, she's from Germany and he's from Brazil."

Barto half stood and leaned to reach a hand across the table to lift Marta's chin. He asked, "That's not right, is it Hermana?"

The touch felt like a baseball bat thrust under her chin, but she started feeling the warmth of it. Marta, past caring about the repercussions agreed with him, thinking, 'No. Only me. From *Vroondijk*. Soggy soggy soggy!' But she didn't have the energy to speak out loud, she was adrift and alone.

Instead of Marta's revelation, Barto made his way out from the table and stood looking down menacingly at Barbara. "You offend and you are wrong. Not Brazil with its *islas* of the very rich in the ocean of starving people more poor than dry dirt. I am from Paraguay. You have something to say about Paraguay, *puta*?"

Charenne Jones came up behind Barbara, the tall Commander frowning over the blonde's head across to Barto, then glancing at the rest of them disapprovingly "Naomi, Cedric, come on back; we're going to watch the 'Teton Charade' in the back auditorium." She waited one more second for Barto to back off, then walked by briskly, pushing an angry Barbara ahead of her down the passageway.

Without further comment, Marta slid out and made her way back to the sanctuary of her cabin, forsaking the innocent little sandwiches. If she had to be alone she'd rather be alone.

chapter 10

confession

few hours later, the blue alert went off again. Irritated with the intrusion, Marta briefly considered ignoring it, then mumbled something about disabling it. The tried and true biofeedback/Zen she wobbled back to her cabin for had done wonders, leaving her with only a dull ache behind her brows. On opening, a contrite Naomi centered the doorway.

After a yawning silence, Naomi softly said, "Marta, I don't pretend to have any idea what it was like for you in that flood, but I wanted you to know that I'm not a Pat in the pejorative sense."

Marta retorted, "Isn't any use of Pat pejorative? I thought you people liked the term 'Patriot' better."

"I guess so. Um, you mind if I come in? I brought burgers and fries as a peace offering. These little bitty square hamburger-like edibles are pretty good if you can eat them warm. You like pickles? Every one has a sliver of dill pickle and a dusting of onions." She frowned contritely. "I thought you might be hungry. Since we never got to the sandwiches earlier, you see."

"I'm sorry, okay," Marta relented, feeling guilty about the poor little orange filled sandwiches. She picked up a burger with a napkin and moved back to the bed, consoled somewhat that any scraps were recycled. "I'm kinda ragged right now. That was a rough lunch." She did not mention heaving in the sink until she almost passed out. The thought and smell of those little burgers burned her stomach so she simply held on to hers for the time being.

"Yeah, tell me about it. I just didn't want you to get the wrong impression. I didn't set that up to be a big mess." She touched at her red eyes with a napkin from her stack and bit half the diminutive burger off, chewing in slow rounds. She seemed to be thinking while finishing the other half.

She appeared to gather some kind of resolve and looked at Marta forthrightly. "I'm here on this cursed voyage because I lost all my civic duty points when I was arrested for protesting for free information about Holland." She dabbed at her eyes again. "It was all blacked out, the big secret and everybody was in denial about it, about a million respectable people displaced at once."

Marta replied softly, "It was only about 703,000 displaced. Many of the rest died. Then nearly half of the displaced died." She stuffed a few fries in her mouth hoping they would neutralize some of the roiling stomach acid.

"Yeah, well you must have got the news first hand being on the edge of it in Mainz. I did go back to my cabin and look up something about everyone. I should have done that beforehand, then I might not have made such an ass of myself and stirred everybody up so much."

Marta was not inclined to pat her on the back and say it was okay; she was too numb from the continuing bombardment of those excruciating memories again so soon to reply at all. The Zen was absolutely wearing off.

Naomi got up and faced the door, head hung low. "I just wanted you to know why Char and Barb seem suspicious yet solicitous, wanting to rehabilitate me and why they pretended to invite me to their soiree. They'd rather have a rattlesnake at their little party than me, rely on that."

Marta replied, "I will."

Naomi placed three more burgers on the bed beside Marta and left, head down.

chapter II

ROSES?

Nearly two weeks had passed since that debacle with Bloom and company. Cedric had become comfortable with the version where he'd lent a steadying hand to a fellow passenger as was expected in any tense circumstance. The memory of the contour of her thigh made his hand twitch. An acquaintance, he lent common aid to an acquaintance. There was really no more to it. He was sure he could meet her again now with no problem whatsoever. He worked his jaw a few times to limber it up; he knew he clenched it too often and he'd have to get his cracked teeth glued back together again if he didn't ease up.

He happened to find Marta where she was working on a laser etching. He'd seen her in passing that morning, fixing a galley convection oven, with no effect on his sensibilities. Now here she was relaxing in a maintenance area on a tall stool carving tiny flowers in a flat platinum oval, at least the sketch she seemed to be using for reference was of flowers. Nothing earth shattering about any of that, though he did admire someone with talent.

She nodded when he walked up, her eyes staying on her work. He knew she acknowledged him and no one else, he knew it in his heart. He quietly watched, allowing her intense focus, savoring it.

He understood he was one of billions of people, nobody special, but couldn't quite put her in the same category. She finished her task and looked up.

His rationalizations fell away. Her immediate smile made him grin back. "What are you so keenly working on?" She reacted with a little uptick of her smile when he said 'working' and he attributed it to his accent; a schoolmate once told him Americans loved the accent and Marta had spent formative years in the US. He was gratified when she eagerly moved the magnifier over for him to look through.

"*Gud Laird!*" He checked the magnification and looked again. "That is exceedingly fine etching." Glancing over, his words flowed. "Miss Van Rijn, that's very fine, it is. Such delicate filigree. What tool are you using? That must be platinum because there is absolutely *nae* melt from what must be a microlaser." Peering through the glass once more he murmured, more engineer-like, "Rather precious tool, a microlaser with such a clean finish on platinum, with a much tighter field than regular maintenance tools. No slag, no skips, none."

"I made this one from salvaged parts; all I had to buy was the right collimator from an ophthalmology surplus site and rechip it for the extra power requirements. I made a little pin money doing custom work."

He thought she looked pleased with his interest; he liked that as well as the lucid description. He nodded and she explained in more detail how she made it. It felt strange to him, the feeling that they stood almost on an even level, two professionals discussing tools. It felt good in his bones.

Meanwhile he couldn't pull himself away from her side or the impossibly dainty roses. 'That crude sketch and the detailed etching was from memory, not vids,' he surmised. His face hardened involuntarily.

He realized he'd done it because she copied it, though her face was not stony; hers was sensually serious. It took him a moment to register that she was speaking aloud, that he was reading her lips.

She was saying, "I'm sorry; I get going on too much detail and don't know when to shut the gate."

"No, no! I was just thinking about the roses." Turning fully to her he felt a little vertigo, but somehow it felt good all over. "My mother used to grow roses, the heavily perfumed damask roses just like that. I haven't thought about the detail of their petals in years." He knew he was at risk of getting lost in her eyes again, unable to recall why there was such a strict injunction against something so sweet.

She meekly replied, "I see." She added compulsively, as if she were afraid to make eye contact again. "I know a million people are trying to genetically improve a multitude of flora to accommodate the warmer places here and drier places there, but I think I could still put my two cents in, I mean the drought-resistant polyanthas were doin' great when I left. Besides, my Aunt hopes I can increase certain understory subspecies' survival in our clime. She's responsible for far more than she can manage well."

What did she just say? "I thought the government only subsidized acclimatization of the best sequesterers?" He spoke low and slow.

"Sure," she replied, also more slowly and softly, "but the black walnuts are dying out and the oaks in general are getting weaker by the year largely because of the warmer winters and the blight." She looked toward him now with more confidence. "With the Coasties taking up every square centimeter of inland ground from there to Saskatoon, the trees have nowhere to go. You can't grow a twenty meter specimen in your rooftop garden and nobody wants them taking up their whole yards. There's a lot in the woods besides those big fellas."

She hesitated, but apparently something she saw in his face made her rush onward. "I did work for the big trees. The white oak and black walnut are premium examples of critical hardwood species as well as great sequesterers and are a critical home to wildlife, the mast sustains a major segment of the whole environment. They may grow slowly, but on top of everything else they're first-class furniture woods."

He was getting into her rhythm. "Cherry, don't leave out the glowing strength of cherry."

"I wouldn't dare leave out the cherry or the weeping willow or the ashes or tupelos, or Lordy, all the maples. I hate to leave so many out right now! Have you ever been in a mixed hardwood forest so vast that there were only trees and the natural forest flora and fauna? The trees don't whisper like pines, they rustle and creak; a strong wind before a summer thunder storm sounds like river rapids. The little gray squirrels and even a few of the big red fox squirrels, 'possums, groundhogs, white-tailed deer? The holler of the big ol' pileated woodpecker surveying his kingdom, loud and proud?"

The sound of her voice was mesmerizing, a music unlike any he'd encountered before. She must have thought she rambled because she stopped abruptly and lowered her eyes with an unspoken apology.

He flinched when he recognized he was falling farther after reconciling against that very thing. Ogres in wheelchairs with spiked wheels rolling didoes in his cranium reminded him forcefully that he did not have time for infatuations!

After a beat, he regained his more studied demeanor, a compromise. "I would like to visit there, to Kentucky that is. The Bluegrass State, isn't it?" It hadn't interrupted his study to look up a few facts about Kentucky earlier, not much. He turned back to the magnifying glass, thinking again, but this time more reservedly, recalling he would never return to Earth.

Lee burst in ranting, "What the hell did you do to my oven! It *stinks*!" Targeting his tirade at Marta, he did not notice Cedric back up into shadow.

She put her back to the workbench. "It's just the new wiring heating up; the odor was almost gone before I left."

Cedric heard her answer him with a strident tone, nothing like any voice she'd ever directed at him. Something in her tone disturbed him although the words seemed benign.

Lee advanced to crowd Marta back onto the workbench, making her lean backwards.

Cedric saw her reach behind and grasp a long, stiletto-like pick by the handle. He stepped back into the light and noticed she dropped it back onto the table.

Lee smirked and retreated, holding his palms out in peace toward Cedric. "Sorry man, didn't know you were involved here." With a quick leer at Marta, he sauntered out.

Cedric stared at the floor, wanting to comfort her and caress her hands, including the hand that seemed to be ready for murder. Instead, he clenched and released his jaw and his fists a couple times and briskly walked out the other way.

* * *

She returned to her project and lovingly powered down the equipment, carefully unclamping the cooled platinum buckle blank, placing each piece of her project just so in the small case she'd made, whispering sadly to them, "You guys are great, don't you worry." She hesitated to touch the long, sharp pick, but gritted her teeth and laid it in its assigned place. She closed the case and murmured, "First it was Barbara and now he's mad Bodine saw him alone with me. Ain't I special?"

chapter 12

Assignments

"Captain, I see you have not yet found the time to write your recommendation for Ensign Bodine. I assure you he is ready for advancement." She loved to catch him first thing in the morning because he was no morning person and would usually acquiesce to anything to get rid of her.

"Commander Umana-Jones, I am not certain he is ready for advancement, unless toadyism is a merit I've overlooked. If you continue to allow him to coast along, I have no opportunity to see his work, his ability to plan and execute orders, his leadership, nothing! You would not want me to sign him off just because he's your mentor's nephew?"

Charenne steamed down the passageway, replaying the conversation in her mind and scaring the little floor 'bot into a utility closet. She silently raged, 'Toadyism! The nerve! Oh, you can't retire fast enough, old man.' She stopped in the middle of the corridor at attention with a brilliant idea. She knew the perfect job for Ensign Bodine.

She checked her locator and found him in the gym. "Lee, I have an assignment for you."

He cancelled the virtual barbell and sat up, toweling himself off with what he must have thought was manly style. "Yes, ma'am?"

Damn, the boy was cute! "Ensign, the Captain won't sign for your advancement until he sees you complete an assignment that shows leadership. Your orders are to reorganize stores according to military specifications. Your predecessor insisted on his own system and now the computer inventory doesn't interface properly with the main. The AI doesn't like it."

"But ma'am, I don't know anything about inventory or the interface to main! Besides, the Franklin AI will already have inventory of everything." He put a singlet on and pulled it down evenly.

"Don't you see that the Frankie's AI has to interface with the thrust ships' inventory to keep track of the available stores? You're the Supply Officer!" He could be so exasperating. "Don't worry, here's a plan to go by, step-by-step."

"But it'll take forever," he whined.

"Part of this exercise is for the Captain to see you exert leadership, so I will assign you San Luis and Van Ruin. You see?"

She saw the beauty of the plan dawn on him like the rising sun. "Yes ma'am!"

Charenne was relieved he finally grasped the possibilities. "You take care of this and I'll mind the rest. This needs to be complete by the time we reach Kuiper Station."

Satisfied with the plan so right on so many levels, she decided to run a few laps around the virtual Magnolia Gardens.

* * *

Lee wasted no time implementing his orders. He swaggered up to Marta as she returned to her cabin. "Hey, Van Ruin" he called out, crooking his finger in a sinister 'come hither'.

Marta turned quickly, prickling visibly at the deliberate bastardization of her name, very glad she hadn't opened her door yet. "Yes, Mr. Bodine."

"You work for me now little Miss Soggy Britches. What do you think of that?"

"Work for you?"

Her homely face fell as she said it; this was going to be fun. "Yeah, you and that Messican." He had hoped for a response he could reprimand her for but she was playing it cool so she must know that he had seniority and was a real Ensign, not a Warrant. Fine. "Here are the instructions. Have it all done by the time I get back. Hah!" He shoved a printed flimsy copy toward her and watched.

Her fingers trembled, a sign that her first impulse was to trash the orders immediately.

She gave him a vengeful look, but her narrowed eyes and tight lips were a disappointment; she didn't give him much of a show after all. He bet her buddy Messican wouldn't suck it up like that, and he bet she'd run around and try to reach San Luis first. As he trotted away to the next target he listened to hear her running after him, to maybe get ahead of him and break the news. She disappointed him once again.

* * *

Barto did not take the news well, unaccustomed to dictates from an *insolente* like Bodine. He decided to walk it off, heading aft toward the exercise room where he could cycle away the nuisance of it. He waited for his favorite Commander to leave with her sweaty towel, studiously not looking at him.

He bent his mind to choosing a rigorous workout. He decided on what he thought of as the race to *Campo de Las Tigres*. It worked well; an hour of uphill took coordination and brute effort and he could watch the generic jungle scenery as he pedaled, superimposing his former world on it.

After his ride, he did some calisthenics to power down and loosen up. He tossed two sopped towels in the chute and draped another over his shoulders. "I hope I don't run into nobody all sweaty like this, *agua caliente pronto, por favor.*" He grabbed the ends of the towel over his bare shoulders and pulled alternately to dry his neck and upper back, then ran his hands through his hair to smooth it, finishing with his comb.

In the corridor before his own, he noticed Barb waiting at Lee's door, impatient like an addict. He could have passed her and got to his shower, but his security habits kicked in. He retreated half a step to the corner and leaned against the passageway wall, watching.

Just as expected, there came Lee, a big toothy smile and a large cup of something in one hand, looking quite satisfied with his earlier commands, clicking his teeth together as if nibbling on something – or someone. Barto turned away in disgust when they started pawing on each other. He heard her say, "That hurts!" and glanced back, taking in the scene in every infinitesimal detail as he had for many years of his career. Lee had reached up with his free hand and squeezed her left breast, laughing out loud.

Barto fell back a few steps to slump down in a crouch just around the corner. It was a blazing and totally unwelcome flashback of the *putas* that followed the camp and it was taking over his motor skills. Barto was there in the forest and it was as real as the original pain. He went to the camp looking for his second in command and close *amigo*. Major Campestos was leaving the *puta* and had grabbed her just so. Just like that! Laughing when he hurt the girl! Barto saw the scenes unroll in his mind's eye as if on vid; he had walked back a way and waited for Campestos to catch up so he could discuss nearby guerilla activity. They walked the perimeter a couple of hours going over a multitude of details. They returned to camp and reminisced about the poor but happy childhoods they had in Paraguay.

The next morning Barto found Campestos with a hole shot through his forehead. Barto vividly remembered lifting Campestos' head and finding the bullet had blasted the man's brains completely out the back of his head, brain bits hanging from the weeds and low limbs, tiny black flies feasting. Barto felt nauseous all over again. He shut eyes tightly and tried to come out of it. Then he smelled her, the *puta* in the here and now, approaching as she moved to pass him in the corridor. He peered at her through slitted eyes, "*Maldita puta,*" he mumbled as she neared.

"What the hell?" She turned, disconcerted. She stepped back against the wall, staying on the balls of her feet. He looked up at her intently, merging her with the girl in the memory. Frightened, her eyes widened as if she'd stepped on an alligator snout; she bolted away.

Barto knew he could not stay on the floor. He did the deep breathing thing, counting like the Martian therapist taught him. After a few minutes, the scintillating aura from the flashback faded and he ratcheted himself up as if he were a couple hundred years old. After a moment of consideration, he headed to the galley for a cool drink for his parched throat. Those flashbacks always dried him out and he'd sweated out a few liters of fluid on top of that.

"Barto, I was just thinking of you!" Naomi spoke brightly as ever from the bench. She wrinkled her nose when she got a sniff of him. "What happened to you? You look like what a cat leaves on the front step. Come and sidle up here with me."

He had so hoped to find her there - he respected her achievements and position but more than that, she seemed authentic. She could be so sweetly ridiculous and that juxtaposition was refreshing. "You want some more tea?" he asked, pouring himself a cup. He drank it straight down and got another with a pitcher to bring to the table. After he refilled hers, he sat opposite, intensely aware he had not cleaned up yet. His tea was gone once more in one long gulp. More relaxed now, he asked, "Miss Naomi, explain to me why that Bodine boy has no work." He drank down the pitcher contents, cup by cup. Her eyes stayed on his chest and arms, roaming from muscle to muscle, so he made sure to flex strategically.

"Barto, I'm sure he has his work on board with the stores and galley and whatnot." She did not look very confident in her answer as she swirled her cup absently, trying to dissolve the extra sweetener she always dumped in there.

"Marta and I now do the stores. We all eat our *comidas* from the automat." He used the empty cup for emphasis, jabbing it in her direction. "His work is to build up his muscles for to show, and to play around with the *puta*." She seemed to appreciate that his physique was earned by her frank perusal.

"*Puta*, what do you mean?" She lost interest in her sweetener-sludged cup because he was sure she had a good idea exactly what *puta* meant.

"His little sex girl." He set his cup down with a deliberate motion and then put his fists on the table with the same firm and deliberate care. He was determined to stay in tight control. "Maybe he no pays money, but she is *puta* anyway."

He watched her look up and to the left and to the right as she considered the thought. "I think he's as much at fault as she is. I mean, it takes two, doesn't it? Or more?"

"Say again?"

"Oh dear. What I mean is that he is as much *puta* as she is. I think. My opinion. Unless you think guys can be mucho macho studlies but the girls have to stay sweetly chaste and quiet?"

He leaned back expansively, understanding the gist of her argument and allowing her naïve view. "I see, you may be right! They both live for this moment and pleasure now. Ha." At least using this reasoning he could differentiate this *puta* from those that haunted him, Naomi's gift. These two were Pat fools while survival instincts drove the ones from his past. "Is the Patriot way of living, yes? Each person for the moment?" With his half smile he added, "I believe in responsibility and family and do not keep different rules for the man or the woman."

He followed her eyes to see she yearned to trace his smile with her fingers, and then perhaps slide her hand behind his neck, pulling him closer as he was, unwashed.

"I am delighted to hear you say it!" She chewed her perfect lower lip as if he would deny her anything. "As much I delight in your company, I have a previous obligation; I need to go check on Miss Marta, okay? She seemed upset about something earlier and I bet diamonds to donuts you know about it but are maddeningly unforthcoming. Something to do with that 'Bodine Fellow', isn't it?"

He volunteered nothing, but he knew she was giving him time to shower and build intensity by waiting.

"You'll survive without me for a while? I can drop by your place later?" She gave him her dimpled grin and went quickly aft.

chapter 13

Travel Agent

Naomi found Marta studying a Supply Management Manual in her cabin. "Sweetpea, do not try to tell me that is your light entertainment."

"Naomi, Barto and I are Ensign Butthead's newest recruits," she replied, waving the orders. "I believe Lee Bodine is a quintessential capital J Jerk. Look, I don't want to dwell on that pig's ass any longer." She tossed the manual off to the side decisively. "Tell me about the places we're going."

"Don't think I've been to any of them, sweetie. Didn't you look 'em up before you left?"

"I didn't have a chance! It was 'sign here', 'thumb here', various samples, and zoom I was on the way to Ecuador and up the Rope with hardly any time to get my belongings stored and tell my Aunt what I was doing, and that was just a message. Now since I've been here I have done some research, but it all looks like propaganda, nothing from the colonies themselves. It's kinda eerie.'

"Sugarpie please go easy with that 'p' word. Let's say that the Patriot Government has the wherewithal to purge the net of those items and opinions that might give inquiring minds the wrong ideas about the subjects that our benevolent leaders want us truly straight on."

"Naomi, That's bullshitting with a heap of words when one focused word means the same thing."

"May be, but the heap of words are not keyed on surveillance systems either. Enough of that creepy big brother stuff. Let's start from the end and work out way up, okay?"

Marta knew AI didn't rely on tagging single words and that 'benevolent leaders' would be higher on the naughty list than the straightforward 'propaganda' in any case. How long had Naomi been away from a college campus where the geeks made it a quest to uncover and publicly post all the classified AI secrets? It was a sport to find and read the postings before the officials ripped them down. Never mind, she wanted to hear what Naomi had to say, so she'd play along. "Here, I'll read the brief descriptions from the net, and you can, um, guess? Yeah, conjecture about what a fiction writer could say about a similar world."

When Naomi stopped laughing, she agreed.

"Roundabout? Here it says 'Rich in resources for industry, Roundabout enjoys a high technological standard and is the major exporter of many of the minerals depleted on Earth. This benign world has a perfect atmosphere and beautiful hydraulic cycle with astounding rainbows.' It says they received the first Eco-Pack with the basic flora and micro fauna, but no higher life forms yet. Here it says that's where they fine tuned the cyanobacteria suite used on Tenembras. Roundabout sounds wonderful!"

"A fiction writer might say a planet like this could be an Eden pillaged for its easily accessed precious minerals, with highly polluting heavy industry making more ways to rape and refine the raw materials that Earth already squandered. They go the extent to extract the oxygen from the very air and liquefy it for export to the dome colonies because it's easier than breaking rocks. The vast farms there help feed the rest of the colonies and provide the textiles for the elite's clothes and curtains. It is a fact that they taketh it from Roundabout and giveth it to everybody else, everybody else of consequence, that is."

"That's horrible; what an evil thing to do to a planet where millions could live and be happy with minimum outside support. What are they thinking? How short-sighted and ignorant of history?"

Naomi giggled, as if it were all in fun. "How's that blood pressure? You going to pop a cork or what?"

"I'm sorry. Here, let me read off another one, it has to be better. 'Lutz, a bustling world teeming with bio-rich wetlands full of well adapted Earth flora and fauna and blessed with abundant transuranics for unlimited industrial power.' It says Lutz is a palette for evolutionary study."

"Translation: A Jurassic environment where any introduced earth creature or plant that could survive in endless hot, humid swamps has undergone unchecked growth with selection for size and aggression, threatening the tenuous population by undermining any structure or barrier they can conceive. There are more carnivores than easy prey, driving the endangered humanity into sealed domes where radon and thorium cause cancers from being trapped inside to decay to polonium – a killer alpha particle emitter. The nasties get in when they vent enough to cut the cancer rate." Bloom walked over to the previously spurned tea dispenser and prepared a heavily sweetened glassful. She tilted the glass to Marta in askance, but Marta shook her head, so she sat back down on the flip-chair.

"Okay, now where was I? Oh, yes. Lutz has the human buffet and as an added bonus, they have to reflect the sunlight off the domes or they'll roast, making existence beyond misery in a dim and stifling place where one must be eaten either by an animal or from the inside. Thus, the planetary population relies on nuclear power to charge the tools and equipment needed to kill off the burgeoning biome and build more domes. This would be a case of trying to make an Earth without considering nature's checks and balances and the effect of an environment similar to what Earth had 70 million years ago, a failed attempt at implementing Eco-Pack 2. The people in charge live up Topside at the extensive docking station complex."

Marta curled her legs up under her as if watching a scary movie, pulling a pillow over to hug. "Yikes. That's more harsh than criminal, though. How about Marguay? It's 'A planet of rugged landscapes and breathtaking vistas, with great skiing near the poles and perfect farming weather in the tropics. Careful bio-introduction has yielded a great balance of sea life as well as a finely-managed biosphere.' Marguay sounds like they learned from the errors they made on Lutz."

"How about this: Extreme tectonic activity means plate collisions with frequent quakes, making mountains faster than they can be weathered or otherwise made into dirt. It's breathtaking because the atmosphere is light in oxygen and so thin a skin on the surface that the mountains poke right through. The tropics may have farming weather, but have poorly eroded and shifting rocks they may one day farm on with the odd volcano popping up. The extensive seas are great for all manner of fish (with excess selenium) and that biome is pretty well established, so the population mainly lives in the temperate zones on massive motorized floating platforms, avoiding the active mid-ocean rifts. The Eco-Pack 3 Marine Suite seems to have worked out pretty well. Since they can't extend their Rope to a land station for any appreciable time it's the only Topside Station that is not normally grounded making it very complicated to use and the one the Bus shuttles test twice for electrostatic charge before docking."

"I don't know if I want to do this anymore, it's too damn depressing. Is Solomon any better? It says it's a new world burgeoning with opportunities."

"No, not by a long shot. It gets frequent bombardment from asteroids chunks as they collide with each other along with the errant comet or two. I'm sorry, sweetie. Don't stop now, though, Chanx is next and that's the best one."

"If you say so. Here goes, 'Chanx is a paradise of indigenous life, a wonderland of exotic creatures and vegetation that excites the most magnificent assemblage of scientists in human history and supports the healthiest and best educated population of any of the colonies.' That doesn't sound right, indigenous life. I thought we hadn't found exotic life, and if we did, the first thing we would do would be to sterilize a planet to make sure there would be no competition for the introduced Earth species."

"Chanx is the officially shortened version of Chankessanderkar. The Buddhist colonists from Manitoba would not allow the death of that world and therefore live there among the denizens of a dense biosphere that bears little similarity with Earth's; that was when public opinion could be swayed and mean something. The air is fine, the sea/land ratio about 55/45 and the tectonics are there, but more calm than on Earth. The sun is only a tad brighter than Sol with twelve little moons."

"That doesn't sound so bad. What's the catch?"

"It would take hours to tell you everything, the place is fascination on an axis. For example, the atmosphere has analogs to krill and plankton that clump together in the clouds and raining critters is a normal part of their life cycle. There's a whole food chain in the sky, extending onto the land and into the seas. The people live in domes because the microbes and tiny mite-things can encyst in your lungs and you can get horrid infections from your own bod's responses and they can lodge in blood vessels causing clots and strokes. There are some wicked acid creatures, and I think something that hums at high volume as it chases you.

"So anyway, they live in these domes in communes with rights but few laws. They have universal lifelong education, health care and childcare. You do whatever work you're suited for to earn your filtered air and water and your food credits, with no advantage for big families or having your uncle on the hiring committee. Industry and other company-type leaders can be voted out! A rotating tribunal balanced with a guy's peers judges any malcontent and tech can catch and confirm the guilt or innocence of somebody in a snap, with punishment being sent up top away from the community. Wild, yeah?"

Marta was starry eyed, ready to go there in a heartbeat. "So when we get there how long will shore leave be?"

"Babe, you don't get it. It's 100% off limits, no exceptions. We leave one-way supply pods or immigrant pods but that's it. They pay with intellectual goods, they beam discoveries and tech solutions right over the net. There is no way no how that any alien microbe is going anywhere."

"What about video? At least if we get close enough we ought to be able to pick up some outstanding ordinary transmissions. What about some of the studies? Educational programs?"

"I'm pretty sure anything like that'll be jammed. They wouldn't want your private recording contradicting their versions, would you?"

"Nothing? That close and nothing?"

"Nada, not on any of 'em unless you want to apply to O'Reilly. This is the kind of bull I've been fighting for! Let's finish up with my new home, sweet home."

"Tenembras?"

"Righto, Tembo. That's our first bus stop where all the Passengers and thousands of the sardines get off." Naomi put a finger along side her nose and peered at Marta. "Thinking of the lovely crew and us gentle folk leaving, maybe you should make friends with Doc Trogden now, seeing how 'killer bee' certain persons in the crew are to you."

Marta leapt up and realized she couldn't pace in the tiny room. Instead, she bounced lightly on her toes, using just enough force to feel the affect in her calves, still clutching the pillow. "The trip back is a long time from now. Now I want to see the see the places we're going! I was so excited about going to another planet! And now I find I can't do anything more than look out the observation bubble at them. I can do that at least, can't I?"

"That I do not know, but I reckon you should be able to gawk at the spinning balls."

Marta settled back down on the edge of the bed and laid the pillow aside. She didn't bother to read the glowing review from the net. "Please don't tell me Tenembras is a horrible place. It has to be a great planet for you guys to want to go there." She halted. "If they don't want any word from any of these places getting out, how are you ever getting back? You have to make a hundred oaths or what?"

"Hold on, honey. We don't come back."

"Never?"

"Not as long as the blackout is enforced, and probably beyond that. You thought this was a contract job or a vacation?"

Stunned, Marta searched for words. She asked the patiently waiting Naomi, "It is for me, why not you?"

"It's a long story, full of fiddles and damp hankies, and I am not emotionally prepared for it tonight. Hate to toss you a cliff hanger, but I am worn down to the nubbins."

Marta was surprised at how easily she brushed the idea of what amounted to exile off; she must be made of sterner stuff than Marta. Naomi looked like someone on a mission as she walked out the door and her spry step indicated it was a pleasant one.

chapter 14

The Rest of the story

Naomi's lab was far more utilitarian and neat in appearance than Marta expected. To Marta that meant Naomi had a much more organized mental state than she typically let on, flowery speech and all. This week's lab lessons were much more interesting than the last few. Polymers! Naomi had a cornucopia of supplies and equipment; even better, she knew what to do with them.

"This is something I learned up on because I doubt the generous endowment of my lab on Tembo. Since we've covered the equipment and processes I'm likely to use, we can go on to some improbables now."

Maybe this was the opening Marta had been waiting for. She couldn't up and demand a story that drained all the joy from her friend that night last month, but now Naomi had brought it up. "What kind of work will you be doing on Tenembras?"

Naomi shoved back from the desk and huffed. "I suppose I am going to need this off my chest eventually. No time like yesterday, and so on. My lab? I expect to work on keeping the oxygen and other gases our friend Cedric blasts out of the sand in the air in a cycle with water vapor such that we can breathe it and we can kick start some semblance of hydro cycle. I expect no replacements when something is broken, I expect theft and I expect the air to be gritty with a fine dust that will foul everything I have." Her speech rate increased with her agitation. "I mean that's where they send the people that have screwed up. I'm not just talking criminals, but not excluding them either. You ever hear about how Australia was populated?"

Marta presented a rapt student look so Naomi kept going.

"First of all, from what I've heard it's a complete and total pit." Naomi didn't even look up. "A misfit pit."

Marta creased her eyebrows with concern. "You don't have to go on if it hurts."

"Oh yeah, I do. This is like a popped zit and the pus must come out." She stood and hugged herself as if freezing, rubbing her arms. "Most people there are the equivalent of slave labor, or at best indentured servitude. The elite among us, like yours truly, get fair jobs, but they're still jobs in hell. I can't imagine anyone volunteering to go there."

Marta now crossed her own arms tight against her breast as another rosy hope crumbled. "But you, and Professor Cartier, and, well, all of you passengers, Cedric and Dr. Tomlinson, all of you volunteered didn't you?"

"I think Cedric actually did just sign up, although there was a rumor he refused to join the local sector Pats, or whatever they call it in the dysfunctional Eurussian conglomeration. That would do it. On the other hand he does appear the masochist."

"But..."

"Honey, listen up. Cartier is a hero to you and probably the general populace, but he made too many Patriot enemies using his clout to try to open up the barricaded Mex-Guat border and increase food aid to meaningful levels. He said we could tighten our belts and save millions not only in our annexed Mexico but all over the world. True, but that's not the party line. Never ask him about East Africa. Saving people would mean having to provide food, water and energy to that many more people. Ten billion is too many, so why not let natural selection thin 'em out a little?"

Marta sat on the edge of the stool.

"Tomlinson, not a Malthusian by all accounts, went on some humanitarian mission to China. Well, he decked his boss's boss when he was trying to sort out the ethnic groups in the evacuation in Szechuan, some kind of chemical fiasco. When the order came down to divert 'em wherever there was room, he went to the top guy and made his case. You see he wanted to keep families and ethnic groups together since nobody would be coming back for fifty years or more. China as a single entity is a misnomer as there are a thousand distinct ethnic nationalities hanging to their identities there."

Naomi sat again, leaned forward toward Marta, hands on knees, elbows flexed, conferring in a hushed tone, "I heard there were words about how the animals would breed with whoever they were put with so it didn't matter who went where." She sat back up and resumed her narrative. "Something like that from the guy in charge! Anyhow our Mr. Thao went nuts and nearly killed the guy. He was slated for execution, but the church group he was with got him out in the general confusion of the place." She shook the visible tension from her shoulders and rolled her head once.

Marta worked at digesting this information, linking what sounded like facts to other things she'd heard. "And you? You were sentenced for asking the wrong questions? About Holland?"

"Sweetie, how do you think I know this stuff? And about those other blacked out colonies? I didn't just fall off the turnip truck and ask a few questions to the schmo on the street corner; I was a member of News Front. Heard of them?"

"You were News Front?" Marta sat up ramrod straight, a jolt through her spine and a flood of pictures racing across her vision. Suddenly the ambient lighting was painful; she closed her eyes. In a scared little voice she said, "I saw News Front people, I have nightmares about them."

"Where?"

"At the refugee camp in Nijmegen."

Naomi, shocked speechless for a good minute, whispered, "You saw them? Nijmegen is in Holland. You're talking about the South Netherlands Mega-Camp. Why were you in Nijmegen?"

"Can I? Can I tell you or am I hanging myself?"

"Let's check out that leaking faucet over here." Naomi spoke loudly and led Marta to the double basin lab sink then started running water. In a low tone she continued, "We, I mean News Front, sent some people over there but never heard from them! Where were they? Do you know?"

With quiet tears and bowed head, Marta trudged on. "I can't ever forget them. I see them so clearly, their hair, clothes, the exposed skin with no spot that wasn't bruised." She snuffled and kept going, "They kept shouting their names and then calling out 'Freedom of Speech', even after the first shot."

"Honey you don't need to keep going on my account" Naomi whispered, gulping, hanging on every syllable.

"They could hardly stand and had their wrists tied together in front. They almost looked resigned to what was happening, like they wished the soldiers would get on with it. When the soldiers lined up along the frontage with their rifles, we all got really quiet. I mean, I had to watch, you know? The mass grave was right outside our box.

"I saw the soldiers laughing and spitting and got very scared. Then one of the tied up ones, the tall one, started shouting 'Freedom of Speech!' They all picked up on it; soon all of them were shouting that and their name in turn, over and over, 'Freedom of Speech, Debra Kaiser, Freedom of Speech'. Debra kept looking at me and they kept it up even as each one was shot. They would be in the middle of saying it and just stop and fall back into the grave."

Marta's gut cramped, but she swallowed hard, wiped her nose with her sleeve and finished. "Everybody stood around and watched, like dummies, like zombies, like it was okay, justice or out of our control or something. Our little place, our box, was right there, all we could hold, Mama and me." The tears dripped slowly off either side of her chin but she did not notice. "All night I thought I heard a faint voice from the trench, singing the refrain from 'Shall We Gather at the River' over and over."

Naomi pulled a few chem-wipes for Marta's nose and stuck a beaker under the running faucet. Marta dabbed her red eyes and drank down half a liter of water in short order. "Naomi, let me finish." She deeply inhaled and exhaled before going on. "In the morning some of the guys had to shovel lime over them, all of 'em afraid of getting shot for no reason except they were already at the pit, anyway they covered the bodies over a bit with lime, but it was the soldiers who posted a sign in Dutch 'There is room for more.'" She slitted her eyes apart enough to reassure herself where she really was.

"Honey, I'm so sorry to have brought that up, how horrible, horrible." Naomi turned aside slightly to blow her nose with wipes.

Marta rocked slowly. "Martin Rosier, Debra Kaiser, Stuart D'Agostino, Farad Adina, Philip Albergenian, Brigit Castanos, Bryce Coleman and Sam Boatwright. Sam was a girl, a redhead. I think the Armenian-sounding guy was not really one of them because he watched what they did and copied them, maybe a liaison or something. I guess since he was cast up there with them he started chanting too."

Naomi rubbed at the back of her neck. "While I was in a comfortable apartment in Georgia getting my Doctorate."

Marta looked toward her with heavy lids. "If you were so comfortable and only passing messages, why are you here?"

"I'm too ashamed to say. I mean it was all so stupid."

Marta waited anyway. There was nowhere she wanted to go until the atomic headache passed. She stood and forced her joints to free up, moving hips and shoulders together on one side then the other as if wearing a straightjacket that limited her range of motion. She forced herself up on her feet and went over to the lab fridge to take out a couple iced teas, offering one to Naomi. Caffeine helped cinch up the dilated blood vessels in her brain that had gone into spasm. She didn't get the iridescent light shows Barto got, just a growing blackness.

Naomi tipped the bottle to her in thanks, opened it and took a sip. Marta downed hers in one long slug disregarding the flavor. "Okay. You deserve to know if anybody does. Here goes." Naomi cleared her throat and straightened as if to recite but still keeping the volume low. "I was rooming with an artist, Marc Crenon. That guy was so dreamy, so fine, I was head over heels gaga devoted. I went over there to have fun, it was New Years Eve. I also thought he was the kind of guy to propose on an occasion like this so I dressed all sexy and spritzed on the perfume he'd bought me from Paris.

Well that's it, la la la, and we got drunk. We were at a party and ended up not at a romantic rendezvous but at a Freedom of Speech rally about the Dutch blackout. Of course, I knew I could never overtly associate myself with the Front, that it was dangerous to even talk about a rally. However, it was New Year's Eve and I was deliriously in love and he had no idea I had an alter-ego, so saw no harm."

Naomi stood and shut off the running faucet. "This is no secret from anyone who might listen." She slumped back into her chair and went on with resignation. "I vaguely remember really getting into the rhythm and beat of it, the rush of the crowd, the sirens, the brilliant lights all around, I was fearless. He'd yell '2' and I'd yell '1' and we'd look at each other and yell 'OH-OH!" Marc drew us up a couple really zowie signs, and we twirled them and pretended they were Mr. and Ms. Sign spouting poetry to each other, all manner of silliness." She paused to dab at her eyes again. "We were laughing still as they loaded us into the van, eyes streaming with teargas.

The next morning I woke in a small concrete cell, with no windows, a hole in the floor, a hangover and a used up Vanitee patch stuck on my left shoulder blade. After what I guess was a few days they let me out, but someone else had moved into my apartment, Lord knows where my stuff went and my bank account was routed to pay for the fees associated with my detention. I had a thousand dollars of books alone in there, and all my beautiful clothes, and my shoes! My parents wouldn't answer my calls; Marc had vanished off the face of the Earth.

I found out from my brother Tim that my parents actually disowned me. Legally disowned, you know? For being a Newsie or for being an idiot I don't know. I'm technically an orphan. I was 'offered' Tenembras."

chapter 15

Alain Gets His Apprentice

Muttering to himself, Alain struck off to see the formidable Commander Jones about his help. He'd been so involved with his own preparations, digressions, obsessions and general study that he'd almost forgotten about having an assistant and now it was nearly six weeks into the interminable voyage. Less than five months to get a neophyte up to par!

'She'd better have half a brain; I have far too much to do than to baby-sit some Patriot waif.' Scowling toward the floor, he shuffled with hands in pockets through the port passenger passage into main corridor forward. 'Probably some sallow-faced dewy-eyed dimwit.' Off to the side at an auxiliary booster pump room he was distracted. That Bodine fellow was blatantly ogling the lower half of a person whose top half was deep under the framework, hips moving in time to a ratcheting sound. He almost put voice to the opinion, 'Sorry excuse for an officer, that one. I'll probably be stuck with a potato-brain like that.'

Finally, Alain made it to the Bridge after several wrong turns and a standoff with the strangely costumed floorbot.

"Ms. Jones, the Captain said you'd assign me my assistant. I have much to prepare."

She looked down her nose in disdain. "You are not allowed on the Bridge without my express permission."

He stood as straight as he could and pulled a crooked forefinger up to wag at her face as if she were a sassy junior. "Since I'm here, young lady, you could answer my question. Where's my assistant? The Captain indicated she was aboard."

She sniffed and replied, "You mean when he called you about the probability of our detour to Lyra 9976? When he so helpfully shared that vital information?"

Flustered by her yammering, he asked again, with emphasis, in case she was a bit daft and could benefit from repetition. "I would like my assistant, please."

She looked over to the clock and sighed. "Yes, I do seem to remember something about that. If you like I can look it up and message you with the result." She walked to her console and sat.

He followed her. "You have precisely ten living persons under you management and I would not think it too difficult for someone of your undoubted capabilities to keep close tabs on all of them, especially since they have only one small ship in which to hide. Either you have my assistant or you have jettisoned her."

She tapped sharp fingernails on the console. "If you mean that foreigner, of course she has a chip. Oh pardon me! You're Canadian aren't you? So sorry, I meant 'that flower from another shore is locatable.' I've been thinking that South American fellow, San Luis, would be much more helpful."

Alain had been given the runaround by experts and this mink was no match. In a matter-of-fact tone he said, "Actually, I was told a Van Rijn has been set aside for me. For me, personally. Something about him having a degree, or so I was lead to hope. A Hort-Botany degree to be specific. Stellar grades. I really do not have the time to bandy this about with you any longer. Pray tell, where is she?"

"Dr. Cartier, I do have a young Van Ruin, but she happens to be handy at repairs and maintenance and is working on a critical project for Ensign Bodine. As an Ensign, we expect to keep her busy on board."

Why was this woman so obstinate? Why would she try to deny him his assistant? With a professorial boom, he declared, "Commander Jones! This is an outstanding opportunity for the young lady to gain valuable experience assessing an alien world! And I need someone who understands what the equipment is and what it does. That she has talents for mechanical endeavors is a welcome bonus. That I have capable help was the entire purpose of the posting in the first place!"

"The posting you made because you knew about the side trip a month before most people." She wasn't even looking at him, she was examining a fingernail!

Alain's patience, not generous in the first place, had thinned considerably with all this. Was it possible that she was belligerent simply because he was given time to get his grip together for the trip? Ludicrous! "Yes, that very posting. It was not filled until the last moment. I was desolate, whole classes of graduate students turned me down."

Char did not suppress a sneer. "Go figure. Ensign Bodine needs someone for the stores project as well as routine maintenance and minor repairs. That must be a factor to any assignments."

Alain remembered seeing Bodine in the pump room and the figurative LED lit over his head: That was his girl under the framework the reprobate was ogling! "Surely that Bodine fellow could help with the maintenance and repairs, he seems idle much of the time. Ought to be part of his qualifications, I'd think. In fact, I saw him on the way up. He was lounging while she was hard at work."

She wafted a hand like she was sweeping the crumbs of his words away. "Never mind Lee, he is assigned to manage and she to be managed." She threw up her fingers with her shiny magenta nails to concede he'd bullied her into something. "Very well you may have her, but you probably already know her kind don't like working for people like us."

He had started to leave but turned back because her thinking they had anything in common was ridiculous. "Like us?"

It was her turn to point an emphatic finger at him. "Dry feet and full bellies, Doctor, we are viewed as the fortunate ones because of our foresight and are despised in some quarters. She was adopted here from the Rhine flooding a few years ago, soggy as they come. If she says something, please let me know, as I will not have any subversive behavior on my ship and discipline will be swift. Do keep San Luis around, he can help keep that girl in line as well. He'll be a good contact for you on Tenembras, heading the Seneca City Police section."

Alain wished he hadn't needed to say a word to the bigot. What made her so superior? The sheer luck to have been born into a 'rich at any cost' country? The country of conspicuous excesses that caused 70% of the problems? The one that gobbled up his beloved Canada to create an even larger Ameri-centric Empire? The gall to give him advice! The 'Thank you' he said when he abruptly departed left a sour taste in his mouth. He left determined to find that girl and take her into protective custody.

Alain arrive back at the aux pump room primed to confront the obsequious Ensign Bodine, but there was no one there. Wandering around to the galley, the exercise room, her cabin and even the observation bubble, he found himself back at the Bridge, sans Commander Jones but plus the Navigator, O'Reilly.

"Lt. Commander O'Reilly, have you seen Marta Van Rijn? She's supposed to be my intern and I have work for her."

"Stand in line, Doc," she replied, pointing at the open closet at the console corner.

Marta was laser soldering some line oblivious to the conversation. Alain waited for her to finish.

"There, all done!" she announced as she locked the closet door. Then she saw him and froze.

"Marta Van Rijn?" Recognition pleased him.

"Yes, sir, I'm Marta Van Rijn." She brushed imaginary dirt from her hands, walked over and said, nervously, "It's so good to meet you at last Dr. Cartier."

They shook hands. He imagined she wanted to make a good first impression with that pleasant but businesslike smile on her face, undoubtedly mindful that her job was at his request. He gave her his 'I'm the good guy here' smile in return. "Marta, I understand you have an undergrad degree in horticulture and botany?"

"Yes sir."

"We are landing first on Lyra 9976 in a slim few months and I'd like you, my assistant, to begin immediately. There is little to prepare even the most rudiment tests and experiments we will need to assess Lyra. How about it?"

"Yes sir," she said energetically. "Real science!"

"A rather broad statement that nonetheless describes the scope of duties. All right then. Let's get started as soon as possible." He started down the corridor, still talking. Not hearing her, he spun around to see her glance at the Navigator, who pointed at him. Marta scooped up her tools and ran after him.

"Marta, I may call you Marta?"

"Yes, sir."

"Oh my, please an old fart and call me Alain."

"I'll try, sir. Pardon me, but where are we going? Your labs are on the port main. Common areas and storage are on the starboard main."

"So true, dear, but I seek the Sky Doc in the exercise room. I saw her there when I was looking for you. And here we are."

"Dr. Bloom! Since we're both going to be working outside in the field I'm sure we'll be able to share the hired help as needed?"

Naomi slowed the cycle to a stop and turned off the endless boardwalk. "It's so pleasant to meet you after all those messages and calls. You denned up in your lab like a bear in the winter. Anyhow, call me Naomi, please, Dr. Cartier."

"I am at home in the great outdoors. Once I get out there I tend to stay at the cost of correspondence, study and my memoirs. Sadly, there is no wide open vista here, so I delved into my work which netted a similar result. Time did slip by me faster than anticipated, though. And about names. Naomi you shall be, if you'll not only call me Alain, but convince Marta to do the same. Reasonable?"

"Alain I can only speak for myself. I do know that Marta was excited enough to pop corn when she confirmed you were *the* Dr. Cartier. I do believe this appointment will be the salvation of the entire cruise for her. However, on the point of first name familiarity, I don't think her respect as a defacto intern will allow her to call you other than by title. At least that's how she strikes me, you know, conservative."

"Alas, you may be right; I certainly got a sack full of 'sirs' as we walked over. Anyway, this little lady seems to have boundless energy and skills according to reports so I'm sure she'll be able to split time between us. With Bartolommeo San Luis as a bonus, according to the Commander. What do you think of that, Marta?"

"Yes sir, I look forward to assisting you both and working with Mr. San Luis. I have been studying with Dr. Bloom until now."

"See, Naomi? Sir, sir, sir. I suppose I'll survive it." He caught Naomi's eye and winked, but she shook her head slightly.

Naomi stepped off the cycle, toweled behind her neck, and then sipped a tall beverage through a skinny straw. "I like the news that San Luis is part of the package." She looked innocently toward Marta who glared gravely back.

"What do you have in the cup?" he said, drawing himself a tall fruity beverage from the dispenser, disgruntled at her sunny attitude toward the big Hispanic fellow. "Ummm, this is good. Imagine the improvement with fresh strawberries whipped into it." A dribble escaped from the dispenser and he found a napkin to wipe it up from the counter, drawer fronts and a spot on the floor.

"Well, yes, where was I. Ah, Marta's education. Your met-Atmo assessment is something Marta should learn about before her gray matter gets fossilized like mine. You know I'm rather disappointed there were no verifiable indications of indigenous life on Lyra 9976 or on Tenembras for that matter, apparently no genesis at all. No fossils of any kind to be had on Tenembras, and I brought my gear." He knew he was rambling, but they'd both managed to make him feel old.

"Have you ever used the Osaka methane detectors? The literature says they have a much tighter error range than the Nakamichi ones. I remember the first Nakamichi I used was in Graduate school and it was the hot item that year. Goes to show how fast technology passes us by. Naomi?" He turned and found himself alone in the room, sucking on a clogged straw and holding a sticky napkin. He sighed in relief they were gone.

* * *

Marta was torn between following Naomi and staying with Dr. Cartier. He kept talking while she beckoned Marta to escape. "Naomi!" Marta rasped, scandalized at the woman's rudeness.

Naomi replied, still in stride to her cabin, "Honey, sure I feel guilty about blowing off Cartier like that, but Glory how he can go on and on. I mean that man could free-associate an ongoing discourse to kingdom come! You are going to have to learn to cut him off; I sure did."

"I suppose so," she said, heading for her own cabin, already daring to hope she could actually work with, not just for, the great man.

chapter 16

interrupted

J ust as Naomi reached her own room where an essential shower was waiting, the Commander accosted her.

"Yes, Ms. Jones, what can I do for you?"

"Naomi, I notice you spending more time than really necessary with that Van Ruin girl. Why not come up in your spare time and we can get to know one another better? You know you need a little boost after that misunderstanding about the Soggy protest or what have you. I can help your reputation. You know I must write a report that will accompany you to Tenembras."

Naomi almost gagged. Was this water moccasin trying to be buddy-buddy? Bleh! "Ma'am, I feel I need to spend time with the persons I'll be depending on when we get to Lyra 9976. I know I'll have to share her with Alain, but that makes it even more important she is knowledgeable and ready. She already has shown a prodigious talent for the lab end of things, but there is much more beyond the lab. I hope you understand."

"Certainly. Carry on."

Naomi watched the Commander march off in a huff, probably running various phrases through her mind like 'The failure to rehabilitate the scientist was wholly Bloom's fault and 'Bloom resisted repeated conciliatory overtures.'

She decided to use her anger for a good purpose. She worked it up a little more, went down the passageway to Barto's cabin, found a strong shoulder to cry on and showered there.

chapter 17
oliuia's assessment

"**M**a'am, you reported a flicker in an indicator?" Marta asked Olivia.

"I reported it to you only."

Olivia looked closely at her with partly lidded eyes, it was intrusive, like being picked apart with tweezers. She let that picture, go, military officers had to assess personnel all the time. Mindful the Navigator was a high ranking Patriot Officer capable of chucking her out the nearest hatch at any time, she seemed less likely to do that than the Commander. Lately she was almost friendly. Almost.

"You did efficient work on the spy line in the closet the other day and I thought you might take care of this now."

Marta flipped open a small worktable to prevent cluttering the control surfaces, cataloging 'spy line' into association with her recent telecomm cabinet job. She popped the lower component cover off and peered inside with her lamp.

"Marta, dear, I've seen you talking a lot to Mr. San Luis, and I have to wonder what you have in common. He seems all business when he comes up here, but perhaps in a way gauged to rankle our Commander. Stimulating thought. What's your opinion?"

The woman leaned over her shoulder, uncomfortably close. "Ma'am, I find Mr. San Luis very personable and he has consented to help me learn Spanish."

"He's a weird guy, though, isn't he? Has fits or something? One of the others was rather alarmed at finding him huddled up on the floor having some kind of episode in one of the passageways recently. I bet he's been through some tough shit."

Marta moved her probe from one spot to another, seeking the problem. "The things that make each of us unique are a gift from God." How did O'Reilly know about Barto's attacks? Surveillance cameras sure, but were the rooms really bugged like Naomi seemed to believe? Like Marta expected from Day One? Was O'Reilly the Queen Bug? Oh, yes, it fit; O'Reilly was the Queen Bug.

"Figuratively?" Olivia appeared genuinely interested. "Do you say 'gift of God' as an expression or do you infer something by it?"

"Ma'am, my reference was intended as a literal one." She stopped troubleshooting and rested her hands on the edge of the console. She had heard that O'Reilly and Doctor Trogden liked to discuss religion and philosophy so the question did not surprise her, but she knew there were probably several levels of analysis going on and that got her nerves jangling.   On another level, the idea the Navigator could do all that along with her duties and that Indian book she kept around made Marta think of her as some kind of super-woman.

Olivia seemed to have come to some favorable conclusion, because she sighed and pointed with a stylus, reaching around her. "The wonky indicator is over here. It flickers in the late afternoon with no one near. Flickering electronics make me uneasy."

Marta cocked her head. The mental mosaic tiles she pictured for thinking of soft subjects always gave way when there was a technical issue. Her synapses flashed her a diagram of the comm circuitry – better than the actual boards or a schematic in this case. She paged through the documents in her head. Aha! "When was the outgoing message circuit rerouted? Maybe for a delay?"

Olivia hesitated and pulled back, as if suspicion was burping up. "Delay? Rerouted?"

Marta picked up, belatedly, that it was probably Olivia trying to cut into the comm for personal reasons. She peered inside the components again and spotted the black carrier wire, with another wire spliced in as well.

"Ma'am, if a jumper was installed from the main to the second peel to avoid the AI, the shortest route is right over the capacitor near the indicator switch. When your evening reports and analyses stream in, the cap and thin jumper probably heat up just enough to cause the intermittent flicker." She smiled her professionally, grateful she'd found and catalogued a treasure trove of electronics supplies in her inventory job. "I have longer and heavier gauge jumpers to route away from that capacitor and could add Spartan connectors to make the routing indistinguishable from the original set-up without scrutiny. Yes?"

Olivia seemed very pleased. "Yes, that will suffice."

Marta prayed that this discrete work could dissuade the Lieutenant Commander from reporting all she heard and decided to earn her Level Three AI Interface qualification as soon as possible since O'Reilly would probably grant her access to the restricted training now.

chapter 18

Man Talk

"Crannog, Cartier. I hear you'll be working on that infernal sand O2 contraption?"

"Yes." He was at a point in his Higgs review where he resented the interruption; the interactions seemed incomplete and he had reread the section several times to try and get a grip on what was bothering him.

"Well, what does the work entail, if I may ask?"

He blanked the tablet, the elusive idea flitting off once more. Perhaps this would be a good time to practice ordinary conversation? "I'm to squeeze more power out of the existing power plant and do whatever else to improve efficiency of the Sand Breaker."

Alain nodded. "Well good luck to you. I understand the only thing the inhabitants like about the behemoth is that it ejects that fine quartz-laden dust so high it actually increases the albedo."

"I read that as well. I believe the result is at least 3 °C lower temps and less of a noon day blaze. Without that lofting the sky is still a pernicious gray simply from having no organics to anchor the dust and sand, with more of a dun color closer to the ground, though, from the heavier ferric particles. I also read you have to filter the air you breathe most of the time. What they really need is much more free water vapor for cloud production."

Cartier had great hopes for creating a true temperate climate with the EcoPack they still hadn't deployed and his expertise. "Yes, the brilliant cumulus and other cloud systems on Earth reflect enough sunlight to make the dark of the moon visible and to create the ethereal vision of the shining blue ball from Dharma base on our lunar companion. Life is a more fragile concept than people realize, except perhaps the unfortunates of Earth who were fated to loose their rain and have their rivers desiccate and their farmland billow away in dirty winds while other places drowned."

Cedric fidgeted and tapped his book. The Commander had warned him that some of the others my try seditious conversation and that he should avoid it for his own sake. So much for his effort to take that advice.

Cartier went on. "I know you're eager to be off, but maybe you could answer me this nagging question. How can this Sand Breaker liberate O2 from SiO2? You can't have a loose silicon wandering around, oxygen is always the preferred partner."

Cedric hated explaining technical issues. Still, he may have to work with this fellow. "The sands of Tenembras are not uniformly or even mainly silicon dioxide, but are predominately composed of quite heavily oxidized compounds of most sub-lead minerals with frequent seams of mineralized sulfuric compounds. We liberate an oxygen molecule from many of these compounds, iron when possible."

"Crannog, you mean a chemical dissociation? Surely not nuclear."

"Cartier, this is not like fission blasting atoms apart nor chemical dissociation, but is a high temperature dissociation; a desktop version of the big Fresnel pyrolysis they ran before getting the domes set up. Our nuclear reactors are the large economy size and provide the power to drive the reaction via lasers. The particle lofting is a byproduct of dispersing the released oxygen energetically enough with the aid of released hydrogen to prevent immediate recombination with the fine dust."

With a thoughtful look, the elder man seemed almost ready to go. "Well I get it somewhat better now, thank you. Speaking of water, have you run across any plans to bring serious water there? I can work in arid zones, but not absolute desert."

Cedric had difficulty answering because all he could think of was 'no, no, no'. "They seem to have a great paranoia about unwelcome exo-microbials, else they could drop a few ice balls."

"Afraid of space cooties! How did Earth get most of its water? Comets! Kuiper comets! I could certainly put an iceball to good use."

"Some of those comets undoubtedly changed the biota of Earth, though that's closer to your area than mine. They may have contributed to making us what we are, but now that we are what we are, there are those who want to preclude any further galactic tinkering." Cedric wondered how to escape before he got further tongue-tied. He picked up his tablet. "You, sir, are too famous to be headed to the far end of driest nowhere. You made central Canada the breadbasket of the world."

"Well, I thought I could use a break and try my agro-wares on the unsuspecting Tenembrians. Tenembreros. Or whatever they're called. Tenembers sounds like the remains of a fire. Might be appropriate."

Cedric said nothing. This could go on forever; Alain was probably gearing up to chat about the expected dust storm profiles or something. He tapped his tablet again suggestively.

Cartier inclined his head in a knowing nod. "I see you're busy, so later, eh?"

"Certainly."

Cedric walked on down the corridor wanting to reach his cabin without further delay, considering conversation overrated. Then he saw Lee. There was one niggling item regarding the Ensign.

"Mr. Bodine."

"Lee, please Mr. Crannog," he replied hyper-courteously, obviously hoping for a return gesture.

"Whatever. I have notice of your being quite beastly to Ms. Van Rijn. There's no call for that, can't you be civil?"

"Yes, sir, sure. I didn't mean anything by it. I could be real nice to her, how about that?"

"All I ask is civility. Thank you." The rest of the way to his room, Cedric wondered why he did that. He was so tired of hearing his father's voice telling him to quit toffing off and get to work every time he thought of her that he had become a hermit in order to avoid her. Not seeing her seemed to amplify the deep yearning to hold her in his arms he experienced at waking. He slammed that emotion away like he did every morning as he stepped back into his cabin and was soon immersed once more into the intricacies of sub-atomic particle dynamics.

chapter 19

comparative trauma

"Hey Marta, wake up! Wake up! Is a dream, *no mas*. I hear you bam bam bam on the wall and I think somebody beat you up or something." He barely deflected the heel of her hand ramming his nose into vital tissues. "Whoa, now. No fight me, I not your enemy." *Madre de Dios*, she was strong!

She stopped trying to punch his face or solar plexus, or his privates. In an instant shift to waking clarity, she seemed suddenly horrified.

"You okay now?" He was breathing hard with a sharp pain on one side; his grip on her arms was slick.

"Barto, oh God...I'm so sorry, I didn't mean too cause a ruckus. Did I hurt you? Oh God, please say I didn't hurt you."

"No rookoos, *no problema*. If Miss Naomi wake you, she be in trouble, but I am one tough *hombre*." With relief at her returning sanity, he released her.

She breathed more normally, relaxing some. "I...I didn't say anything *loco* did I?"

"You say like someone choking you, *no creo*. It was not clear."

She got silent, obviously embarrassed and confused, but putting a brave face on it. "I'm okay now, you can go on, and *muchos, muchos gracias.*"

He didn't go. He suspected he was a better friend than she'd ever had. From his own perspective, the whole scene seemed too familiar: the unrelenting nightmares, fighting phantoms and paralyzing night terrors. Yet he would not assume anything, he didn't want to superimpose his hauntings on her.

"Marta, you tell me. Tell me your dream."

"No, Barto, it's not important. I'm okay now, honest."

"That's what I say about my bad dreams. I say, grow up, bad dreams will go away. But they don't go away, do they?"

She massaged her throat as if it pained her, as if feeling for bruises long faded. "No, Barto, no they don't."

"Tell *Tio* Barto."

She smiled at the Uncle Barto remark, a good sign. She steadied her breathing further and he watched her set her mind to relate the dream. She closed her eyes loosely and spoke softly, rocking forwards and back gently.

"I am at the secondary seawall west of the Delta Works, where Papa works, I'm looking for him. I have on a pretty blue pinafore and have my blue bunny Moog with me like I was five or six again. I walk along the top of the far seawall which you really can't do because it's the wall way out there and gets really rough waves and weather, but anyway I'm always there in the dream and then I see Papa and he waves at me. I start running to him so happy and soon my brother Benjamin and Mama and Papa and I are all having ice cream at the overlook on top of Vermeer Tower in Arnhem. I am so happy!

Then the ice cream is gone. I look over to the sea, of course you don't really see the sea from Arnhem, but still I look over and tell Mama 'hey, it's like the shower curtain, but so big.' Our shower curtain was blue and shimmered like water, you see. Mama starts crying and Benji fades away and Papa looks right at me and says *'Tut sins, liebje.'* Yeah, see you later, huh.

"Then it's very dim and cold and I'm in a soot black place and cannot move from terror - then without transition I'm suddenly being raped by some man in uniform, his uniform changes, on and off. It's crazy and he laughs and paws and I scream and he gets angry...and..." She was shivering, arms wrapped tightly, rocking hard now.

Barto's muscles were so taut he could have deflected bullets. He felt her anguish as she cleared her throat, struggling to come out of the dark place she was in. Her words were wet and phlegmy. "The bad part is he never really did say goodbye. Papa never said goodbye, just 'see you later'."

"That's enough, little one, *Tio* Barto is here, *si?*"

She leaned on him, his arm around her shoulders. He might not have known her long but he knew her to be a fellow survivor. "How old were you when this happen?"

"I was thirteen the week before the first time. It doesn't matter now. Tell me yours." She felt around and located a sock to blow her nose.

"Marta, I better not, my dreams they too bad, you think I *am muy loco, muy malo.* You think I am evil man." He pulled his arm back and made an ineffectual attempt rub the tension from the back of his neck.

She wiped her face with a drier part of the sock and sat up. "Maybe you tell me about your devils and maybe they won't hurt you so much?" She seemed so innocent, so much in character like his dear sister. He could tell by the way she made the offer to listen that talking did not work for her. He didn't want to burden her, but he felt she deserved to know. "You will hate me, but I tell you one of the short ones."

She started to speak but he placed a gentle finger to her lips. "Shhh, say nothing."

She instead caught his hand. He held on.

"I am in the jungle as *Sequestero Primo,* in charge of *un mil personas, El Jefe de Pantana*l, when we tried to control the place ourselves. This was before the Patriots took over Columbia and started pushing south and I had to move to meet them, you know? In the dream I am master of all I see. There in the jungle among the trees and vines is a beautiful jaguar. I see him through the trees, but he fast and I start to run, he's so beautiful and he makes me feel so free. Then suddenly I am in the dirty camp town that follows us, with *putas* all around. They are so many and so big and they make the whole circle around me. They smile with pointed teeth and say 'I show you good time' but they smell like rotten meat.

"I put my hands over my ears to shut them out but is no *bueno*. Then one touches me, pulls on my arm. I become the jaguar and I tear out all their throats and blood and meat are all over the ground, I have the ripped veins in my teeth, I see the ropes of steaming guts. I roll in it all, worse than any beast until sticky blood is all I can smell and taste.

"Then my little sister walks up with a mango she wants me to cut open for her. She's about six and has her white church dress with a little lace cap and she reaches out holding the mango in both hands. I don't know why she cannot see me as I am, she should run, but no, she stands there smiling so sweet. I rise up with bloody claws and I kill her. I rip her up like everybody else.

"My friend who was shot in the head for grabbing a *puta*, Campestos, walks up and says here, take this tree. He has a pulled up tree in his hand but is sharp on the end and he pins me - I am a man again – he pins me through my belly to the ground and as I lay pinned, it hurts so bad, I am pinned to the ground and the jaguar walks up and looks at me, into my soul, with glowing eyes of love and sorrow. I cry. I cry so much the pillow is wet in the morning."

Marta hung on although he was sweating and trembling. They rocked as one through the telling, slowing to a stop when it was done.

"Barto, you are a good man and a good friend. *Mi amigo, si? No Tio, su es me Hermano.*" She banged his shoulder with hers, shoving hard to knock him out of that gruesome focus. "Let's both calm down. These are dreams, they cannot rule us."

Barto sat in the dark on the bed with his arm around her, sometimes humming a soft tune, sometimes silent, until he felt he was under control again and she seemed calmer. Softly he asked, "Marta, su es mi amiga? *Verdad?*"

"*Si*. Truly."

He stood and urged her to lie down. He tucked her sheet around her and kissed her brow. "*Buenos Noches, Hermana.*"

chapter 20

A Bad Reaction

Marta only sought an iced tea after working on her etching project, plain if she could program it to leave the sweetener out. Rounding the corner, she was disturbed to see Ensign Lee Bodine, her nemesis, standing over Thao trying to intimidate him. Marta, a fellow albeit junior Ensign, perceived that Bodine was in a fair amount of danger, that he was an idiot to provoke an outburst he'd be sorry for. Her first thought was that he would get what he deserved, but then knew it would be Thao that got the blame.

Bodine was saying, "Look if you're not going to eat this food don't take it in the first place. There's not enough to just waste you know, or do you even give a shit?"

So far Thao was holding his temper but Marta found herself getting angry on his behalf. She stepped over to the table and looked at the plate in question. Lee frowned at the interference, but that didn't worry her. "Ensign Bodine, he might have eaten it if you hadn't scraped it off the floor. Not nice."

"I did not!"

"Well it looks like it and (sniff) smells like it. If there's a problem with the galley, I should check it out. I'll have to clear my time with Commander Jones first."

Lee moved up close to her, very close. "You wouldn't, sugar. I know we can come to an understanding that will keep you in your superior officer's good graces." He raised his arms to take hold of her.

She swiftly grasped his Adams apple and said sweetly, "No, I think I'll leave the XO out of it and manage my own time." She squeezed enough for him to feel it, but not enough to damage. "Yes?"

At once Thao's thick hand tugged her arm down. He pulled her away and they left Lee standing, goggle eyed and massaging his throat.

Around a corner the little man spoke, that high voice that belied his stocky stature. "Miss van Rijn, thank you, but there was no need to intercede. That boy can do nothing to harm me, but I fear he can do you much harm. You will have to travel back without any of us Passengers to look out for you, will you not? Please take care."

She nodded agreement, but added, "I had previous scores to settle with him anyway. I think I can handle that punk."

Thao used a chopping motion to highlight his words. "That may be, but would not harmony be a better environment for travel? And you know he has the sponsorship of the Commander."

She sunk to the floor with her arms draped on her knees. "Yeah, and the Navigator's probably got a fine recording of this whole scene. All those officers have to be in the same rat hole together."

Instead of telling her to be more prudent as she expected, he said, "No, you paint with too broad a brush; please do not make such dire assumptions about all of them."

She certainly cataloged that; was the Captain a good guy after all? "Okay, I've calmed down. I will behave more circumspectly and with more discernment. Thanks for getting me out of that before it got out of hand back there."

"There is your cabin. Will you be all right now?"

"Sure. Good night." She felt low enough at her loss of control to crawl from the corridor into her room, but walked in spite of her mood. When she got inside and closed her door, she reviewed it all in her mind, fixing it as a lesson. One thing that was clear to her was she'd blown the definition of what constituted a situation being 'out of hand'.

chapter 21
chat?

"So, Olivia, what do you think of our Mr. Crannog?" Char Jones had run three klicks in place this morning and felt great.

"He's picked up everything I can think to show him that might be helpful, he's a quick study."

"He was chosen for a highly restricted installation on Tenembras. There is no doubt of his expertise from our files and his resume and references. Will he carry the load, though?"

"You mean 'can he physically stand the conditions in the Sand Breaker' or do you wonder whether he will agree it's worth it once he's experienced it?"

Leave it to O'Reilly to throw a rebellious ball into play. "You should have more concern about the common interests we serve instead of taking every opportunity make a snide remark. There is no question that sand breaking is the cutting edge technology that he was bred for and besides, the workers have to go inside, not him. I think you know I mean whether he will he stop sitting on the fence and join the Patriots as a full member? He has an excellent chance to pull himself up by the boot straps and would be a fool to let it go, with possibilities in the government."

Olivia asked the obvious question. "What makes you think he's a fool?"

"He's smelling after that Van Ruin girl and it worries me. Those Soggies are the ones who protest, who sabotage, who try to tear down the future the Patriots are making. What he does on this ship affects his attitude on-planet and my report."

"She's crew, they're the dissidents and I thought she was from Germany. An Immigrant."

"Semantics. Immy or Soggy, she's here because of some natural disaster, sucking on America's hind tit, walking around like she's some angel and then bellyaching about it. I have plans for her after her big shot buddies leave."

Char shook her head turned to leave in despair. She paused just outside the doorway and sure enough heard Olivia with another ill remark, "Her name is van Rijn, you blowhard." She mentally added that comment to her long mental list of grievances attributable to the Navigator.

Charenne ran into Barb in the corridor. "Hello, Barbara. Are you looking for Lee?"

"No Ma'am. I stopped by the galley for a late lunch and that Tomlinson guy was there. He gives me the absolute creeps! Ma'am, who is that guy? I get the shivers the way he stares from those hairy eyes. Yuck!"

"Calm down Barbara, he's a linguist, I think. He's getting off in Tenembras like the rest of them and will probably continue stay most of the time until then locked away in his cabin."

"Not another refugee!"

"Not as such dear, he's listed as being from Minnesota whatever that's worth. It would have been better to shove them into steerage with the sardines or cram them in a pod and shoot them at Tembo instead of mingling with them, rubbing up so close. Ugh!" She shivered dramatically and continued, "Now, have you studied your advancement materials? Becoming a Petty Officer is a great way to show your Patriotism and gets you a significant increase in pay."

Char patted Barb on the shoulder calculated to be sufficient to show concern and encouragement without coercion. Although she felt she was more adept at coercion.

chapter 22
lab star

"So, Marta, do you have a question on the Mark 57? Or the Elisa 6? We're getting ever nearer to the grand mysteries in the realm of the Great Lyre and there are not to be enough figurative sunrises and sunsets to accomplish all I wish."

"No sir, no questions. I've finished the books and both machines seem straightforward with the basic Canterbury Interface."

"Finished? Bah! I need you to study and fully comprehend this material. A quick scan is unacceptable! We'll be on an inhospitable planet with too thin air, excess cosmic ray bombardment, heavy gravity and with a very short time. I need you to hop when I say and be able to maintain the equipment. I know Bloom will depend on you, too."

"Please sir, I did study. Since about 0300. I believe I could set-up, operate, troubleshoot and repair anything you have." She squirmed, aware that bravado is often balanced with come-uppance, something she rarely recognized until she was too deep in it. "If we have the parts, that is."

He frowned at what he perceived as a lack of confidence in her caveat. "What size seals do you need to couple the air pen to a Fairfax Gentron in a corrosive environment?"

"Silical 0.2 with lithium gel rings, sir, two sets of both parts, with an over coat of Starseal – the blue kind."

"How long does the Elisa 6 have to warm up before analyzing an organic specimen, pH 1.3, in the expected conditions of Lyra 9976, at 15 degrees?"

"The Elisa 6 requires no additional warm-up time above freezing sir. It should indicate 'green' within ten seconds as the components come on-line. The sample would not be a problem as long as the planchette is rated for the acidic pH."

"Okay, so you remember some details. He screwed his lips around a couple times in anticipation of asking a real poser, one he had no answer to, yet. "The Elisa 6 is a phenomenal advancement over her predecessors, faster and capable of both better accuracy and precision. However, she is more vulnerable to harsh treatment. I did bring a workhorse 4.5 for Lyra, but I'd much rather have the 6 immediately available on-planet. How are we going to keep from contaminating our little Elisa and having it destroyed by the chemical decontamination required to get it back onboard?"

She grinned, couldn't help it. "I made up some DeBoer membranes in Naomi's lab. I'd really like to test Lil' Liza with a standard to see if I can run cal verifications on her with the membranes in place."

"A what membrane?"

"DeBoer. I made some up in Dr. Bloom's lab last week using a spare Elisa 6 sample assembly as a mold-template. She has the most incredible chemistry set!" She waited a tic, but he still looked puzzled. "The membrane fits the assembly like a glove and has an extended edge to mate with a standard enviro-wrapper. This way you fuse the DeBoer to the wrapper and that seals in all parts of the machine except the disposable planchette."

"You mean this membrane will be between the sample and detector during analysis?"

"Yes, sir. I would like to test it out if that's okay." Marta paused once more to make sure Dr. Cartier was amenable to the experiment. "If it works, we can do a chem sanitizing, preferably not straight peroxide, pull the membrane and scope it for any residual.

It's very thin but should easily come out in one piece." She stifled her grin and pasted a serious look on her face. He looked skeptical.

"My Dear, the Elisa 6 won't come up with a membrane, it's been tried. The thinnest membrane is seen as opaque or it leaks, either of which fails the purpose."

"Sir, please let me try it with doped samples. I really believe that this application of a DeBoer will win the blue ribbon."

"We do have a bit of time, but not unlimited materials! And this had better not damage the Elisa – I depend on it. I have no access to the equipment sent ahead to the Franklin for Tenembras."

"Sir, I hoped you'd agree. I do have a sample set prepared. Here, you run the test. Use this assembly with the membrane here." She pulled open a drawer and set each required piece out.

"It has color to it! How can it possibly be transparent to the detector if it has color? It is as green as a Coke bottle."

"A what?"

"Before your time. But it can't work with any color at all." Nonetheless, set up and sealed the unit. He packed a test sample into a planchette. "Sliding this in will probably damage the membrane anyway." The drawer slid in smoothly and the analysis commenced immediately. In 30 seconds they had a result.

"Sir! Look!" She pointed emphatically to the Elisa's display.

"Amazing! It read right through it! To the 6th decimal place! What did you call it?"

"A DeBoer membrane, sir. We got them as leftovers from a past PhD dissertation and used them in school to prevent cross-contaminating diseased plant samples in equipment that operates with the same spectroscopy principles." Which was a lie because her mother used them in her lab and taught her how to make them.

With her simple, happy smile, he came to an internal decision. Perhaps he was finally ready to treat her as a colleague. What he said was, "Don't call me sir. My name is Alain. And this is simply amazing, how could I have missed it in the literature? Not published yet! From a Kentucky hillbilly botany lab! It solves a whole stack of problems at one blow."

She left him to play with the equipment and felt a twinge of pride. She got over it quickly when she misjudged a bouncy step over the hatch that unbalanced her landing, making her catch herself with hands flung out. "Oh, yes," she chided herself, rubbing her wrist, "we be decelerating, and we be findin' out the hard way."

chapter 23

sling Time!

The docking with Cerberus went smoothly and was completely uneventful. Marta was disappointed the there was no 'slinging' to it. She'd expected being whipped around like a bolo and then released to zoom to the outer reaches. She grunted and reprimanded herself, 'Bad analogy, bolos are aimed to hit something.'

Instead of a whirling sling it was more of a slingshot of sorts, or better the plunger for a pinball game. From what she could understand it was a field dampened yet accentuated acceleration transfer from the smaller but much more dense Cerberus. When she thought about it, she realized that a small increase in acceleration goes a long way in the vacuum of space.

She pictured that desk toy of the row of suspended chrome balls – pull one to the side and let it fall toward the others and the momentum is transferred; Newton's Toy or something. Of course, the toy's frame absorbed counterforce and she knew of no analogous frame here. Being this far away from Sol's pull had to help, but the 'how' was going to bother her until she had a chance to study it. She wished she could ask Cedric, he was bound to know. She'd find time to study some first, though, with whatever she could find in the ship's net.

* * *

In his peripheral vision, Cedric saw someone peering around the corner at him. Perhaps if he ignored the person he or she would go away, especially if it was that garrulous Bloom or even more garrulous Cartier.

"Mr. Crannog?"

He paused his book and turned to Marta, an automatic eyebrow inquiring about the urgent need she apparently had to interrupt his study. He'd used that supercilious glare to push away the impertinent before, but regretted it as he saw her hopeful face wilt. He raised his hands palm out to shoulder level as if pleading self-defense. "Sorry, you surprised me. I haven't seen you here in almost two weeks, not since the sling and we didn't even speak then."

Her mind swarmed with inferences. He missed her? Had he kept his schedule hoping she'd come around? Off subject! "Um, do you mind if I ask a dumb question?"

"If you expect the cliché about 'no dumb questions', you've come to the wrong person as I know there is a plethora of them, nor am I an oracle." It pained him to see her afraid to approach him and for her to treat him like a senior. She couldn't be that young. Did she rebuke herself for their unaccountable fusion reactions as ruthlessly as he did? Well she should; his heart beat faster already and he feared a painful and sleepless night ahead.

Suddenly he felt as if a solid being of compassion burst from his chest, a living creature. The thing stationed itself between his icy heart and her, indeed he seemed to have difficulty seeing though it and blinked repeatedly to try and clear his eyes. It was intellectually surreal but had a solidity in some critical dimension that pressed against him, softly but with weight.

The thing made him say, "I'll try to answer your question if you'll refill this beaker with very hot water." The beast made him smile, but he was able to restrain it to a bare movement. This manifestation was quite worrisome. He tried to push the thing away when her attention was diverted, but it pushed back so he only accomplished moving it to center over his sternum. He noticed it was warm and plush, the wretched beast.

He called after her, "Bring yourself an empty cup, I've something I think you'll like." The creature raised its impossibly large paws up, one on each of Cedric's concave shoulders and pushed them back. Cedric shifted in his seat to accommodate this straighter posture.

She returned with the liter beaker, her slender wrist seeming to have sufficient strength to hold it by the caddy's D-handle which pleased him for some reason. She sat opposite him. "Here you go. What do you have?"

"Tadme Estate Assam. It's a centuries old estate on Earth, but this came from the Tadme Estate established under license on Mars' Kramer District." Why did the creature pressing his ribs insist on explaining such unnecessary details? He held a waste cup in one hand and a perforated metal tea infuser in the other; when he squeezed the handle on the infuser, the two hemispheres parted. He bumped the used leaves into the cup. He reached into a pocket and produced a pouch from which he reloaded the device.

He tapped the leaves into it much like he'd seen the horse wranglers on North Uist do as they would fill their cigarette papers with local tobacco, wondering why he hadn't made that connection before. He had a fond memory of the sea-foam flecked standing stones of the Hebrides, still erect through the turbulent centuries, the Callanish collection on Lewis in particular. She reminded him of the free wet wind that whirled leaves about the jagged monuments.

Surely she'd seen his handled beaker before and the infuser was much like ones sold anywhere loose tea was bartered or sold. It appeared to captivate her anyway, so he moved briskly as if presenting himself on a stage, a thing he'd never consider actually doing.

"Your cup, please?" He passed a steady stream of the hot water through the side of the infuser and into the cup, the aroma blossoming. Then he did the same to his own, finishing by placing the infuser directly into the half-full beaker where the tea continued to color it. "Cheers?" When she also raised her cup and grinned, the creature kneading its paws on his vest purred. He sighed inwardly, thinking, 'It would be a cat, wouldn't it?'

"This is surely the cat's meow and it beats dispenser tea by a country mile. That stuff is way too sweet and syrupy. And some people put more sweetener in it! Mmmm, that feels good going down."

He could see her nervous unease and warred within himself to address it, disturbed by her 'cat's meow' remark. He shoved the snuggling cat away from his mouth and demanded to hear her burning question. The creature's thick fur softened it into a simple reminder that she had a question when she came in.

She got that focused look, the same look he remembered from when she was etching the flowers. He sharply remembered how much he liked that. In truth, her face was rather plain and the intensity gave her character. It occurred to him that her plain face was the perfect pallet for an extraordinary number of nuanced expressions.

She finished the tea and asked, "How does the sling work?"

What an inane question. "Do you have a week and the necessary background in calculus and Quantum Mechanics? That's for the simplified talk show version." The cat growled and he could feel its tail twitch.

She held her ground. "I think if you wanted to you could explain an overview so even a botanist could understand it. We do have a couple months before we reach Kuiper."

'I deserved that,' he derided himself. He'd give it a try; she'd not asked him for anything before. "If I get too technical, stop me." Taking a deep breath, he considered where to begin. He winced at the huge razor-toothed shark in his skull that patently hated the cat on his chest. The shark took it out on him, ripping at his brain as if to tear a cavern to fill with cat bones. The black shark with his father's faced wanted him to stop wasting time. Cedric rocked his head, chin to shoulder, a couple times to release some of the accumulating tension.

"Right, then. Our good friend Sir Isaac Newton said that if there is a force between two objects, each object acts on the other equally."

"Yes, Newton's Third Law. The one that says whatever you push, pushes back," she replied with a tentative widening of her enticing lips.

He looked away from those lips. "So here we are in space, a more perfectly frictionless environment that Sir Isaac ever dreamt of. The Peck maneuvered arse-first into the sling field, bringing its great wad of momentum with it. Why didn't the Peck push the bloody Cerberus away? We have a very large ship, visibly larger than the main sling module."

"Two reasons, I think." She chewed her lower lip a moment, frowned and quit. "Sir Isaac says acceleration is force divided by mass. Now remember we're talking about the acceleration due to gravity, so it's attractive. The sling is constructed to be a much denser mass, therefore for the same gravitic acceleration, its fraction makes the force from the sling very large and its larger force would attract the Peck to it."

"You can't make up physics as you go along, dear, nor mix and match on whim. Omitting the essential vector components of his Second Law grates, but I suppose we don't need them for this special case. And the bit about density is rubbish. The sling is simply more massive *at times*, not intrinsically; a variable inertial mass. It occupies fewer cubic meters than the Peck thus can be denser but that's irrelevant although the resultant gravity wave of the transition is not. What you've told me means the Peck could have landed on the sling in mass-naught mode and sat there, perhaps both of them slowly drifting back in recoil, depending on the mass difference and the Peck's incoming acceleration. Why did the Peck need to not only exert a force toward the sling, but use its engines to accelerate as it approached?"

"The other reason. I don't understand how the force field works, but I can picture the sling as having a great spring that the Peck compresses as it approaches. The spring takes more effort to compress, more force per time I mean, um..."

"You're on the right track, but in the wrong county. It's so simple to show with vector analysis, a wee bit of calculus and a dram of q-mech and so confusing to verbalize. There is a well that stores potential energy on a relatively very large inertial mass that the Peck pushed up to with accelerated force. Peck pushed harder as it went to fill the energy well, your fabled spring. In addition to the conversion of the 'compressed spring's' potential energy to kinetic energy pushing the Peck away, the sling also multiplies the pushing force with energy it stored since the previous sling, the previous vessel's recoil included. The so-called spring facilitates the Peck's vector change and regurgitates the initial force in that direction with the extra oomph of the stored energy acting on the Peck's mass-prime."

She made a comical face. "Yuck, regurgitated forces with oomph."

He did not think that kooky expression very attractive. On the other hand, it was becoming clearer to him that her physical attributes mattered less and less.

"I told you I was better with the symbols; that explanation is utterly inadequate and false in part because Newtonian Mechanics is stone age and not applicable. It doesn't account for the effects of the sling's phase-shifting mass at all. You obviously researched this in some superficial way before coming here and it appears you were unable to grasp the material beyond three letter expressions containing the letters F-M-A. There was nothing novel that I could add to any of the references you would have found, no resident epiphany for issuance."

He shoved his tea paraphernalia away, angry with himself for being so mean to her. He wrenched his head around to her direction and demanded, "Why did you seek me out? Anyone around me for five minutes should be able to discern I am no patient tutor and I communicate in mathematical symbols or notes, not words. Those who can, do, etcetera." He felt bad about challenging her like that, but the demented shark in his head had frightened away the cat and there was nothing to stop him from being a monster.

She hadn't broken down. "How would you find out about how to genetically modify a peach to resist blackspot?"

"I would buy resistant peaches. Barring that, I would hire someone to do it for me. I assume that person would have researched it, learned the theories, constants, functions. If you demand that I might desire such a thing, I suppose I'd have to do the same, meaning study. Only after achieving competence in the underlying bases would I pursue the applications, and then only to the extent of that competence."

"You mistake me, sir, let me rephrase. What if you were simply curious how it was done and wanted a glimpse of the mechanics behind it?"

"Were I prone to dabbling, I might review summaries of the materials and try to make broad inferences from it. Genetics are a far cry from my field, so inferences would be broad indeed."

The way she answered was a parody of a conversation. "How would you know if you got it right? Tell it to Olivia and ask for feedback?"

"Certainly not. I would test myself with someone possessing the appropriate skill set, likely Cartier." He hesitated, "Or you. I am no dilettante, but I understand your point and apologize. Your paradigm differs markedly from mine. You muster up a concentrated focus for working on a problem which could have little or no relation to the previous problem, a non-contiguous form of world appreciation resulting in shallow packets of knowledge scattered around like so many flung pillows."

He blinked hard several times to banish the picture of a large carpeted area with multi-colored pillows strewn strategically, as if to make a cozy nest. He tightened his jaw to suppress that idea. "I maintain my focus on my profession and allied fields in a constant manner for in-depth penetration and hold it tight about me." Part of him felt like he was either making love or beating her, but he was accelerating downward toward the buried bones at too fast a rate to worry about that now.

"My shallow knowledge," she retorted, then steadied her tone, "My breadth of knowledge allows me to work on electronics, electrics, hydraulics, optics, farming, sewing, tractor repair, bread baking, woodworking, polymer chemistry, dowsing, tech writing, marksmanship, cake making, genetic manipulation, canning, hazard analysis, pottery, AI programming, cheese making, spectroscopy and *what have you*, as well as the requirements of my field. I find that a fulfilling way to spend my time. You show little appreciation for anything except your chosen field, wearing it like a turtle shell, keeping the extraneous flotsam and jetsam that make Creation so interesting on the outside."

"You have made me into a dull caricature." He sighed aloud and parked his sight on a chair support, the shark having Cedric's head in his jaws with the point of a particularly large tooth pressing his right eyelid down to half-mast. "I do not deny it is justified, I see it myself in the mirror daily. Let me resume my monomaniacal study, please."

Marta cleared her throat. "I do appreciate your time and for your attempt; I pushed your desired caution aside, so it's my fault. And thanks for the refill while I was desecrating Sir Isaac's memory, however ancient he may be."

She failed to hide the disappointment from her voice. Was it from her own errant display, his reversion to that professional façade or perhaps she disliked his allowing himself to be a cartoon of who he really was? She slid out from the booth with her cup, now empty, and he felt she took something essential to him with her.

He tried to rally and called over to her, "It was no trouble and a pleasant diversion." Drivel, it was exhilarating to converse about a common experience even if the theoretical business was bollixed, at least to an innermost part of him. His right eye was now closed completely, the tooth point stuck in his cheekbone. "Do look up Hook's Law if nothing else. It merges nicely with Newton with regard to the recoil effect and will give you something you can visualize." He expected her to move on, but she lingered, teasing him. 'Why is she still standing there?' He heard a distant purr in response.

She came back to his table. "One more thing," she said, shyly. "I shouldn't mention it but it seems significant. This is the first time we've talked together where one or both of us didn't rush off in a huff or bleeding. I liked it, even with the well-deserved jibes." She balanced on one foot, then the other. "Good night." She seemed to attempt a better smile than resulted, swiftly rapped the wood patterned laminate table twice and left.

chapter 24

Barto on the spot

Barto wore his summons to sickbay poorly, with surly impatience and disdain after a hard night and too little coffee.

"Come on in San Luis," Doc said, pressing the desk actuator to shut the door to her office behind him.

He looked around sharply, suspicious at having his exit taken away. He noted the switch panel was green, indicating the door was not locked and he could leave at will. Mollified on that count, he asked, "Doctor, I am here. What is it you wanted?"

Doc's practiced eye saw the typically crisply turned out man was haggard about the eyes, ashy cheeked, with one sleeve and pants leg rumpled. His slitted lashes indicating an oversensitivity to light. She reached over to dim the ambience and motioned toward the seat in front of her desk. He sat with the clear intention to bound back up with the least provocation. "As a security professional, you understand the need to maintain order on a ship like this."

"I have done nothing."

He was supposed to agree, not get defensive! She decided to disregard that reflexive statement. "A part of that effort is surveillance. You have done plenty of surveillance, haven't you?"

"You see me have a bad dream. Enjoy it?"

"No." She looked at him square on, eye to eye. "You have seen this before in many others, you know what is going on, you recognize the symptoms and you know you are in denial. You are much smarter and more responsible that this, San Luis. You know you need help. I can help you."

His gaze was more normal with the dimmer light, but its directness was more than she'd anticipated and it made her twitch. 'What is clinking through that sore brain?' she asked herself, feeling her way into his mental state.

In a low, sonorous tone, he said, "The Doctor at Ticonderoga did not help. I was sent there to take a security job at the Central Dome, they wanted someone who was effective, they said, without a history of 'excesses'. That Doctor, *el Diablo*, he was not happy with letting me work, he said I had too much 'hidden aggression'."

When he spat on the floor her mind flashed to a video of someone who'd sucked poison from a snakebite victim.

Louder but lower and with close control, he continued with a new, emphatic staccato, "Not to tell me, he start me on dope. Dope in my *comidas*. I never take dope! NEVER!" He bolted to a fighter's stance.

Trogden did not stand or portray anything but peace. "Hey, San Luis, calm down, you're here on the Boris Peck."

He tilted his head to the right and sneered in retort, "*Si*, the Peck, ship to hell because *el Diablo* feed me dope." He abruptly jammed his fists into his pockets. "He dope me and play tricks, like poking sticks at *el jaguar* in the cage. He would not stop, jab, jab, jab. Nurse say 'Doctor, that not a good idea' and she say, 'Doctor, let's start again tomorrow' so he tell her get out then he call me a coward for no facing my fear. He come up and jab me in the chest with his crooked finger, his Devil's Claw." His face registered disgust. "I push him away."

She waited a beat and softly picked up the rhythm, smoothing it out, "Breaking his wrist when you grabbed it and his back when you hurled him into the desk. You watched him die."

She connected his version with the documentation. The report said he stood there in a stupor until the nurse found them. San Luis was detoxed and sentenced.

She shifted in her chair and waved an arm across her desk as if to clear the air and start anew. "You know the words, to sweep?" He seemed to be at a loss, a much less aggressive stance, probably predicting questions about the treatment or attack; he'd watched her clearing motion and was on the tipping point of accepting it. She saw the decision in his face.

"*Si*, sweep with broom. I been studying English." His volume was lower than usual and his words were uttered with less individual force.

She propped her chin in her palm, elbow stilted on the desk casually. "In your house that you keep clean and in order, a pig comes in and messes in the floor, roots through your belongings, chews up family vids. You strike at the pig and he falls. Now what?"

With no hesitation, he replied, "You dig a hole and line it with charcoal and banana leaves while somebody prepares the pig and the spices. Leave him in the hole, covered up, with a small place to blow air in to keep the charcoal hot. Next day this devil pig is now a very good pig."

He took the 'pig' bait! Great! And he appeared more relaxed, more normal now, wonderful. "Okay smart alec, what was the answer you know I wanted?"

His eyes narrowed at her a moment. "You have to remove the pig from the house and clean up as good as possible. Somebody probably want you pay for the damn thing. Some *objetos de valor* are lost and is too bad. Sweep out the bad things and start over."

"That's much better."

With the slightest up-tick of his half smile, he said, "That's a waste of pig."

What a relief to see him lighten up, a marked change in body English. Body Spanish? And he retained his personality throughout, very good. This is why she got into this profession in the first place!

"Senor San Luis, you need a broom; I have brooms. You choose a broom then it is up to you to use it."

"Dope?" He assumed a military-style stance except he crossed his arms, fingers gripping his biceps.

She could tell he was contracting and relaxing his biceps against his strong grip without showing the tension elsewhere. She hypothesized that he had ironclad faith in his innate control and when that shattered with psycho-drugs, the loss of control flayed him, terrified him. She had some damage control to attend to.

"Apparently that guy was doing experiments that weren't allowed on Earth. That was illegal and unethical." She could tell he was struggling with the phraseology. "The Doctor was acting against the law and against what good Doctors have agreed is right." She saw his slight involuntary nod and the muscles in his upper arms loosen enough to allow freer wrist movement; his inner wrist rested on his chest while the outer one slid a bit toward his elbow. Very good, he was deciding to trust her.

He countered, "You are far away from Earth and nobody will ever hear about what happens to San Luis in the lake of fire we go to. Here I am another passenger in Purgatory. You get many chances to try new methods on the broad river Styx, don't you Doctor Charon?"

Not the direction she expected! She knew she was staring, knew it to be unprofessional, but being characterized as the boatmen to Hades had her on the brink of a convulsion, she felt the edges of it, dammit! It was exactly the theme she'd been dwelling on all the previous night, tossing and turning, reliving a screaming match in Carolina! She couldn't reach her medicine, she couldn't move, numb.

His face filled her view, noses almost touching. He forced her backwards, supporting her firmly and prying her rictus jaws apart. The spoon stopped the choking and she blessed him. He gently dipped her up and down, crooning 'breathe' in her ear and the intense comfort of it slowly melted her spasmed muscles. She had not gone all the way into it, thank God, only a glancing blow. He pulled her to his chest, still rocking and somehow he had her legs, holding her like a baby and humming a lullaby.

She rested her head on his chest a moment more, breathing deeply and slowly to center herself. Taking the coffee spoon from her mouth, she tasted blood where it had scraped her upper palate and refused to tell him that one should never stick something into the mouth of someone having a seizure. He stood her up with a hand on her shoulder to steady her until she nodded and sat. He sat, his concern clear.

"I am very sorry to cause that, Senora."

She sent him a standard 'don't worry' hand gesture. "It's not your fault. I have medicine and a mouthpiece and usually enough time to get to them. They started some years ago. I hid it for a long time, or denied the importance. Then I was offered this run instead of mandatory retirement because of it. I have participated in too many decisions on who will get expensive treatment and who is too close to death, I have been unable to save children because there was no medicine left, I have closed the door in the faces of gaunt families and allowed dysentery to course through a sector and burn out because it would have been too costly to stop it.

Those things are what a Doctor has to contend with in this age. I can somehow deal with battling an emerging zoonotic disease better than packing people like a Mumbai ferry whose only crime in most cases is a difference of opinion, delivering them to the doorstep to exile in hell. You hit it on the nose, I'm Doctor Charon." She buried her gray and deeply lined face in her hands.

"May I try some of that brandy, *Senora*?"

Had he smelled it on her breath? "Before you drink with me," looking up at him, "you should know I found out about your problem weeks ago and did nothing." She was gratified at his trust and humbled by his care, but wanted it to be pure, to be honest this time.

Anyone could have seen his smile this time. "I have also known about it for many weeks and done nothing."

"Touché." The flask of the straight stuff was at her left hand, the unclean hand, she thought. She swigged and passed it over. No fastidious wiping, but an immediate tip and generous squeeze. It hitched his throat a millisecond, making his eyes bulge perceptibly; perceptible to her eye.

"*Senora Doctor, es agua fiero.*" He passed it back.

His inflections were low-key and didn't reflect the recent upheaval. She'd likened his voice to a growl before, but now it sounded to her practiced ear to be a crystal mountain stream rippling over sharp rocks converted into a voice.

"My special recipe." A referee blowing a shrill whistle in the back of her aching head kept shouting 'do not get involved with the Passengers!' She knew the voice would not hush up no matter what she did now, so she brushed it aside.

"So, Senor San Luis, what happens for you? Not the convulsions yet, but bad headaches?"

"Migraines."

"Marta has helped you with your English and has shared some of the common vocabulary?"

"You see much." Narrowed eyes again.

"I have each of your vitals monitored and got an alarm one night, I couldn't sleep anyway. She was thrashing with her heart racing a mile a minute. I was clearing the cobwebs out and considering how to intervene when you came in. How did you finagle access to all the rooms?"

"Passenger rooms only, I don't know. I try a door and I get in or not. Maybe I have magic fingers."

"That's a good enough reason for me." She was certain Char did not know about that, but Livy had to know and must be allowing it for some reason. "The fact is, she was trying to kill you and came damn close. I came within a hair of gassing the room with a sedative, but you subdued her. Should we do this all together, a big happy family?"

He seemed to be picturing the girl he knew as his Hermana, eyes cast to the side. "I am already in chains, she is not. I have been seen 'in an episode' by a member of the crew in a passageway, she has not. I have lost control of my mind and myself in a horrible, violent way and she has not."

In sympathy, she continued, "You have killed and she has not." Instead of confirming her assumption that his past of killing was a major component of his illness, he raised a disturbing implication with his troubled silence. The room monitors had sound pick-ups, but Doc only got the video for emergency assessment purposes. She'd have to apply to Olivia to hear what they said, but was suddenly reluctant to bring all this to her friend's attention. His arms braced squarely out in front of his chest once more, in Marta's defense this time?

"San Luis, she does need assistance, she has shared information with you, and probably Bloom, that is vital to treating her trauma."

"She tells me this nightmare thing did not happen much at school and not at home since she was much younger. She uses 'biofeedback' and 'meditation' to fight it. This is a very bad place for her, with the Commander and Ensign wanting her to suffer, so is worse."

He flung his arms loose, plunging his wrists out and hands at a right angle to stretch and continued conversationally, "You like that word, suffer?"

She did not want to answer that question.

He reached for the flask and did not flinch at all this time. He had to tilt it high, not much left. "What do you think will happen to her when we leave?"

There was no viable solution. She already had an aide, the Captain was off in his own world, Olivia would have no excuse to keep her near and Commander Jackal and her two pups were hungry.

"I can at least put her on a treatment program that will give her a reason to come see me daily."

"You think that will help her the other 23 hours of the day?"

He was negotiating with her! "I can help her cope with what they will put her through and can intercede if it gets bad. You think I can't help without harm, but I can." She didn't believe a word of what she was saying and it shamed her. What happened to her resolve to be honest with him? 'Down the toilet with my other resolutions,' she answered herself.

"I think you mean to help, but the system you are part of is a great harm. You are one person and they are legion, as it says in the Bible. I can tell her of your offer but I think she will not come unless I recommend it."

He had made his point and she had to acquiesce. "Okay, laddie, let's work on you then."

"Tomorrow, when we each can see only one person before us instead of two or three?"

"Deal." She was already lining out the treatment as he left, planning to make gate adjustments in the time allowed before the Frankie split. As much as she scorned the AI, she'd need its guidance to identify the brain's overextended controls, then reset the signal gates to prevent the exaggerated and oversensitive stimulus avalanches; any hospital would have a sophisticated unit that did real-time diagnostic imaging and adjustment, but her two-part method would work. She'd explain all of it very carefully so he didn't misconstrue the injected nanites needed to make the physical change as 'dope'.

chapter 25

Anxiety

"Miss Naomi, can we go someplace quiet, private?"

"Why Bartolommeo, I thought you were too fuddy duddy for a quickie!" She switched off the scope and pushed a drawer shut, then directed him over to a spacious supply closet. He had helped her move the empty pallets out weeks before. Last week they'd moved inside the little cot she'd brought to the lab for the nights she wanted to stay with her project.

She closed the door and activated the inside light. "Don't tease me, Tarzan,' she giggled, whispering, "The pick-ups are outside and I accidentally sprayed silicon on the two nearest audios a couple days ago. The vids are pristine, so take care when you leave." The heat of him arm to arm was making objectivity very difficult.

"Naomi, what do you think these piranhas are going to do with Marta when we leave?"

Marta. That threw cold water on her libido. "She's a tough girl, she'll survive." 'And go back home!' she cried to herself.

Barto looked befuddled. "What is happening to us is a result of our past actions, our poor choices. She is a school girl who needed money for classes, so she could be a doctor like you. She admires you so much, you are a star in her eyes."

"I don't believe it! She treats me like one of her farm buddies, there is not one gram of respect for me or anything I have or want." She knew that was too loud, but the collected drip-drip-drips of discontent gushed out that way.

"You amaze me, Miss Naomi. I though you would help me think of some way to protect her, but I forgot you are Americano and so must be superior to us foreigners. We get closer to *azufre* daily, who cares what we leave behind?" He tousled his hair, pulled at his tucked shirt and left, closing the door with a 'snick' behind him.

* * *

Barto found Marta encoding the revised part numbers from her supply system realignment plan on some bins in Supply Room B. The project was nearly complete, and most of it her work. Contritely, he said, "Hey I would've been doing my part but stopped by to see Doc this morning." He put a finger to the screen and saw where he could start on another row. He punched it into the handheld encoder and crouched down at the row's end about three meters away. "You went to see Doctor Trogden? Good for you! I worry about you so much. Do you think it'll do any good?"

"Not really, but she caught me on surveillance. You thought the lightning bolt would come from the Bridge, but it was from Sickbay." He rested the encoder to his knee. "We talked about you."

She stopped mid-motion and simply asked, "Why?"

She was withholding judgment, good. "Doc saw me coming over to wake you from a nightmare once, maybe more. We are both worried about what will happen to you when I leave."

She laid the encoder on a shelf and leaned back on the shelves close behind. "I wanted to bounce a plan off you. What if you teach me self-defense? I remember when we first met you said that if anyone jumped you, you'd kick their ass. I want to be like that. I took some karate classes in college, but never used any of it."

"You do fight like a girl." A girl who could crack two of his ribs and bruise a kidney with knuckle punches and solid chops, but that was a dire secret. They were healing well.

Marta's pensive look meant she knew he was minimizing the damage she'd done. "Maybe Naomi would like to learn, too? Tenembras could be a rough place and it might give her more confidence if nothing else."

"She a good friend?"

"The closest friend ever, except for you."

He saw fat tears run down her cheeks like summer thunderstorm raindrops on a windowpane, drops big enough to have been icy hail moments before. "Hermana."

"What those Pats will do can't be worse that what I already know I can survive. What breaks me up is to think of you, and Naomi, Doc Cartier ... I'll even miss Thao."

If he started crying it would only make it worse. "Let's get this done and then get some coffee, very strong, and plan out our classes, *si*?"

"*Si, bueno.*" She wiped her face with her sleeves and resumed encoding.

chapter 26

Anticipation

"**D**r. Cartier, do you expect any living organisms on Lyra 9976?"

"What's that, Marta? Alive somethings? Yes, I surely anticipate it. The atmospheric analyses that started this whole epic indicate probable photosynthesis so there may be living vegetation with chlorophyll, typically an unmistakable signature." Alain hadn't budged from his modified stool, modified to make his butt stick to it in the decreasing gravity, still examining each of his slides in the microscanner and comparing the computed results. "Please get started putting the slides I've finished with into those cases over there." He looked around peevishly. "All this must be stowed soon or we'll have damage."

She wanted to ask where the detected chlorophyll came from, what alien process or what crash, but he seemed intent on maintaining the classified info as such. Searching for Lyra 9976 on the net had come up empty so she supposed she'd have to wait; maybe they'd brief everybody closer to deployment.

"Naomi and I have secured most of her loose items and put the sensitive equipment in cases. Do you want me to start palletizing the bulky stuff so it can be tied off to the floor links?"

He leaned away from the scanner and rubbed his eyes. "Plunder, all this plunder. I despise moving and shoving, something is always lost or broken. No doubt doubly so this time since it's all irreplaceable." He peeled his pants from the stool seat and shuffled over to stare at the equipment in question, as if blaming it for his displaced state.

Marta saw Cartier behave older and more bent each day. He absently mislaid things and was losing his boisterous, confident style.

She'd seen him the day before when she arrived at the lab for a very early start. A flicker of light around the corner to his darkened personal room had caught her eye and she naturally went on over. He perched on his chair pitched forward, gazing at the wall in his office he kept blank, a wall now filled with fulsome amber wheat gently rippling in a fresh breeze. Tiny brown birds twittered in and around the feathery grain awns and a pair of Viceroy butterflies wafted by, surfing on invisible currents, a splendid sunny morning with scudding cotton puff clouds. His rapt attention and outreached hand with beseeching fingers assailed her heart; she crept away red eyed and ended up late to work that morning.

* * *

Doc was beside herself in frustration. Her ale turned out marvelously smooth and hoppy, a second a-one batch and now this! "I'll take a hatchet to you, you damned piece of trash! Little shards that I will flush into space, you hear?"

Cedric heard her just before he entered the exam room. The only person he could picture her shouting at was Doc's assistant Barbara. Alarmed, he rushed back to the closet to see her leaning with the heels of both hands pushing down on a waist-high barrel lid. His hackles settled and brain engaged to decipher what was going on.

"Cedric," she said, standing and slapping her hands across each other in a gesture of finality. "Another question about the intricacies of Health Physics? More on the radiation effects on squamous tissue?"

"Ah, yes, but that can wait. What?" he asked, pointing at the big bulgy brown barrel.

"Sir, as a Scot I value you opinion. She went over to the counter to a white bucket and shielded her actions with her turned back. She caused a distinct gurgling noise.

Cedric recognized the noise before she turned back to him with the mug, an authentic pub tankard-style mug. He salivated and swallowed hard.

"It's too heady because the carbonation is liberating more and more as we near Kuiper, but it's still quite potable. I had to deal with this at the sling, too."

He took it from her, blinking as if the scene might dissipate into a mirage. He sucked his lips and touched them with the tip of his tongue, like a safecracker preparing to spin the tumblers. He looked over to her. She, the physical signals expert, was grinning maniacally.

After a long, savoring draft, he reported, "Supreme, a triumph!" It went down so easy; he could almost hear the clink of glasses and chatter in the Fettered Ferret. He reverently gave her the empty mug. "I had no idea! This is jolly good!" He burped and they both laughed.

"If I'd known about your reaction I'd have shared this all along." There was a real regret. She loathed the necessity of all the subterfuge this took, as if zymurgy, the brewer's art, was immoral or something. And here was someone who understood. And he was a Passenger.

"It seems your pressurized keg there is not sealing properly?"

"Right you are. We could binge and finish all this up now, or bottle it in lab ware for dispensing at our leisure once we get under Frankie's spin. What do you think?"

He removed the lid and scrutinized the lid seal and bucket seating surface, no observable flaws. He studied the way the lid should fit and the other aspects of the pressurized system. "Dr. Trogden, I think your vent valve is clogged though it's hard to see. You're not getting a seal because you aren't strong enough to compress the air inside enough."

"Holy moly. Okay, let's fix it. Thirsty?"

chapter 27

wheel on the way

Olivia focused total attention on the passage through the Kuiper barrage with such heightened awareness that Doc Trogden's magnetic soled clomp made her hiss in irritation as if an extraneous noise might make her miss a betraying 'ping' on the hull. The sound of it, muted as it was, snapped her out of the fixation.

"Hey, didn't mean to startle you, Livy. Bad time?"

"No, not at all Ronnie Sue. I am simply enthralled to the point of obsession with regard to the intricate microthrusts and minute corrections the AI does to choreograph this transit.

"I thought we had to go though at a constant deceleration to wind up at Kuiper Station without ramming it."

"All true, but remember AI has to match the actual velocity with the projected optimal while dodging blocking bodies. It appears its damn close already."

"I know there's not a blessed thing I could do if we blundered into one of those things, but I can't get the history out of my mind; I know it's in yours."

"Maybe you're picking up the signals from the rest of the persons on board, you know, like an antenna. Clairvoyance? You've researched that I think." Olivia liked to tease Ronnie Sue, sure that finely tuned observation plus experience could give a person a psychic aura.

"The general fear level does seem thick enough to cut, regardless of the nonchalant veneers I saw pasted on them in the galley at dinner. That's not what I see when they're alone."

"You mean when you 'look in on them'?"

"Yeah, Livy, when I do peek-a-boo. It is the Doc's prerogative. Nobody's had an anxiety attack on Kuiper's account yet, except for me that is." She stretched as far as her fingers could reach, arching backward, extending her spine. She thought she could hear it creak.

"You're the psychiatrist. Why invest the energy to worry if there is not one jot of difference we could make?"

"Would it surprise you that the Scot is truly unconcerned and more involved with balancing some equations? Van Rijn and Tomlinson are up in the observation bubble. He sits like a stone, but she's whooping it up, pointing out the closest ones and making sound effects; it's pretty funny to watch."

"Why would he be up there, that Thao? I thought he never left his cabin."

"Van Rijn went to his cabin and invited him. He shut off his screen and followed her. Meanwhile Barb and Lee are in his cabin alternately fighting and smooching and Jones is immersed on a different plane on Nervana.

I actually went to the exercise room and discovered Bloom and Cartier talking a mile a minute about a quite eclectic array of subjects. Those guys are true whiz kids I think, besides the IQ and what have you. They can casually chat in more depth on more subjects than I can even identify, and because of their combined Kuiper and Tembo anxieties they're jabbering almost faster than I can understand. I aught to record it!"

"And reveal yourself as a bigger spy than me? Right! Got any hooch?"

Doc reached into a side pocket and extracted her flask. "Try this; I got a better grade of brandy crystals to flavor it this time."

"Wheee-oo! That does the job."

"Careful, there, it's about 120 proof."

"Ah, yes. Not much at a time, then." She sucked another mouthful out and returned it to Doc.

"Rest easy, I watered down the lion's share of it as I bottled it." Just a white lie! "I had to bring you up the high octane for a taste, though." She glanced over Olivia's shoulder to the screen. "Looks like they're thinning out now, doesn't it?"

"Oh, look! We're 93% through! Kuiper Station will be in hailing distance soon!"

"Livy, I will leave you to your tasks. I might go up to the dome with Tigger and Eeyore and try to catch a glimpse of ol' Frankie. By the way, the Captain spent the time playing music and watching vids of his family, no unusual stress at all."

"Your conclusion is that the Americans were the nervous ones and the others more calmly accepted their fates?"

"We Americans tend to believe we have control over our fortunes however adverse the circumstances. We were raised that no matter how we started, nothing could keep us down or stand in our way, that we could turn bad into good and could skip some of those rocks out there across the sea of stars if needed."

"Plain hyperbole, Ronnie Sue. As an Irish-Indian American, I certainly had no desire to EVA."

"Not too far off, really. I believe some way to show defiance would have done us a whopping lot of good." Doc looked down to her boots, suddenly morose. "Later. I think I might go on to bed after all. Good night?"

"Yeah, good night." Olivia was concerned about Doc's sad change of mind.

* * *

Olivia was aroused from her mediation by the chime indicating hailing had commenced. She switched views and got a well-framed picture of the Franklin, docked at the central hub to one end of Kuiper Station 3. Small and at high magnification now, by Thursday the interstellar would completely dwarf the relatively tiny Boris Peck.

'There,' she confirmed to herself, 'the comm buoy has acknowledged the Pecker's arrival.' She checked status one last time and was satisfied that the trajectory was true, with deceleration on schedule.

O'Reilly, reared in part within site of the Omaha Aeronautics complex that masterminded these intergalactic marvels, rose and stretched once more before heading back to her cabin. There, the Navigator reviewed some of the vignettes observed over the last few months and pondered defiance and its worth.

chapter 28

on kuiper station 3

As much as Marta wanted to explore Kuiper 3, she was obligated by her sponsor to supervise each load as it was hoisted and carried over to the Franklin's shuttle; both Cartier and Bloom were frightened stiff of the robots mishandling their precious equipment. To her initial dismay, there were no people, only the mechanical-looking robots. It was far more important to have each pallet tag complete and legible, learning that the extra lines on the tags were to designate what storeroom or cabin it went to and details like 'place on top' and 'store at -20 C'. She wanted to ride a load over to scope out Dr. Cartier's storage area to better understand what kind of directions were needed and how much room she had to work with, but found it forbidden.

She annotated and verified the tags on the remaining equipment and went back to the waiting room where Dr. Cartier glared at her. She shrugged and hop-sailed carefully over in the very light grav, using the handholds as taught and taking care of her ankles and wrists.

Cartier wagged a finger at her, "You have missed the crew tram! They've gone on ahead without looking back."

"Alain, don't chide the child, she was only doing the shepherd bit you assigned her," Naomi reminded him, neglecting to note her own part in it. "Marta, dear, I do wish you had gone with them. This looks ominous."

Marta looked at the downcast faces; even Thao was more glum than usual. "I'll go with you guys, there has to be enough room, right?"

"Hon, that's not the point," she replied, sniffling. "This dog and pony show is for us outcasts."

Cartier gruffly told her, "Don't get snot in the air!" He sniffled, red-eyed, and slumped back slack into his depressed reverie.

Barto was lost in another mental place and didn't seem to notice her presence, his hair uncharacteristically ruffled, mumbling what she thought might be a catechism; his fingers seemed to be counting invisible beads and his head bobbed with the rhythm of it.

It was Thao that motioned her over and quietly murmured that this was where they would be severed. Then he also drifted into his thoughts. She sat carefully on the stool between him and Barto and pulled the strap across her lap to hold herself down.

The door she'd entered through closed and the lights went out, leaving no reference point except the cold hard stool she sat on. Marta's heart thumped hard and unevenly; picking up the mood, she yearned to keen like the disanchored soul she felt she was, a wretch cast aground on a treacherous reef, shivering, missing the ministering touch of the absent Cedric. She uttered no sound, no moan nor whimper nor shriek; the word 'severed' careened around her skull.

Abruptly, a giant screen on the wall across from the stools lit up with a very large bald man, pale as a ghost with oily black eyes and a grim red slash of a mouth, a Patriot Official according to the seal on the podium. He stared malevolently into each person's eyes for a total of several minutes, wresting each of the exile's attention, and Marta's.

"Attention." He thundered, "Two doors will appear and open before you."

The voice was blaring from all around the room, inundating the matte black space, the light from the screen failing to illuminate the coal sack blackness around them. The metal-echoed stentorian voice affected them far worse with no visual clues to hang onto, no visual at all except the executioner himself.

"If you choose this door (the one on the left glowed for a second), your case will be reviewed."

All eyes riveted to that door as the only alternative to the screen.

He went on relentlessly, "Choose this door only if there is a creditable reason for your plea. The penalty for error is death by expulsion."

He let the idea of a body cast away into space sink in.

"If you accept your lawful and just exile from Earth and the Solar System that contains it, choose this door (the right door glowed).

You have one minute to decide and act if you choose the review."

One minute was ticking away and Marta, dazed, tried to understand what he said and what it meant; at enough volume, words are difficult to distinguish. The left door opened to an inviting pale light.

'I'm not convicted of anything!' She quickly decided to use that left door and let them know she was in the wrong place. She released the restraining strap and rose too fast, rising fast toward the very high ceiling. Barto grabbed her ankle. He arrested her momentum and held her there like a balloon until the door on the left closed.

He pulled her leg gently to get her moving toward the floor and held her hand as the lights came up with a dull red glow. She saw he was standing, holding Naomi's hand on the other side. Naomi's far hand grasped Alain's. They all stood in grim anticipation and she had fallen in with them. So be it. Marta reached around and took Thao's hand; he gripped it hard.

The guillotine-like, unforgiving voice resumed. "You have pleaded guilty to your crimes and acknowledged just punishment. Once through this door (it opened to blackness, a wan yellow frame defining it) you will have no further contact with any person on the face of the Earth, no breath of Earth's breezes, no taste of her waters and shall not partake of her beauty or bounty except at the mercy of the countrymen you have despised.

You shall not communicate in any way to the birthplace of mankind, nor will any bit of data reach you forever more except by mercy. You are cast away from the cradle of humanity and land of your forbearers. You shall never return." He hit his podium with a gavel that reverberated like a steel drum dropped ten meters to a concrete floor, striking it three times, echoes overlapping. He continued to stare until the aural effects dissipated, then said in deep bone-chilling chords, "You shall never go home."

A great sob broke out when the screen blipped out, from the way he was jerking, Marta was sure it was Barto. All was ruddy near-darkness except the sallow glow of the right-hand doorframe.

Naomi yelled, "What a steamin' pile of horseshit! This melodrama has not changed ONE SINGLE THING!" She made a mucous-sucking snort that started deep in her throat and fought its way up noisily. She spat the accumulated gobbet onto the floor and the gushy splat of it shook the mood, pulling them back from the ugly echoes. No one complained about contaminating the atmosphere.

Angrily, Naomi pushed the listless Alain ahead of her and Marta shook the men on either side of her into motion. Soon they all filed through the dark doorway. When Thao cleared the door, it clanged shut making everyone duck and cringe. Then pale yellow lights along the floor showed the passageway that led to the Franklin. They shuffled apart in silence.

chapter 29

Franklin

After a sandwich in his room for dinner, Cedric headed to the monitoring room allotted to this group. He knew the remaining arc segments of the enormous wheel had loaded in the last few months before the Peck arrived with supplies and immigrants for all of the colonies on the agenda. He couldn't go to any other allotment or find out anything about any of those others, but he could walk about and see all of what they allowed him to get to in this part.

One thing very different since the transfer to the Franklin was the bare animosity between the passengers and the crew, excepting Marta. The only saving grace was that the crew area was in a different arc section, on the other side of the shuttles and cargo pods. Marta was with the Passengers; how she managed that he couldn't understand, but he was heartened by her proximity.

The comm center and the exercise room sat empty; with all of their equipment already on a shuttle they had little to do except fret on the completeness of their plans so he really thought someone would be working off the frustration. He discovered San Luis, Cartier, and Bloom playing Monopoly in the common room. They snubbed him coolly so he moved on.

Marta was in the library reading about Vikings of all things. Despite the pervasive gloom weighing everyone down, he was sure he could chance talking to her, that she was least likely to mind. He stood in the doorway a moment more and realized his childishness, afraid of the boogieman. They had talked before and he'd survived; there was no need to make a fuss of it now and he still wanted to know why the Passengers were all so depressed. Sure, they were going to another planet. They knew that from the beginning and seemed resigned to it. In the moment after that, Marta laid the tablet down and said, "Yes?"

He spoke like letting off high-pressure steam. "This place is like a graveyard after a plague, with the weeping and moaning spilling from a private crypt. What happened on Kuiper?" He hadn't thought of that scene from his past for many years, why did it have to surface like a bloated body now? He shivered and loosened his jaws with effort, working them a few times to dissipate both the rotten memories.

"Have a seat. I'll tell you, but you won't like it. Sit!"

He forced himself into movement, pulled out the chair next to her and sat quite close. Marta rubbed elbows with him, perhaps a Kentucky greeting.

"You missed out. It was horrible. The authorities did everything possible to humiliate and denigrate them, and hammered in the fact that they were going to exile 'away from the cradle of mankind.' I think they're more angry at the Hollywood horror treatment than the intended message, surely Naomi is."

"You aren't exiled, why did you stay with them?"

"I watched the cargo loading like Dr. Cartier told me to. When I got back it was too late. I noticed you weren't there to get the big speech."

Her slightest reproach felt like sleet. "I volunteered."

"Still, the 'never more to feel the sweet breeze of Earth' should apply to you, too, if I read the blackout restrictions right. Yet those guys were subject to personal ridicule, no scraps except for Patriot mercy. Skunk stink! Isn't it enough to be sent to sent to a place like that without getting pitchforked? And my ears have not stopped ringing from the din, either."

She could get under his collar faster than anyone alive. "One, I did sign the contract before I left Earth. Two, I did petition to go back and get you when I saw you were not among the crew; I was refused with a disagreeable degree of mirth. Three, I fear you are correct about Tenembras. The more I learn of it the more desolate it seems, but it's too late for recapitulation."

She sank back in her seat. "I'm sorry, I wasn't blaming you, not intentionally. Tenembras. Sulfurous clouds, right? Air fit to choke you? People go blind from the alkaline dust storms? From hot to hotter to hot enough to boil blood?"

"That's at the equator and then only in the summer. Otherwise, the great hazard would be the massive dust storms. It's much more habitable in the cities, though it is dry and desolate as you say, with the sulfur-tainted dust. I don't believe anyone has been outright poisoned in years."

She was becoming increasingly emotional, tight features and lips, reddening eyes. "You're so nonchalant, but it's all that with no reprieve! It scares me to the marrow and I'm not even going!"

With more emotion than he knew he contained, he barked, "That's right, you are not going. So why are you crying?"

"People I love are going," she whispered. She caught his eye for no more than three seconds and jerked away as if he'd burned her. She scooped up the tablet and went behind him to leave, bumping into his chair.

When he turned to see her shuffle out, a sharp pain alerted him to how hard he was. Elbow to table, he rested his head on his left hand's fingertips and pictured gradients of heavy red, dusty orange and fine white sands and how they would look from various vantage points until he could comfortably go back to his cabin.

chapter 30

Franklin Arrives

Marta spent lots of time on her classes, but checked in with Dr. Cartier and Naomi every morning during the transit; with all of their gear in the shuttle, there was no piddling around with experiments or hands-on training. She'd passed her Level 3 AI course on the first try early that morning. As she entered the Communications Room, she confirmed her guess that nobody would notice her tardiness.

None of them mentioned Tenembras or their separation from Marta soon after Lyra, so she let it lie as well. She chalked Naomi's aloofness to anxiety and sympathized with the futility beating one's head against it. Cedric discovered a dartboard with real darts and punctuated his studies with aiming sharp objects at a small target with a degree of mastery.

Marta, bored with her usual biology studies, took on ship electrical systems so she could be more valuable to the crew on the way back. It might not work, but it was a subject she found she knew relatively little about so it carried a high distraction quotient.

Barto spent afternoons teaching Naomi and her self-defense until Naomi dropped out, then it was just the two of them. The controlled aggression felt exhilarating and her firmer muscles gave her a sense of power that carried her day to day. Barto, a strict taskmaster, pushed her until she could punch with sleeve-snapping speed.

On the eighteenth morning, a synthesized utilitarian female voice came over the section-wide speakers, "All persons, assemble 1300 in the Communications Room for a briefing on the expedition to Lyra 9976." She repeated the same at ten o'clock and at noon. Marta marveled that they'd traveled light-years with no tactile or otherwise sensed indication; indeed most of the time was spent getting into position around Lyra 9976 after coming back into real space.

Commander Jones presided over the briefing with the Navigator present but silent as if carved of marble.

"The mission to assess Lyra 9976 begins tonight at 2019 hours. We will have a thirteen day transit to Lyra 9976 orbit. Once there, we will immediately begin atmosphere and general environment assessment and initiate transit procedures for landing, the Captain going first in the gig. You will refer to the gig as Shuttle One. A few hours later, I will follow in Shuttle Two with your equipment. We will assay the planetary life indications as possible in the six days allotted and return to the Franklin in twelve to nineteen days depending on factors you don't need to know about. Departure from the planet for both vehicles to dock with the Franklin is on June 16th. All you will need is on the shuttles or in your pod. You may go aboard Shuttle One at any time but no later than 1900 tonight. I want you all seated and ready with no issues of any kind by 1930. That is all."

Dr. Cartier smile surprised her; he even came over to pat her on the back.

"Marta, my dear, we've survived transit and are here! I must say, I'm intrigued more than ever with the mystery of Miss Lyra. Most scientists have discounted the indications as spurious but we are in the position to find out for certain if they reveal life or not."

"So that you're looking forward to this? It's not just forced labor to you?"

"Dear, I have never been on another planet and find myself truly eager to see what it's like. You must know what I mean! I may not have chosen to come here, however here I am and the closer scans confirm chlorophyll down there. Chlorophyll! And we get to discover how it got there! What do you say we go check on the job those rude mechanicals did with my lab on that shuttle?"

The task of reorganizing the mayhem on the shuttle daunted Marta to the core. All of the carefully packed and tagged cases and crates were stacked neatly, but they were stacked high and in no discernable order, several rows deep.

Naomi stalked in front of the main equipment massif. Speaking at large, she said, "I would surely love to toss a porcupine to whoever thought this would be funny."

When Cartier went to commiserate, Marta skipped back to her little cabin and looked up the material handling capabilities aboard. "Aha-di-dah, it is all indexed and retrievable robotically. Too fine!" The instructions looked simple, so she started back to relieve a couple of tense folks.

On the way back to the shuttle, she ran into Cedric and fell down after a split second decision not to grab him for stability. "Yike! I'm so sorry!"

Cedric looked down and held out a hand. "You're the one on the floor; I was thinking and not watching."

She accepted his hand in a comradely way and let him pull her to her feet. He did not let go.

"Marta," he whispered, very close and intimate, "Why do you spend all of your free time with San Luis? What do you do in the cargo hold that makes you return so flushed and vibrant?"

With her eyes closed, her sense of touch seemed accentuated. She felt his breath warm with a waft of alcohol and what seemed to be a magnetic force, one curiously attractive, that kept her from pulling away or reclaiming the hand he'd placed over his heart. She was surprised at the amount of control she had to expend just to stand still, to neither defend nor flee. Marta wanted to place her ear to his chest to hear the heartbeat she felt with her fingers at the same time a feral part of her urgently wanted punch him in the same spot and watch him fall.

"Marta does not answer. I wonder what that means?" He leaned and lightly kissed her brow, his free hand tracing a scintillating fingertip across her temple, perhaps to tuck errant hair away. His hand smoothly slid to cradle her head.

"Stop, please stop. I am tainted beyond hope and can only hurt you." She dropped suddenly from his clasp and rolled backwards to her feet. She was close enough still to kick his head off his shoulders and knowing that, being able to visualize the sequence of motions and the resulting mess, saddened her piteously.

She chanced an indirect look and saw he'd defused his magic hands, letting them hang flaccidly at his side.

"Marta, dear Marta. I only wanted to reach you, to touch the garden in your heart. Instead, I have made a fool of myself and frightened you."

"If you hadn't been drinking, you wouldn't have tried anything. I won't ask where you got booze from. I'll forget it all if you will." What a stupid thing to say, how impossible. She went back to her room and stared at interlock configurations.

chapter 31

Landing

Commander Jones droned, "The initial landing will commence at 1800 with the Captain piloting Shuttle One. The passengers will be inside Shuttle One ready for departure at 1730. I pilot Shuttle Two with the Expeditionary Survey cargo pods will arrive at 0600 tomorrow morning. The focus of work this evening is to set up the Shuttle One Portico and perform on-site testing at the Captain's direction. Upon arrival, you shall set up the Portico and all Passengers will exit to remain there or on the planet for the duration."

This after lunch announcement was a recording of the one from the morning, when they reached orbit. Cedric almost resumed his reading, looking up only when the vid went live.

The Commander looked quite excited now. "Any activities deemed contrary to the laws and tenets of Greater America will be considered contempt of exile and persons committing such activities subject to summary execution. Don't think for a minute that I don't mean it! Out!"

Naomi burned with ire and erupted as soon as the vid went dark. "Contempt of exile! Eat shit and bark at Tembo!" She paced tight circles with clenched fists slamming her hips in time. "Makes me want to stay on the flipping ship and let 'em do their own damned analyses." She plopped into a chair.

"Don't lop off your nose to spite you face, dear." Dr. Cartier advised, "Go about your work cheerfully and with gusto to show them you value what you do much more than what they do. As with compost, waste nothing."

"Here, here!" Cedric knew that most of what Jones threatened was bluster because she was a sanctimonious bully who got off on kicking the mighty in disgrace. "Emotionalism only feeds her ego. We all need to go about this professionally, impervious to her threats and jibes. Show nothing."

Everyone except Marta turned to look at him, each seeming to think some version of how he practiced what he preached to a fine art. Or perhaps they simply acknowledged his comment? They had, after all, acquiesced to his plea to have some time to create a sweet memory at landing.

Barto spoke up from the rear of the room, "Remember that this is the last chance you may ever have to run your own work and to work with each other. I have no doubts they will separate us and drive us like cattle later. Use this time to sweep out the old and face the new like the strong people I know each of you to be."

Naomi dropped her hands to her lap and drooped back, admitting that success was better revenge.

* * *

They landed nose south on a barren, sandy spot about 120 meters west of the edge of some mighty sea cliffs. The entire planet was barren of course, except for the remains of the ill-fated Van Damme that, according to repeated scans, had no human survivors. Marta had no idea the mythical Van Damme made the signs of life seen from distant Earth until assigned to do the close-in scan.

The Van Damme! She still couldn't come to grips with the thrill of it, the actual Van Damme! She considered the amount of Earth tree cover they'd measured from orbit and tried to imagine how many of the crew had survived long enough to plant them all and still longer to nurture them in this hostile environment as she finished the last round of exterior scans. If they lived long enough to plant a forest, what happened to them? "Captain, scans negative for animal life, the atmosphere matches projected components and levels. The checklist for deploying the Portico is complete."

The Captain responded, "Scans and checklist sat, aye. Deploying Portico 10 by 6 by 4 starboard, 3 – 2 - 1 deployed."

The shuttle rocked, a brief tremor, to indicate the Portico did indeed deploy. Preparation and further scans took over two hours, the alien sun already setting. It would be dark by the time Marta got the chance to step onto the strange planet. What stars might she see?

She reported, "Portico indicates amber, caution."

"Initiate sterilization sequence for Portico."

"Sterilization initiated." They would be in and out of the Portico every day all day long; this sterilization was only to allow the cargo hatch access for the initial equipment transfer and personnel egress. Once unloaded, they would shut the cargo bay and the personnel hatch. The impersonal instructions sent over earlier said that if they needed something else inside, only Marta as a crewmember could requisition anything for delivery through the relatively small cargo airlock.

"Sterilization completed, green go." She switched the comm off and walked around to the outside hatch, very conscious of the heavy gravity making her feel as if she carried a dead burden. She did, figuratively, but it couldn't diminish the wonder of being there, the thrill of it.

Giddy, her thoughts sped with variations of 'This is it!' and 'I'm on another planet!' Soon she guided a pallet of folding chairs up as Cedric released the starboard hatch. She nearly ran the chairs into the portico wall at her glimpse of the sky. Even through the slightly hazy force field, the stars seemed so thick and so impossibly near she almost reached out to touch them. The Captain cleared his throat behind her so she shook off the reverie to start setting the chairs out. Cedric came out with lights and began stringing them on provided hooks.

"You'll see the Portico has access to the starboard cargo bay for the suits you'll need," the Captain explained, "also the rations, the water, etcetera. We won't open it until the morning; Bloom and Cartier are still fussing over what to leave in the cargo bay and what to hold back, with San Luis keeping the peace."

Marta turned in alarm. "They need help! Gosh, I didn't know they wouldn't take it all. Why bring it if they weren't gonna use it? Sir."

Fajar smiled at her near lapse. "They didn't realize everything would require hard sterilization for return, not the just standard chemical decontamination they anticipated. The majority of the equipment and the consumables are in Shuttle Two's cargo pod, but I believe they wanted to share some of Bloom's gear that we have here."

"Hard sterilization?" She knew that would fry the fragile innards of the scientists' precious equipment; it wasn't made to stand up to that kind of punishment. "Sir, we detected nothing alive except those trees. If this is where the Van Damme landed, those are Earth trees."

"Yes, but they've been exposed to the elements here and may have mutated in some strange way. You know we can't afford to let any virus, mutation or any alien thing threaten old Earth. Commander Jones has made it clear you and those inside will implement the survey and analysis plans as submitted, no substitutions. The hard decon for Planetary Protection is her call based on conditions. They really do have it under control, you would be superfluous."

"I see. Thank you for explaining it, sir. Maybe Thao or one of them'll get a chance to come out later."

"Ensign Van Rijn, I rather think you might enjoy the peace without the crowd for a change." He flung his arms wide and announced, "In any case, I will leave this personnel hatch open and we'll start the work at first light, about 0500 local. Good night!"

When Cedric attached the last light and switched it on low, it diminished the stellar show somewhat but allowed them to see what they were doing once their eyes acclimated. He followed the Captain back in, leaving her surrounded by an alien planet night.

Seeing the brighter Portico perimeter lights come on, she stepped forward to the Portico wall and dabbed at it with her left index finger. It felt like glass, though she knew it to be exponentially more resistant to damage, including the sandstorms Naomi determined were possible.

"You don't appreciate the moon until you don't have one, do you," Cedric asked as he settled into his seat, long legs stretched out, crossed ankles. He had a guitar with him!

Flabbergasted, she watched him slip off his shoes. While there was no chance of dabbling toes in the sand because of the glassy yet not slippery Portico field, it still seemed like a good notion. She hesitated only until she saw him grin and start twisting on the guitar's tuning knobs. He seemed sober and the Captain had latched the door open. Why not enjoy the music?

"Yes," he said, twanging a string and twisting a knob, "the moon is an underestimated piece of real estate. Granted the starlight is about the same aggregate magnitude brightness as Earth's moon, but it's not the same being scattered o'er the breadth of heaven."

Marta curled up in her chair by the window-like wall and soon got caught up in the sparkling panorama above her. His presence and words made her feel cozy as her eyes adjusted to see the alien landscape. She was aware of the straggly Earth trees discernable further southwest and of Cedric's reiteration of the scales as he tuned his instrument. A gladness floated on the fringe of her reason that Cedric was there with her at this moment. Then guitar music with lilting chords met utter stillness, still but for the stars twinkling in time with his magic fingers. Neither of them spoke.

First he played something feisty in the Spanish style, with tapping and fast picking. She stretched out and commented on the music with her hands, though she tried to minimize the motion.

He turned the tuning knobs once more and said, "How about a song?"

The tragic story of Dutch explorers planting those trees before dying here kept her eyes roving the terrain as if one of them might troop up to the shuttle to greet them. In a dreamy voice, she replied, "Is it one I know? I'm not a very good singer."

"I doubt you've heard this one."

(The tune is picked nearly mandolin style and is bouncy with fun flourishes)

> I want a parade!
> I want a parade I want a parade I want a PARADE!
> Drum and pipes
> And horns and fifes
> Uniformed marchers
> Flaming arrow archers
> Miniature horses
> And all-boy choruses
> I want a parade!
> I want a parade I want a parade I want a PARADE!
> With fine ladies dancing
> And polar bears prancing
> Peacocks and cockatoos
> Lemurs and kinkajous
> On enormous floats with palm trees
> Swaying in the cool breeze
> Maybe today
> It could be today
> I want a parade!

At his final flourish, she turned to him exclaimed, "Mr. Crannog, that was fun!" She settled a little and demurely added, "That's not in the popular style at all."

"Don't you like the modern pop music? I daresay the false free association endlessly repeated makes no sense to me."

"I agree; there's no music to it, just noises with anything that will squeak or rattle with random hoots and hollers over and over and over. Do you have another?"

"If you're sure. I've only ever played this once."

She heard him hesitate, but dearly loved live acoustic guitar; it reminded her of the Flint Springs campfire nights she'd missed so sorely while at school. "Yes, please, and then I won't badger you anymore. I stopped listening to music for so long it feels like you've opened up a new world for me. Ha, sorry, this is a new world isn't it? I think I better hush up and let you have the floor."

> Further out and further in
> I really don't know where
> to begin
> Further out and further in
> This new sensation leaves me feeling wild
> Within
> (Break, humming and quickly picking variations)
> My feelings run
> They run away
> I want to run away
> With you
> I want to fly among the clouds
> And feel the morning dew
> With you
> (Return, picking more slowly, more sliding chords)
> Further out and further in
> I really don't know how
> This will end
> Further out and further in
> Further out and further in
> Further out and further in
> With you
> Let me run away, let me run inside
> With you

All was silent when he finished, when the last note faded. Replaying his smooth, warm voice in her mind, it took a minute to understand he awaited a verdict. "Oh, I didn't want it to end! You have such a compelling voice and it matches that song perfectly. It seems to me that the person who wrote it had to have experienced a long journey like this and he or she must have fallen in love."

"He, I believe, and I think your guess may be true." He returned for Spanish style and played softly with no further comment.

Marta kept that song near her heart, letting it wander through her mind just as he sang it. The following music was more of a general entertaining effort, beautiful but not so emotionally moving. She drifted in and out, the strings creating a lovely atmosphere for her introduction to the world where the great heroes of the Van Damme lost their lives.

Marta gazed out into the midnight coolness and tried again to imagine those pioneers who braved the primitive interstellar technology and got this far, only to crash. She remembered the model ship her brother Benji had on his bookshelf, the proud *Nederlander* 'Van Damme' emblazoned on its side, out there somewhere in ruins.

Her heart lurched at the ridiculousness of telling her beloved brother she'd gone light-years to actually track it down; he would have been so jealous. Cedric stopped a minute to adjust another string and segued to another classical sounding piece. He whispered, "Segovia."

She heard him peripherally, the vibrant memories of her childhood filling her mind. The Van Damme launched in the heady years following the breakthroughs that ushered in the true space age. Of the first four ships that went out with such fanfare and expectation, only one was ever heard from again, the Gloria Benson AKA Glory Be, the ship that founded Roundabout. In the ensuing twelve years the navigation systems became much more reliable with special proximal positioning controls.

How did these Dutchmen get so close without those things? Was this really their target? Once they did get here, what made them crash? Some of them must have lived for a while to plant all those trees. Did they have some intact equipment and think they might live somehow? Did they hope for rescue? Sensors confirmed no animal life, no survivors. She wanted to see what memorial they left, those heroes who tried to found a new land, she owed it to Benji.

In the midst of her musing, Marta saw a 'tree' move on the far right of her vision. She diverted all attention to the tree in the halo of that farthest corner light. That tree was most definitely closer than she remembered seeing before and now two new ones, bigger, moved near to it. Not like the wind, but completely moving location. As was her habit, she held it to herself and thought about it. What in creation could it mean? She watched more carefully after that, but saw no more movement. Imagination?

Cedric kicked her chair support lightly and startled her. "You're really out there somewhere, aren't you?"

She then noticed he had his boots on, holding his chair in one hand and the guitar in the other.

"Sorry, yes, you're right." A huge yawn overtook her as she arose. She snickered when he yawned. She put both chairs back on the pallet and hurried to her little cabin, waving good night to the musician left standing at the Portico door.

chapter 32

Day One's Busy Start

The next morning when they began staging the needed equipment from the cargo bay to the Portico, she noted that the closest 'trees' at the south light were gone.

* * *

"Mr. Tomlinson, is there anything I can do for you? I could bring you a shade. This sun seems weak but the thinner atmosphere lets in much more UV and cosmic radiation through than you're used to, including the hard UVBs. Some of that cosmic grab bag might zing right through your suit."

Her friendly offer and homey manner genuinely surprised Thao, so absorbed in the tangle of events that brought him thus far. She'd defended him and included him and then had shown humanity at the sundering at Kuiper Station. Had so many shunned him for his grotesque appearance, his violent repute, that he took it as a natural byproduct of who he had come to be?

Did she see something in him he'd lost sight of, like a misplaced and forgotten pearl? The very idea stirred cool embers, causing a warming flush. Perhaps he would accept the advice he'd been given by another and awaken his heart to the greater good.

"A shade would be most welcome," he replied.

* * *

Marta nodded to Thao and slogged off to get his shade. She'd agonized while arranging the Portico, had neatly organized it and checked it twice against the scientist's lists so that she shouldn't have to requisition anything as that signaled poor planning for routine needs and would depend on bothering the Captain or other officer.

A critical part of set up consisted of ensuring the environmental protection suits had all the parts needed and passed the final pressure test. The mandate to wear the thin but impervious suit system made sense to her, but a redundant barrier suit and then a sacrificial outer barrier? She hoped they verified the plumbing through all three suits. Movement seemed as if through mud, a constant reminder of the xenophobia presented by this extraordinary increase of safety margins and the rejection of the scientists' arguments that the planet was D-E-A-D except for Earth introduced vegetation.

Dwelling on the Patriot, really, the Earth-wide xenophobia and all its manifestations could have led to depression, but she was here on an alien planet and was determined to make the most of it. Like Dr. Cartier said, if manure is thrown at you, make compost!

She reached to a shade on a tall cabinet and tucked it clumsily beneath her arm and turned to stoop at a parts bin for some shorter stakes with more streamlined but aggressive serrations for anchoring Naomi's main work station to a harder than expected surface. She tried to place the stakes in her shoulder-slung carry pouch while still pinning the shade with an elbow. Annoyed at missing the pouch opening twice she finally released the shade and lifted the pouch away from the bulky suit so she could see the opening. She crouched so she could rest the pouch on a knee, opening it wider. 'Possum poop' she muttered. Rising and retucking the shade, she then waddled smartly toward the Portico outer doorway. She walked with a regulation shuffle and tried not to kick up too much dust in the boot-deep sands.

"Here you go Dr Tomlinson, and when you want to move it, collapse it this way." She made exaggerated arm gestures with her elbow angled high and arrowed finger pointing in the approximate location of the controls. He seemed even shorter with his chair sunk in the sand so.

"I thank you Miss Van Rijn," said, inclining forward in his folding chair with his whole body.

"You are very welcome, sir." She bowed in return, stepped back one sliding step and headed for the main Atmo station. Incoming, Shuttle One had released bright lime green monitoring modules of three meters in diameter on two cliff edge sites about ninety meters apart north west and southwest and two about 100 meters out across the sandy eastern plain seventy meters apart. This morning, Barto flung two away from the cliff to float on the ruddy sea twenty-six meters below. The bobbing color of the north cliff had caught her eye for a moment and made her laugh; it was not some exotic creature.

Once she had the main station anchored, she'd likely have time to check out the fascinating and out of place straggly tree line due south and southwest. She thought of the poor trees as dissonant, as if the music of the planet, stark and alien, rejected the painstaking efforts of the pioneers to make them harmonize, as alien as the neon green monitoring stations. The Earth tree line troubled her more than the simplicity of the rest of the landscape; the ruddy sun told her he did not want organics here, the affront at the audacity of these puny humans seeming plain. The imagined message sent a sharp shiver though her bones.

There was not much conjecture on the identity of the tall bulky figure at the Atmo station with Naomi. Barto San Luis cruised the perimeter frequently and had made it his base, bringing supplies on the return trips. He set up shop at Naomi's station 'for the strategic view'.

She straightened up her attitude upon approaching the station. Erosion by wind and rain erased most sharp physical distinctions in the landscape and the triple suits eroded any sense of facial expressions or any but the most exaggerated body English, making the scenery seem blurred. The helmet pick-ups superbly carried voice by virtue of speaker membranes so life-true that she was sure to detect nuances in speech, and was sure that the Listeners on the ship would hear all just as well.

Soon Marta held the stakes in position as Barto pounded them with a sledgehammer into the as-yet inadequately studied rock. All they knew at this point was the hardness and thickness. Naomi leaned on the front frame of her bench, jittery in case the sledge slipped or something blew out of an undetected void and jarred her equipment.

"A snapping turtle couldn't hold that bench any tighter," Marta announced. She stretched upward, extending hands high and starting to arch her back. When she felt that instantaneous panic at passing the point of balance, she also felt a supporting surface at her back.

"Not used to the extra grav yet, huh?" Naomi's thin laugh was arrested by her having to pick up and gently brush off a now dented aluminum sample can; she'd bumped the table herself.

Barto took a step back. "Si, ladies, all falls faster including you!"

Marta was chagrined because of her error but not embarrassed among these friends. A thought panged her stomach, the idea of losing her first 'adult' friends, better than she'd ever had. With a huff, Naomi prodded her out of her introspection by poking her in the arm with a long rod.

"Hey, how about hustling some water up here? I have several tests I need to calibrate with ours. Then we'll lower buckets or something for samples."

Marta turned slowly to fetch the water and saw Barto methodically sweeping the environs with binoculars, scanning once then backtracking to a few degrees of land and sky in sequence to overlap and miss nothing.

Apparently satisfied, he waved and called out, "I will bring you some empanadas on the way back."

Marta could easily imagine the curl on his lip as he said that, watching him start another patrol.

chapter 33

Jealousy

When Marta trudged back with the Earth water as requested, Naomi greeted her saying, "That Barto is worth ten of any other fellow, don't you think, Marta dear?"

The tone of the question caught Marta's ear. "He sure saved my bacon earlier. If I'd fallen backwards I'd probably still be unconscious, or might have broken something."

"Honey, I gotta ask. Naomi's helmet angled down, her arms like triangle legs stuck to the bench frame base by the thick gloves. "I know you and Barty spend boo-coo time together and I know you share secrets." Her visor tracked toward Marta. "I do not want to interfere with anything y'all have going, okay," she stated evenly.

Stunned, Marta took a couple seconds to reply. "We're just friends, honest cross my heart!" Tears were not the easiest thing to take care of in an expedition suit, much less a triple decker, so she earnestly tried to hold them in.

Naomi rose up and turned fully to face Marta. "I know you all worked long hours side by side in supply and did that self defense stuff and that he goes to your cabin at night; I have seen claw marks on his arms."

"N-Naomi, I told him not to come over like that, that somebody would see and think it was something it's not." She eased herself into a folding chair. She breathed in one-two out one-two in one-two out one-two, the blindsiding accusations having knocked the wind out of her.

Naomi moved her chair half a meter from Marta's and sat. "If it is not what it seems then what is it?"

Marta fumbled to a tablet in her left thigh pocket. The stylus felt like trying to write with a strand of spaghetti. She stroked the tablet in the daintiest motions possible in the gloves and handed the tablet to Naomi.

'Bad Nit mares' it said. Naomi handed it back.

Marta knew Naomi must be skeptical, but how could she explain with the suit monitors and recorded voice comm? You could direct the comm to only the person you wanted, however she'd seen the circuits in the bridge console for surveillance. She blanked the tablet and stared at it. It was probably bugged too.

"That's what drew you together, hmmm? Common trauma?"

Frustrated over the inability to say what she wanted, she wrote and passed the tablet again even though it was probably a futile gesture.

'Brthr ONLY swar to G' it said.

Marta held her palms up together at eye level, looking at Naomi through prayerful hands.

Naomi reached for the stylus and wrote in a shaky script 'wors thn u tll me b4?'

Marta deciphered the scrawl and nodded, her helmet a great weight on her stiffened neck. Seeming to continue the conversation from the last voice com, she said as nearly normal as she could, "Oh, Dr. Bloom, he just worries about me. I tell him he's way too protective. He calls me his little sister."

Naomi must have decided to accept that they were not romantically involved at least for now because she responded with the same tone, "You mean like when that coconut head Bodine has been cracking his whip?"

"Yeah, well, I wouldn't want to show any disrespect to any of the officers."

"How about the animated manikin Bodine, not wanting to show any disrespect to robots?"

There was hope that she and Naomi could still be friends! The guarded relief was reflected in her response. "Remember, I'm going to have to deal with the Ensign for the rest of the trip," she replied, giving Naomi a thumb's up in agreement. "I couldn't lock the door before, but maybe with us all in the Portico it'll be okay."

"Honey, I have no doubt he's man enough for both of us."

Marta wanted to see Naomi's face for some reassurance but it was impossible.

Naomi gave her loaded bench some focus and made a pointed suggestion. "Looky, you want to take these last two gas monitors over to the trees? They are big but not heavy, you can roll them if you like. Try these coordinates, using your judgment for exact placement. Go far enough in to minimize the edge effects if you can."

Turning from her waist to reduce muscle strain, Naomi noted Barto's return. "I see our fellow coming up from the other side of the ship and bee-lining this way; you're going to need help since there are two of them."

Maybe that was Naomi saying she wanted to be alone for a while? That sure killed two birds with one stone. Marta saw the distant trees rustle in the breeze, and it affected her like a siren's call, a third bird, if it was allowable to stretch the metaphor that far. If only she could hear them! She reminded herself of the priority to implore Barto to behave as soon as possible, and in the midst of the trees would be a fine place out of visual surveillance.

When Barto arrived, Marta left Naomi to explain about the monitors. As she sipped the nutrition he'd brought through the carefully articulated sterile tubing systems in the suits, a beep-beep warned Marta of an incoming comm from the radio.

"Marta Van Rijn?"

Marta recognized the Doctor, the medical Doctor. "Yes, Dr. Trogden?"

"If you have a moment, I have a question for you."

"Certainly ma'am."

"Okay, I was monitoring the suits a while ago and followed you setting up a comfy spot for Thao Tomlinson. You guys had a conversation or something like one. He came out of his cabin so few time times the whole trip out, so I don't know how you guys could have got chummy. How did you get him to talk to you coming into Kuiper in the Bubble and again just now?"

"Thao Tomlinson?" Marta took a moment to think about it, then replied, "Move in a non-threatening manner, talk with a friendly tone, be respectful, and mean what you say. It works with most people."

"Look Marta, it's my duty to keep up with the mental health of the Passengers and my reports will help on Tembo. I'm not being a voyeur for kicks. I honestly just wanted to know what he responded to. I know next to nothing about this guy, you know what I mean?"

"Yes Ma'am." Marta was thinking it was too late now, the good Doctor was on the verge of deleting the passengers she professed concern about.

Trogden sounded resigned now. "He doesn't speak to me outside of a rare direct inquiry. So if you know of anything I can do for him, I'd appreciate the heads up."

"The only thing that could have helped was lowering the temp in his cabin, but that's moot now."

"Yes, he mentioned that metabolism thing at the post-launch exam. I didn't realize it was serious. I asked, but he clammed up." She paused and clicked the actuating button twice, articulating her loss of words for her. "Thank you, Marta. Out."

* * *

Charenne Jones shut down the last of the systems and transferred controls back to auto-standby. The landing had been a good one that morning, nose north about 50 meters aft of the relatively smaller Captain's gig, parallel to the cliffs and much closer to the trees. Her shuttle with two cargo pods was not as agile, much more of a challenge to maneuver in the augmented manual mode she could and did opt for.

She'd have brought only the one pod loaded for the work at hand but the shuttlecraft needed the ballast of the other, for both weight and aerodynamic balance in manual. She'd get to log more manual time leaving this rock and that should top off her last skills signoffs. Char, smug, had a commanding screen view on the shuttle bridge.

"Olivia, I think that little monkey is following that Soggy van Ruin around. Just look!" Although Olivia stayed aboard the Franklin, Char knew she'd be watching the same panoramic video feed.

"You mean Dr. Tomlinson?"

"Don't let the name fool you, I went deeper into his files before we left. He's Vietnamese, raised in a cage at a research farm or some baloney, befriended by busybody missionaries in Minnesota who got him involved in some fracas in China. Look how long his arms are to his torso! Like a monkey!" Char hit the magnification and pointed, agitated, "And there, see, he's parked that chair within sight of van Ruin again now that she's at Cartier's spot. I think it's gross."

"Is that why your eyes are glued to them?'" More circumspectly, Olivia replied, "Maybe he's just trying to stay with people, or at least the one person who's shown him any kindness. He likes to sit outside and it would be spooky to be alone on a bloody dim world like this."

Char faced her. "Making excuses for the little ape, are you? I'd like to know what your parents think of your misguided …"

* * *

Olivia had heard her superior's diatribes before so she cut the Commander off before she got up to speed on it. "Spare me please, Ma'am! It's my breakfast time and I would like to keep my appetite." As she cut the comm she wondered what past sins had stuck her on board with Charenne Jones. She was not a spiteful person, but Char Jones begged for revenge and Olivia weighed the Karmic cost.

A cat-in-the-cream smile spread across her usually placid demeanor. Char stuck down there left Olivia to enjoy the freedom and leisure to touch up her handiwork; Van Rijn had given her practical pointers on two occasions and Cedric had unwittingly contributed valuable theoretical tidbits. Olivia had applications in mind. The layered suits gave her claustrophobic hives and Char's fear of leaving the place unattended gave her a fine excuse to 'hold the fort'.

"I shall attend the fort, Commander, indeed I shall."

chapter 34

Last One Out

Shuttle One was about to lose its last expeditionary member to the outside as Cedric suited up. He looked around at a noise and watched the Captain stroll up to the airlock, thumbs hitched into his waistband.

"So, Crannog, sleep in late?"

"Hello, Captain Fajar. Ah, no, sir. I was waiting for Dr. Cartier. He's just entered the Portico and wanted to check one last time that he missed nothing he needed. He thought I could grab any overlooked item on my way out."

"I seriously doubt our Miss van Rijn of any oversight."

"Miss van Rijn?"

"Yes, you know, pretty girl, studious and diligent. She's the one who put the ears and tail on the Passenger Deck floor 'bot."

"You mean she's the one who animated Jethro?"

"I give you my word there was no Jethro before she met the 'bot in the hall."

Not wishing to continue on the subject that could so easily throw him off balance, he asked, "Any handed down wisdom for getting around out there?"

"Outside? Oh yes, you've never been. Damned uncomfortable. I gave Jones authority to promulgate the personal protection requirements to accelerate her promotion off my ship and she went insanely overboard for a dead world; the monitors don't support her paranoia at all. Be that as it may, there's really not much to say about getting on out there aside from using your common sense."

"Just go slow and think ahead, then?"

"That's about it, remembering the extra grav."

The comm from the Portico flashed and Cedric pushed the pad. "Crannog."

"Crannog, yes, I believe it's all here. Nothing critical will turn up missing until we're all out here, ask Mr. Murphy."

"Right, then, I'm coming out." To the Captain, he asked, "Are you sure you'll be alright here by yourself?"

"Spoken like a neophyte. I can help you on with your gear."

Suited up, he backed into the airlock. "Thank you Captain."

"Enjoy yourself, but do take care. Twenty percent more gravity is not immediately recognized as a problem, you could easily snap an ankle, albeit you can't bend an ankle in triple suits. You should take a few minutes to acclimate moving in your new milieu in any case. You could fall and not be able to get up or could fall from even a short height and break bones or perhaps your helmet."

Soon Cedric stood on very foreign soil, or more correctly, sand at that point. He raised his arms slowly, doing a force analysis through a range of motions, gauging the stress, estimating the addition torques. Once satisfied he could account for the affects of the forces with the help of imagining the vector indications, he called the agronomist on the comm only to discover him on the far end of the Portico bent over some packages of equipment.

Ducking back into the Portico, he called out, "Dr. Cartier, how may I assist you?"

"Mr. Crannog! Marta and Bartolommeo were supposed to help, but they've run off on some errand for Naomi. First come, first served I suppose. Do gather up the perimeter stakes and proceed with your planned deflector establishment, that's a main concern for us living creatures. Bloom might be able to neglect them for a short time, but I have more sensitive body parts and equipment and want the field as soon as possible."

Cedric had duly mapped out the locations in the planning phase according to the scientist's data, but hadn't really paid much attention to it. "I thought the suits were made to stop anything short of a 2 meV cosmic ray?"

"We detected higher in the initial surveys, but I'm not that personally concerned because we're only going to be a few days. My babies are a different story. One cosmic bazooka at the wrong time could destroy detectors and hours of work, extra detectors and hours that we don't have. I'll set up near the ass-end of Shuttle Two because I have to be near the trees. Even with that, fifteen or sixteen poles ought to do. That would be Plan B, although any poles we don't use are wasted anyhow."

Cartier raised his glove to his chin and made a rubbing motion. "Wait, considering the latest scans, you could include all of Bloom's area and enough of a perimeter to get a more even effect around the pod entrance, that would be your Plan C, modified a bit. That'll be all twenty, right? And do use the cart, they're about three kilograms each without the additional grav burden here."

As he went on about the quantity, Cedric already set about to load the cart with all of the meter long poles. Cartier kept talking as Cedric placed the plug-in deflectors into baskets hung on either side of the cart. On the way out, he slung a laser drill over this shoulder; the heavy cart's wheels sank ten centimeters up the balloon tires, a third of the way to the axles. No matter, it would get lighter faster if he got to business.

Well aware of the requirements of field damper installation from helping his father with his trade, be began at the north edge of the Portico. He concentrated on his work and shoved away the memory of his father's terrible accident with a failed force field in a gust of wind. The fall from the high castle wall to the sea below crippled his father's body and curdled his soul. Cedric beat the memories back harder.

chapter 35

work

First Cedric used the drill to scan the ground where he needed to insert the pole's lower extension. Then he set the depth, degree of burn and the diameter of the hole. He placed the serious end of the industrial sized laser firmly to the ground and punched it. He moved the laser away from the side, avoiding the steam from the new hole. As it cooled, he assembled the deflection poles.

The deflector and light assembly popped onto the pole securely, the solar flap fanned out properly and the catches released without a snag. As soon as mid-hole registered less than 100 degrees C, in went the pole to almost half its height. It fit like a glove. He telescoped the pole segments top first until the deflector was four and a half meters from the surface. The little LED verified deflector activation, but the area light just below the deflector wouldn't activate until dark.

He looked for the next sites - one between Shuttle One and the cliff and then one between that and the point the cliffs swung east. At the cliff edge he fought momentary vertigo before installing a pole; anyone could walk off into the sea without knowing in the dark. Working his way around, he arrived at the angle between the cliff and Dr. Bloom's main bench. Doing actual work felt so good that while accurately employing his instinctive force compensating motions, he barely noticed the cumbersome suit. He did notice Bloom's bench was not where it should have been.

"Good day, Dr. Bloom. I've started putting up the deflector field. Dr. Cartier sends his greetings with regrets that he could not tell you in person."

"With all the tech he uses you wouldn't think he'd be so scared of using the comm system. He told me he thinks it too impersonal." She pointed a gloved finger at her temple and made circles. "Actually I am having more of a problem with the scatter off the ship than the direct UV or cosmic goonies. Can you set a couple more poles on either side of the Portico? If you think that will suffice? The scatter of the hard solar radiation off the hull was showering me with lots of fast little particles, I had to get outta that."

"Bremstrahlung. That's why you are not at the planned coordinates?" The initial survey put her location 20 meters closer to the ship. He turn to the shuttle, turned back, annoyed they hadn't shared the latest energy profile with him at the planning stage, he would have foreseen and integrated the compensation instead of this extemporaneous malarkey.

He estimated the distance and made the energy compensated calculations in his head. "From here you shouldn't have much of an effect; the field should drop off at least five meters from your equipment." He took extraordinary pains to be courteous since he would need a cooperative relationship regarding the atmospheric mess on Tenembras. "Of course anything energetic enough to traverse the distance will cause a surge that may encroach. Your requested two poles should do it."

"Thank you, sir."

"Very well Dr. Bloom. This perimeter pole is not too close to you station, is it? I can resurvey and move the further stations apart a bit. That would leave three for Cartier who will have an even bigger issue with his proximity to Shuttle Two."

"If you think so. I brought monitors with me and so far so good, but I'll be sure and let you know if that changes."

"Very well. Do let me know if you get interference from the completed field; I expect to have it finished in about an hour and a half." He turned and took up the wagon handle.

"Wait a sec, before you go."

"Yes?" He really did want to go. He was kicking himself for not taking the responsibility to ask for the latest energy profile so he could have accurately factored in the effects of scattered radiation in the first place. Why defer the blame? Dunce!

"Are you listening sir? This is rather personal, but I have a stake in Marta's emotional affairs. I have seen her go gaga over you and you squirm away like an eel and avoid her for months. Meanwhile an incredibly handsome and eligible man of Hispanic heritage dotes on her and she considers him as only a brother. Now that suits me fine, but do recall your time is running out."

"Dr. Bloom, I have a good deal of work to do before midday." He was suddenly itchy and sweaty in his suit.

"Hold on just one more moment, jackrabbit. I'll put it plainly: You can't have a serious interest with a long term commitment considering our assignments, so in the short time left, please desist with the cruelty of teasing Marta the way you do and let her down with something less than a fiery crash. She's been through living nightmares and you could push her too far. It's clear to me you're attracted to her, so maybe a sweet little affair with no expectations? I think you'd both be better off if you got some, and who better with than each other?"

"What on Earth? Bloom, are you mad?"

"Crannog, she thinks you are the golden gander and she's rube enough imprint. Maybe she goes for that gaunt, emaciated look and it's not your personally at all. What I do know is that she puckers up around you as if awaiting her first kiss. Is that what you want?"

His suit felt oily inside and was clearly overheating, the thought of her wanting a first kiss from him. "I certainly do not want to present myself under false pretenses. I have never said anything to her that I thought might construe any permanent attachment and am sharply aware of the date of our parting." What else could be say? A cornered rat could not fear a terrier so much.

"Don't get so huffled up. It's probably just my maternal instincts jumping to a conclusion. You claim to be unaware of any difficulty. I apologize, no harm done? I'm feeling the guilt of supposedly misplaced jealousy and I'm trying to make it up to her, not wanting to know her heart was broken as well as having to contend with the monsters she'll have to travel with for so many months on the way back."

He clutched the cart handle and began pulling it to the next position. "Please contain your conjectures, Dr. Bloom. I must be on my way."

At the next spot, he went through the sequence and calmed down physically. His mind would not let it go, though. He finished a hole and pole erection and verified operation. At the next position, he hesitated and tried to sort through the puzzle of Bloom's words. Had he really inferred a lasting relationship? Had he not? Absurd! Did he care what happened to her when they'd been dropped off at Tenembras? Did he not?

He stopped and leaned, hands stacked on the cart handle. He closed his eyes. He heard no exterior sounds, soon lost to the present. Without volition, he fantasized seeing her not in a bulky landing suit, but a simple ship's jumpsuit. He could detect a hint of her curves from behind as he crept up in the ruddy sunlight. She was intent on assembling a solar collector or something, as she was always so beautifully intense with her work. He knew that look, even turned away from him, because it was indelibly inked on his animal brain.

In what other tasks would she be intense? In his fantasy, she twisted around and smiled broadly at him then turned back shyly. Did she blush? Hard to tell in that light, but he thought so. He treasured her blush, her physical reactions to him. Then he drifted to a vision her lying under the console doing some kind of repair. He heard the clink of her tools, he watched her writhe to reach a particular spot in the back with her tools. To see those hips rock and then hump up and down twice trying to ratchet herself back, feet pushing, knees spread made him breathe faster.

Marta herself jarred him out of the impromptu peep show! Merciful angels in heaven, there in the flesh. Could she see him redden? The evil, ugly guilty red covering his face like a hazard sign? Could she see how hard he was through the suit? He straightened as if there was no discomfort, physically or emotionally.

As steadily as he could muster, he asked, "You need something, van Rijn?" Damn, his head still hurt from his sleepless night, a thorough payback for the wonderful evening he'd shared with her.

"I didn't mean to interrupt. I was asking if moving the field back was going to be a problem. We had to move the Atmo station, too many zinging particles."

"Dr. Bloom mentioned that. It's a small thing you should not concern yourself with." Cold bastard, he just couldn't do any better right now and felt worse for it. Why must he always pay in such painful currency? Why must he make her pay?

He saw her happy demeanor fade like a spent blossom and was doubly shamed. His unexpectedly frigid reaction was obviously much more than she was ready for. With her head bowed she said, "Sorry, I'll leave you to your work."

His eyes locked on a slight sway of her hips as she trudged away until the dusty plume of her steps blowing toward him obscured her. The vicious mental slap that snapped his head to the side from the force of it caught him completely off guard. He should have been prepared; he could feel his Father's handprint and hear the derision in high fidelity.

He winced at the accusations of adolescent sentimentality once more. "Get up you pathetic sniveling excuse for a son. You make me want to puke, you hear me? You'll never make anything of yourself if you can't grow up and get on with your WORK. Grow up! WORK, damn you! You will stop playing with flowers and keep your deviant hands off the girls. You will be a damned Engineer, the one I can't be. Do you hear me boy!"

"I hear you," he mumbled as he scanned the ground and burned another hole. Work, force applied to an object.

chapter 36

The Van Damme

"D r. Cartier, sorry I'm late. I had to place monitors in the trees over there with Barto for Dr. Bloom." She pointed and added, "Those are real trees! They have signs of damage and irregular growth, no revelation, but look how they've grown here! I saw seedlings!"

He seemed glad to see her from what she could tell. "They were actually planted? Not simply dispersed from the crash?"

She reported, "The planting is in a complex but recognizable pattern, with the holes still distinct from the surrounding soils. The lower canopy is much healthier looking than I feared, seeing the mess on the fringes." She waited a beat, the added with a tinge of mystery, "There aren't any boot prints or other visible signs of them, the Van Dammers." She knew each of the twenty-six crew and scientists by name, rank and by holograph; they were the greatest, if also most tragic, heroes the Netherlands had seen in generations.

She and Benji had pretended the Van Damme heroes had made it to the new Eden and set up an exciting paradise for them to go and explore. No imagination needed now - she threw up her hands, exclaiming, "Dr. C, they did it! This may be no Eden, but they got here and they got trees to grow in a place like this! With 8.8% ox and less insolation and in spite of the hard energy blowing in!"

"Settle down, Marta, you're making me dizzy and you're going to strain a muscle with all that gesticulation. Besides, we have to follow the plans I slaved over while you were fooling around with that karate stuff or we will not accomplish all I want to do in the short time here. Five and a half days from now we shove off! Chop, chop! Without so much dust!"

She contained her outward excitement for the moment and got with the plan. The tree stems looked bigger around than the height would suggest, concurrent with previously studies done in high CO_2 hypoxic environments and her estimation of the gravity effects. Nothing in the literature really matched what she had here. She'd have to measure the girth, height, cambium and xylem densities, the cell wall shape and densities, the percentage of stomata closure. Would she have time to determine photosynthate distribution? She had to, yes, yes, but for how many species, locations and soil profiles?

Either Cartier or Barto had already unlocked the pods and left them open. The nearer one contained reloads of the consumables staged in the Portico, all in deconable clear bag-like enclosures, most of Cartier's gear as well as the more sturdy and bulky supplies that both of the scientists would need. Climbing in was more strenuous an activity than she'd anticipated with no visible step or ladder and the triple suit made it much harder. She finally heaved herself belly flat on the pod's deck and had to use a handrail to rise up to her knees and then to her feet. She decided to look around and cool off before resuming work.

First had to be the lights and she found a control panel on the pod wall. Next to the light control she saw the ramp extension and it was out and ready in no time, no need to climb out. The scientists' pod had relatively few supplies in it compared with the interior dimensions; she'd helped them plan ways to share quite a bit to save even more in case they couldn't keep any of it after all - good thing, too. To take up much of the remaining cavern, four enormous film-wrapped mechanical yellow beasts crouched in the shadowy back. Tractors? "You beauties must be for Tembo or one of the other colonies. I reckon the hard strip will take care of you as long as you stay in your cocoons back there." She checked the shipping label and found it was Tenembras, all right. Excellent, now it wasn't just hearsay that this pod would go to the first colony on the ticket. Cartier seemed sure he wouldn't be able to retrieve anything from here, but he said the deconned pod would be delivered straight to his domes so there was a chance of getting some stuff back.

The procedure called for taking everything that belonged to them out, sterilizing the interior with the peroxide-Bagnold fog and closing it up with only the encased machines. They could chemically decon anything they wanted to salvage at the end with the peroxy fog and load it back. The last hard gamma sterilization would activate automatically after the pod doors shut and they got through the stratosphere, followed by overkill via vac venting, all governed by AI.

That was the plan, anyway. Cartier had already told her he wanted his pod left open as a nearby supply base as opposed to piling everything in the sand and as a shelter when the rad monitors went off indicating solar flares. Bloom, on the other hand, didn't seem to need the security the pod presented.

With her breath and temperature back to normal, she found the cart and proceeded to load it with all manner of frame members, equipment and various supplies for putting up the benches and equipment stands on location near the trees. She couldn't help but mourn for Dr. Cartier's probable reasons for siting his main bench so near the trees; they were the last Earth trees he was likely to see since she'd heard Tembo hadn't yet terraformed past alga on the sea.

She eased the cart down the ramp at a somewhat faster rate than desired without stumbling. The other pod was ajar. She thought there shouldn't be anything for them in that one. Pulling the wide door open, a sunbeam fell on a recessed but easily accessible floor panel for the ramp controls including lights and the ramp, duh! Climbing for nothing! Since the pod was already open, there was no reason not to deploy the ramp and take a peek.

Though this one was a twin to the Ag pod, it felt smaller inside from possessing only one gargantuan item. Curious as a raccoon,

Marta poked about the folded satellite that took up the entire back half of the pod and had an attached grav sled to move it, none of it wrapped. Back at the entry, she flipped on the interior lights.

She couldn't do much more than admire it and note the thousands of cool parts in it, folded up like an immense sleeping insect. She snooped closer, spying the connections to a dual rail on either side for the convenience, no doubt, of a remote launch. Why in a pod? Satellites launched from a launching bay. Unless it was some kind of secret? Pats learned to sneak before they could speak. Charitably, maybe the Bus shuttles didn't have launch bays and they had to make do.

Anticipating some fun, she reminded herself to stay mute, thinking, 'Something else to decon, but I'll get to play with that slick as snot sled!' The next second she corrected herself; there would be no need to decon something going directly into independent orbit and the pod would be open to vac if not the rad-kill. Still, it didn't need to be open to wily contaminants like this. Why would Barto have opened it? He'd been integral in the planning and should have known everything for the expedition was in the one pod. She left the enigma, retracted the ramp and extinguished the lights so she could push the door almost shut and get back to work.

Tugging the heavy cart with both hands and walking backwards, she labored her way slowly back toward the Ag bench. The sand was only a couple centimeters deep closer to his bench, so she made better time without the dusty auburn plume and without looking like a struggling waif. She and Dr. Cartier worked continuously with set-up, calibrations and other preliminaries until they simultaneously looked up to realize it was twilight.

As the ruddy sun bowed ever lower, Alain stopped Marta from trying to assemble one more soil frame. "Marta, dear, do come and walk with me to the cliff. Neither of us has seen a sunset on another planet, eh?"

She eagerly joined him. On the way, she side tripped to the Portico for two folding chairs. Her mentor appeared rapt as she unfolded the seats so she stood by him in silence. The sun glowed maroon now, with part of it touching the sea edge and with an optical illusion of horizontal stripes of turquoise sky shimmering through it, melting from one layer to the other liquidly, as if molten precious stones.

They relaxed on the cliff, listening to the crash of the surf below and watching the panorama above, the sea and sky merging, absorbing the splendor of it. The scattered cumulus clouds catching the radiance seemed afire while the sea complemented the blaze, a vast sky of surrealist crimson and saffron, tangerine and magenta, all backlit into a flamboyant optical fanfare.

The sun fell inexorably lower and the heavens slowly lost their brilliance. Then with a greenish-blue flash, the alien star melted away below the horizon; the clouds, even more starkly outlined, dimmed as if the sun had pulled his colors with him, unwilling to share them any longer. Then within a minute, the encroaching darkness began allowing fleeting glimpses of the brightest stars between the clouds.

They sat speechless. Because the perimeter poles brightened after sunset, Marta and Cartier lingered at the cliff, watching the enveloping night for any sign of life, scanning the sea for a glimpse of any wave-defining phosphorescence a indicating biology. No, only the growing shimmer of starlight from millions of tiny points and a respectable naked-eye view of a neighboring barred galaxy.

"Sir, isn't the planet so different by starlight? It could almost be Earth with the waves below and the 'normal' night colors."

"You don't think the red atmosphere during the day is due to the sun's slightly more orange color, do you?"

Affronted, she replied, "No, sir! The winds die down toward evening, stirring up less dust to color the sky, just like Mars."

He tested her as usual. "But why is the sky so clear so quickly?"

She remembered the sand blowing in from the right all afternoon, remembered having a stray thought of there being sufficient blowing sand to fill her ear up were it not for her helmet. Now walking back from the cliff the breeze blew the dust from their footsteps ahead of them. "The direction wind changes offshore as the sun sets."

"Very good, it's harder to make observances in these suits, with this time line and with all that dust." He halted a moment as if he had more educational questions, but suddenly did not have the heart for them. In a weary tone, he said, "Marta, I believe we'd best go on in before they send a search party, eh?"

They carried their chairs and followed the line of pole-light back to the portico. "I'd like to do that again," She told him as they neared the entrance. "I love a blazing sunset!"

"As do I," he said wistfully.

chapter 37

Tree Talk

"**M**arta, I've seen you out with the pentameter. Which tree densities match Earth standard? Any?"

"The oaks are faring the best under the duress here, sir, with that stand of quercus albs over there the best so far. I suspected that from Earth, where the insects and diseases did them more damage than the positive CO_2 effect could overcome. Here, no bugs and disease, just the cosmic radiation to contend with."

"You mean aside from the lack of symbiotic biota and native nutrients that aid Earth trees."

"Ah, yes sir. Even considering that, annual rings from the core samples showed 35% more growth than Earth standard, with xylem densities corresponding very well. I mean, considering the age of the trees on arrival and time since, the pentameter showed impossibly high numbers so I had to confirm it. Preliminary results show a phenology consistent with the atmospheric composition, but not the general nutrient availability."

With a perplexed expression, she continued, "Somehow when they planted the trees they enriched the nitrogen, potassium and other nutrients in the right proportions at each planting site. I haven't found any appreciable concentrations of any of those anywhere. How they could do that without having an idea what the soil condition would be in the first place? Serendipity? Or did the bring everything including the kitchen sink? The first results indicate plenty of available nutrients and enough ox to fuel photosynthate transport! Next, I'll start on the root-to-shoot and woody root protocols."

"That's for the oaks, but what about the conifers? They look scrappy."

"I was surprised at how poorly the pines in general showed, and the spruces and firs were not much better; they should have had the least sensitivity to UV like you predicted last year at the Toronto Symposium. I did a quickie test and found excess starches in the needles causing the drop and evidence of accelerated germination and senescence."

"Good thing there aren't any of those pathogens or pests here, they'd have succumbed readily. I expect a poor response to the short year is a part of it, too, only 0.7 of Earth's. Did that seem to disrupt growth of many species?"

"The maples as a whole are doing well in nearly all categories, but their densities average on the low side, compared to the oaks that is, so the rapid seasons could be a factor. Does that make sense for a more adaptive successional species? It wasn't defined very well in the literature how much of the maple's annual cycle depended on temps and how much on time. Here the temps probably average three degrees C low across the board with about twenty degree summer and winter differences."

"So in general the biomass of most trees was stimulated, agreeing with the lit." He continued in Professor mode, "This increased biomass effect was shown on Earth with only a doubling of atmospheric CO_2; is there evidence of increased fruiting and seed production?"

Marta knew he hadn't paid attention to her personal preparations and was now pleasantly surprised. She bounced on the balls of her feet as possible, charged with intellectual excitement and a young woman's joy of discovery. "The only fruit trees that seem to have acclimated well are the apples and peaches. I would not have expected the apples to do well at all, but there's lots of evidence they've fruited many times, with some seedlings surviving, especially where the canopy shades enough to absorb some of the harder rays and still let sufficient light in. The peaches are kinda knobby, big pit-to-flesh ratios."

"What other fruits have you seen? They should have brought a wide variety."

"The guavas and mangoes have all but died off from what looks like not finding that happy medium between UV protection and light and the complete lack of non-tree organics. The pears seem less affected by the UV and are surviving well in the cool temperatures, but don't seem to be good at holding on to their fruits to seed maturity. Go figure! I have it all in a report I can have ready by morning. Unless you want it sooner?"

She'd seen much more, but purposefully tried to contain her delirious elation at being able to roam the Van Damme's forest! She could almost sense Benji with her and had to refrain consciously from speaking aloud to him while conducting her studies for her innate fear of who else listened.

"Marta, I did not assign you the tree assessment. That was a shortcoming on my part. I am impressed at you progress, I really am. You absolutely have to record every detail so you can fold all this into a thesis on the way back.

"I have to tell you, however, that our task is to assess the planet, not the spurious Earth trees. We need to get on with the soils assessments. I'm sorry, kiddo. I'm glad you did it; I was dying to know. I will read your report very carefully. It really is too bad they won't make it."

"Sure they will, they've made it this far."

"No, dear, the Commander will want the evidence erased, I'm certain of it."

"Erased? The Van Dammers and these marvelous trees?"

The relics of the expedition without doubt and not enough doubt about the trees to even consider. Any evidence will give Eurussia precedence on this planet and I don't think the Pats want to cede it to them, not with the resources they could get."

Marta grudgingly saw the point. "But sir, can't we make an exception? I understand Tenembras relies on dome gardening to feed most of the population. The emphasis has been on soy with some grains and vegetables. These trees are the ones that have survived and thrived in excess CO_2 and perpetual dust! Fruit trees would provide vital nutrition, the maples and oaks are important for shade and timber. I read that the oak may be the species that enabled civilization to take hold in the first place, what with the acorns and wood for shelter fabrication and fuel."

"Yes, yes, and the primitives could climb up in the oaks to escape the saber-toothed tigers." His exasperated tone lightened. "All right, we can extract the particular DNA from the best examples. We might incorporate them if we ever get to light off the Eco-Pack. Remember Tenembras has virtually no readily available fresh water and trees are thirsty fellows."

"DNA? Seedlings are what you needs, lots of seedlings!"

He looked back at the ships. "Your quest to take something back is moot because we cannot take any organic materials anywhere unless they are oxidized and zapped hard enough to kill them. You know this." He seemed determined to remind her that she was Crew. "Your commitment to uphold the extremely paranoid tenets of the Patriot Hegemony is safe by virtue of not being allowed to do otherwise."

She hadn't forgotten, she wanted a better outcome and thought he might sympathize. For the comm, she stated, "Sir, I do not have any thought of breaking or even bending any Patriot requirements!"

He chuckled. "I accidentally installed some equipment and diddled other bits nearby that have the unfortunate effect of blanking out our communications, too bad, yes? Why else do you think I suffer this rather poor position well beyond Shuttle Two in this blowing sand next to these mutant trees?"

She didn't believe what he was telling her; Dr. Alain Cartier a subversive? To the extent of tinkering with the surveillance?

"Marta dear, don't look so stricken. I am nearly to the edge of my personal precipice. What secrets should I keep anymore? What risk do I not dare? I'm doomed already!"

She stuttered, "Y-you are the man to turn Tenembran agriculture around, the one to show them how to feed themselves."

"There is NO WATER!" He slammed his gloved palms on the bench, rattling it. He knew the suit's med pick-up was on a different freq than the comm and didn't want to arouse suspicion; even if it weren't that important any more, it was still ingrained in his brain to starve the monitors so he took a deep breath before continuing.

"Dear, they sent me there to die under falsely advertised pretenses. These are the same people who decree we won't just leave these miracle trees here so we could build an outpost and perhaps a research facility. I heartily agree they are worth study!"

Miserably, she asked a question she already knew the answer to. "Can't any be saved? There won't be any proof they ever existed?"

"Nothing except in encrypted Patriot files. They'll go back and tell Eurussia that the life signal was an artifact of the peculiar sun or some such falsehood. They will paint the place as hostile as possible and so easily get the rights to the place and then mine it with robots because of the heavy energy spectra. None of our data will get through uncensored. Yes, they have to burn off all the evidence that the old EU's Van Damme made it here and started terraforming and it was working!"

"Why couldn't they keep the trees and add to them? Make something instead of destroying it? This could be a beautiful world, and already has all that water, abundant water and a working hydraulic cycle." She had little success trying to quell her bubbling anger.

"I know, all this water here and they probably won't touch it except for local mining. I know I'd like to take a million liters of it to that dust ball we're going to. No dice."

"All for politics!"

"No, it's not only politics. They won't cart foreign microbes home and they will not leave Earth DNA scattered around for any unfriendly race to trip across and build a bioweapon for. Who knows what may happen when we turn our backs here?"

"That's crazy!" He sounded like he went along with the nutty notion!

"Not that crazy, and I know it was in your orientation materials. You know I read that according to the survey of known systems with habitable zones, about three quarters of them would have had longer to evolve intelligent life than us. And remember our evolution was blown away several times by comets, very low ox, excessive ox, what have you - what if we're the laggards and there are warrens of them out there, all with sharp teeth? Go no further than Chanx for the chance for life, you know about Chanx? You can bet that if little green men in spaceships exist, those steely-eyed beasties would love to swarm upon us. We don't need to leave them Earth scraps to tailor a threat with."

She couldn't believe she heard this from her mentor. "Why would they have to be antagonistic?"

"Because they made it this far, child. The fainted hearted do not overcome the obstacles to the stars."

chapter 38

And who Are you?

The next day, technically Day Two, Marta dragged about, debilitated by her overwhelming nightmares. "I haven't seen it sir."

"Nonsense, it's under your left hand!"

"Sorry, um, here." She fumbled with the wrench a couple of times; in a pique of frustration shoved it across the table, knocking his tablet to the ground. "I'm sorry!" came out raspy and quavering. She picked the tablet up and laid it carefully on the table.

Barto watched this as he walked up and worried. Everyone bunked in the Portico last night and no one could have missed her thrashing and crying out or him sitting with her, trying to comfort her in silence. He gave them both a cheerful *buenas dias* that landed flat. He grabbed her wrist and pulled her at a diagonal within the zone he'd helped Cartier establish, stopping a few meters away.

"Hermana, you wouldn't talk to me last night and I think is because of you don't want to make Miss Naomi mad. I understand that. Now I see is something else. What is it?" He raised her chin and touched his helmet to hers. "*Que paso*, Hermana?"

She shook her head slowly as if unwilling to let her voice betray how distraught she was, how powerless and worthless she felt. He'd seen her this way before, but not with this immediacy and not while fully awake.

He walked back to Cartier, took her tablet and returned to tow her towards the woods. After a few steps, she jerked away.

"I can't go in there!"

"Why?"

"I can't!"

"I drag you like a twenty kilo *bolsa de zucar* unless you tell me a good reason why not."

She slowly shook her head.

He did drag her, so fast she barely kept to her feet. He did not stop until they were about twenty meters into the trees, nothing but trees visible all around. He held her still until she stopped trying to escape. Then he did something very peculiar. He took a step away and pulled two devices each about the size of a mashed plum from his courier pouch and handed them to her, then poked some suit controls on his arm. He exaggerated taking a deep breath and released his helmet! To the open air!

Her amazement made her clutch the devices he gave her to the extent he had to pry one from her glove so he could loop the strap around his head and press it around his nose so he could breathe. Since she didn't move, he repeated the process for her, allowing her to fit it snug to her nose.

He made a show of holding the helmet's opening against his torso and she did the same. He mimed holding it tight and she did.

"These should last about an hour or more, depending on how much you work, your breath activates it to release oxygen to make up for what the air don't have. You see this world is not the terrible place they say, acting like it is contagious with some exotic disease or fungus, is just low on oxygen, is a good world with good trees. Now, you tell me what is wrong with you."

He'd got the word on the atmosphere from Naomi, whom they both trusted completely. Now, freed from that traitorous helmet, she *could* tell him.

"These trees are alive and were planted by my countrymen. My brother Benji and I worshipped these guys as more than heroes, more like gods pointing the way to a fantastically bright future. Then my homeland drowned, Papa, Benji died, and Mama who couldn't stand the rigors as well as I went psycho. I struggled to come out of it all with something Papa and Mama would be proud of."

Barto took her helmet and handed her a visor wipe for her oozing nose. Despite himself, he found it amusing to watch her blow her nose without breathing through her mouth or inhaling through the mask. She spared a visor wipe of her own to clean out the mask and put it back on. The story resumed with less emotion.

"Barto, I tried making something of myself, something I thought Papa and Mama would value so I could forget what happened to our happy family and my idyllic childhood. Then I lost all my financial support and came on this miserable cruise. And what do I find here? Benji's and my Shangri-La, the paradise we'd dreamed the Van Damme had founded. All here and alive!"

She stopped for some deep breathing through the small mask and it had the effect of stopping the incipient hyperventilation. More stable, she continued, "Yesterday Dr. Cartier told me those rat-ass Pats were going to cleanse the planet when we leave and we could take nothing, not even samples back. They're going to burn these trees to less than cinders with intense incendiaries, hot enough to melt the damned rocks, and let the powdered ash scatter on the breeze."

He knew she was defying him to deny the circumstances warranted despair. Instead of empathizing, he started asking her questions. "What is this one?"

"Barto, please don't. I can't get to know them any better, it hurts too much and I don't care."

"Hermana, you cannot tell me you got as far as you have by running away. You face this and get it right in your head or it will make you *loco*. Now I say again, this tree is called what?"

"An ash tree. This is a healthy and vigorous ash, what the general carpenter at the farm called a piss elm. It has little helicopter seeds that kids play with. They make baseball bats out of it. I do care, you know, I'm a caring person."

There was several of that kind together, so he moved to the next grouping. "This one?"

"You know it's an apple, you can see where they've fallen to the ground and dried up because they can't rot without bacteria and fungi. This one is a Macintosh and it looks like we missed the peak fruiting but if you could find one, they're tart and great for pies. Jimena married an Austrian guy and made strudels with raisins for him."

He made his little half smile to have missed that obvious indicator of the windfalls, but was happy she talked more normally now, with less volatility. He walked over to a place with disturbed sand, perhaps wind eddies. He pointed to a small grouping of tall faded black-brown trees with bark that looked like smooth, parallel rods. "This one?"

Marta studied it carefully, taken comically aback to be unfamiliar with it, with its exceedingly odd build. "Barto, I have no idea." She shoved her despair into an internal compartment to let her deal with this new conundrum.

"A tree you don't know! I gonna tell Alain and he laugh his ass off! Write it down so you can look it up and I take pictures. Maybe I not tell him, but it would be funny."

"Barto, you don't get it. My bread and butter is trees, my whole future is trees. I may not be able to recognize every subspecies, but I am confident I could identify the genus!" She put her curled glove tips to her chin. "I wonder if they can move?"

"What you mean, Hermana? Any tree can move or they break in the wind."

"No. Let me tell you what I saw the first night I was here when Cedric and I sat out on the Portico and the rest of you stayed inside. It was dark night, only the stars and the Portico perimeter lights outside, just enough to see the south end lights but not much else. I saw trees move to the light near the farthest Portico edge. There was one there when I first noticed it, then I watched another move up next to it, then another."

It was his turn to stare at her. Had she inherited mental instability from her mother? Had clouds made enough shadows to fool her eyes? Had that Doc doped her food? He did not know what to believe. "You say the trees move *across* the ground?"

She walked slowly around the group and spoke her observations aloud. "They are of varying heights, but all with the rod-like cambium, that's bark, the same rod-like structure. The slim interior stalks are strange, with some kind of weird berries at the branch tips. Three interior stalks only, note that. They are too thin for their heights in this atmosphere and gravity and they exhibit atypical outer branch structure, leafless branches pulled up close to the trunk."

"I think they're aliens." She summed up flatly. She backed up a pace, still staring at the nearest tree and absently asked, "How long do these masks work on one charge? I'm getting light headed."

Barto shook himself and pulled out two more cartridges. He replaced hers and kept his in hand until needed, slipping the spent one into his satchel. "You don't be talking about aliens and they last longer."

She stepped up close and put her glove to the bark, and realizing that yielded no information, pulled her mask under her chin and pressed her cheek against it. It was cool and slick-smooth. She straightened and replaced her mask. "Barto, you have to figure out a way that I don't have to hold this damned helmet all the time, I want to use both arms and try to estimate girths."

"I get right on it, as soon as we see what these alien things are and what they can do." Barto let go of the worry and let wonder guide him. He came around and pointed at some of the berries. "Is this a part of the tree or one of those bug nests?"

Immediately he laughed and corrected himself, "No bugs! It has to be the tree. If it is a tree. It looks kinda like on a palm tree, the long yellow sticks that come out with the berries. How does a person know if is a tree?" He reached to pick a berry and she grabbed his arm.

He jerked away violently and wound up to deliver a chop, then let out an explosive breathe and bowed his head with a grimace.

"Barto! Hey! I'm sorry! Hey, It's me, Marta, snap out of it buddy! Please? I'm so sorry, please forgive me, *por favor*!"

"Used to be you do that I have a flashback and maybe I knock your head off, but Doc she fix me. I guess I gotta learn new habits before I hurt somebody." After a second, he stretched and rolled his shoulders and his anger faded. "Why you do that?"

Relieved, she explained, "Barto, what if you touch that and it squirts acid on you or something? This planet was lifeless, sterile except for what the Van Damme brought with it. The Van Damme did not bring these. We have no idea of its defense mechanisms or anything else."

"You put your face to it."

Pleased he had his smile back, she agreed, "*Si*, that was foolish. Maybe we need to put the helmets back on as a safety precaution."

Barto jerked around as if hearing a call. "Is that Naomi looking for us? She gonna get lost."

"I didn't hear anything, are you sure?" Marta stepped away a pace to listen.

Barto reached up and tried to touch the nodule on the mid-sized one. It retracted and settled out of reach.

His movement alerted her to whirl around in time to catch the movement, barely maintaining her balance. "Yeah, buddy, I saw it. This must be the mobile alien I saw the other night. Great greasy groundhogs, it has to be!"

They both stepped back about a meter. In an absentminded effort to relieve tension and think more clearly, she closed her eyes and attempted to reach a heavy hand behind her, over her shoulder for a tension-reducing stretch. The bulk of the suit prevented her from the extension she wanted, but the effort helped. When she opened her eyes, Barto stood gawking, white as a sheet.

chapter 39

Monkey see...

Now the both stared. The smallest 'tree' had reached a limb-rod and made a similar motion to hers. The larger 'tree' next to it bumped it, emitting a high-pitched note. The smaller one straightened up. Marta and Barto looked at each other then back at the ... aliens.

Unbidden thoughts raced through her mind. Aliens. Mimics. A...child? Corrected by it's...parent? Not from here. *Alien!* Where are the rest? Where are they from? We are first contact! At least the first contact of us to them. Unless they met the Van Damme people. Contact! A parent and child! Aliens! The trade of ideas, the learning of each other's cultures. The vast expansion of knowledge possible!"

Then Dr. Cartier's visage filled her mind; she heard his words again. Was Cartier right about aliens, or her heart?

She nearly fell to her knees but Barto caught her and waited impatiently for her to explain as he changed his air cartridge.

She stood, shaky, gripping her damned helmet to her belly. "The Policy toward alien life. Barto, this is First Contact or close to it and we're not allowed to be civilized. We must kill these guys and sterilize them into oblivion unless they can get outta Dodge. The paranoid black widow Patriot Policy!"

"Marta, we just leave them alone, *si*? I mean for now, until we learn more about them. Maybe they got a ride on the other side of the planet." He tried to smooth his hair with his glove.

They looked back at the little mimic, now still and treeish. "Barto, we tell no one anything unless we agree in advance, okay?"

"*Si.*"

They looked around at the trees as she repeated Cartier's pronouncements to him, her eyes drifting from the apples and leaves and bark, to each other, and then back to those impossible aliens in a lost kind of way. When her O_2 cartridge started running out, she took the mask off and donned the helmet. Barto sealed it, and then they got his on. They kept the rest of the masks away for next time.

chapter 40

Now what?

Barto and Marta made their way back through the little forest quietly, neither willing to share their thoughts with the secret listeners like remoras in their helmets. Back at the Ag bench, Cartier shoveled a hole in the ground. Barto politely took the shovel from him and dug more efficiently, knowing the plan to dig to rock and sift particle sizes, to observe structure and to inspect for anything identifiable. Marta got to her knees and sifted from one screen to another.

Dr. Cartier seemed pleased she'd come around and didn't inquire how it happened. He sat to rest a minute; Marta knew digging in heavy grav didn't figure on his list of preferred activities.

Cartier had explained to her that he expected nothing from the screen survey, selecting the test because was easy to do and it required little of his highly valued equipment while producing reams of data. Soon complete for that location, Barto headed off on another security round, promising to bring back lunch.

"Marta, dear, what did you find in those trees to make you so happy yet so worried and secretive? I must say it's an improvement, but I am concerned."

Instead of feigning embarrassment or making up some story, she asked him a question weighing on her mind. "Dr. Cartier, how do you know when a commitment you have made is the right one? How do you judge the merit of the existing commitment made for convenience but in good faith against a new one that seems more worthy of respect, more noble, that may be diametrically opposed to the first? How do you know it's not sentimentality or some angst from the past overly influencing the decision?"

He got in her face, visor to visor. "You swore to Naomi your relationship to young Bartolommeo was platonic and now you're had a rendezvous in the woods and are torn. I submit to you that in a short time you two will be forever parted. My advice is to get what you can while you can and let Naomi fend for herself later. She'll have plenty of time and is more flexible than you might think."

She sputtered, "Dr. Cartier! There was no 'rendezvous'! We identified some trees and talked over my problem, the one you so clearly illustrated yesterday."

"About scrubbing the planet? Absurd! No one can alter that, so there's no reason for your emotional ricochet. Don't try to put one over on someone with my amorous history. I put forth the hypothesis that your blatant involvement with the attentive stud is why Naomi snubs you and Crannog usually keeps his distance. Naomi's perfect picture would be that she gets Barto while you get stuck with the stick, Crannog. I like Naomi, but I have to side with you. The comparison between Barto and the stickman makes it self-explanatory."

"False! False! Why must you and Naomi think with your gonads first? Barto and I are a team working on a serious issue, an issue we would like help on but are afraid of your resistance."

"You might convince me if there wasn't a leaf in your hair."

Stricken, she wildly wondered if jumping up and down might loosen it. The alternative was to go back into the woods and try to take off the helmet. She fretted getting it sealed back on with no supplemental oxygen. She'd have to do it soon, before anyone else noticed.

"Marta."

"Doc, I can't explain right now. I have to go back for a minute, but I'll return in a jiff."

"Marta, stop." He put his glove on her arm. "There is no leaf, but clearly you've had your tin can off. Deception is fun but it can get too confusing for an old fogy like me."

* * *

Alain Cartier smiled when Marta turned back to her work, relieved. Let her think he was omnipotent; the red smudge on her chin was all he needed to know something secret was going on.

chapter 41

who's the alien?

TaaTaa said more forcefully, *"No! Our history is always of peace. We shall do no thing to harm these aliens!"*

R'noot challenged him. *"They are of the same kind that crashed into our ship and stranded us here. It is the fault of these things that half of us have succumbed to the bad sun's poisons; we should have completed our job and moved on long ago. Now your little one has revealed us. We must strike before they come at us in force."*

"Wait!" Kreeek said, twirling a left limb. *"I saw them approach. They looked carefully. One reached to poke my eye and the other one stopped it, but the one fooled the other into looking away. My eye was not harmed, but it was I who betrayed our presence, not LeeLaa when I pulled from its reach. They looked for what we are, not in harm. When LeeLaa moved they did not attack nor did they run, they talked words to each other and only then left."*

"There were seven of us around them, they would have been fools indeed to show mischief then. They will come back with many more." R'noot's unhappiness was clear.

"Friends," big BinThaa said, *"do not forget that when the alien ship of years past crashed, they could not navigate away from our ship. I was there at the first to help the three survivors and you all know they were peaceful, only planting trees to the end. We have always parleyed with other races for*

our needs; this one is different only because of that accident. Let us ask for assistance."

SaaTee, the sole representative of her family still living, spoke, *"No, you and the rest have allowed two to see some movement. I was there too and I perceive the aliens are stupid and weak. All we must do is hide until they leave and await our kind to come and rescue us."*

This caused many jeers and derisive flashes among the unharmonious survivors. TaaTaa had waited a long time for some change to signal an answer to his prayers. BinThaa led the group, but TaaTaa felt it his duty to direct his fellows in faith to the peaceful solution that benefited both themselves and the aliens, though he knew no possible road to that end.

TaaTaa twirled for attention. *"Hear me! I alone will go among them and learn what I may. I will seek out how their systems work and try to determine if any of them would help us. I will discern if they are angry or stupid or generous. I will not lead them back here. All we do know is that the light they can activate at will is so like our own benevolent Sun that we can be nourished. I will attempt to gain this light for ourselves and our children."*

"TaaTaa, your family supports you in this." Kreeek gathered LeeLaa between her and TaaTaa. *"We shall meet them together in the emanation from He Who Rends and She Who Mends and find the right way."*

"You have lost your reason to go forth this way! There is danger and you risk us all!" R'ooot looked for support, but found none.

BinThaa stood in front of the family and faced the others. *"Those of you who believe, pray. Those of you who do not, hush and hide. I will keep watch on this family and contemplate the will of the Render and Mender. I have spoken."*

chapter 42
important questions

"**D**r. Cartier, do you *approve* of the policy you told me about yesterday?"

"No, not entirely, but that's the way it is, dear. I think there should be a way to do carefully controlled studies so we can learn what's out there and add to mankind's store of knowledge. I think the current policy has its head in the sand, er, if I said that right."

"Wild blue question, just so I can better define where you stand," Marta asked, "what if an alien walked square up to you and said 'Eek! Eek!'?"

"I would wet my drawers as I ran away."

Chin as far back on her neck as the suit would allow, her puzzled frown lingered as she tried to maneuver her mind into a response.

"I see you don't like that reply, but like I told you yesterday any sufficiently advanced alien is most likely aggressive and would probably either take us out or perhaps cage us in a lab somewhere while they seek out Earth for subjugation."

She countered, "You would kill off first contact out of emotional anthropomorphizing and conjecture-based fear?"

"What do you mean, first contact? Chanx resounds with alien life. There is a research colony studying it and the planet is strictly quarantined."

He purposefully tried her patience. "Sir, each alien species is an opportunity for contact and that includes the bugs and critters. *First* contact is meeting an intelligent being we can converse with, one that knows prime numbers or something. What if they could converse and share technology or even share an inherently alien culture, you would still want to kill them without provocation, even the children?"

"This is more than a 'wild blue' question. What have you found? Something resembling a glyph carved into a boulder? Three-fingered claw marks on a tree? A saucer with blinking lights off to the side that evaded our scanners? A glyph-like mark can be a question of perspective and shadow; erosion produces marvelous figures in rocks. Something that resembled claw marks would be intriguing and I would be interested to determine what natural process caused it if I had the time. If it was the saucer I'd expect the Captain to tune our scanners to detect the sighting and then judge if we can take them out or not." He faltered. "We could never lead them back to human habitation." He sat again and picked up his magnifier. "Enough red herring distractions. Go bother Bloom for a while if you have the nerve."

She noticed a disturbance in the trees behind the cargo pods and soon saw Naomi and Barto lumber out with sloshing buckets. She took Naomi's and they kept walking. "How does it look?"

Naomi had a grin in her voice, "Crystal clear. Preliminary probes indicate it's a bit heavy but potable straight out of the river." They bypassed the Ag bench and headed for Naomi's spot.

Marta remembered the charts showed a river winding behind the forested area and around to the west; she'd like to see it - maybe it made a waterfall where it ran off the cliffs. She gratefully parked the buckets on the bench where Naomi indicated; they weighed much more than she'd expected.

"Ladies, I get us Kentucky Fried Chicken today, okay?" Barto started across the sands to Shuttle One's Portico.

Naomi loaded water samples in her analyzer, an old, dinged up campaigner by the looks of it.

Marta thought Naomi's slow, encased fingers caressed its surfaces in melancholy, like apologizing for putting an old draft horse in the traces one more time before you shoot it. Would the sterilization process kill it? Marta shivered.

"Barty said you guys found something odd in the woods and I ought to ask you about it. He's not usually so cryptic."

"He told you we found something?"

"Yes, honeydew, about a half second before I accosted him for literally dragging you into the woods this morning. My tender self-esteem is so battered that one more eruption of jealousy would maim it for good, or for bad I suppose, and so I must trust you two have an immaculate story."

Marta had no immediate answer, so she stepped over to a sand-free rock outcrop and climbed up onto the flat thirty-centimeter high top to think. The outcrop sloped gradually down to the sands in every direction but the Atmo bench. She turned around slowly like a music box ballerina in a full set of armor, thinking about how little experience she had with social interactions.

"Miss van Rijn, is something the matter?" Cedric came up a slope from the side, appearing cool as usual, but she thought she could see a hint of concern in his voice. It warmed her heart, the way he stood, slack hipped with a bent knee in front to rest his gloves on, ready to listen.

She would like him to understand her predicament and offer aid, but could not directly tell him anything for the same reason she'd left Naomi stewing down there.

"I understand Tenembras is a percent low on oxygen despite the cyanobacteria mats and the Sand Breaker and that the method of using land flora to exchange the abundant CO_2 for O2 is stymied because no one has authorized the Eco-Pack and they won't try anything independent of it outside the domes."

"I believe you are correct that the only effort for a green solution is the sea algae, the filamentous cyanos and various other epilithic alga and some planktons and forams. The oceans are well colonized now and the oxygen balance with them is still too low. Thus we break out the ox of matrices that would not otherwise ever give it up short of subduction temperatures and pressure; I refer of course to the Sand Breaker."

"You sound like you're looking forward to working on the thing. I heard it is immense, very hot and dirty and requires the output of several nuclear reactors."

"The CO_2 levels remain too high and the Breaker does produce prodigious amounts of particulates. I do anticipate a challenge in making it more efficient and a better place to operate, but believe I'm ready for it."

"Would it be helpful at all if some trees already selected for high CO_2 were established?"

"I understand the first ones out of the domes tried trees and they ended up with brown twigs in the dry ground. The CO_2 wasn't the issue as far as I read, but the poor alkaline soil. And there is also the dearth of fresh water that cannot be underestimated. You are imagining you could accomplish this green solution where others could not?"

"Professor Cartier is a premium resource, there must be water to have limited irrigation and the trees with a CO_2 affinity are already here." She raised her arm to point a gloved hand toward the scraggly trees. "I believe I'm up to the challenge."

"The CO_2 was not the primary issue. It was the media misnamed 'soil' and the freshwater, not seawater, availability. Maybe you can make a super-tree that can overcome these obstacles, but I don't think you can genetically modify a tree already grown. Or are you wanting to take seeds? DNA? These were Earth trees to begin with and would be no different than the Earth trees brought directly there."

"But these trees in this energetically bombarded environment have shown a rapid directional selection toward meeting the non-Earth environmental challenges far better than expected. There have been multiple generations of seedlings and as an example, the seedlings' photosynthesis rate has acclimated to the environmental CO_2 levels faster than theory would predict with high CO_2 and low Ox environmental immersion alone."

"Miss van Rijn, natural selection takes ages and the Van Damme only crash landed about a dozen years or so ago. Presumably, there was at least one survivor who planted all these trees. Earth to wherever here is, directly planted. No natural selection."

She wondered why they didn't teach the story of black moths and white moths in sooty 19th century London in Scottish schools. He'd told her he only studied his own field, but this was worse than she'd expected. "But Cedric, many trees were planted but some died and some survived, but several species have actually thrived given the additional grav and the solar radiation difference. The reproduction rates increase with the environmental pressures and there are many annual sets of seedlings thriving, a grand array for selection!"

He didn't respond, so she kept going." Tenembras has a whiter and brighter relative sun even if it's further away, a more highly oxygenated atmosphere and is overall significantly warmer. I bet candy apples that with the implied lower solar wind and cosmic ray burden, the better quality light and the less inhibiting grav, these CO_2 selected trees would take off. And they are principally timber and apple species, too. I can't fathom the right nutrients aren't on Tembo, they would simply need to be made available to the trees. A win-win?"

"You are maintaining a sentimental attachment to these particular trees. And you dodge the problem of the lack of free water." He looked over toward the sea, standing straight now with crossed arms. "Too bad you can't bring anything back from here not doubly sterilized, because it would be interesting to see how they'd do. I do like to see green and growing plants and know I will miss them terribly. One thing Americans fear is contamination. If you brought some trees and a few tonnes of water it might work, but no, this is a dead end. I don't think they would consider the water alone, though Bloom assures me it's Perrier. It's a grand thought, Marta, it's a drat shame it can't happen."

He'd actually thought saving the trees could work, then, as an experiment perhaps, the idea was viable! Stubbornly, she attempted to confirm. "If I could get them back, do you think they could eventually make a positive difference to the atmosphere?"

He shook his head. "You're an idealist. There are too few and the conditions too harsh. It's probably best to leave it at that. It was pleasant for you to call me by my given name, though. You even pronounced it correctly." He jumped down the Atmo-side of the rock with perfect balance and flexion.

Naomi had studiously not been watching, but heard his puff of breath when he jumped. She reached with both hands to lift one of the full buckets Barto had left on the ground, aiming to put it on the table without sloshing it.

"Bloom, do you need help shifting that?"

"Sure, I can always use the help of a tall, strong, handsome fella."

"Shall I go find one? Where do you want it? Here?"

Marta came down the gentler part of the slope and stood at the opposite edge of the bench.

"Closer to the middle, please. It's going to rain this afternoon and I want plenty of room for the hood clamps. I know it seems weird to not want the water to get wet, but I'll have probes in it and don't need it getting diluted. Thanks!"

Naomi peered around Cedric's bulky suit. "Marta! Looks who's turned beast of burden!"

Naomi sounded so pleased, as if presenting to Marta that Cedric was an honest-to-goodness human after all, worthy of affection. She could almost hear she comment something like, 'see how darling he is?' or some such. Did she really not see that she and Barto were not 'involved'?

Conversationally, he turned and said, "Hallo, van Rijn."

Marta wondered, 'What is up with that? Am I supposed to answer him? We were just talking a couple meters away! I'd give a dollar to know what goes on in his head sometimes, I honestly would.'

"Me Naomi, she Marta." Naomi instructed. "Not too hard is it?"

"Not anymore." He froze. "Oh my, I'm late to the shuttle Portico to, um, do something. I will see you ladies later!"

"Marta, did he just make a Freudian boo-boo? Marta?"

chapter 43

Rainy Day

Marta came back to Atmo after finishing with Dr. Cartier's rain protected projects because Naomi lingered. Naomi forecasted a series of brisk showers lasting a few hours all together, maybe to twilight, and thick clouds rolled in to corroborate.

Walking up, she asked, "Is there anything else? Or are you waiting for Barto?"

"I was rather hoping he might escort me over. He is sure to be by shortly, worry not flowerpot."

Marta worried about the aliens. If work was on hold, she'd have free time to go see them and perhaps establish some kind of communication. "Why do we have to go in? Do you expect gusts that could blow us into the sea or something? I mean, the rain won't hurt these suits."

"No, nothing like that. There could be lighting and without a better feel for the meteorology I can't rule it out."

Idly, Marta said, "The trees don't show evidence of strikes, no burned out tops as far as I can tell."

"Yeah, I saw that, too. To tell the truth I tire of standing on these poor little feet and my shins are aching. The official story is 'lightening hazard'. Then she added, 'I mean it is true, there is a hazard, but I have large error bars."

Cedric came up and looked from Naomi to Marta and back to Naomi. "I abhor large error bars, don't you? Bloom, do you need any assistance battening down the station or bringing anything back to the shuttle?"

"Thanks, no. Barto has promised to come back and carry my poor carcass in."

Marta spoke impulsively, fudging on her pledge to Barto. Her time ticked away steadily! "Would you guys like to go with me to check on the met stations in the woods? This could be important data, with the rain."

"Like I said, doll, I need to prop these dogs up a while. You kids go on ahead." Naomi patted the cover and sat in her folding chair to wait.

"If you are serious about checking the met stations, I will go with you if you like." He always sounded so suave.

"Yes, sir, if it's no trouble. I have something odd to show you while we're there."

They checked the stations and found them exactly as they should be. The rain began filtering through the ragged tree canopy and left wet trails on their visors. Marta got an absurd sense that he was a large heron stalking beside her, intent on possible frogs. That picture segued to one of them approaching a lake, captioned 'Leda and the Heron'. "The trees I meant to show you are over here."

Marta went to the spot at about 340 degrees south, a left-hand diagonal from the apple trees. They looked at bare ground. The dimmer sun with the shade of both the trees and rain clouds made tracking difficult, but she thought she saw a recent disturbance in the sand at about due south from that spot and branches pushed aside the path. She followed it and found a grouping of 'them'. "Here they are, these are the strange trees I was talking about."

Cedric walked slowly around one off to the side, peering closely at the outer structure. "This is a tree, I suppose. Look at the bark, though, it looks like carbon tubes or rods." He started to reach a hand out, but apparently remembered the heavy suit glove as soon as the effort began. "The corrugations appear almost more like joined tubes." His courier bag yielded a magnifier. "Smooth a glass. I wonder how conductive they are? Potential lightening, you know."

"I can't identify them," she admitted, trying to hold his attention.

"They're funky yes, but remember the high UV has buggered everything and you did say the reproduction rate was accelerated. I mean look at those knobby bits on the upper branches, probably tumors." His bag also provided him a utility knife. He thumbed the mechanism to expose a blade and reached for a red nodule.

"Don't touch that! How would you like them pointing a blade at you?" She tugged at his arm.

Stepping back, he said testily, "Come on, Marta, it's a tree. Maybe a mutated tree or an experimental tree, but nonetheless a tree. Please don't fantasize about trees."

She grabbed his arm and guided him back to the area behind the Ag bench where she hoped their conversation would stay private.

"Mr. Crannog, those different trees are not native and are not from the Van Damme. Do you hear me?"

"Marta, yes, I hear you of course. How certain are you?"

"I don't have incontrovertible proof yet since we didn't bring DNA assay with us."

His head nodded inside his helmet. "Okay, let me get some tools and we'll cut one up. I'd like to see if the carbon rod structure is only on the circumference or chock through."

"Cut one up? No!"

"Why not? Do they seem dangerous? We can don even more protective gear. I thought taking something apart was an accepted method of investigation in your line of work."

"No! Yes it is, but not this time. Come see, I can't explain." She motioned back toward the aliens and tried to will him into understanding.

"I don't believe that. You are one of the most articulate persons I've cared to converse with. I was rather glad when you asked be to walk among the trees with you. Now you try to draw me into something disingenuously. Why?"

She rested her head on her right hand fingertips and made the futile motions of massaging her forehead through the helmet, not prepared to take the hated helmet off. When she straightened she asked, "How do you stand on the Policy?"

"Which policy?"

"The one about leaving Lyra 9976 a bare rock with no organic residue of any kind."

"Didn't we go over this before, about how we Earthlings in general are paranoid and we can't bring your trees back?"

"Don't be dense. I meant the Policy to sterilize all life here to prevent any aliens stumbling upon ingredients for weapons or whatever to prevent them from threatening any human habitation. Any life, including these alien trees right here that have not threatened us in the least. The policy does not account for finding friendly aliens."

Nettled at her tone, he responded at a rapid and more heavily accented clip. "It makes sense to protect humanity, don't you think? We've protected our biointegrity since we first left the thermosphere and have carefully left places we're trod upon sterile. You want to take these trees back and plant them? My opinion is *no*. You think these odd trees are aliens and you want to bring them home like so many stray puppies. My duty is to tell you *no*. Study all you like with or without dissection and make a grand report, but unless you apply to Captain Fajar and Commander Jones, you can't take any of any of this with you and whatever is here will be burnt off the planet, leaving no trace for an alien species to capitalize on. How's that for not being dense?"

She waited but her voice still quivered. "If on another planet we ran across sentient life, the first intelligent space-faring contact, would that policy still make so much sense?"

"Doubly so!"

She swallowed surging bile and turned to walk quietly and sadly away from him, back to supposed civilization.

He hit his fists together and yelled after her, "What the blue devils do you want from me?"

She yearned to tell him, but the way was now closed.

Marta found Dr. Cartier under the tree verge looking up at the clouds and stepped over toward him. They watched Cedric as he stalked on toward the Portico, hunched over. She stood companionably by Cartier, longing to feel the rain on her neglected skin. She felt very near a precipice of her own.

"Marta dear I don't understand. That Crannog comes around and you fuss and he leaves you in an emotional mess, yet you watch him as if he's some kind of prize. I tell you dear, that scarecrow has no heart and can do nothing but wring your poor soul dry."

"Dr. Cartier I know you mean well, but he does have a heart, it's in there somewhere."

"And you who can fix anything think you can fix him? Women have suffered though that vain hope for eons." He shifted his stance, no longer bathed in the afterglow of rainy day memories. "I'm only trying to help."

"I know and I appreciate it. You know Barto would just as soon punch him as look at him." To clarify, she added, "And, not it's not jealousy, it's protectiveness. He said that if I liked the accent so much I should download a recording."

Alain heaved a body-encompassing sigh and they listened to the rain pattering through the leaves until the current shower tapered off.

"How about that nice Bodine boy? About your age, fit and handsome in that Aryan airhead kind of way." In a sec he twisted to her and asked, "Are you laughing?"

She was laughing dangerously, because she was nearly certain 'that Bodine boy' would try to force himself on her and she'd kill him, ruining everything she'd endured.

* * *

Olivia edited a few minutes from the comm system off of the official record and filled it in with a similar but less suggestive line of conversation between van Rijn and Crannog. She liked them both, idiosyncratic and refreshingly not hypocritical. She added her copy to her continuing study materials, highlighting the word 'alien'.

chapter 44

equations

Cedric had a meeting scheduled with O'Reilly. He'd arranged the time to see if she could down load some sensitive data from the Sand Breaker power grid docs in hopes of using his remaining time constructively. The Passengers were now only allowed to respond to messages, so he had to register his presence and wait until she rang him. The vid light flashed and there was Char Jones.

"Oh, hello Commander Jones. I expected Lieutenant Commander O'Reilly."

"She went potty and asked me to have you stick around. I haven't seen you poring over your books so much lately. Not picking up too many of those nasty UVs out there, are you? Skin cancer can strike other places than Earth, you know."

"Ah, yes ma'am, I know, and no ma'am, I have not allowed myself to be overexposed. These suits are adequate and the deflectors help for most of the energetic particles."

"Good. However, I saw you with that van Ruin girl earlier and outside the deflectors at that. What can you be thinking? It's not in your best interest, professionally."

"I was only talking to her about some odd trees she's found."

"Trees? There's nothing from the Lost Dutchman that isn't already in our gene banks. Did you straighten her out, or does she need Authority?"

"Surely not ma'am. I did iterate the impossibility of any action beyond local study and she respects that."

"If you find any recalcitrance on the part of our least crew member, please let me know immediately. I have to maintain discipline and it's difficult to do when I'm in here and she's running amok out there."

He did not voice the obvious solution, for her to come outside. "Commander, perhaps you can assist me in obtaining my data? I have encountered a knotty problem with the Esterhane catalyst functional sequence and Olivia was going to let me know if I was cleared for that yet."

"She mentioned that and I have okayed it. You'll have to come in for that, though, it won't transfer to a non-secure station even if you're personally cleared."

This vexed him since he knew she could override that Portico station if she wanted; he was not keen on going back in while the other remained outside working. "I can wait until we all come back aboard."

"Nix on that. I was told to make sure you got whatever you needed and the only time you'd be able to study it is here on the shuttle bridge since it can't be printed and you won't have access on the way to Tembo."

She maneuvered him for some reason, but her rank him relent. "Thank you, please let me know a good time."

She reached to disconnect when he blurted out another request. "Ma'am?"

"Yes, but make it snappy. I do have work to do."

"Since the scientists tell me their projects are in hand and don't require my assistance, I request the buggy so I can go back to the wreckage we saw coming in and take a look."

"Hold on, incoming comm." Char put him on hold a couple of minutes. She returned with a smile, saying, "How about the morning of Day Six? You can come in early and pick up the buggy keys on the way out. Lee was going to get the buggy out then to place the incendiaries in and around the vegetation site, our insurance of a thorough job. Instead he can check the Passengers in." She smiled tightly. "About those Passengers, you know they'll be at their worst now that the fun and frolic of this place is ending, so watch out."

"Yes Ma'am, I will, and thank you." Special privileges like going in and shucking the protective gear for a while would rile the others and spur distrust. What worried him more was that he'd just agreed to set flames to the trees so clearly dear to Marta.

He straightened his slump and clamped his jaw tight. The silly girl had no importance; getting a leg up on his new career had priority. If he took on a task that someone would surely do whether he volunteered or not, what of it? He wanted to see the wreck and bloody well would. That girl had no claim on him whatsoever and in a few short weeks they would part forever.

chapter 45

Dichotomy

"Now what has you so upset? Not Lee again?" Doc did not want to hear her snivel about someone picking on her again; it happened on both the previous trips and was getting old.

"No, it's that messican. Are you going to do anything about him?"

"San Luis is outside on the planet and will be on Tembo in a few days. What do you want?"

"He kept calling me messican names that I know are dirty just by the way he said them. I never did anything to him!"

"Did he do it every time he saw you, or what?

"He'd wait until I was alone, like after saying goodbye to Lee or talking to Cedric. The damn messican waits until the guy is gone and then gets an awful expression and cusses and flaps his hands around. I'm going to complain to the XO about him if you won't."

What a pouty, self-centered troublemaker. If she wasn't so aggressively brazen sticking her tits out at anything with a weenie and verbally antagonizing the women she wouldn't attract so much unwanted attention. Doc particularly hated the snooty sniff she did around any of the women Passengers. "Wait, wait, how about we take him as a clinical study subject? I can advise academic credit for it."

"What do you mean?" She was haughtily indignant. "I have to put up with this? From damn Passenger?"

"We're segregated now and will be for the duration, so that doesn't matter anymore. Let me explain Post Trauma Stress to you."

She swelled her breast out and reared her elbows back, heightening the strutting peacock effect. "I'll go to the Commander right now and she'll see he's demoted to sewage treatment."

Doc was tired of going through this rigmarole staged so Barb could garner attention and feed her ego at the cost of others. "Barb, you are only doing this for a feeling of personal power. You don't have to be a Tech all your life; you could have personal power of your own. Look at Naomi Bloom. She has her Doctorate and is not much older than you."

"And look where it got her – Tembo! Besides, there's always something else to do. Studying is so boring."

"So what field is more exciting to you? What would you like to study?"

"I don't have a nose-in-the-book personality." Her expression changed to resemble a cat right after licking a paw and wiping its face. "I can't imagine wasting my youth to study. Either I can do something or I can't."

"Barb, honey, making something of your life is not going to be as easy as spreading your legs. Think of something else that interests you, something else you're good at."

"You're gonna regret that, bitch!" Barb stomped out angrily, and Doc did regret loosing her temper. She knew the girl was inexplicably protected no matter what excesses she committed. She leaned back in her chair to her personal stash and plucked out a porter. She was on her last slug of the dark, hoppy ale as Char came in.

"Got another one of those?"

"Sure." She pursed her lips in aversion as she reached behind her, thinking Barb didn't waste any time, the spoiled pinhead. Her face blanded out as she passed the opened bottle to Char.

"Doc, there is no one on board this trip that understands what the Patriot Revolution did for us. The foreigners fear us and the youngsters don't know any difference. Like Barbara, she sees this duty we're on as a game. We have an important role and are supporting our country. When did it get this way?"

"Hell, Char, I remember back when setting up a space station outside the Kuiper Belt was beyond reason and there were good arguments for placing at an angle to the ecliptic instead of on it. Now we taken it for granted as an interstellar hitching post and the dire problems predicted with the ecliptic position have nearly evaporated. Barb has never known a time when all we had was Earth. I remember the dedication of the first permanent station on the moon, where they made eloquent speeches about Apollo guys."

"I don't go back that far, but at least I did study it in school. What do they teach these kids these days anyway?"

"Not to think, certainly. AI has sucked their crania dry. None of 'em now could figure out the star drive, or the hurricane plug, or the microtractor to fix schizophrenic brains without cracking the noggin open. AI run our lives now, all to our supposed benefit." She waggled her empty bottle at Char, who nodded languidly. Doc opened two more brews, noting there were only seven left; she'd have to reload tonight. Most was in the kegs; only a half case of bottles left.

"Gross, Doc. You and you medical horrors." She tipped up the first bottle to drain it and screwed her face up with a *yuck*. She washed it away with a slug from the second bottle. "Forgot about the sludge." She settled more comfortably in Doc's cushy office chair with splayed knees and the bottle perched on a chair arm. "Remember the solar power breakthrough and we didn't have to jam ourselves on those slow-as-molasses buses anymore?"

Doc did not appreciate the sludge comment. There were a few dead yeasties, that's all, and they should be saluted. "Amen. They'd get so ponderous you could walk faster and smog would soot the roof panels so fast the driver, or his helper if he had one, was in and out, in and out. All the old-timers complained about not having gas for their great and mighty combustion engines with no regard for how criminal they sounded to the rest of us who had to live with the consequences. Daddy did have a Corvette, though. What a sweet machine. He would get drunk and go on about how it sounded and what it felt like to cruise at high speed, but I never knew him to start it." She pulled a long swig.

"We had a neighbor at our first house that had a Fiat Mobius that he swore ran on olive oil. He'd say, 'Essstrrra virrrgin olive oil', rolling those r's. It was a real showpiece, grass green, low to the ground, convertible."

"They made an electric version of that, didn't they?"

"Yeah, but it didn't rev, and man oh man he liked to gun that engine. Ended up stuck on some tracks and got smithereened by a freight train."

After a few minutes of reflection, Doc said, "I wish I could forget the first panicked coastal evacuations, with all the pollyannas out in full force while everybody kept saying their town was 'another New Orleans'. I got so sick of hearing someplace was 'another New Orleans'."

"I don't miss those terrible scenes, either. Nor do I miss the bombings, the sabotage, and the constant 'credible threats' from soggy bastards of every stripe. Daddy had a bomb shelter dug into the back yard twice as deep as the house."

"Oh yeah, we had a bomb shelter, too. We used it as an old-timey cellar." Kicked back with her sock feet propped on the desk corner, in a posture akin to one in a hammock, she continued alternately gesticulating with the bottle and tipping it. "Teed me off cause that's where my swing set belonged and when they moved it to excavate the sliding board wouldn't fit and was tossed in the recycle heap. My little beagle Herk loved to slide." She had loved that frenetic pooch, even when he dribbled wee-wee on her.

"We moved around too much to have pets."

Doc veered the conversation to less personally painful subjects. "Remember when that town in Arkansas voted to paint their wind turbine blades blue and gold for the high school?"

"That was all over the news, wasn't it?"

"Yeah, first for how pretty it was and then for why it was stupid, changing the thermal properties and weight of the blades. I image every other town that did it got out at midnight with cranes and mineral spirits."

"Everybody wanted the wind to be the answer to all the energy problems." Char shifted a leg, knee up.

"Remember the sailboat craze?"

Oh, yeah, everybody had to have a personal sailboat. I think a couple percent of all those toy sailors ended up drowning and they say space travel is dangerous!"

"Death by barge. They weren't really the 'good old days', were they?"

"Doc, that's what I meant about the Patriots. These kids think they can walk to a friend's house at night like it's a right. I remember kids getting snatched right off the sidewalks. A friend of my brother's, or his cousin or something was coming home from the grocery store and we never saw her again."

Doc suppressed the immediate response, 'That's a patented Patriot story, they teach that in tyrant school!' Aloud she decided to concede Char what she could. She agreed, less than whole-heartedly, "You do have to hand it to the Pats, they did get a grip on the violence when we had massive droughts simultaneous with floods that disrupted food production."

"Doc, I heard that unspoken 'but at what cost'. Maybe we have gone a little overboard since the coup, but it's a fact our borders are finally regulated. It was out of control! And we kicked those undocumented sponges out, too."

"It did isolate us from the rest of the world even more."

"Granted, but where was the rest of the world when we were begging for grain after that second freaky hot, dry winter in a row? Who helped us with the Southern California dengue fever outbreak? Who cared when most of Des Moines died from a poisoned water supply? How many food riots were there? Those foreign bastards didn't lift a finger. Our founders left those other countries for a good reason, to make a better life here."

She almost retorted, 'How many of those incidents were because of our policies? How about differentiating what you call food riots; many of them were to try to get food aid sent somewhere else.' She knew she should stop thinking, because sooner or later, the wrong thing would come out.

"Char, I won't argue; I spent my childhood under lock and key and Mama feared every loud noise. You know we lived a while a couple klicks from the hydrogen plant that blew, the one that took out half of Shreveport? I had to get a hearing aid when I was twelve and wait six months before my ears were fixed."

"I read about that, zow. What was it, about a square mile incinerated by the fireball?"

Subversive thoughts raced through her brain again, 'Was that a line or two in your history book? Making the country think it was sabotage and that we needed a more robust government, hint, hint? Or did Pat history say that it was because of a minor earthquake from New Madrid fault system that had a little more strike/slip to it locally than was officially detected that broke an underground pipe, and then the operators didn't believe their indications and ended up shutting the exactly wrong valves allowing the conditions for auto-ignition. Geez, I'll have to calm down!'

She drained the porter and got another automatically. "At least a mile, yeah. We lived in one of those '30s underground neighborhoods, you know the first floor in the ground and the 2nd floor above grade covered with the low efficiency photovoltaic tiles stilted up over sedum? We were down stairs going over my science lesson, weather terminology. I said, "Barometric Pressure" and "WHOOSH-BOOM" the top of the house lifted off and caught fire as it went up. I remember having the wild idea it was an instant tornado." She took a long draw from her bottle. "We dove under the desk until Daddy got home and moved to what Mama called a secure place shortly thereafter. That house was completely underground and we didn't need a bomb shelter, we lived in one."

"When's the last time something like that terrorism happened? Explosions? Or somebody getting to a city's water supply? If we didn't contain the folks in the Displacement Camps, we'd have every service overrun." She wagged her head at the past tragedies and then brightened. "I can go shopping without a bodyguard!"

Doc held the thought, 'Bodyguard, for crying out loud!', but it was close to the surface. Offhandedly, she said, "But Char, what about freedom of speech?"

That phrase jerked Char's head to full alert. "You can't have everything," she snapped.

Doc cooled her brow with the side of her beer bottle. To cover the slip, she decided to play senile so Char would attribute the charged phrase to age-induced innocence. "I know, I can't have everything. What I wouldn't give to have my little Herkimer back. We'd run in the grass and play fetch again. I wonder if we have any Cattle Drive around here, he loves that stuff."

Char drained her beer without tipping it all the way up. She made a show of checking her watch and set the empty on the desk by the other one. "Hey, I gotta make time for my Art Appreciation class. Thanks for the beer! Later!"

Doc muttered, "Its porter, not beer, and the United States Constitution guaranteed us Freedom of Speech." She collected all the empties, rinsed them and went back to her compartment for music.

chapter 46

what about those trees?

Thao sat outside drinking in the cool, damp pre-dawn of Day Four, nearly dying to feel the dampness on his face. He would miss the glory and promise of such a morning, remembering the lush greenery of his home on the lake in Minnesota, the geese honking and the crickets chirping and the feel of the dawn's dew most of all. There was so much he wanted to do, so much wonder to experience and behold but he'd frittered it all away. Someone approaching quickly, wade-walking apace. It startled him, but he stayed stock still as Marta hurried by, apparently unaware of him and also apparently on a mission to those peculiar trees he'd spotted.

The morning dawned clear, the air washed and rinsed, the dust dampened down. From his vantage at the far south corner of the Portico, he could make out the general form of the trees well. He'd wondered about those odd ones clustered almost under the light just to the side of the Agricultural Bench, wondering why they'd planted trees there to all to be burned off anyway. He grimaced at that. Why kill off such valiant examples of survival in a hostile territory? For the sake of killing? Would they who commanded the destruction point and preen over their handiwork, clinking sparkling wine glasses, their conceits preparing them for the Hell that surely awaited them?

* * *

'If I talk out loud to get all this straight in my head I'm done for; it's too friggin' important to mess up, but no, they had to have pick-ups in the helmets and we have to wear the friggin' helmets even though a mask would do and how am I supposed to think properly this early in the morning with only about two seconds before everybody else gets up and probably in full view of the friggin' surveillance and how am I gonna be able to address the gang aliens at the Ag Bench if I can't talk? Sheesh! Yeah, yeah, think. They damped the signal at Ag, at least that, of course I can talk however I have no friggin' idea what to say.'

Marta got nearer to the aliens and smiled automatically, plainly for her own benefit. There were four of them clustered around the Ag bench light: tall, taller, even taller and real tall.

'This is way too obvious, they're going to see this for sure and come out with flamethrowers or something.' She slowed as she closed in and held her arms out from her side, palms out with some idea of demonstrating she had no weapons.

Trusting the comm interference, she spoke rapidly in a low, soothing voice to relieve the pressure in her brain and encourage some redemptive brilliance to germinate and blossom as if the flow of words were the water her creativity needed to bloom. "Hey buddies, how you doing this fine morning, golly it's a surprise to see you. Thanks so much for dropping in but would it be an imposition for you to move you alien behinds over to the pod where we've fixed the vid instead of out here sitting ducks for slings, arrows and pulse rifles?"

She walked carefully around them twice, hoping to detect some sign they were awake, aware that they wouldn't yawn and blink, so what would they do? Were they watching her and wondering if salt and pepper would be enough or if a crab boil was more appropriate? Boogie damn woogie, she had to get these stray thoughts out of her head so it could do its job. She decided to speak everything else aloud regardless and get to business before the posse arrived.

"Those nodules on the branch tips may be light receptors," she opined, noting their orientation to the light. She stepped directly in front of them and said, "Take me to your Leader."

This defined not working. The idea that came like a flash of light made her run as well as she could to the rear of the Ag pod. She heaved it open and switched on the rear loading lights. She blinked when the silly notion popped through her head that the lights would attract bugs. She could hear Auntie, "Quit fiddle-fartin' around and shut that porch light off and shut that screen door, or do you want every skeeter in the county in here?"

Coming back to the present, she knew there was some risk the power drain might show up and raise questions, but not as big of a risk as seeing Ents in the yard. She ran back and lowered the telescoped upper sections of the deflector pole. She bit her lip and switched it off. That seemed to wake them up because all of the 'branches' twitched.

The sun reached halfway above the horizon and people would be about shortly. Expediency! She took a steadying breath, reached over to a short branch to the side of a mid-height alien and very gently clasped it. She waited very still for several seconds and then tugged on it ever so gently. It did not move a micron.

chapter 47

TƏƏTƏƏ

TaaTaa knew this was his plan and he had confidence, but actually being here with his family left him far more exposed than he had imagined. At least they had the light to wait by. Still night, naturally they fell asleep and suddenly woke to one of the first aliens circling them like a wild *nerrrg*. His confidence eroded as the alien ran away. Now what?

"TaaTaa," Kreeek asked, "*What farce is this? Where is the delegation of leaders to greet us and share water? This is not my idea of civilization. The garish display of personal body heat yesterday was enough to make me want to hide behind the trees and today is little better.*"

"*Peace, Kreeek, we are station afar and so may these creatures be a forward group with their main station elsewhere. We have not arrived at this place in a gleaming ship with formal water service that would pronounce us as civilized either. Are we not dusty and dull? Have we not lost our references? These beings may think us vagabonds!*"

"*Hark! It returns!*"

TaaTaa flashed greeting to it automatically. There was no response or indication it could comprehend the message except it moved a branch in the direction of the ship. What could that mean?

LeeLaa piped up that she had picked up a good signal over in the direction the creature had gone.

Kreeek, said, *"I wish we'd stop wasting time. It still seems to me this creature doesn't trust the other creatures from the way it runs about alone and so I do not think we should expose ourselves any more."*

Then the creature touched one of Kreeek's grasping rods and encased it in the resilient substance at the end of its branch. The branches had to be the creatures arms, TaaTaa decided. He thought it odd that there were so few arms; were those two multifunctional? Did they regrow if severed? If not, they must be very strong and withstand hazards well. Strong enough to crush his mate's reproductive appendage?

He felt the discomfort his mate radiated and sympathized with of her fear and with her embarrassment; the grasping rods were for grasping one's mate. She quivered but did not move for fear the fleshy thing might dissolve her shell, or who knows what? *"TaaTaa, it does not hurt, but it is so creepy!"*

TaaTaa felt his mate's distress increase and decided to try something bold. He placed one of his probing rod tips between his mate's arm and the alien creature's flesh. The alien was warm and soft, not unpleasant at all, just as LeeLaa told him from the encounter yesterday.

He could feel a fluid akin to blood pulsing through and beneath its skin. The limb had so may inorganic layers wrapped around it; somehow the soft inside skin held the blood in. Did their blood circulate under so much less pressure? How could it circulate in a soft sac like that without sturdier shell protection? Did they always require the multiple layers of material? It didn't seem impervious to hazard at all! Or was there a completely different system for powering their internal functions? They seemed more like Tooli than anything else, but Tooli could certainly be hostile even if not inherently dangerous. He wanted to probe for structural support data, but didn't want to go too fast and hurt or scare or provoke the creature.

Kreeek decreased her arm diameter and slipped it away, leaving TaaTaa's limb within the alien's fleshy bag. *"BinThaa LeeLaa, the touch of the alien did no harm, but it did feel like poking my arm into a live nolaar, ugggh!"*

TaaTaa said, *"The pull is in the same direction of the limb pointing and in the same direction as the ship. It wants us to move to the ship and I agree with LeeLaa, there is good light there. Shall we go together?"*

"You act like we have not seen this kind of people before. I know we kept many of us back safe, but all us heard the stories each day. I see nothing hurling from the sky so if we're going to, let's do it," said BinThaa.

They found a bounty of light that nearly made Kreeek swoon. Soon LeeLaa begged to look around the immediate vicinity so Kreeek agreed to go with her to search for hazards at the end of the ship. TaaTaa conferred with BinThaa and established that based on the quality and intensity of this light and body parameters, these were indeed the same type creatures as the ones who'd landed so badly and destroyed their transport so long ago.

TaaTaa stood under the delicious light and wondered about the ways of providence. What were the chances of that ship hitting in the exact spot as their only transport considering all the available area of the planet? He to this day made himself think it an astronomical coincidence and not the work of the Render. That did not explain how the Mender could allow such senseless death.

* * *

Marta had kept a light grip on the slippery branch-thing, but the alien next door made it clear he was the one for the job. She tugged and was trying to think of a way to say 'giddyup' in alien when he abruptly came at her. She almost tripped in her haste to guide them properly, the thought 'be careful what you ask for' dancing across her mind.

She glanced up at the vid pick-up again to assure herself it looped, but questioned herself again on whether it happened to be the only spy-eye as two of the aliens began exploring. Again, she got that gut conviction that she could not do this alone, while simultaneously her brain told her she had no allies except Barto, and maybe Naomi. Maybe. Definitely not Cedric. Cartier was the key, though, and nothing could work without his input and expertise. Even if she had to chain him up and put him in diapers, knowing the mess made when one was chained up without diapers, she must convince him. What to convince him of, she wasn't sure yet.

chapter 48

Help?

S he looked over at the tree-creatures, now reconvened as a quartet, and fancied them drinking the light in. She corrected herself: Not fanciful! 'See how their nodules,' she saw it was the clear ones now, 'see how they angle to the light, ja, ja, ja.' She saw the little one's sensors inch closer, then the taller one tap a slender blunt rod on the little ones upper quarter, on a bundled rod, then the little one retract the sensor a few centimeters. Was this a child being admonished by her mother to not be greedy? To be polite at a strange house?

It was hard to leave them there, but they seemed happy enough and she had to check in before anyone missed her. On the way back around to the Portico she bent her thoughts to the pitfalls of applying human feelings and motivations to non-humans. But how to avoid it? She'd already thought of the cooperative one as a 'he', the 'family' arranged in size like the three bears, um, and a Grandpa bear.

She pulled Barto aside as he headed out on a patrol. "We need to talk." She clenched fists and hit her visor in frustration. She looked back and saw his undivided attention. "I thought you and Naomi might like to hear about some old friends of mine, like about the time I invited them over to my house and the folks got so mad because of what we did to their dog. It's really funny!"

"What makes you think she would want to hear your stories, funny or no?"

"I thought it might get us back on a friendly basis. We could talk about anything. I wish we could draw Dr. Cartier in, too, he's getting so tense."

"How about Crannog?"

"Naw, he's immune to small things like missing Earth."

"I see. It would be nice to meet in the trees, no? *Bueno* Earth trees?"

"Sounds fine to me. Let's bring a couple lights. It's bound to be dark in there this early."

He went to get Naomi, already at the Atmo station. Marta went back to the Portico for a cart. She loaded it with four big lights, all of the biggest yet portable solar-rechargeable battery ones. Around them, she stuffed water packs and a few food packs in case they stayed a while. She put a poly cover over that and artfully stacked four folding chairs on top. Barto trotted over and reaching up high, brought down a carton of air masks and a pouch full of O_2 cartridges and tucked them under the cover among the lights. He stuffed some long S-hooks, some elastic straps and a bundle of wipes into a satchel and nodded at her as he looped the satchel strap over his helmet.

There was no hope of eluding surveillance for any point up to the edge of the deflector field, so Marta hoped her thin story would hold. It ate at her nerves to put her friends at risk, but this was worth it! As she neared the Ag bench she glanced over and could discern the 'roots' from under the hatch that conveniently blocked the view from the bench, not that Dr. Cartier had arrived yet.

"Hey," she shouted over, "I left a light on over here while I was looking for something this morning. Let me go turn it off." She could see Barto's eyes grow wide as saucers when he also saw the 'roots'.

She slipped between the door and the pod interior where the light controls where. The bluish nodules wavered in her direction, as if triangulating her position. She could think of no way to warn them of the impending blackout, amplified by the fact that the lights for the rear of the pod were all on one switch. At a loss, she put her hands together as in prayer and bowed to them.

When the lights went out, they moved back as one. Before they could leave, she reached for the next-to-biggest one's handshake rod. At least she hoped it was the same one he offered before!

She led them directly toward the trees behind the pods. She let go and pointed toward the central part of the trees at this end and walked two paces. They did not move. She mimicked reaching for the alien's 'hand' and pulling, the pointed again. They followed.

Marta found where Barto had chosen to set up by the increasing luminescence. She ran ahead to find Naomi with her helmet off and respirator on. Naomi raised her hands and shoulders in a 'what's up' gesture, then scurried back into Barto's waiting arms when the group arrived.

Barto had rigged the lights to tree limbs with some S-hooks in an array that lit an area about ten paces in any direction. Marta went over to the cart and set up a mask, a hook and a strap on a nearby chair.

"Hi, Naomi. I hope you don't mind getting dragged away from your work. You hadn't experienced these trees yet and I really wanted you to get the chance."

Naomi snaked an arm to her back to lift an edge and spoke into her helmet, "Amazingly thoughtful of you, sugar pie," sounding small and faint. Barto squeezed her shoulders in support.

"Instead of hearing me yap, would you rather just sit in the quiet and watch the wind rustle the leaves?"

Barto released a strap and pulled his helmet close to say, "That is my vote, how about you, *corazon*?" He rubbed his stubbly cheek on the top of her head, which smoothed rather than tousled it.

She nodded weakly. "Er, okeydokey."

chapter 49

communication

Barto reconnected himself and came around to help Marta with her helmet, strapping it tight to her back like he'd just fixed his and Naomi's. "Ladies, I think now we can talk softly, *si*?" He made sure Naomi nodded before he continued. "Hermana, how are our Amigos today?"

"They've had their breakfast, assuming they consume light for sustenance."

"They eat light?" Naomi asked, edging up to clutch at Barto's arm.

"From what I have observed, the clear nodules collect light. See how they're angled at ours? And the blue ones are the ones watching us. The red ones are some kind of sensor; I don't have it all figured out yet." She waved side to side palm out, at the little one, who promptly waved back with a rod that Marta identified as one of her handshake hands. "They were at the Ag bench deflector at dawn, so I led them over to the pod and lit it up for them."

"They waited there for you. Then you led them here?" Naomi sounded stronger as scientific curiosity overcame her fears. "Do they talk or otherwise communicate?"

"I've heard some high-pitched screeches and you can see their red nodules blink, but I don't know what any of it means."

"Where's their ship?" Naomi stepped in front of Barto, but not far.

"Ladies, they enough arms for the calamari, si? Maybe they can draw."

Naomi twisted to look him in the eyes. "Calamari? Squids? Tree squids?"

Meanwhile Marta moved the chairs and found a long switch in the accumulated tree litter to smooth the damp sand. Finding a long, pointed stick, she stooped over the smoothed area and drew a large 'M' as seen from the alien's perspective. She stood by it and said 'MARTA'. She passed the stick to Naomi.

She drew an 'O' and stood by it to say 'NAOMI'. Aside to Marta, she commented, "An M and an N look too much alike, and are dependent on orientation."

Barto approached and drew a '+' sign, saying 'BARTO'. He then backed up and walked around the perimeter to the aliens.

The second largest, the one Marta figured as the leader, took the stick in a long, very thin arm and walked close to the sandy chalkboard to draw a symbol resembling an ampersand. He seemed to visibly shorten his main trunk and said, "TaaTaa." To her ears it was still high pitched, but audible. She repeated in as high a pitch as she could muster, "TaaTaa."

The little one twirled the ends of two arms around away from her truck and emitted a squeal. She rushed up to TaaTaa and took the stick from him. She shortened a greater percentage than TaaTaa, emitting a clearly audible, "LeeLaa." She pointed the stick at Marta. "Martaa." She pointed at Naomi and said, "Omee" and then at Barto to say, "BaaarTow." She pointed the stick at and identified, "Kreeek" and "BinThaa." She straightened up to her full height of about 2.2 meters.

Marta's brain labored hard in full data acquisition mode. The alien's main tubes that appeared to form a central barrel got shorter and wider when they wanted to talk, or be audible to them. That meant they understood acoustics. Maybe? She swore at her musical deficiency, only able to conjure some details for frequency and wavelengths. This was going so fast; was the 'little girl' 'precocious'? Cedric knew about music, damn him!

Naomi called out, "Water" and Barto handed her a pouch. She looked over quickly when she heard Kreeek screech. LeeLaa stepped around and placed her arm ends in a prayer orientation. She bowed from the middle, more like an arc. She shortened and said, "Waater."

"Barty, get the baby a water, did you hear that? She said water!" He gave it to Naomi to hand to her. She was considering whether to open it when LeeLaa put a curled arm around it.

LeeLaa took the water to Kreeek who made a prayer sign and bowed slightly.

Even Marta winced when Kreeek and LeeLaa skewered the bottle with stiff darker colored tubes, the immediacy of it making her think of a javelin hitting a target. When the pouch collapsed nearly half way, Kreeek screeched with a varying modulation and gave the pouch to TaaTaa and BinThaa. They finished it in the same manner. TaaTaa flipped the empty pouch neatly to Naomi.

"How phenomenal is it for them to do the Japanese bow thing!" Naomi was excited now, repeating their names and laughing as the humans shared Naomi's water.

"Uh, guys, I have a confession to make." Naomi and Barto stilled, apparently apprehensive at what other surprises Marta might have for them. "I think I taught them that. I mean, when I wanted to turn out their lights at the pod I did it and when I wanted them to follow me I did it."

Naomi was excited about that. "The first communicative gesture they learned and repeated was about manners! That's a great sign! We have to record all this, this is too, too, too much! I wanna see their ship, how do we ask about their ship?"

Marta used the branch to erase the drawing surface, but it wasn't working well with the thin switch. She felt herself getting warm with embarrassment, showing incompetence when she wanted it all to be so perfect.

BinThaa came around and walked into the middle of the effort. He extended lower 'root' rods onto the surface; where he walked was smooth and packed down. He spiraled outward ending up by TaaTaa.

Marta did the bow and started her sketch. She drew a circle and in the circle drew an M, O and +, and said the alien's names. She had to stop then for an O_2 cartridge.

When she resumed she pointed toward the ship with her whole arm and stick. She said, "Sheep" in a high pitch and made a divot there, repeating, "sheep". She tried to pass the stick to TaaTaa, saying "TaaTaa sheep?" but he did not take it. He did the bow and Marta went back to her place.

Marta booted herself for making an assumption about syntax and the meaning of a word when there were other senses in play. What else did she have to go on? Time was running out!

TaaTaa used an extended lower rod to draw a depiction of a circle within a circle and a lozenge shape on the inner circle that the humans agreed amongst themselves could be this planet and its atmosphere. The lozenge could be their ship? Next, he drew an 'H' figure, a middle bar twice as long as either of the bookend bars. He used the point of his – leg? – to make a curve from the H to the small lozenge on the planet. He wiped out the lozenge.

Marta was staring to feel ill; she recognized that shape. TaaTaa was depicting an interstellar craft, not shuttles.

TaaTaa stopped for a minute as if he needed to compose himself. Resuming, he drew the 'H' again, but it was broken in the middle and the larger part had landed directly on their ship. He shortened and said, "Vaan Daamme".

Marta went over to a white oak and wept. This tree was planted by the Van Damme survivors in the aliens' presence; the only way they'd know the name was if someone had told it to them.

Barto came over and collected her from the tree. He led her to a chair. He said, ladies, that means what I think? The Van Damme crash into these guys ship and the ones that survived, these guys, they been here every since?"

"Barty, you don't think they killed the human survivors, I mean, look at the way they jabbed that pouch? They could pop anyone of us like a balloon."

"Miss Naomi, if these the same ones, why they bein' nice now? Why they not pissed at us? I think maybe we better watch our backs."

"Guys," Marta said, sniffing, "I think maybe they are treating us the same way they treated the Van Dammers. They're friendly. I wouldn't think they'd present themselves that differently, a matter of disposition if you will."

"Sugar, I'd be ornery as a cat hung by his tail if it'd happened to me."

Barto shook his head slowly. "The scatter of the wreckage we see from orbit makes me think not many Van Dammers survived, maybe none."

Marta wagged her hands at him. "Barto, they knew the name Van Damme and the only way was to hear a survivor say it in the right context. And somebody had to plant these trees. Every hole I've seen is prepared, a visibly different soil mix at each tree."

"So they were friendly to the survivors. After what the humans did, they no revenge." He hesitated as if needed to force to words out. "So let's burn the planet and kill the rest of them?"

"Marta," Naomi said, fists on hips, "you have to get Alain in on this. There ain't a thing in this world or any other we can do without his blessing and expertise, you know that."

"I can't tell him!" Marta protested. "He told me point blank that any aliens, especially smart ones, should be shot first and examined later. He'll turn us in!"

"Shut your mouth! Alain would never turn us in, never! And don't be so sure that what he says in character is what's tick-tockin' behind the little doors of his cuckoo clock. You just wait until he hears darlin' little LeeLaa say his name and he'll do somersaults to help."

Marta was having a difficulty following Naomi's increasing southern-speak and the more exotic metaphors. "You mean that his decrepitude is a sham? And maybe his paranoid opinions?"

"When you *mujeres* get this settled, please tell it to me in *Englais despacio y mas claro, por favor.*" They took little notice, so he went over to an apple tree with several bright yellow fruits. The ones he'd seen on the way in were old and soft, but these here were firm.

He chose one of the roundest ones and bit into it. The succulence nearly made him keel over! He snatched a wipe from the satchel to mop up the excess juices.

Marta and Naomi were at his side the moment they heard the crunch.

Barto said, "Mmmm."

Naomi chose one and took the wipe he offered. She turned to see Marta fumbling for her helmet and nearly laughed to see her able to touch it but not get hold of it.

"I'll go haul the good Professor back here even if I have to conk him first." She turned to the direction of Naomi's shifted gaze. The aliens were gone. Marta shrugged, more annoyed with the suit than ever. She imagined herself a turtle trying to take off her shell. "We gotta have an apple together, anyhow." Barto rescued her from her predicament and latched her lid on. She trotted toward the Ag Station in high hope Dr. Cartier would be there by now.

After the deliciously cool breeze that had reached all the way to her shoulder blades, this newly generated sweat was like having used lube oil, gritty and viscous, rubbed on her skin, much worse than yesterday. She slowed as she approached the Station, planning her pitch.

"Sir?"

He turned to her, still holding a beaker of red dirt, and frowned in her direction. "And where have you been? You know we had every minute planned, and at this place where you should be and where you were contracted to be you are not!"

She found it much less heartrending to think this peevishness was a put on, but was annoyed he reminded the Listeners that she was lax in performing her contract duties. Unless he was right and they were deaf here.

In either case, he was pushing her contrition and duty buttons; Lor-DEE he was good at it. Penitently, she said, "Naomi and Barto and I were in the woods, just being with the trees. Sir, it's such a powerful experience to sit there quietly. We all wanted you to come join us."

He immediately sat the beaker on the bench and grabbed his toolkit. He stepped over to drape his arm around her and they proceeded into the wood.

Barto had his arm around Naomi, chairs pushed together. Marta didn't see any of the Amigos, which was fine. Barto got up to fix Alain's helmet.

"I knew you children were going native out here and was quite affronted you didn't invite me." He leaned back to inhale long and deeply as if it was the air of Earth. "Now, Marta, tell me your secret."

"Our secret is standing behind you. Please turn around slowly!" Marta was glad it was only the playful LeeLaa. "LeeLaa, meet Alain!"

He stared open mouthed as LeeLaa shortened and said, "Aaa-Layn, draw naaame, AaaLayn."

"What in creation? This tree thing talked? It has talked to me?"

"Dr. Cartier, LeeLaa has asked you to draw a symbol to represent your name, 'draw' your name. She is sharp as a tack to have picked up the way to say a sentence."

Marta fetched the pointed stick and gave it to him. He stood there moving his pursed lips around. She took the stick from him and gave it to LeeLaa, who backed up and drew an 'M', saying "Mar-taa". LeeLaa gave the stick back to Alain. He frowned as he took it from her, but made some kind of internal decision and heaved a sigh. He bent to the sand and drew a lobed semblance of a pointed clover.

Naomi stepped closer. "Alain, we were trying to draw simple things, mine is a plain O and Barty's is a plus sign. Do you want to be known as the ace of clubs?"

"Dear, I appreciate the simplicity idea, but this is the only symbol I wish to represent myself with." He turned to the little alien. "Is a maple leaf alright with you, oh scourge of heaven and Earth?"

Marta interjected, "Professor, that's not funny. She's just a kid and hasn't hurt anybody."

She'd forgotten how expressive his looks could be. "A long time friend with an excellent community reputation, eh?"

LeeLaa seemed to loose interest and did something odd; she threw an apple at Barto.

Barto caught it and threw it back.

LeeLaa threw it at Naomi, who passed it to Barto, who tossed it to LeeLaa, then Marta, Alain, Naomi, LeeLaa, Barto, faster and faster until Naomi dropped it. LeeLaa's hands whirled in the direction they interpreted as 'good, yes', and then stopped.

"Kreeek!" she tweeted. She turned to the humans, *"Martaa Omi BaaarTow Aalen (yes hand twirl) TaaTaa (unintelligible) oooine?"*

Puzzled, Naomi asked, "Do what?"

LeeLaa took the long stick and pointed at the light, repeating, *"Oooine, TaaTaaKreeekBinThaa (unintelligible) oooine."* She pointed the way the others had gone with her stick.

"It appears our little buddy has received a request from on high," Naomi conjectured. "They're asking politely for the lights, do you think? They certainly have taken a cotton to them."

"Corazon, maybe we watch and see what she does."

Marta grinned. "That sounds like the only available option until we learn a little more. Well, Alain, how do you feel about the dangers of the steely-eyed aliens now?"

"Girls, I don't know what to think. This one seems innocent enough, but so does a little grizzly bear cub. What have you people gotten into?"

Marta faced LeeLaa and bowed as low as she dared, saying, *"TaaTaaKreeekBinThaa oooine,"* followed by what she trusted was a 'yes' twirl. LeeLaa bowed and left.

"Senor Cartier, Marta and me find these in the trees, there are at least three more. We been talking to them and they tell us a very sad story." He looked over to Marta as the obvious choice to relate the crash.

"They were marooned here by the Van Damme's crash; they were here and told us the name Van Damme before we mentioned anything at all." Marta sat heavily in her chair. "I think they must have planted a lot of these trees."

Cartier lowered his head as if at a funeral. After a minute of silence all around, he walked to the edge of the clearing and stared in the direction the alien had gone.

Marta watched him, the legendary man she knew so little of, a man she couldn't predict. Could she predict what any of them would do?

He walked quickly back to them. "I may seem squeamish and cowardly, but I advise us to go back to our duty stations and get some work done. Having that thing appear behind my back gave me the shivers and I have to think long and hard about that, so I'm heading back." He took a step away and turned, pointing a crooked forefinger at each of them as he spoke. "You wouldn't want to press your luck by being away too long either. We have assigned work to do and our watchers will not miss our extended absence."

"Alain's right," Naomi drawled, "I think I need a chance to mull this all over myself. We do need to show the flag out there, so come on Marta, Barty."

They worked at their assignments the rest of the day, but the aliens were never far from anyone's mind.

chapter 50

Join the Party

TaaTaa felt in a whirlwind. Kreeek had asked for the water and the creatures were forthcoming, all good. The gestures for following and drawing were clear enough. Why did they stop just when the communication was going so well? Then make noises among themselves? Did they blame his people for destroying the big ship? It seemed not, but how to be sure?

Kreeek said, *"I will not wait more. It is wrong for us to be here in comfort while those behind suffer. Let us go tell them and bring those who will come."*

"Well, spoken dear Kreeek." TaaTaa noted an agreement flash from BinThaa; LeeLaa was over at the fruit again, had he not warned her about alien foods!

"Dear TaaTaa, LeeLaa has pierced several fruits and I have tasted one, no danger. I think our dear little Paaath did not die from the fruit."

BinThaa said, *"You ones are slow when you know the others worry. If we are going, let's go!"*

Several of the community had stood vigil for them. Aashta wailed when she saw LeeLaa missing.

"Aashta," Kreeek cried, going to her friend's side, *"LeeLaa is with the aliens, they are friends."*

R'ooot interrupted, saying, *"Foolishness! They are killers and you have left your small one with them! Shame!"*

"No," TaaTaa said, flashing to all. *"These creatures said their names to us."*

"What of it?" R'ooot twirled his 'watch me signal. *"Perhaps these creatures share a name before setting a person's home on fire!"*

Kreeek slapped him. *"They showed no harm and shared water. Stay quiet when you know nothing!"*

There was a great deal of murmuring about sharing water, a sign of complete trust.

Aashta, calmer, asked, *"How was the water shared? Was it given freely?"*

Grateful for Aashta's intervention, he told her, *"Kreeek asked for it, and it was given."*

Kreeek, insisting on accuracy, said, *"I remember LeeLaa took it from them, they did not give it directly to us."*

After more murmurs and bright flashes, SayLaa said, *"I don't care! You signaled good light, so where is it? My little one needs wholesome light!"*

"BinThaa," SaaTee asked, *"What do you say?"*

"I say the light is good and I will carry those too weak."

There was more murmuring, this time much of it fearful.

TaaTaa interrupted. *"Wait, I saw BaaarTow put lights in trees, the lights move easily and can be turned on and off. BinThaa and I will go with two others and each will bring a light back."*

AaTeh came forward. *"We will anger them when they see we have taken the light. Remember Tooli angry when we took ingratesta to study. Do you know how to ask?"*

"I believe they brought the lights for us, there is no reason for lights at that place except for us. I think sharing light so freely with not asking is far more important than the water."

AaTeh countered, *"You do not know what they think or why they do anything, they are aliens! You will anger them! You put us in danger!"*

Kreeek surprised TaaTaa by piping up. *"We speak with them, less than baby talk for they do not flash, but we speak. I believe Martaa may be trusted. Martaa bring us to light, Martaa tell Bartow to bring more light to us. I will have LeeLaa ask Martaa for the lights."* She emitted a keening sound sequence, the only clearly audible part sounding line *'oooooine'*.

It was not long before the lights shined brightly inside the community shelters and the murmuring stopped for the day.

chapter 51

Analysis

"Well hello Mr. Crannog, I heard you were up here for some technical arcana. Is Olivia on the comm?" Doc settled down in her chair she'd adopted for her morning chats with the Navigator. This was her closest and best opportunity to learn more about this austere young man.

"She went for tea. I can leave you two," he offered.

"That's all right, I was just loafing. I promise not to peek over your shoulder, okay?" She was pleased no one else was up so early, and probably wouldn't be until 8 or 9 o'clock.

"Ronnie Sue, I'm back!"

"Hey, Livy, got an extra cup?" She said it jokingly but was not too surprised when Olivia pointed to the comm console.

"Why certainly, look over to my little warming pad."

"What a marvel you are! I think that our companion here might have had something to do with that." She stretched over to get her tea from the pop-out pad and saluted Cedric with the cup, gently so as not to spill any contents. "To you, sir!"

Doc could tell Cedric was waiting for the chatter to die down with the most pleasant demeanor he could muster so he could continue delving through his data before the rest of the crew awoke.

"Cedric," said Doc, eyeing him speculatively, "Livy and I have been discussing ESP. As a proponent I thought I was getting somewhere, but not with this logician here. What's your opinion?" She intended that line to simply wrench his attention from the complex mathematical formulae and soften him up for more interesting topics.

Cedric's chin pulled back toward his shoulders in consternation. "I have none." He stared in annoyance.

Olivia responded, "Nonsense! Everybody has an opinion. Don't be shy."

"Very well, I think its rubbish, no offense."

"Hah! See Doc, the Engineer knows!"

"Hold on a sec, Livy, Mr. Nuts and Bolts has his mechanic's hat on. I wish to pursue further, with the guy who plays that lovely guitar." Hold the comm! Why did this seem to spark such a defensive response? "Cedric, I recognized the Segovia and loved those songs." She appreciated a few other tidbits Olivia had shared with her, too. When he scowled at what he must think of as her intrusion into his intimate setting, she sighed and turned back to O'Reilly.

"Doc, if you think you can salvage a point on the ESP question, he's you witness." Olivia leaned back in her chair, arms folded as if awaiting the outcome of a figure skating feat.

He crossed his arms, obviously distressed with the interference and waited for them to get done with whatever they were up to.

Doc turned the chair to face Cedric fully and with hands on the armrests and elbows akimbo feeling ready to pounce on him, playing on his defensiveness, bringing the cause to the fore, asked "You mean you're never been around anyone with, say, uncanny empathy? Someone who knew things that she or he really had no way of knowing?"

Cedric clearly did not appreciate this balderdash directed at him with his very limited time allowance, but it seemed to the psychiatrist that he could not quite dismiss some notion he had on the subject.

"He does know someone, Doc, you can tell. Who is it Cedric?"

Doc noted that Cedric was diverted for a second by Olivia's striking resemblance to a cat watching another cat stalking a robin just outside her window. She hadn't had this much fun teasing out tiny signals in years. While not entirely sure of the appropriateness of the aggressive pose, it did seem that Cedric switched gears, responding to the demand. "Yes, out with it, who?"

"I," he faltered, "I don't want to prejudice anyone."

"Not with us, we are gathering data, not evidence," Doc assured him. His voice had softened and become less strident. She pictured reeling in a big lunker, keeping the line taut but not wanting to break the line.

Olivia added, "We have control over what gets recorded and your two surveillance monitors are right here before you." She waited a moment. "If it is regarding Ms. van Rijn, we both would like to help her get safely back home."

Cedric leaned back in his seat, paler, apparently succumbing to the rumor that the Navigator was psychic. "Alright, Marta is out there talking to trees and seems to think they are intelligent beings."

Olivia, her eyes revealing her joy with the chase, quietly asked, "Does she think they talk back?"

Cedric seemed snared by the Navigator for a moment. When he looked away, he said, "I can tell she thinks they're trying but she can't understand them. Now I have come to know her as a highly competent and level person and this fantasy astounds me."

Startled by his movements and gestures that greatly amplified the evenly spoken words, Doc felt he was beseeching her to explain this dissonant behavior and the thought set the wheels in her head spinning to make sense of it all. She'd seen his change in posture when he was alone with her in the ale closet, she thought of it as 'unbuckling', but this was more than that, a distinction with a completely different set of mannerisms.

Olivia excelled at keeping this channel of communication open. "Well if she is to be trusted, either she has a mental link ala Doc's proposition, or the tree is really saying something."

Cedric stared at the space between Doc and the monitoring screen.

"Expounding on the second premise, we could suppose the alien is speaking and she doesn't understand alien." Olivia laced her fingers and rested her chin on the back of them.

"You ladies really can't believe either option, can you?"

His tone was exasperation, a 'what can you do' attitude. Doc noted his body language showing they'd hit the nail on the head. He was torqued tight, all right, and she was impressed with his typically taut muscle control that even now gave him a kind of grace. He was afraid of more than his inquisitors, though, much more afraid.

Olivia pursued further, "Have you any evidence of either premise?"

"She asked me to come look at the met station in the woods and of course I did. I fancied she might want to be alone with me, as awkward in the suits as it may be, but what she wanted was far different. She showed me an odd tree, well, several very odd trees and told me they were aliens."

Doc could detect a great deal of regret now, but was it for his disappointment in her motives or for his reaction to the aliens? Or both? "You felt let down in favor of spurious aliens and discounted them?"

Indignity blossomed on his face. "I did not; I'm quite used to not getting what I want. In fact I offered to help her investigate, having taken precious time from the brute work of an engineer to peruse a couple of general flora texts; I refreshed myself on the parts and processes of plants so we could speak on the same terms. When I volunteered to fetch the tools to cut into one she became irrational and then insulting."

Olivia grabbed the baton, "Irrational? Cedric, I've seen her fighting off phantom attackers in her sleep. Even in her most volatile mental states, she acts in a purposeful way. There is no flailing or thrashing, she uses her elbows and knees for maximum harm and throws punches hard enough to damage the wall partition and our good friend Senor San Luis."

"But that's clearly irrational, reacting to dreams so."

Doc saw him react to the idea Barto met up with Marta at night, could be jealousy. She clarified, "Cedric, I've seem her miss knocking San Luis out or even killing him by a hair, only his reflexes saved him. I wouldn't be surprised if he didn't have bruised or broken ribs. These actions were brought about by real traumatic events in her life, not fantasies, I'm sure of it. Flashback-type reenactment is not in the same league as hallucination."

Cedric slumped uncharacteristically, his jealousy seemingly mollified but with puzzlement evident on his features. "In all that either of you have seen you have not found her acting on caprice?"

The way he stated that sentence signaled some kind of decision to Doc, but she was still not clear on what decision it might be. This wasn't the engineer or the ale-savoring musician, perhaps this was the man beneath them all? "Has she said what she intended to do? I mean about this alien?"

He sat still and seemed so sad.

Commander Jones came in and looked around the bridge. "Cedric, were you able to find what you needed?"

He straightened in his seat in one motion. "Not yet, ma'am."

"Maybe if this little jamboree broke up you'd have better luck?"

chapter 52

More Angst

Olivia rang up Char on schedule to give her redundant report; the AI had recorded every mechanical nuance and supplied a summary that could be mined for as much detail as desired. "Good Afternoon, Commander Jones. All systems green, no problems."

"Fine. What did you and Dr. Trogden learn from your grilling of the inimitable Mr. Crannog this morning? You cut the comm on me pretty quick."

"Just following your suggestion to let the man work in peace. All we learned is that the guy is obsessed with his job and won't voluntarily converse."

Char was rankled that she didn't have access to the recording of what went on; she'd have to ask O'Reilly or the Doctor for it and she'd be damned if she'd do either. "He left about an hour ago. I'm not sure if he dug up the diamond he was looking for because he looked really unsettled. Did you notice that?"

"I think he's nervy over leaving van Rijn behind."

"What a waste! I warned him about chasing that Soggy!"

"Char, why do you like Crannog but despise Van Rijn? They're from European countries a couple hundred klicks apart."

"Olivia, don't get that tired old prejudice horse out again, he's worn out."

"It's a simple question and I think I know the answer but I do so hate to assume."

"What do you think you know about me?"

"I think you hate a loser. Now she's from our ally Germany, but the name sounds Dutch. The Netherlands drowned, ergo losers. Scotland did not, so they are winners notwithstanding their several hundred feet elevation advantage and numerous submerged islands. It's a good thing Ireland's not on your trash list; O'Reilly would be summarily out even though I was born and raised in Nebraska."

"Bait me at your own peril."

"Oh, Char, I mean it. He is one cold fish and ghastly looking at that. She's a vibrant young lady who has a name she had absolutely no control over and has made it through a degree and is headed to her Master's at only twenty!"

"It is nothing personal about the individuals living in whatever country. If they can collectively carry their own weight and support American policies, I count 'em as a Friendly. If they let themselves get overrun with violence, get wiped out with an epidemic, export terrorism to us, or if they can't see that a below sea level country might get wet I have no use for them. Take Holland for example, I used to like Gouda and Edam cheese. I still admire Van Gough and Rembrandt, that's not the point. We have to choose our friends wisely, Miss Olivia, and the Soggies and Sickies and other sorry weaklings are not our Friends. The survival of the American way of life is at stake and you should never forget that cold fact. That's regardless of a thousand other factors and above any personal feelings. Satisfied?"

"Yes ma'am."

* * *

Olivia maintained her composure, the Commander's blatant attitude cementing her own convictions. To herself, she replied, 'I am very satisfied with your reasoning, classic Patriot logic. By the way, art lover, Rembrandt's last name was van Rijn.'

chapter 53

The open Book

C edric spent the rest of the day in his own cabin. He took a long
shower, scrubbing until red from scalp to toes. He felt guilty
being able to come back in and clean up when the others
had to tough it out. Guilt also assailed him from his interrogation
that morning; he knew Marta told him about the tree-things in
confidence. What confidence, though? They all knew the comm
was monitored, so how secret could it be?

He paused, realizing both those Patriot agents had played
him for a fool. Angry at be treated as a dupe, he determined
to get away from them and rejoin his Tenembras-bound fellows
outside. Out there, where she presumably still poked about those
trees.

When he went to the bridge to get permission, both the Commander and the Lieutenant Commander were there. "Pardon the
intrusion," he said hastily, turning to retreat.

Char called after him, "Crannog, what is that Van Ruin up to
out there?"

He got a hot coal in his gut as he came just inside the room to
stand ill at ease. "Ma'am?"

"She goes off into the trees when she should be working and San Luis is always trailing after her. You don't think she's found a way to cavort with him out there, do you?"

The woman repulsed him so much he had to force himself to be civil. Did they all need to get a clawful of him, one bloody piece at a time? "No Ma'am." Why were they all attempting to make him jealous of San Luis? "I believe she's trying to identify the trees and see why they look so poorly. She has the perfect project here to use for her thesis if she works at it."

"The trees are puny because this ain't Earth and all this is classified, so no thesis. If you see her, do tell her to stick to her work. I will not have her sneaking around."

"Yes, ma'am. I request permission to return to the outside."

"What possible reason could you have to endure that suit again, until tomorrow anyway? You know they don't even like you? You knew that, right?"

The jealousy angle didn't work so she's trying to cause division from personal dislikes? He'd lived apart and had been disliked all his life! "Ma'am, I have no illusions regarding camaraderie, but would prefer to execute the remainder of my planned duties."

"About your duties, Ensign Bodine has staged the explosives to attach to the devices you are to set up day after tomorrow. I don't want them out any sooner than necessary. That San Luis probably knows all about explosives and could rig a bomb or something."

He could not reply to such a ludicrous suggestion. San Luis no doubt *did* know about a thousand destructive methods, but Cedric was positive he would do nothing so reckless, something that would endanger the ladies.

"Scares you speechless, eh? I'll get you the key to the trunk compartment and you can leave them stashed them in there. You can take the keys with you, but beware and keep those keys safe!"

"I shall."

"Yeah, well see if I care if you all blow yourselves up! These jewels even burn the ox right out of the air, *whoosh*! Soggy Soup! O'Reilly, I'm going to relax in my stateroom a bit before dinner.

See to it that Lee gets the word I want something edible, will you?" She stamped out.

Olivia pounced on this opportunity with Cedric. "So how do you feel about traveling with Soggies, sir?"

"I think the term insulting and think the Commander's attitude toward people like van Rijn is unprofessional and uncalled for. The pervasive Patriot attitude that you people are some how superior in any way except current circumstance to any of the so-called Passengers is abhorrent and pompous."

"Wow. That's a real opinion, front and center. Must be something about van Rijn that stirs you up?"

"Is that relevant?" It was all he could do to not gnash his teeth.

"When did you know?"

"Know what?"

"That you were the Pharaoh of Denial, that's what. Anybody ever called you dense?"

He pulled shoulders inward and looked down and away. "Not long before I came in. Marta, van Rijn, and I were discussing a point and she called me dense."

"Nothing to it, huh? Calumny?"

He straightened. "To respond to your original question, I don't believe I am unduly biased about any of the Passengers or Crew."

"Unduly?"

"Do you always pick apart a person's replies and reiterate them?"

"Touchy. I only wanted to know why you added the adverb there."

"Very well. I do have a positive disposition toward authority and order. I find it easier to deal with persons who follow established rules. I don't care for spying and manipulation. I have developed a bias against such persons, but not one so strong as to detract from my duties or professional relationships."

Olivia drummed her long red nails on the console. "Marta is cooking up something contrary to the established rules, so caring for her you try to talk her out of...ruining her career? Her future? I've see her and San Luis nosing around those trees a lot, then they congregate over with Bloom and Cartier at the pod.

"The pod? Their supplies are in the pod."

"Right, but they're spending more time running between the woods and the pod than at their stations or equipment. She wants to bring some back, eh? Don't look so surprised, it's well known I can read minds. Just ask Bloom, poor lamb. She's afraid I'll pick up her mental tide and glean her deep secrets from all the other flotsam and jetsam."

"When you would probably need a couple of sentences from her. Between you and the good Doctor, what a person gives away in turn of speech and body language allows you to make inferences and gauge the correctness by the subject's reactions. Do you keep score to determine who's easiest, the most pliable? Where do I fit in?"

"You are an open book."

"What is this game?" He directed his revived ire at her image on the screen. "Are you titillated by the private interactions of others, or is there a more ominous reason for all this? The Passengers and I are shortly interred on the Planet of Excess and Disagreeable Persons. Are we a private psychology project or is there some further evil awaiting those of us who don't make the grade?"

"Cedric, I am not you enemy!"

"The hell you're not! You and the Doctor took turns today poking at my weaknesses, probing for gems to add to your black collection. You tease me with intimations of some kind of plot involving a girl that, yes, I do care about. It's not your business. Stop this!"

"Okay, I knew Ronnie Sue was running you and I was complicit, but I am neither your enemy nor Marta's enemy."

"Why do you keep bringing her up? She is not a Passenger; no, she will be your continuing victim. You know she applied here to earn money for her further education and you wrested from me that she's gathering data for her thesis that Jones says she can't write. Tell me, do you expect her to survive the trip back?"

"I already told you that Doc and I both want to see her safely returned home."

"If that is the case and the rest of us will be out of reach on a planet far away from true humanity, what is the meaning of all this?"

"Look, you can dance around gravestones all day and night looking for conspiracies if you want, but I'm a student of heart and motivation. That's it. I have a tragic fault of caring. Why do people react the way they do? Why the unending number of mechanisms we exploit to cover our real aims, our innermost feelings. The original question was simply, when did you first know you were deeply, madly in love with Marta?"

He wanted no more of this; his throat was gummy and affected his response. "That is an insidious interference into my personal affairs." He looked into her eyes for bare mercy, "In a few days I will see her nevermore. Please keep to your word to watch out for her."

She acquiesced with a solemn nod and cut the comm.

chapter 54

Day Four: Who Will Listen?

"Naomi, I don't want to compromise you. If I tell you and you decide to keep the secret it will be in direct violation of Patriot regulations."

"Pity that. I swear by the rabbi's yarmulke. What?"

They strolled through the trees, helmets off and affixed on their backs, looking for the elusive aliens. They weren't at either of the previous gather points and Marta couldn't find a path. They turned at the sound of Barto's laughter.

Marta wanted to get professional input about these aliens, getting uncomfortable about all the assumptions she'd been piling up. "Come here and tell me, objectively as a scientist, what you see." They got within sight of Barto playing ball with an apple with some of them and stopped.

"They're kind of ropy looking. Sort of like string cheese, you know what I mean? What's the composition? I can't know that without equipment I don't have with me."

"Composition?"

"Yeah, like what do they look like inside? Do they pull apart like a Bavarian with vanilla custard in the center?"

"Stop, please. You sound like Cedric."

"God forbid. Out with the secret. I assume our stallion here is in on it."

Marta waved at Barto.

Barto swirled a quick 'watch me' and 'no' and bowed. The smaller aliens screeched and continued their game, excluding him. He came toward the ladies with a simpleton grin and said, "Ma, can I keep them? Please? I promise to take care of them!"

"Naomi? You okay?" Marta saw her react to Barto as if struck by a fist.

"Marta I am in SHOCK! Yesterday was a thrill, but now the novelty is wearing right off. These are aliens!" She hesitated, as if assembling puzzle pieces in her mind. "I have just seen the fiery script, saying, 'These aliens need a ride home' and it's because of us, because the Van Damme rammed 'em. Marta, I'll have nightmares about this - they'll kill 'em. They'll kill' em all, you know that. Look at 'em over there, like a bunch of kids chattering away playing hacky sack. What are you going to do?"

"Me? I intended to convince you to lead an effort to save them; Barto and I could help."

"No, no sister. I'm a follower, a follower prone to dithering and babble. Either you or Senor Stud here has to lead. Not I."

Barto said, "I know how to protect things, I know how to keep secrets. I can assemble and discipline an army, but I do not know how to put this together."

Marta's disappointment made her plead, "Barto, we have a short fuse on this and need strong leadership, don't you see?"

"Si. I am no coyote; I cannot organize the moving of these Amigos to different planets."

Naomi nodded and said, "I think that puts it very well, this is a completely insane piece of organizing you want to do, not a mission with any sense of order or control. If you truly mean business, let's ask Alain."

"Ask Alain what?" He'd found them and had a bulging satchel with him. He stepped up to TaaTaa who was off to the side, also watching the kids and made the bow; TaaTaa bowed back. They walked over, curious about Alain's intentions.

The professor took a scanner out of his satchel and pointed it at Barto. "Bartolommeo, I am scanning you with an infrared detector. Do smile, because I want to point this at our friends here."

Alain scanned Barto a few times and TaaTaa gave him a slow 'yes' twirl. Alain waved the detector across one of TaaTaa's grasping arms and waited for a reaction. TaaTaa and the two aliens that appeared from the trees flashed at each other, but TaaTaa did not move away. Alain hit the recorder and proceeded to do a full scan starting at the ground and working up.

"Dr. Cartier, do not touch the ends of the lighted sticks up top!"

"Worry not, Barto, old boy." He stuffed the IR meter away and pulled out in succession a UV detector, a Geiger-Muller tube based gamma detector and then an ion chamber radioactive contamination meter (shielded on top against cosmic interference) capable of picking up betas and, pulling a slide back, alphas. TaaTaa was very curious about the radiation and contamination meters and the aliens passed them among themselves.

"Marta, my dear, are you watching this? I think you're right about the light and sound sensors. And, my children, there is no reason to believe they detect light or sound the same way we do, at the same wavelengths or intensities. I'd bet they detect infrared and UV since they didn't bother to have a show and tell with those meters."

"You mean maybe like *perros*? Dogs? They hear very high sounds and smell very small smells. But we still can talk to *perros* and they hear us."

"Yes, but that's because we and the dogs evolved together on Earth. We all grew to be humans and dogs under the same sun with the same sounds of the winds and sea, of thunder and the call of other creatures."

Barto tilted his head to peer squinting through the foliage towards the close, large but unfamiliar sun and then back to the alien. "This tree man did not grow under this sun, or under the sun of Earth. What sun, *Senor* Cartier?"

Marta and Naomi took advantage of the lull after Barto's question to accost Dr. Cartier about fronting Operation Distant Trees.

"Sir," Marta began, we have plenty of room in our pods and I think we can save these stellar emissaries from a sudden and fiery death. We have voted and elected you to lead us."

"I suspected as much. Children, you speak treason not only to the authorities on this ship but to the human race. This is not some trivial hobo in the boxcar deal."

Naomi ran a gloved hand up one of his arms. "Alain, honeydrop, I don't know hobos from Hoboken but I do know these guys are made of carbon and are likely to flame like matches and that they wouldn't be here except for the Van Damme."

He raised an eyebrow at her hand on his bicep until she flexed the fingers up and removed her hand with a curdled smile.

"I too feel sorry for them, but remember the little bear cub I mentioned before. You scoop the little fellow out of a pit and he's soft and cuddy. You coo-coo at it and give it a cutesy name. Then Mama rears up and rips you head off."

Naomi suggested to Marta, "Sweetie, why not make up a preliminary plan for laying the waterworks and atmospheric regulation and a place for a grand selection of trees so our friends can be among them, homey-like? I'll work on the Wise Man here."

Marta knew to vacate because Dr. Cartier wouldn't change his mind with her present. She looked around a saw all the aliens had vanished again, so she decided to return to the Ag station to begin work. That would require the helmet, but she'd be visibly working, an important factor since Cedric's update via Barto on the matter.

She walked through the pod, made measurements and scoped out the available services and the functions she'd need to disable without alerting the ubiquitous AI. There were multiple systems to coordinate and several ship systems to adjust or reroute with no further access to the inside of the ship. Every time she started it felt like it was the wrong place to begin and beginning at the wrong place could be fatal. It all sounded like a fine plan in the woods, but required severe focus when it came time to do it because AI was insinuated into all systems and was formidably intelligent. It also had a strong defensive system that she'd have to crack without it knowing she'd cracked it.

She caught a peripheral vision of Naomi, but that meant Naomi was already upon her because of the helmet's limited visibility. She turned toward the woman, disgruntled about the severe reduction in her vision on top of the extreme discomfort. "How did you make out?"

Naomi may have shrugged. "The man is still quite reticent and I didn't want to push him too hard. Let's give him a little more time to get cozy with the idea."

"We can't wait! This is an enormous project and any rational person would want a year to tackle it. We only have a couple days!" She willed herself to get control of her emotions; only reason could advance the plan.

"Sugar, be prepared for dissatisfaction. I know you're the type of person who's kind to the farm animals, naming them and them tearfully refusing to eat little Miss Piggy. It was a mistake to do the name thing, cause names stick in your head. Just be mentally prepared to stop this before it starts."

"First of all, I learned all the farm jobs including butchering, and nobody turned down real meat. Second, I don't only hear the names I remember, I see every feature, hear every sound, I feel the texture of the concrete curb I gripped and I remember the smell of their rotting corpses. I don't want this to be another chapter of the book illustrating the worst abuses, depravities and evils humanity can come up with. I don't want this to be an unbroken continuance of the past. I want to make a better, more civilized future."

Marta felt her willpower crumbling and tried to shore it up. Then, with clenched fists, she grated, "The hell with it. I will do this myself, by myself if I need to."

Naomi clapped her hands. "Sweetness, that's the heart I wanted to hear from! This is a serious matter that could rate us summary execution, not unlike those of your nightmares. If I'm going to be a part of it, I want to be sure it's a real commitment and not some sport. I will get the recalcitrant elder statesman to straighten up and fly right, count on it, but it's you we'll follow."

Marta felt like the weight of her past had fallen away, like she'd transformed into a bright being. With confidence of purpose, she ordered, "We'll need lots of water, if you can start on that."

"I'll check it out and let you know." Naomi waved her fists and walked away.

Alone again, Marta envisioned Mama with her contained smile and morose eyes, seeming to agree with her metamorphosis, something she couldn't resist being proud of. She pictured Daddy with the wind off the sea blowing his sandy hair into his face, into his laughing pale blue eyes, saying, *"Ja, m'leibje"* She reached out and held her brother's hand, squeezing it gently. She let the vision slide away, but kept it in her heart.

She stood, trying to keep her composure, coming to terms with the larger person she'd become. She concentrated on her outstretched arms, hands inward as if gripping a huge ball from the side, a very heavy ball, working to compact the great big medicine ball problem into something she could manage, gathering the ideas.

* * *

Naomi walked back to her station and used her time to work out the method of getting the water they would need. The river ran near the far boundary of the trees and a creek ran from east to west that eventually met up with it much nearer. She knew the creek would be the best bet, but she had no magic pump and hose system available; no had one planned to pump anything and so had nothing suitable staged in the pod. The best she could think of at the moment was to gather up buckets.

* * *

Barto was amazed and gratified at the change in his Hermana. He bustled around smartly, looking like industry personified. If the monitors watched him, it would draw attention away from the scientists, among whom he counted his Hermana proudly. He would be her right hand man.

* * *

Alain dug into his satchel and took out more sample bags. He collected soil from several tree root radii for analysis; the data might be useful for preparing the pod; he also wanted data on the alien flora and what dangers they might present to them, exposed as they all were from the careless helmet games. He put those samples in the box with the samples from where the aliens had stood and a couple wipes off their carapaces.

He didn't think anything would come of all this anxiety. Of any of them only Marta had the faith needed, a mere child. Too bad because he felt a degree of fondness of little LeeLaa, but letting his wrath descend and end the business at the first big hitch was probably better for the preservation of humankind. Sooner would be better than later, before they became irrevocably invested in the scheme, before the Commander busted them for treason. The idea of quashing her exuberance saddened him, but everything had turned sad since his exile anyway.

He took his samples back to the bench but couldn't lose the vision of firebombs engulfing LeeLaa; he imagined her screaming like a hurt rabbit. He fell onto his work stool and buried his face in his hands. After a few tears he got a tissue, wiped his face and neck and put the infernal helmet back on.

chapter 55

Please?

Marta regarded her tablet carefully and jammed it in a groove in the pod floor to crack the case. With it forced apart, she inserted needle nosed pliers and carefully disconnected the antenna. She held her breath as she released the case and tried a basic function. It worked! Then she tried to access the AI database. 'No signal' it said. Wonderful! Hoping she'd downloaded all she'd need beforehand, she set to work stacking one layer of services onto another, drafting the proposed pod layout.

Already deep into the options available for the tree pan, Cedric appeared from thin air. She jumped up and clutched the tablet proprietarily.

"I didn't mean to frighten you, sorry." He had automatically reached out supportive arms, but dropped them in haste.

"No, that's fine, I was thinking, that's all."

"About those trees still? Why? None of them can back. You know they'll sterilize the pod with the vents left open for insurance. I wish it wasn't so, but we need to face the facts."

She thought she'd give him one last chance, though Naomi said he was a mole for the Pats. She thought she could have really cared for him, maybe even been a good companion if circumstances had worked out differently. If wishes were fishes. "I would like to go back to that odd tree we talked about the other day. You're right, we need to chop it into pieces and at least take pictures. Can you do the chopping?"

"I know this is painful, but I appreciate you allowing me to share it with you. You can always blame me when you think of this later." He went back for the tools.

She concentrated on the task at hand. Why did he have to act like a real person now of all times? All this journey together and he waits until now! She stiffened her resolve; he would not tempt her to lose focus. As he returned with a heavy toolkit, she reasoned to herself that she wanted him for his skills.

They walked closer together than she would have preferred, but she allowed him to stay near as long as he kept quiet. They stopped a moment just inside the tree line to allow their vision to adjust and then made their way to a large tree.

"Okay, Crannog, this is the one. You saw and I'll photograph. Don't expect me to say anything, you know I didn't want to do this and I don't want to get emotional again."

"Yes, I saw, you shoot, no talk."

She popped the latches of her helmet and donned her mask. She hung the helmet on a pair of S-hooks and handed them to him. She turned around and pointed at her nape. He hung it.

When she reached for his, he retreated a half step. She pulled out another mask and tilted her head in entreaty. He allowed her to set him up.

"We can talk now, but keep it low."

He stretched his chin up to allow some air inside his sweaty suit. When he found that didn't work, he said, "I suspected as much, all the time you people spend back here. This is just a tree, not an alien at all." He dropped the heavy tools. "I'm the world's fool these days. Why have you lured me out here with another fabrication? You have no intention of harming these things, do you?"

She did not like what sounded like anger; it did not bode well. "Forgive me, will you please? How else could I get you to this point without alerting our overseers?"

"Yes, I will concede you that, but why?"

She had a strong urge to kiss him, but squelched the thought ruthlessly. "I will not demean you with demanding your secrecy, and I won't beg you to not interfere if you disagree. All I ask is that you let me say my piece before commenting."

She suddenly felt as if she floated. She knew she looked dreadful with matted, greasy hair and dark blue-gray circles under her eyes, but her heart said that she would soon loose him forever with never having shared a kiss; her mouth moistened with an acute ache for a taste of his lips. With a shock she realized she was caught in his gaze once more, the windows to their souls open with loving breezes blowing gently through. Her need to roll in the comfort of his embrace warred with her purpose to keep the strict timeline.

"I will wait," he said softly. He edged very near.

His voice and expression entranced her for a moment more, but her purpose was urgent. She broke contact and turned her head aside. "I have discovered that the things we looked at are indeed alien beings. They are intelligent and communicate with us, showing nothing but friendliness."

He retreated a step but said nothing.

She feared looking into his eyes again, so pinned her vision to his chest and kept talking. "When the Van Damme crashed over a decade ago, it destroyed their spacecraft. Only the ones in a remote area survived and they are weak since the light spectrum they use doesn't match the spectrum that this sun provides. Our light does match."

He started to speak, but she raised a hand. "If we leave them, the Patriot policy will murder them, burn them with the trees. We are going to save them by rigging the pod for them. Tenembras may be bad, but it will be better than outright incineration."

She looked to him with hope. He looked like a total stranger, his face hardened and his stance rigid. With crossed arms, he said, "You wish to bring back some alien thing that infects the ship and locks us in quarantine like that reckless comet hunter and his iceberg, left near Topside until who knows? Maybe he's still there. Study whatever is here and take a few samples that can be sterilized. You have time for that and I'm sure Alain would let you have the materials."

"But Cedric, they're intelligent, space faring beings. They have families and we can speak to each other. Their voices are musical and I know you could discern so much more than I can. I want you to listen and tell me what you think."

"There are real reasons for the century old biosecurity rules."

"Don't you think that if they were an aggressive conquering race they'd have found us already or done something to us here? You'd be fascinated at the way the act, the way they talk. They appear to be bundles of carbon fibers and they seem to have sensory organs at the top ends. We can go watch the kids playing ball! I can't just mince one up and smear it on a plate and I can't let them burn! Come with me and meet them."

"You cannot afford to be sentimental. Warn them if you must, but you can't take them home like some shrubbery from a nursery. You have work to do and this is not it."

"Have you no respect for life?"

"My obligation, and yours too, is to ensure the biosecurity of the human race. If Commander Jones were to catch wind of this…"

"Halt! If you refuse to listen to anything I say, if you parrot that arrogant P-pat," she stuttered in anger, "Well, you are a Pat at heart anyway aren't you? Go have an Assam from an estate on Mars because all northeastern India is now a plague area with sanctions that prevent meaningful aid from reaching them. You and Char Jones and Olivia O'Reilly go have a damned party and I'll stay here and burn with the most beautiful life within light years. I will burn with them and curse you!

"You have no call to accuse me and you will not deflect attention from your crime." He spoke low, but very coldly. "You want me to abet your risking all of humanity because of an accident."

She could tell he was on the verge of saying he would not, that he was heading straight for Commander Jones to put an end to this mania. She knew she should try to ratchet the anger down, to defuse the situation, but her ire flamed. She spat, "Okay, Crannog. Forget it. Don't come near me again."

"Marta, see it logically…"

She heaved him back with both hands and he barely caught his fall grabbing a tree. "Get the hell away from me! To think I wanted to kiss you makes me want to vomit!" She could not stop her tears, nor could she rein in her fury. She stood belligerently watching him lay dazed against the tree, strong emotions roaring inside her. He would not look her in the eyes now. She uttered a long, frustrated cry and stalked away.

Marta knew the chance had passed for him to see the depth of commitment, the rightness of it; he would never see that the risks were acceptably low and the benefits extraordinarily high. Her stomach churned with the failure to convince him, the failure to win him to her side. She stopped in her tracks and breathed steadily until her heart calmed somewhat.

She turned back to see him staring at her from where she'd left him. At once, her red fog cleared and she realized the horrible things she'd said. She took a tiny step toward him and started to raise her hands, praying he would see her and forgive her. All she could see was that an ugly spirit had blinded him to her entreaties.

Frigid as ice he called out, "No good can come of this. They will be killed. You will be arrested. Your friends will be implicated and demoted, or perhaps executed with you. You are destroying your future and theirs. I find no satisfaction in telling you this."

Coming closer, she softly asked, "Come meet them?"

"I will not." And he ripped away the mask. He loosened an S-hook on one side and the helmet swung around to his waiting hand. She heard the latches snapping shut as he hurried away from her.

She dropped to her knees, then hands and knees, head hanging with her shed tears plopping to the sand.

chapter 56

commitments

When she came to herself again she sat on a rock leaning on TaaTaa who stood behind the rock, with two smooth, thin arms guarding her. She spotted a spent oxygen cartridge at her feet. The load of doubts Cedric Crannog brought with him dispersed as she leaned back onto her friend's strength and gazed at the steel-strong arms of the being who'd saved her from asphyxiation.

She understood at that moment in her gut that no one else could accomplish this. Her previous commitment was ideological, based on a grandiose idea, almost an academic exercise. Now she felt it viscerally. She must lead the others and work them hard. She would assign Cartier to the growing medium and tree transplanting. Naomi must do the environmentals and water. Barto must provide support, the best support any of them could have. Her had to do her best with the engineering tasks that could have been easily performed by, well, an Engineer.

She considered feigning illness to get back into the ship to heist some more supplies, but discounted it because she'd be watched and therefore unable to bring anything. So she might well fail. It occurred darkly to her that her superiors might let her die out here instead of leaving her friends, not caring if she made it on board or not. She held that thought until Barto came with water.

"Hermana, what's wrong? I thought you were working at the pod." He greeted TaaTaa and crouched at her knee, peering at her. He got out a wipe, moistened it and mopped her face gently.

"I don't want to tell you, Hermana, but Dr. Cartier says is impossible to save our Amigos, that it is wrong to give them false hope."

She brushed his hand away and stood. Both TaaTaa and Barto backed off a step. She aimed a chopping, rigid hand at Barto, emphasizing her words. "I'll tell him what is possible. Will you help make the parts we need and move stuff around? Maybe you can scrounge up more gear I don't know about?" His grin gave her confidence. "Here, Barto, leave me a couple more cartridges and I'll meet you back at the pod in an hour or so."

"Why you not come back with me?"

"I need to chat with my Amigo, here."

He appeared torn, but when she smiled for him, he trotted away.

She faced TaaTaa. She bowed. She took out her tablet and used the tablet drawing tools to show a circle with that lozenge and dots in the same places as the drawing before to indicate it represented this planet. She knew from previous efforts to communicate that there were only seventeen of them remaining; she drew seventeen sticks. With the stylus, she moved the lozenge into orbit and produced lines radiating from it toward the trees. She made the planet opaque red. She blanked the tablet and passed it to him.

TaaTaa used the tip of a rod as a stylus and drew seventeen sticks and many circles she knew to indicate trees. He passed it back.

She solemnly drew a thick line through the sticks, then through each tree. His red and blue orbs hovered over the screen and retracted sharply when she used a graphic technique to cover the screen with opaque red, a few down-pointing triangles at a time.

He screeched loud and soon Kreeek and LeeLaa stood by him; they flashed and squealed, then faced her silently. TaaTaa used a leg to draw a circle in the dirt with a smaller circle above it, their icon for days but drew no lines.

She knelt and used her finger to draw two parallel lines, two days. She signaled for him to erase it all and he complied. She drew a straight horizontal line with tree pictograms on either end. She drew a sun circle at the eastern horizon, then an arc of nine more circles to end at the western horizon. She motioned with her finger around the arc once and put a single 'day' line within the arc. She drew three-quarters of a 'day' line next to it and pointed at each sun position up to the sixth. The last three circles she put a thick furrow through. Looking up at three sets of attentive orbs, one smaller and paler than the others, she nearly broke down.

She stepped back and pivoted twice to show a new subject. Meanwhile TaaTaa cleared the surface again. She drew a lozenge at the far end and one at the near end. At the near one, she drew smaller lozenges to indicate the pods. She waited until they stopped flashing each other.

Off to the side she drew a large lozenge, then an arrow from the starboard pod to the newly drawn pod enlargement. TaaTaa pointed at the starboard pod and mimicked pushing something up. Marta rotated her wrist rapidly clockwise twice to say, "Yes." She went to the enlargement and pointed her finger at each of them in turn, then drew seventeen sticks in the enlargement, with an 'M' figure. She pointed at the figure and then herself, and then approached him as if to lead him to the shuttle. She stepped back and bowed.

He erased the surface and drew an arc with a straight line to close it off it for the surface. He quickly drew three ovals, the central one much larger, in orbit over the arc. He stepped back and they all watched her make seventeen lines in the starboard pod, with an M. She bowed again.

LeeLaa squealed, *"Barto! Omi! Aalen!"*

Marta updated the drawing with a little circle, a plus and a barely recognizable maple leaf placed in the shuttle itself.

TaaTaa erased it and drew a small circle on the far left side. As she watched, he started from that circle to scribe a large one ending offset from the small one. After a pause, he scribed another circle, offset, ending a bit over two thirds of the way through the arc. He took two arms to point at the western horizon and then pointed at the sun visible through the trees.

She pointed at the sun and continued his drawing of the unfinished arc to the equivalent of 1800 hours. He reached over and drew a deep wavy line from the arc on down to the eastern horizon. They were silent as far as she could tell, probably stunned. She stuck her left hand out and rotated it quickly counter-clockwise, meaning, "Watch this." Using his drawing, she drew seventeen lines in the center and an arrow pointing to the shuttle midway, at noon.

LeeLaa scampered over near Marta and hunkered down to say, *"MarTaa, Barto, Omi, Aalen, Kreeek, TaaTaa, LEELAA!"* She used several arms to point up and was bouncing.

Marta rotated to show 'watch this' and 'yes' until they all came back together. She stepped back and bowed, they did the same and the parted on their separate destinations, for now.

chapter 57

Day Five: The Big Plan

"**H**oney, Barto said you had bad dreams again last night, and you surely do look like old lettuce."

"Thanks very much. I'll have to speak to Bartolommeo about privacy." She did have a residual headache, but her resolve helped her dampen its effects. It took a smidgen more concentration to remember her lines today.

"Honey, don't be that way, he's just trying to help. Why not tell me? I'm a sympathetic sort and have really soft shoulders."

"No offense, Naomi, but it's not something an American can understand." It pained her to talk to her friend like this, but they'd agreed to the script.

"An American? Pardon me, but you are now in America. Isn't America a mite better than where you were?"

"Please don't be angry with me, Naomi. I don't know what it is. I find it easier to talk to Barto, that's all."

"Don't do that pitiful act to me. I want to know why *Senor* San Luis is good enough to hear your problems and I'm not."

"You ever seen a family member beaten to death for not giving up a crust of bread? Have you ever lost color vision from acute starvation, having to eat roots and worms to live one more day?

How many days in a row have you endured diarrhea, squirting your stinking life into the fetid mud? To you what I confessed about the refugee camp was a story that you paid close attention to because of the Americans involved. But I endured that camp getting beaten and raped and I still feel the hairy stinking Americans pinning me to the gravel in my dreams. First hand. Okay? It is more real to me than a manicure or matching shoes and more a part of my life than a Stars and Stripes pin."

The throb in her head worsened, but the secrets were over. This was not according to the agreement and Naomi had a look of horror.

Suddenly Cedric materialized at her shoulder from behind.

"Hey, I heard an angry voice coming from someone I would never have expected, at least unless I was present. What's the matter?"

Marta's incredulous expression was lost behind the visor, but her voice betrayed it. She swung around and shouted, "You want to know what's the matter? So you can report it accurately? I told you to get the hell away from me!"

Naomi put a hand on Cedric's arm and had to jerk to budge him. As Naomi pulled him further, Marta heard her telling him, "She's upset. She was putting me in my place."

He would not be led away, but instead rushed her face back, retorting, "Shame! Treat me as you will, but Dr. Bloom is a scientist worthy of your respect and was your friend."

"Ashamed?" Marta backed away. "Ashamed? I suppose I should have swallowed it all until I had not one emotion remaining exposed like one psycho I know, but I want to be alive as an ordinary human being for whatever time I have left, not a damn Soggy! I get so damned sick of hearing it. To hell with it! I'm sorry about Naomi, but I will not be ashamed for speaking up for myself!"

Barto muscled Cedric aside, "What is this?" Barto rose on his toes to tower over the thin man, staring menacingly at him.

Cedric waved him off, saying, "I walked into a fit in progress and am sorry for it. Good day."

* * *

Olivia excised the incriminating part for her own file, wondering why the kid would come out like that after all the work that must have gone into her alias. What was the payoff? She thought she might have an idea of what they were up to, however outlandish it seemed, but Marta's purposeful estrangement from these two puzzled her, as well as that bit about the time she had left. In her estimation, the camp experience story was a melodramatic touch too much. On the other hand, if what she said were true all of that might have been uncontrolled. Could the poor girl be less resilient than expected? Should she tell Doc?

chapter 58

It won't work!

"Whew, that's a little heftier in this gravity. You don't notice it so much walking around but try hauling this plunder!" Alain exaggerated wiping the sweat from his brow with a theatrical flourish, beaming at Marta.

They unpacked the last contingency pallet and sorted it into constituent piles like the others. Barto brought more from the Portico while performing his sleight of hand with the modified cart. To surveillance, it looked like he regularly got food and water packs, the lowered deck not readily observable from that camera angle. They all cheered Barto for finding another carton of ox cartridges.

Alain tapped her shoulder for attention. "Marta, dear, let me get this straight. You want me to configure a habitat for trees and aliens in the cargo pod within twenty or so hours. Even if I agreed to the entire plan, which I have not, this undertaking is a much larger one than I have ever attempted and there is no guarantee habitability is possible with such restricted working hours and limited resources. You have no idea of the preparations that should be done! The air units for example were not built for this use, although yes, perhaps they'll be suitable if they stay on in-flight."

Marta did not need his wavering again. "They were designed to operate in flight for the troops!"

"These pods were designed to double as troop carriers, okay, but AI knows there are no troops in there. What about the fact there is no water supply and no air regen beyond what would be needed for a limited expeditionary unit - sorry but that's the basic design - if AI can be persuaded to leave them on. Of course the trees themselves are regen units of a sort, but they regen at a much slower rate than you choose to remember."

She smacked her lips and gave him a stern look. "I expect the pod opens to vac unless I can disable it. While calculating what the trees need, be sure to leave room for LeeLaa and her extended family; each needs a minimum of a meter and a half diameter floor space. I'd rather have the air regen on in there, but if they can get by in this air, they'll be able to make do with the pod air without mechanical regen for a while. I couldn't get too specific with TaaTaa, but he said they could survive if there was enough water and soil, meaning they can modify what they need to some extent."

He waved a hand at her. "It's not soil; it's regolith with proportioned mineral content. Hold on." He took out his tablet that Marta had modified for him and poked at it, concentrating and posing some more. Silent, he swished his pursed lips while frowning in deep thought.

He shook his head and frowned. "Since you refuse to see reason, I'll give you my best shot. This is it: You will jimmy crack corn the lighting to be Sol equivalent at 30,000 lumens at two meters from fore to aft on the port side. The starboard is for stores, with the center to walk in." He paused only long enough to lock eyes on Barto. "You will bring me at least 400 cubic meters of whatever passes for soil here, the kind from the planted areas with the 30/70 composition we talked about earlier, remember? Okay." He switched back to Marta. "You will rig drip irrigation in a net throughout the TOP of the planting area, in meter increments. I will use the medium from the mulched trees on top, if we can get that little grinder to accept more than a gram of branch at a time." Back to Barto, "You will remove the unneeded equipment from the area and put it out of sight somewhere. I must approve of anything you want to take out as unneeded. Now, who is leading this flagrant parade to Armageddon?"

Marta enjoyed the speech until he said 'Armageddon'. "Sir, you don't think, I mean, Armageddon?"

"Marta, these loveable stick things could exterminate the entire planet of mom and apple pie. How do we know any differently? The little bunny rabbits brought to Australia as pets contributed to the extinction of several native species and became a menace. A cute little snail rode into the Great Lakes with the tankers and ended up clogging the nuclear intakes as well as municipal water intakes, fouling vessels abominably all the while. A tiny genetic tweak in the Clostridium humboldtii bacteria that was introduced to interrupt the incubation of Dengue fever also somehow crossed over to dozens of other species before it inexplicably stopped.

"We have shown we cannot predict the outcome of the introduction of a foreign species. How much more so for a highly advanced species not of the Earth at all? These tree-things could not only decimate but eliminate our species. If you haven't seriously considered that I beg you to do so now."

"Dr. Cartier, the risk is not negligible, as you say. However we're not going to Earth, the planet that kicked you out. I cannot decree that Tenembras is marginal anyway and of relatively low population so it's a good place to try this. I cannot say our Amigos are entirely benign; they have shown no hint of hostility but I cannot conclude that will continue in that mode if provoked. All I can say is that this is first contact with fellow space farers and I ask you, are we going to cudgel them with clubs or what? Let's take whatever precautions are needed but let's define what it means to be human and get on with it!"

He truly appeared tired of vacillating. "Oh, Marta, you bring tears to my eyes. No more reservations, I am onboard. Come here and I'll show you about the lights and we'll see if the air will do. Two days are impossible, but we'll make the effort to save a few of the, ah, visitors. Deal?"

She hugged him. With him working with her, it was possible and his expertise in play meant she could focus on the tech issues; the pod seemed a bigger peril each time she went in there. What surprises would AI have in store for her?

chapter 59

TaaTaa's worries

"**F**riends, there is no reason to doubt Martaa, the planet surface will be destroyed and there is no need to debate it further. For those who desire another outcome, I am sorry that a better outcome is not here. I know you fear the confines of a simple alien shell that you cannot control; I fear it too. I cannot see how it will sustain us through the great void. I cannot see where we will go, or what we will meet when we arrive. My faith rests on the emissary of the Mender. If Martaa says it is needed I will do it."

SaaTee, the one who had lost her entire family to the Van Damme crash responded. "*TaaTaa, I have always respected you family and your beliefs, but now is not the time to commit us all to a magical plan with the only religious assurances. A physical ship crashed and marooned us. There is no need to blame that on the Render. Another ship of the same people arrives. Why color them as Menders? The first was a danger and so is this one. Please try to be logical.*"

"*Logic gives me no comfort, SaaTee, the risks loom large for any choice. The first ones came and did not molest us. Why? Who knows? Martaa and three more of her kind have made friends with us, nay, do not interrupt! I say they are friends to my family if not others yet. I say it is part of their nature and that leads me to trust them in general. Martaa saw we starved for good light and she provided the light, look about you, these lights have given our weak ones hope. That endears my specific trust."*

More listeners came up to hear the debate. TaaTaa said a silent prayer to the Mender and continued, *"Martaa could have left on her ship and thought no more of us. Instead, she sees through into the future, telling me of the destruction and invites us, all seventeen of us, to her ship. She did this without asking which of you were worthy or which could be trusted. That is of the Mender."*

R'ooot flashed and retorted, *"They cannot speak properly, they cannot flash, they are alien and unknown. We have only bad experience with these beings!"*

There was no need for TaaTaa to raise his volume, all sensors attended his words. *"Friends, did you see how she and her friends hide? I believe they are intent to do the Mender's will against the will of others that control the ship. Martaa is a farseer! Through her, we know the day and hour of destruction. Will we wait to see if that future of fire is true or take the chance that this is the Mender's will? If I must choose between fates, I would choose the one containing hope. BinThaa, what do you say?"*

"TaaTaa, you are persuasive. I have listened and studied on this. If Martaa is a true farseer and there is to be fire, we might survive the fire that they send, but it would destroy the trees that shield us, leaving us at the mercy of the harsh arrows from the angry sun such as we endured before the trees grew. It takes no magic to see we live on an edge now and would only do worse. Old ones have died and young ones have grown tall since we were marooned; though we look daily for salvation, it seems our people will not come. Both logic and the Mender tell us to trust Martaa and leave this place by any means possible."

R'ooot flashed respect to the elder BinThaa. *"I resist the notion, but will join with those who proceed with this plan."*

BinThaa flashed to those assembled that the discussion was over. *"Tomorrow let the ones that know alien devices best come with me and we will assist Martaa to make this craft a sustainer of life. Let us all prepare to quit this planet of woe and let us together look to the next horizon."*

chapter 60

What are They up to?

Cartier looked skyward and made a show of checking a watch he did not have. "Marta, where's Barto please? It will be dark soon and we have so much left out."

"He went to gather up dinner. He's going to bring it back here because we need to be busy beavers."

"Dinner here? I get to suck the straw of flavorless mush here? Yes, why not, we could work after dark, I suppose. We do have the lights in here. Naomi will have to pack it in, though."

* * *

"Mr. San Luis, I have called for you multiple times and could not get through. Is your radio off?"

He tried to come by at unpredictable times and leave quickly, but this time she caught him. He knocked his helmet against the hull a couple times and shook his head toward the monitor. "I can only pick up anybody if close to me, maybe happen when I fall, almost knock me out."

Char frowned knowing it's damn hard to break one of those. There was nothing to be done about it now, but she could check them out later. "What have you been working on?"

"I have been helping Dr. Cartier finish some tests and starting to bring his *equippas grandes* back to the pod. I think I can work the peroxide sterilizer now," he reported, smiling. "I must return, we have not much more time."

"Very well. When you do get back remind Dr. Cartier of that fact and if you see that Van Ruin girl send her to me. I will not have her lolling around when others are working. There are too few hours remaining for idle hands."

When he got back to the pod, he relayed the messages. "She said nothing about why we don't come in, so is not a problem. Where is *mi* Hermana?" He looked around inside the door into the pod and was mildly surprised to see BinThaa acting as a scaffold for the lighting framework he and Marta had cobbled together. She climbed across the permanent lighting bar framework that ran the length of the pod's apex, attaching the agglomeration of lights and wiring them to the point of hacking into the main.

Dr. Cartier came around and shared the scene for a moment before returning his attention to the modular grow pan corners. "Bartolommeo, my boy, we may get there yet, but not tonight." He critically surveyed the grow pan joints and did not appear happy.

chapter 61

The Last Day

At the first glimpse of dawn's rays, Cedric came to the Ag bench to find complete disarray and nobody present. He wanted to get an early start with his investigation of the crash site and came to ask San Luis along to spite the Commander. The whole cabal of them was missing from the Portico, but those odd trees were blocking his way to check the pod; the door stood ajar but he saw no sign of movement. Did they bunk in there last night? He scanned the tree line, unwilling to wander around in there on foot on the chance of finding someone. With no sign of Marta or anyone, the tree things worried him; he couldn't shake the idea they knew he'd spoken out against them.

"Mr. Crannog, you look confounded."

It took Cedric a second to separate the voices in his head from an external one, to realize a soft, treble voice spoke. "What?" He shifted to find the speaker, but had trouble picking him out from the shadows of stacked equipment and materials.

Thao stepped into Cedric's sight, off to the side and still in partial shadow. "I hope I do not unwisely intrude."

"Tomlinson? Confounded? I surely am, but I am unclear of your interest in it." He crouched to see the man eye to eye, but immediately regretted it as he thought about how to stand up again.

"I have many interests. One that applies now is that you are at a crux of the fervid beliefs of the two factions among us. In common parlance you ride the fence that divides two camps and when you finally choose a side, you will impact the balance in a far greater degree than your current status would suggest."

"I am aboard with you for all this time and the first thing I hear you say to me is an embroidered commentary about my state. What do you mean by this, sir?"

"I mean to unbalance you by my intrusion," he said, with a fluting lilt, "and so help you to choose the side you fall into, instead of watching you fall by the whims of circumstance."

Cedric was more confounded than before. "What business are my choices to you?"

"I am not accustomed to civility, so I will forge ahead to ask you what your plans are toward the Lady's project."

"I would not have expected you to discuss such a matter on the comm."

"I appreciate your discretion. The communication signals are disrupted in this area. We may speak freely."

"Fine, then. You mean Marta and her disastrous scheme of bringing trees and Heaven knows what to Tenembras? No good can come of it. Authorities will shut that down before any potential contamination can reach the biosphere. I have told her that. What, were you lurking in the shadows then, too?"

"Sir, do not confuse your hostility toward my appearance or style of communicating with the line of inquiry. There are important issues here that go far beyond my part."

"All right! You think I'm wrong about the trees? I could tell you I'll reconsider, but the fact remains that the deal is dead before it begins and that doesn't even touch the 'other' issue."

"If so, why do you struggle with your conscience?"

"Whoa, who said anything about conscience? My conscience is just fine."

"You would have the aliens exterminated like so many vermin, crushed underfoot and maintain your fine sensibilities?"

"You don't believe that rot about some of the trees being aliens? Come on, man, there are some freaky trees that will be cleared off with the rest. Period." He looked nervously over to the trees that seemed more unsettling in the growing light, seeming to stir out of time with the breeze. How did they come to gather around the pod?

Thao did not reply, but stared implacably at him at him steadily, silently.

He refocused on the enigmatic Thao. "You believe they are intelligent aliens? That changes nothing. The fate of humanity is at stake and the authorities will not take a chance."

The little man remained silent, gazing through the shadow.

Cedric fidgeted, becoming more and more anxious to get into the waiting buggy and be off. "No one knew about any of this alien business before we arrived, so this has to be some kind of one-off speculation. If they are aliens, they aren't native to here and this isn't a civilization." He spoke aloud to prioritize the line of thought that sought his inner motivations, the voice in his head that was so often drowned out, the one that grew from his own self. It was proving elusive. "You're a linguist, what is your interest in this in the first place? This is a straightforward biosecurity deal that you need not become involved with."

Thao faded back into the long shadows with Cedric unable to follow by sight or sound. He shuffled around to face the pod and fell forward, palms to pod, so he could walk his hands up the side to stand. Then the pod door at the end opened wider and the tree-things parted for San Luis to pass.

"Hello, San Luis, have you seen Marta?" The moment he asked that he was vexed for not asking San Luis to join him on the investigation.

"*Si.*"

Annoyed at the man's clearly obstinate stance, Cedric decided he would not invite the man along after all; he could well do the job by himself. He might have a quick word with Marta, though. Might she like to join him? A basic part of him warmed to that concept, bringing her to the wreck site so they could peruse it together and he could make amends, discussing what clues they could tease from the debris could allow them to at least speak to each other again. "Well, sir, which way is she, I'd like to talk to her a moment."

"No."

"What do you mean, 'no'? I want to see if she'd like to accompany me on a survey, I have use of the buggy."

"No. She has not the time not the energy to fight with you today. Go fight with the trees and try to hurt them. They too will soon be gone forever and I know you would be sorry to miss the chance."

Cedric was stood dumfounded with an unaccustomed anger boiling up. "You sonuvabitch, you get out of my way." He tried to slide between a bench piled with parts and his adversary.

Barto picked him up, mashing Cedric's forearms against his ribs, and threw him bodily against the pod, his back impacting hard and his helmet clanging loud. He slid down and landed hard on the packed sand.

Dr. Cartier tore around the door, hand gripping the door edge to maintain equilibrium. "What is this? Stop it this instant!"

"Dis *flaco* always come here to fight. I say no, not dis time, Marta is busy."

Cedric pushed his back up the hull and raised himself on shaky legs. He shook his head as briskly as he could with the damned helmet to settle the reverberations in his skull. "Dr. Cartier, there is no reason for this person to ..."

"Stop! Mr. Crannog I have to agree with Barto. Every time you leave Marta she's distressed if not in tears. I won't have it sir, I will not. I'm sorry, but please go on your way immediately."

Cedric stopped the impulse to brush off and sneered at the staring fools. He pushed his hands out, arm muscles tensed hard as if trying to fend them physically until he got by them; with clenched fists and jaws he marched back to the Portico to get the buggy.

He saw the Portico's comm monitor blinking red 'incoming' as soon as he entered and saw Olivia on screen the next second.

"Cedric, why so upset?"

"Sorry it shows. I had a dust up with that San Luis."

"Why on Earth?"

"It's not Earth, is it? He can push anyone around here he pleases. All I wanted to do was talk to Marta."

"And her bodyguard wouldn't let you. I've seen some things on this monitor here. See?" She split the screen and showed triple-speed scenes clearly showing the moving trees around the Ag area. She inquired sweetly, "What are they doing back there?"

Even with the altercation hot in his mind, he could not freely expose them further. "I could explain some things personally, but not over the comm."

"See that purple button on the side? No, higher up. Yes, press that and hold it down. Now it's just you and me."

Either he trusted her or not; his control over his emotion was tenuous. "I think Cartier is helping her get specimens against the express orders from Ms. Jones. San Luis is egging her on. The aliens are helping load the trees. I tried to get her to desist before she gets into trouble but she won't listen!"

"Now, Cedric. She's a smart girl." Olivia's voice cajoled him, trying to exert a calming influence. "Don't you think she's considered her risk and decided whatever she's doing is both possible and worth it?"

"They won't let me back there and they won't let me talk to her." He worked at keeping his jaw loose enough to talk and concentrated on keeping the purple button down.

"You have greater success finding out more by being sweet than antagonistic. Have you listened to her reasons? To understand what she's trying to accomplish?"

That hit him harder than San Luis's blow. Part of him cried out but another part beat it back. Cold and acute, he told her, "I am amazed you are siding with her without even knowing what she's into."

She seemed taken aback. "Crannog, I am amazed you are siding *against* her without even knowing what she's into."

He released the purple button and turned away.

chapter 62

Diagnosis

Olivia cut the comm and finished a bit of editing as Doc Trogden rang her up. "Doc! I just had the most interesting chat with dear Cedric, want to see?"

"Surely!"

Olivia ran the newest version for her. "What did you think?"

"It looks like I was right; there are three or four in there, warring for control. He not only acts like a different person, but his entire physiognomy changes to match."

"I take it you've seen this before. How was this missed in the initial screening? I thought nutcases had to be sedated for the duration."

"Don't jump to conclusions; Cedric is highly functional as an engineer and appears to be breaking only under the emotional stress resulting from his attraction to Marta. He can't escape her in the confines of our transport, although you yourself have noted his attempts to do that very thing."

"Yes, he'd meet with her and usually get upset in a strange way; like starting out as a regular professional guy and transitioning into some kind of beaten animal and then he'd barricade himself in his room for a week or two. That's not what we saw a minute ago, though, is it?"

"No, that was more like a teenager crying about being outdone by a bully. Emotional development arrested somehow at the teen stage? Dunno. I don't think Teen comes out much."

"I picked up on the professional one when he was up here spelling me on the nav console, but I chalked it up to style."

"Yes, most people have different personas they present for certain occasions; you don't present yourself the same way at a funeral as you do a horse race or they way you want to appear at a job interview. This goes beyond that."

"Who is the mean old ogre that he flinches from? When the bogey seems to take over, it's scary."

"It could be that a father figure inflicted some kind of mental trauma in his formative years. I see no maternal influence past that."

"You said three or four. Is the forth one the guitar player?"

"Yes, I met him when the Professional came by to ask a tech question and I asked him to help with a bucket seal. When I passed him a mug of the Porter, the transformation floored me. He became the poet, the musician, I don't know, the sensitive lover of what's beautiful in the world. When Marta saw that one the first night, that's why she fell for him."

"That's right, he serenaded her that first night here."

"I think that's it. The Poet is badly bruised, though, and the Bogey is a powerful antagonist."

"What's going to happen when he goes downside and she stays here?"

"I think he'll go back to status quo, the professional engineer with music as a private outlet. Lots of people live that way and it shouldn't be a problem. On a planet he should be able to escape any such intense amorous urges."

"That doesn't bode well for fatherhood, unless…"

"No, he doesn't fit the attacker profile. He's peaceful at heart and shows no unusually violent tendencies. Remember how he tried to slide by San Luis? He probably will miss out on having a family and that is a shame, but you never know."

"No meds? No treatment?"

He's distinctly uncooperative and I can't act without the suggestion of harm to his self or others. There's no such suggestion. Face it, Livy, he probably will work himself to death at the Nukes and Breaker anyway."

chapter 63

Advice

"Hey, Cedric!"

"Naomi, I'm in a hurry." He slammed the buggy trunk, assured the needed supplies were secure.

"In a hurry to get away from me, I see that. Fussing at Marta again. You gotta stop that darn quick and I mean it."

"I though you two were rivals and I see she must have won out. Unfortunate for you, now make way." He plunked into the driver's seat and switched on the ignition.

Naomi leaned on the windowless door. "You are a worse klutz than me, but you trip on words where I trip on stones. I know you can't mean some of the awful things you say to her. Why do you try and go outta your way to hurt her like that? It's like whipping on a dog that just wants to please you."

"What the blaze do dogs have to do with anything? How does she treat you? And why are you privy to my private conversations with Marta? If you must know I think she's being silly going on about those trees. Well you needn't worry about it any more, I'm going to see the wreckage site and then we're away. Tenembras is desert with no damned trees! Good Day!"

chapter 64

Problems

"Children, we have about seven hours left and it's a no-go. I cannot get the weights to balance, not even close. Even with you moving the tractors to the other pod with all the extraneous equipment, the aggregate weights and the distribution are all wrong. I've hauled too many Ag Packs in-system to think this has a prayer of working."

Barto preempted Marta, "How much weight where?"

Walking to the pod gate, he pointed in. "See that long trough under the lights? That's where the trees will go. If you pack them in, that side will be heavy because of the moist media, the density of a living tree and the ridiculously heavy aliens between them. And we can't add any more on the port side because that's for habitability equipment."

Alain shook his head and scrunched his lips around. "I've tried different configurations in an attempt to balance better; if I try to stack the trough on top of some of the lighter gear and heave the heavier stuff port we'll have to top the trees and then have the gear at moisture risk. And then it won't balance with the other pod!"

"Excuse me!" Marta insisted. She looked serious and upright, like reciting. "To get out of Rotterdam to America I had a passport for an older and heavier girl. I stole some fat meat and cut it into strips to tape to my body, then covered them with leather from God knows what animal. The immigration monitors showed it as my extra fat. Anyway, I gained ten kilos in the right places."

Dr. Cartier had no idea of Marta's alternative past and his jaw dropped. Her matter-of-fact admission of her illegal entry caught Barto by surprise as well.

"Wake up, guys! What will we use as bladders and how do we get water to them?

Cartier shook his head at her rambling logic, pensive. "We don't have enough water as it is, a couple buckets at a time."

Naomi trotted up, raising puffs of dust. "Y'all we do not have the means to store or provide any more water. I have rooted through the Portico like a pig smelling truffles trying to find any container we could use bigger than the teeny buckets we lugged all night, but aside from filling the grow pan reservoir, we're high and dry."

Cartier responded, "That's part of what I was trying to explain to these two. We are stuck in the doldrums without the sizeable bladder that my protégé recommended, but also the means to fill them much more quickly."

"Leave it to me. Professor, please finish that nutrient solution and make sure anything we have to palletize for the other pod is moved back at least three meters. Naomi, please scope out where to drop the hoses and start laying the markers out. Barto, can you work on that palletizing? The straps are around here somewhere."

"*Donde va*, Hermana?"

"Liberating the parts from the spy satellite was a crime, but this will be a work of art."

chapter 65

Hitchin' A Ride

C edric backed up to the Portico, having forgotten his stash of two masks and half a dozen ox cartridges, loosing an hour in wandering before his return. He'd regained sense enough to know he wanted the freedom from the damned helmet and comm as soon as possible. With that vital equipment in his satchel, he went back out to the buggy got about ten meters away before getting a comm signal. He pulled over so he could collect himself for the call. Before answering it he glanced up and blast it if that wasn't Marta coming his way. She seemed to be looking his way, too.

'Every time I turn about there she is again. Doesn't that peripatetic girl ever say put? What the hell is she up to now? If it were the Corpsman, I'd say she was trying to implement some kind of showcase for her grace and energy. Not that Barbara has her grace or energy.'

He slumped and worked at loosening his jaw. His imagination seemed ignited around her. 'I bet she could do anything she put that prodigious mind to. She'd be great as teacher. She has a wide range of knowledge and a nurturing spirit, yes, she could raise a fine lot of children. I wonder what her children would look like. Our children?' The comm beeped again and this time he acknowledged it. "Yes?"

"Mr. Crannog, this is van Rijn. Can you hang on a minute? I have a passel of cargo I hope to requisition and it would be a professional courtesy if you would offer that conveyance in assistance."

He switched the motor off and rested his arms on the steering wheel.

Marta jabbed at the green call button every two seconds until Lt Commander O'Reilly responded with a cup in one hand and a flimsy in the other, something that appeared to be an electronic schematic. "Thank you for responding, ma'am."

"You're welcome, Ms. van Rijn." She laid the flimsy out of sight.

"Ma'am, I wish to requisition a Fargo HP pump and four in-line water pumps with 200 meters of three centimeter water hose. I have the inventory numbers if you like."

"You'd come in clearer if you'd press and hold the purple button at 1 o'clock. That's right, much better. Now tell me what you need more equipment out there for on the last day."

"Ma'am, nearly all of the non-consumables can be salvaged; I do understand that the pod will be transferred directly to the Ag Research compound, yes?"

"If it's properly cleaned out and sterilized, yes."

"Well, you see dust and sand has inundated the pod and saturated the equipment. I've tried wiping and sweeping until I'm worn like shiny leather and there's still grit everywhere. The only way I know to get this stuff clean is with the universal solvent, water. If you please. Ma'am."

"Won't the water be as bad as the dust and dirt?"

"Oh, no ma'am. The water is sterile in the first place and will displace the particles. Then in the sterilization process, the water will evaporate leaving much less of a trace."

"What do you mean, 'less of a trace'?"

"There are some few dissolved minerals in the water, just some iron and traces of other sub-leads."

The girl's inventiveness and plausibility pleased Olivia, all the while knowing the equipment would be used other than as stated. "Is that all?"

"No ma'am. I also need sixteen of the utility water bladders with taps and at least four of the two centimeter utility hoses, the six meter lengths and spray nozzles to go with each."

"I'll buy the hose, but not the bladders. Why would you need them?"

"The Fargo is an HP pump and with the hose diameter it takes it would give us too much too fast, worse than a fire hose. Also, there's only the one big hose. We'll run the big hose to the river and fill the small bladders. By using the bladders with the smaller pumps and hoses, we can regulate the water flow and each of us can work in a different spot, cleaning at different rates. Filling all the bladders at the start will save having to fool with refilling them repeatedly. That will be much more efficient given our time constraints and reduce the mud hole effect at the work areas as well. Ma'am."

"You said you know the inventory numbers?"

"Yes, ma'am, they're ones I had to rekey and they stuck in my brain somehow."

"You have that good a memory?"

"Yes ma'am."

"Here you go, plug your numbers in and I'll authorize it."

As O'Reilly spoke, the screen split to show an inventory withdrawal page. Marta started keying the numbers in, wondering why the Navigator bypassed the req system and went straight to inventory withdrawal, but didn't wonder too much. It was awkward to key the numbers with her left hand, but she had the right hand occupied with that special purple button. She knew that button activated the new circuit she'd installed a while back in addition to the usual 'dampened transmission field' function, the one specially requested by the Navigator. Before she closed the requisition out she added a reducer for river hose-to-bladder line and another case of ox cartridges; they'd run out late last night and the suits were worse than ever. She held her breath to see how it flew, readying a story for it.

Instead, the Navigator smiled politely and waggled a little wave as she cut the comm.

In a couple of minutes, the cargo airlock door to Marta's left slid up and a pallet of equipment slid out. It sat there on the deck looking very, very heavy. The compartment filled with a fog and the door slid shut again. Marta inventoried the lot. All there! Including the cartridges and bless the Navigator, all on a wheeled tow-cart with a long hitchable tongue!

She looked behind her to see Cedric hipshot and leaning with crossed arms against the doorframe. She imagined him without the bulky suit like that and her heart skipped a beat. Why did he have to alternate from darling to demon so fox fast?

He helped her roll the load to the buggy that he'd backed up to the door without comment, him pulling and her pushing. She was glad the cart and contents were bundled together tightly on the pallet because she knew the bladders to be slippery and she did not need to try to corral sixteen very heavy eels. The cart's wheels sank more than half way to the wheel's hubs. He drove slowly to reduce stresses on the trailer hitch and because the drag would overcome the buggy's traction if not. Marta rode beside him far beyond touch in the shotgun seat, but near enough to see across the chasm they'd created between themselves, neither speaking.

When they finally reached the Ag area, Barto stood guard like a mastiff straining his chain. He broke the aggressive stance when he saw the cart contents and stepped over to it as Cedric came to a stop. Marta and Barto unloaded the cart, heaving to lift the hose reel and big pump. When they finally lugged the last bladder away, Cedric sped off at high speed, a billowing brown cloud obscuring the cart, pallet and straps that bounced behind.

chapter 66

Finishing Tasks

"Come on Hermana, let's put these stuffs to use."

"He left before I could tell him thanks."

"You need to get back to work and forget about that guy. Come on, let's make good use of all you bring, *si?*"

She could hear his eagerness to shuck the helmet, so he followed him around. "Dr. Cartier," she called via the comm, "We can thoroughly clean that equipment now! I got everything we needed!"

He stepped carefully off a ladder over by the plumbing control plenum, saying, "Everything?"

"Yes, sir, we'll start all over, moving everything out and use the big hose to blast the pod clean. The filled bladders will provide us the control needed to carefully rinse inside and outside every piece before it goes back in. You know we have to get every speck out!"

The heavy grav obviously wore on Cartier, but not enough to stop him. "I see Naomi coming back. Since I know you two had a spat, I'll get her started on prepping the bladders. You and Bartolommeo can run the hose. Put your Fargo pump between the fifth and sixth sections, okay?"

"Yes, sir. Here's the remote for the pump."

"Wonderful, I'll wait at least a minute before activating it after you press the reset in case it blows. It shouldn't, but it could cut you in half if it did, so step away lively after that reset."

"Will do, sir. I'm turning the comm down now to prevent that loud interference past the deflectors, it gives me a headache."

"That's fine, dear, none of us will have much to say anyway."

With that last comment, Barto unlatched her helmet and rigged it. She donned the mask gratefully. Naomi suddenly stood before her with arms wide and they hugged happily. They had the water they needed!

Running the hose may have been hurried, but the result was outstanding, with no fishes or moss to clog it. Yet the sun showed late morning and they were still filling the bladders had to be in place before they could redeploy the big hose as the main header section of piping they needed for the pod, one small pump in each internal piping section. Relieved the Navigator hadn't questioned the excessive hose length or extra pumps, Marta arranged the utility hoses would be the piping from the system to the gauges. She knew she was getting reckless, but she found it harder and harder to identify the hazy line between bold and fey.

When they got back, Marta found Naomi filling the first big header bladders in the Ag pod. She had a matrix of four of the 1000 liter bladders across the nose of the pod with two more rows adjacent aft. Lord, what if she hadn't procured enough bladders! They nodded at each other and Marta left Naomi to concentrate on that task.

Checking the other pod, the tractors now sat in back and the marvelous grav sled parked in front of it ready to load with balancing bladders. She hated the idea of throwing the parted out satellite away but it was a wreck. If needed, she supposed they could pile heavier bits of it in places.

The total system would be somewhat heavier, but as long as it balanced they'd be okay. Probably. Marta banked on the thrust off of this irregular foreign surface introducing enough variables to drown out the effect of the slightly greater weight; the pods themselves were significantly more massive than the load, making the increase almost irrelevant. Hopefully.

Barto scoped out the placement of the remaining bladders. They'd planned on two tapped for the grow pan recirculation. Dr. Cartier said the inline filters with the integrated auto-cleanouts were up to the job, so she once again told herself to put that worry out of her head, that there was no room for comforting redundancies. She couldn't help but remember her mother emphasizing the special needs of a closed system. She and Barto unfolded a bladder and nudged it to her satisfaction. Once the water works were in place, she'd start installing the air system Naomi had slaved over and laid out on the deck as components.

She woke as from a dream, a dream of her mother showing her as a small child how to transplant trees. She stared in the direction of the air system components. Dr. Cartier crowded her elbow, jostling it.

"Where were you, dear? I have to tell you this worries me more and more."

"Worries you more?" She focused on his face to see real concern.

"Marta, I've been talking and you haven't been anywhere in the vicinity! To recap, we've gone along with you, but it worries me that with all your plans you don't seem to have a plausible outcome mapped out. It seems like 'bring them and all those wrong-minded oafs will see the light and make them and you welcome' or other such pie in the sky tripe. You shake my confidence to the core. We might be able to hide them for a slice of time, then what? And what would they do to you?"

"Sir, I am more concerned about the trip there. I feel like a fat tot scheduled for Cannibal Daycare and Barbecue. As for our Amigos, I'm on it, Professor. By the time we come out of slip I'll have the whole picture together." She projected all the self-assurance she could scrape up, knowing that she had no such plan.

"Dr. Cartier, don't lose faith now, is too late!" boomed a basso voice.

"Bartolommeo San Luis, do not sneak up on me. And it is never too late to put the kibosh on a bad idea. This could stop right now before anything compromising is actually loaded."

They gauged each other's resolve for a few moments, like a triad of gunfighters with twitching fingers.

Marta shook it off and put on her foreman's deportment, saying, "I'll need some help positioning the upper frames, Barto. Would you mind? Dr. Cartier, the tanks are ready for leak testing, if you'd take the pump from Naomi there. Naomi, if you would, explain me a bit more about how this air system goes together and hand me up the pieces. Our guests will be here soon!

chapter 67

T MINUS 3

"Hydro recirc," Marta called out.

"Hydro recirc GO," was Barto's reply.

They were all satisfied now that the pod was rigged as well as could be done, all systems green-go, with three hours to spare. The aliens had been collecting for the last couple of hours and BinThaa with a new one they didn't know inspected the pod along with them. BinThaa did his clockwise right turn thing with a 'hand' and Marta rotated her hand the same way in agreement.

She'd been able to tell TaaTaa that she wanted to save some young trees, too. They walked through the woods earlier and she showed him the kind she meant, the young and healthy ones of nearly all the healthy types. The aliens now commenced bringing the trees with good root balls into the pods, planting each one personally to Dr. Cartier's joy.

Cartier grinned happily, "They're natural gardeners! Look at that, will you!"

She gauged that the planting phase followed by the 'moving alien plunder in' phase would take a couple hours, enough time for her next performance. "Sir, I don't want to curb your exuberance, but I need to talk to you guys."

His grin vanished and he followed her at once. The other two waited apprehensively for them at a little seating area they'd set up between the pods.

"Out with it honeydew, we're on pins and needles," Naomi drawled. "You can't defuse something, right? The gamma sterilization doesn't have a bypass."

Marta knew her accent strung her words out when she was nervous. Without preamble, she began. "When we load up I have to go with the crew, so this will be good-bye."

"But we have a couple weeks before we get dumped! Your skinny hiney belongs with us until we shinny down the rope to perdition!"

Marta persevered; it was not the time to choke up. "I don't imagine I'll get to talk to any of you at all past this afternoon, so I wanted a hug from all of you before the last call."

Dr. Cartier looked wretched. "I suppose that means I have to conduct the rest of this train and do something clever with our friends here." He cleared his throat. "In charge regardless."

"That's right, sir, and I regret not having the marvelous plan I promised." That much was true, she hadn't thought much farther than the pod.

Barto walked away swiftly, around the far side of the satellite pod.

She watched him leave and almost started crying herself. "I thought that by getting it out in the open now, we could come to terms with it by time."

Naomi's face suffused with emotion. "Sweetest sugar, you have labored to surpass Hercules to get our Amigos here safe and upward bound, but you'll never know what happens to them! I will not bawl!" She walked swiftly the way Barto went.

Her mentor's pale and sorrowful face struck her heart and made it thump. "Sir, I know you can do this, have faith that love and light and the good Lord will see us all through."

He held his heavily gloved hands up as if to study his calloused palms. "I haven't attended church in decades; I spent my time in the fields."

She put a hand of her own on his arm. "You gloried in the bounty of creation! You struggled to provide for others and shared you gifts without stint or fear of reprisal. You are a shining vessel of love and light." She got so emotional she had to stop a moment. "Doctor Alain Cartier, you have taught me more than you can know and I will keep you in my heart forever."

He laid his face in his dirty gloves and sobbed.

Marta rose quietly and released her helmet the way she'd seen Cedric do it, put it on for appearances sake and went toward the Portico hoping to find him but not sure what she'd say. She didn't see him or the buggy. She lingered in the Portico too long, though, and the monitor started flashing for an incoming call, Olivia O'Reilly. Marta pushed the answer button and the purple one.

The Navigator smiled and asked, "Why are Bloom and San Luis standing at the cliff with no helmets on?"

"The air is pristine, just shy of oxygen. With the ox mask we can adjust the ox delivery to compensate and be free of these damnable helmets."

O'Reilly peered steadily as if to pin Marta to a card. "The leadership would consider that activity an abrogation of orders punishable by whatever certain leaders wanted to justify, the least being a lengthy quarantine Topside to ensure no biohazard got into you bodies."

Marta stood her ground. "We understood that, ma'am. The dread of Tenembras eclipses all else."

"You are not going to Tembo."

"I am with them until we part."

"Goodness, girl, you're crying! I will make deal with you, you who have disabled some of my eyes and ears. Tell me what you've stashed in the pod and I'll let you stay in the Passenger's section until final transfer."

Marta pretended to consider the offer; actually assembling the bits and pieces of information the Navigator should already have wind of. "Cartier told me I couldn't keep anything, but I said I'd take responsibility. I have sectioned every species of tree and double wrapped each specimen and triple wrapped sections of the specimens I think are alien. I wanted Cartier to take them with him to Tembo for study."

"You don't lie as well as you think. I have seen the tree-things move and I know you have learned to talk with them."

Marta was afraid of that, it was too difficult to circumvent all of the ubiquitous spyware and she'd been busy with other priorities. "They came to say goodbye because I warned them. They are evacuating as we speak; I got the bit about the coming fire and brimstone across to them."

That was to cover the activity among the trees; she probably had seen more of them as they gathered at the pod. "It does not surprise me that you cannot detect their tech, their ship has to be eons past ours."

"Great Shiva, you can communicate with them! What are they like? Up close? How does that bark-material feel?"

"Their exoskeletons are composed of flexible, strong, smooth carbon rods, they absorb nutrients from the ground and catalyze them with light. They've been living in small caves and under the trees. Our solar spectrum is more like their home sun so they gathered at our Sol-calibrated lights. They treated us with kindness and fellowship and I am shamed that I had to hide them from you people."

"You misunderstand me so, van Rijn. I would have loved to have met them. I thought they might not be able to get away."

"If they stay, so do I."

"I'm going to scan for their ship. You may report with the Passengers." She cut the comm.

Marta felt deep guild lying to her friends, her enemies, and to enemies that might have been friends. She went back to the pod and saw to details.

chapter 68

Treasure

The assembled incendiaries were easy to stab into the ground and arm and he did so coolly and without compunction. He'd planned his route to end at the wreckage site and soon arrived.

His initial survey revealed nothing that could aid in determination of the failure, not that he was any expert. He hadn't found the black box, but he could study the photos later if he could recognize the wreck through the dust and dirt that partially buried it. The early pioneer ships were a long, segmented affair, bristling with antennae and solar arrays. He searched around some of the larger segment pieces, careful to avoid getting snagged by the sharp curled back jagged metal around a couple of very suspicious holes. Those certainly rated pictures. He wished he'd remembered the segments better because it seemed there were excess chunks of debris of a different material. He took photos of both.

A large section of the bona fide Van Damme caught his attention. It protruded around a clump of mimosas and appeared open and empty, the presumed primary cargo fuselage. So there must have been survivors here long enough to plant all the trees that must have been in there.

He noticed a knoll to his right. He crossed himself when he found three branch-made crosses with placards naming each poor soul. As he sang them a soft Kyrie Elysian, he thought about the sad conclusion to their epic journey. How they must have anticipated arrival!

The others must have died in the flaming inferno as the stellar craft hurled through the atmosphere and broke into ruin, here at the brink of success. He looked around fruitlessly, wondering where the one who buried these people ended up. The thought of the man, or woman, alone on this alien and inhospitable world, knowing there would be no rescue, caused a cold bolt up his spine and into his arms. He shook the chill off and crouched graveside. He placed the placards one by one in his toolbox to give Marta. She would see them enshrined in honor. Somewhere. He nodded solemnly and carefully stood by, leaning on a crate.

Behind him, the Van Damme's secondary cargo fuselage appeared intact. Cedric took his last photos and walked around to the hatch; it had sunk about twenty degrees below level on this side. He attempted to start the manual override, but it proved balky. He worked up a sweat in the cool air getting the interlock to flip over and hesitated before trying to open the wide gang hatch.

When he shook off another chill, he pulled hard on the handles, rocking back and forth, hoping to find no bodies. The door abruptly popped back. His reflexes took him a giant leap backward when two crates fell out. Holding his splay-fingered hands palm out before him, he teetered on tiptoes a few seconds until he determined the cases were simply loose boxes obeying gravity. He calmed his respiration and returned to the hatch. He approached it circumspect, but nothing else leapt out at him.

He slid the door over until it locked in place. The door spanned two meters and admitted the breeze easily, flushing it with the air that his mask was adjusted to. The light of the dim sun through the dappled shade did not reach far into the compartment, so he relied on his utility light. He had hoped a black box was in there, since he'd looked at every other accessible location where one might be. The wreckage had scatted over a long and wide area and this looked like his best chance.

Shelves lined the whole compartment, some broken to account for the scattered jumble of crates. They seemed mates to the ones that somehow stayed stowed, all different sizes and with Dutch labels. After checking each corner as well as he could with his light, he climbed in and peered around, pushing and tossing crates out of the hatch to make room.

'Yes, behind these crates, quite possibly,' he told himself. He methodically moved and pitched the crates as needed to access the panel where a back-up box could be.

"Eureka! Heh, heh, gotcha." The compartment with the box lay open, jarred open perhaps. Once he had the box in hand, he returned to the entrance and dropped the short distance to the ground outside, sidestepping the crates. He checked the officially sealed fireproof flotation case and decided not to force the lock; he'd have a chance to use tools when he got back to the shuttles. Checking his watch showed it was only now noon, so he had a little more time to look around.

He dropped the case with the prized black box in the front seat of the buggy. He thought about following the debris trail, but a peculiar smell kept tugging insistently for his attention, an Earthy smell, remembered from childhood. Cross about the insinuating memory, he chose a crate at random and set it on the trailer. Removing the placards from his toolbox to the front seat, he found his pry bar in the bottom. He pried the crate open.

Bulbs. Big bulbs. Tulips? Go figure the Dutch ship to bring a bit of home with them. He wondered if he could bring them back; it would surely make peace with Marta if she had a way to find out. He should be able to add them to whatever set up she and Alain and all were cadging together for the trees and supposed aliens, she'd see them then. He tried to decide which box to open next, sort of like Christmas.

Marta would love them and smile, much like at Christmas. With her smuggler's heart she could doubtlessly take a few of the original Van Damme bulbs home with her. She might forgive him and remember him fondly. Perhaps she would find a way to accomplish her dream after all.

At peace with that thought for the time being, he acted on his curiosity about the rest of that cargo. Choosing a longer crate, he expected it to be heavier but it proved to be the contrary, much lighter. He popped the lid off.

He looked up at his Mother and placed a red rose in her basket that hung from her prosthetic arm. She had clipped some for the piano vase, but she allowed him to carefully hold each rose while she clipped. He got to help arrange them in the vase, too. She coaxed gorgeous blooms from deep reds, sunshine yellows, the venerable peace roses, fragrant fat pink ones and snowdrifts of tiny sisterly white ones.

With the scent of the roses in the air, he sat at the bench and played an etude for her and then a song she liked. Her smile so warm and true, her eyes so porcelain blue, like her Delft tea set, and yet so tragic. He played and she would softly sing nonsense syllables, la-la-tra-la-la-di. He heard her clear as the sparking dew on a velvet petal.

He realized he sprawled on the cold hard ground clutching rose canes so hard it took him a few moments to understand why his hands weren't bloody. What lax command! He threw the roses to the dirt. Angry, he wrestled his way to his feet and stood with hands clenched into fists, disappointed to not feel the pain of the broken off thorns, a real pain that might help him draw the line in his muddled mind.

His father had mourned his mother too, but had held the grief inside until it festered. He must have loved her, anyone who met her did. That deep grief probably contributed to his accidental fall off Edinburgh Castle while repairing the parapet force screens. One bad gust and one failed transformer resulted in one bitter, cruel and wheelchair bound invalid, made more bitter by the fact that he'd used up all the family's medical benefits and spent every last farthing of savings on trying to save his exotic disease-riddled wife.

Stop thinking about it! He knew one thing and that was rehashing old memories helped nothing.

Cedric watched his green-handled clippers snip-snip as he tended the roses he'd transplanted from their house near the stockyard with diligence and love, his Mother's roses. He thought they brought some of her loveliness to this rented, run down cottage. He thought about school and how he had a paper due and how he wouldn't have time after his shift at the crematorium, but he was drawn to the fragile beauty, recognizing the obsession but not caring.

The collage of scenes changed to that day, the memory he knew would come, the day he came home with some bone meal for the roses, to find his father waiting with a look of angry satisfaction that worried him very much. Father, already red-faced, sucked in a great gout of air and demanded to know why he was late, howling that he wouldn't tolerate it, getting redder with his forehead vein pulsing. Cedric knew a fit was coming and tried to brace for it, he tried to prepare his gut for the burning pain that felt like a creature inside was trying to escape the stress. When his father turned away and demanded supper, the Cedric in the memory thought he was reprieved. The Cedric doing the remembering felt acid rising.

He got the chicken wings from the refrigerator and put out a skillet, hoping his father would see subservient compliance and leave him be. He hadn't intended to look around, but Father chuckled as he rolled away. Where his father had been, he saw the muddy tracks. Part of him wanted to run fast and far, but in the crystal clear memory, he coated the wings in seasoned flour as the tracks nagged at him. When he placed the wings in the pan and bent over at the cabinet to choose a dehydrated veggie, he noticed bits of leaves and petals in the muddy stripes, red petals. He knew Father was impatiently waiting around the corner as he neared the tracks, but he couldn't stop.

He walked past his grinning father into the sitting room, past the ticking clock, past the bedroom, sharp claws digging through his belly because he could see the tracks led to the patio and his precious garden. Opening the door with badly shaking hands, he found what caused his father's glee. Mother's roses, uprooted and rolled over, narrow wheelchair tracks creasing them with dark, moist stripes, a container of Eradicat weed killer tossed among them. Nearly hysterical, he started to pick up the largest of the busted bits, trying to salvage some canes.

Father hit him hard with his stick and told him to stop being a momma's boy. 'Be a man! Men don't play with posies! Men work!' He ordered Cedric to put *all* the rose pieces in a trash bag. Cedric cried, desolate as he followed the command. His Father struck again and again as he knelt, knocking him over again and again. Father screamed "She's *dead*! Get over it!" He rolled to a different vantage point, hoarsely screaming, 'Bet you wish I was dead too, don't you?'

He struck Cedric so hard and so much that the fiber reinforced hickory cane cracked, the last dozen centimeters flying off, skittering across the patio like a scared mouse making a frantic escape. That made Father so angry he frothed at the mouth, a rabid, crippled wolf.

His father hunched over, a demented knight, and pushed Cedric against the low retaining wall with the sharp cane end jabbing, screaming with great heaving sobs that his sniveling boy was going to be a man or die.

The next day in the free clinic his father, matter of fact and seemingly full of pride, told him that he had been accepted to the next semester's classes at Glasgow's prestigious Engineering Institute for Power and Propulsion.

Cedric's plan to study environmental science, majoring in endangered coastal habitats, the dream he'd planned to the extent of discussing schools and curricula with his mother, evaporated, leaving only a briny scale in his heart. He could not gainsay his father. There was the fear, but the real reason was the deathbed promise to his mother that he'd do as his father said and make him proud.

As his bones mended and punctures suppurated and finally healed, he ditched all his loves and dreams and banished all else to be an engineer. In a secret and locked compartment deep in his soul, he kept the vivid memory of singing a requiem for the roses, Mother's and his, as they burned in the human crematorium.

chapter 69

Time to Go!

Gasping, he dug for a cartridge and inserted it clumsily into the mask. 'That should have lasted longer,' he thought when he was re-aerated. Stable again, he checked the time. "Oh my Gracious God!"

With little more than two hours to get back and gain admission, he gaped around bewildered. How did he loose all those hours! Think! He saw spent cartridges on the ground, but for the life of him couldn't remember changing them out.

A stentorian voice in his head commanded him to take the Black Box and leave the rest; it would prove he was over the childish fixation with mama and her posies. He could go in early and clean up. His fists clenched and loosened, the pain in his gut and head bringing spates of focus to his confused mind.

He wasn't convinced of his sanity until he could count the piled and strapped crates on the trailer twice and get the same answer both times. Heart aching for leaving the others, he drove as fast as he could without bouncing crates out of the open trunk or off the trailer

"Thanks to Merciful God in Heaven!" he shouted as he braked hard in front of Barto at the pod hatch.

Barto had pulled up the ramp and vigilantly prepared to close the door, and the only reason Cedric could think of was to make sure Marta didn't try to get into the shuttle. Barto shouted, "Shuttle *uno*, he's ready go, you leave that with me and get to the front. *Capitano* waiting for you!"

Cedric climbed out of the vehicle shaking. "Look, is there a way to put this in a sealed container or something, its organic and I want to take it back. For Marta, please!"

"I take, you go. *Run!*"

"But..."

"Go! *Go now* or I kick your ass! Go!"

He waited just long enough to see Barto deploy the ramp and get in the buggy.

* * *

Barto drove the buggy up into the pod and parked it on the starboard side by the water bladders, a tight fit. The standard pod came with vehicle tie downs and he lost no time in securing the buggy in place with the two he located in reach. He did one more walk down with his light, checking behind supply pallets and water bladders, peering through the trees and aliens in the grow box and in any other nook or cranny he could reach swiftly.

He hopped out and sent ramp up, but before he heaved the door shut, he said, "Look you tree things. Marta give herself to you, you better be good or I find a way to make it right. You are not people, but I pray to God you be good. Do not hurt humans 'cuz you know she never forget you. I will be there to see, I'll know. *Vayo con Dios, mi Amigos.*' He could think of nothing else to say, nearly strangled by the reminder of losing his Hermana, of leaving her to face those cruel people alone. He clanged it shut, locked it up and ran forward.

chapter 70

Back on Board

Barto came in winded and saw Naomi seated with Alain. "Notice the dear old captain didn't even show his face? He practically ran to the safety of Hypocrite Central."

Alain moved over a bit to make a gap between them as they felt the shuttle take off, replying, "Naomi, dear, you didn't want to see his ugly old face anyway, did you? It's probably a rule to avoid mutinies or some such nonsense."

"No, but it chapped my butt to have that kid Bodine's voice tell us to hurry on inside like good little exiles. I mean, why prod at us like that, hustling us into our cages? Hell, we'll probably have to wait a week on the Frankie before we get a good slip probability."

"*Cara, por favor, silencio.*" He sighed heavily and bowed his head, hair shaggy from plunking the helmet on to make it through the portal in the last seconds, then pulling it off with the rest of his despised gear in the decon chamber. His skin tingled from the laser-like treatment.

He found his comb plied it, trying to relax. All he could think of was their big attempt at honor on the planet they'd already started calling Van Damme. Would his Amigos survive?

Alain looked around and declared, "It seems our Engineer has the right idea, he must have gone straight to his cabin. I believe I shall do the same, to shower and sleep with my head on a soft pillow."

"Sweetie," Naomi asked, nudging Barto's shoulder gently, "Walk me to my cabin?"

"I go to the big screen and watch the trees burn." He heaved up and trudged toward the Comm Room, feeling tired and lost.

Naomi looked over to Alain with a puckered brow, saying, "You think they'll have the vid on?"

"I do, because it will hurt us."

They shuffled after Barto and saw that the vid on planetary pan as expected. Thao watched slack-faced.

The red-brown sandstorm from their precipitous takeoff left a minor smudge compared to the star-bright flares of the phosphorous based incendiaries. They saw the ring of fire fill out like a clock ticking off doom. The flames rose high and mixed with curling gray smoke that roiled up high into the sky where it dissipated into the wind, leaving nothing discernable but a small black smudge. There weren't that many trees, after all.

Naomi, her tears cleaning the grime from slim channels over her high cheekbones, collected as muddy on her jaw line. She reached over and set the vid to replay from takeoff. "They must be too cheap to use the big boys. Overkill, anyway. It looks like the incendiaries were enough firepower to do the job ten times over."

"Yes, my dear, I think you're right. They advertise the big planet-killer light show and then renege. Still, dead is dead. Someone must have looked at our reports that indicated the UV would sterilize any microbe that could possibly survive."

"I think they just not gonna show that part, they not gonna take no chances. Don't cry, Cara, we done the right thing, we worked hard and done the right thing."

They knew better than to openly congratulate each other on the stupendous effort expended and the precious cargo they held, but their eyes shone with satisfaction. Many trees burned, but some would live along with their shepherds. Cartier already started planning his arrival at his new domain, the Ag Domes.

"Attention Passengers, assemble immediately in the Comm Room. All Passengers assemble immediately in the Comm Room." The Navigator's emblem preempted the replay at the point of seeing the first little fire on the horizon. They waited in place, keeping an eye out for Cedric.

The screen blipped to show the Navigator, looking a bit frantic. She didn't say anything at first.

"Senorita O'Reilly, why you call us? I think you can tell us what you want without us being together. I think you can tell who is here without seeing us like little ninos in a classroom, no?"

The Navigator's eyes were big and glassy and she seemed flushed. She blurted, "Marta Van Rijn is not aboard Shuttle One or Two."

Alain shot to his feet, waving his fists. "Of course she is, you people wouldn't let her stay with us these last weeks, she told us so! She's over there with the crew!"

"I tell you she is not on Shuttle Two." O'Reilly's clipped voice brooked no argument.

"Hold on," Naomi cried out, standing to hold Alain's arm. "She came up with us, but said she had to sign off on the final sterilization and closure of the pod, so she ran back to you, honey." She looked at Barto, pleading for him to make this right.

Barto got to his feet, too, gripping the edge of a partition, leaning on it. "She come back to me and say to hurry up, she go over and check the other pod seal. She say to me that the latch, he does not look right. I go over to see the latch is fine, no problema, and I seal it up. I come back around and she gone. I think she go the Shuttle *Dos*?" He started replaying every step in his mind. "Maybe to this one instead?"

Naomi shook her head and stamped a foot. "No! Alain and I came in, then Cedric, then you."

They stared silently at each other.

Olivia sounded more ragged. "I know about your tree rescue deal. I have to inform you that as soon as we left orbit both pods were vented to the outside and hard sterilization commenced."

Naomi gaped.

"I know one of you, probably Van Rijn, disabled the aft vent and several of the indicators in the Ag pod in an attempt to hide your work from the AI and me. There were several vents and several indicators, most not visible or easily accessible. All of these indicate vacuum throughout both pods and a complete sterilization cycle. Every one. But she doesn't seem to be there, not in either pod or anywhere on either shuttle. She had an embedded immy chip affixed to her shoulder blade and it should blaze like a beacon. No scan picks up Marta's chip anywhere. If you can think of any other way she's up here somewhere, for pity's sake tell me!"

"We thought," Alain began, hawked up some phlegm and swallowed it, then kept going, "we thought the pod might not be secure so we kept her away from it and in our sight the last hours. Barto kept watch at the back with the hatch shut. She said she was going with you."

Barto interrupted, "She did come back at the last, but I know she was not in the pod because I check it real good one last time, with a light." He wrinkled his face, recalling every tiny detail, "I check it good." The phrase 'I check it good' repeated over and over and over in his head.

Cedric trotted in, not even clean yet. He saw the anxiety and measured his words, "What has happened?" When no one answered, he looked directly at Olivia, "What has happened?"

Olivia curtly asked him, "Did you set the incendiaries at every mapped location?"

"Yes, of course I did, and verified function."

"Do you remember what she said about staying behind to burn with beauty the last time you argued?" She cut the comm.

The vid resumed with the ring of fire ignited one by one.

Naomi grabbed his shirt with one hand and pointed accusingly at the screen with the other. "O'Reilly scanned for her immy chip. She's not up here!" She pumped her fist, yanking him then thrusting him to the limit of his shirt and then, unable to speak further, shoved him against a counter.

Alain stopped the vid at the completed ring of fire, with the billows of sooty smoke, his face bunched and red-blotchy as if he were a physical witness to the flames. "Crannog, they didn't send anything else, your incendiaries were the only fire there." He flung an arm with an accusing finger at the screen. "You set them."

Barto fell to his knees, vomiting bile on the other side of the partition.

Naomi went to Alain and they consoled each other.

* * *

"Marta is on Shuttle Two," Cedric said, trying to achieve a confidence that eluded him. Why were they so intent on that picture? She'd said she would stay and burn, but that was in anger.

Barto whipped around the partition jaguar fast and picked Cedric up to heave him over his head to slam him into the screen, wailing, "She is *there*!"

Cedric's head and body bounced off the screen and he landed heavily on the floor, a leg emitting a sharp report as he landed on it. A moan escaped him as he rolled on it. Had the wall been of harder materials than acoustic tiles, he believed it would have killed him.

All seemed silent for several more minutes, although he had no idea how long he was in-and-out, groggy from his body's response to damage. They all still stood around him, staring. The acute pain in his lower leg helped him to concentrate on consciousness. He raised shoulders up and rolled to sit, bracing with his hands on the floor behind him.

He sat that way until the reverberations in his skull subsided. His vision cleared some and he saw doubles of the incendiaries he personally planted on the creased and torn screen. The incendiaries he volunteered to set up to burn the beauty left behind. He looked around to the others to scratch away some hint of subterfuge, some secret they cruelly withheld as he tried to stop his uncontrolled trembling. Please let then be playing him for the fool again and have it not be true! All he saw was demented grief.

Every straw he flailed for failed him and he could barely control his limbs as he reached to stark conclusion: He adored her, he denied her and he murdered her, burned her like trash. The sea roared in his ears, angry swells crashing into his shipwreck head. Good God in Heaven, he'd murdered her! Wrenching up on his knees with sublime pain, he pounded at the killer within using knotted arms and fists, pummeling the evil that lurked as he plummeted deeper and deeper into a dreadful black abyss.

"I killed her!" he croaked, his eyes bulging at the horror as he fully connected the image in his skull of her being alone on the inhospitable planet with the agony of seeing a firestorm seconds before being burned alive, when his last scrap of reason admitted it *must* be true.

He fell onto his back, feeling himself float into deeper and deeper darkness, the pressure squeezing every drop of humanity from his heart. The last thing he saw was the screen, his tunnel vision centering on the inferno, searing a hole into his brain, as he tumbled into a sulfurous, superheated rift chasm, hideous hagfishes thrashing each other in their haste to taste his fresh flesh.

By the time Barto got himself under control again, Cedric had already clawed one eye into mush and was digging at the other. Barto throttled him and held him like a superstructure holds a rocket until they docked and Dr. Trogden arrived.

chapter 71

Excuses and Goats

The XO shouted shrilly, "O'Reilly, are you certain the pods are vac'd and cooked?"

"Yes, ma'am, AI and I have checked it from every angle, every indicator." She didn't mention that there was no indication of any alien ship anywhere at all, no fabulous rescuer. Marta had stayed with her friends.

"How about weight discrepancies?"

"As reported, no discrepancies. The weight equivalents for the returned supplies and including the other materials stored in that pod show that all is accounted for." There wouldn't be a discrepancy, she'd reset the balance just before take-off to cover the odd goings-on with the water bladders and such.

Char marched from the XO's Station to the Nav Station furious and edgy. "Is there any reason *whatsoever* to alert Tembo Topside of a breach?"

O'Reilly stiffened her spine. "No. Even if there were some tree samples stashed in there, both Cartier and Van Rijn knew how to wrap them securely and they were sterilized. If somehow that screwed up, the vac and gammas have taken care of them. The only organics on that planet were Earth trees, all else was sterile. There is absolutely no threat of biocontamination."

Char's elbows clung to her ribs as she fidgeted with her hands. "Why are you so eager to convince me that all is hunky dory? What are you hiding up your sleeve?"

The Navigator didn't blink. "Ma'am, we always run a clean bus. We pick up Passengers and drop them off like clockwork, no hitches. They trust us with an Expeditionary assignment, six days on a place like that and then resume schedule. What will they think of us if we mishandle an assignment so simple? They'll hang us by our nipples and leave us on Tembo!"

Char chewed a thumbnail and hugged her chest tighter; the other fingernails already gnawed to the quick. "What if they suspect something? What if they find out we had, er, a problem. I mean that damn Van Ruin is *gone!*"

"Commander, they will see what they expect to see. We are set up to divvy out supply pods and passengers and to be the Caesar that Tenembras Topside renders unto. When we get back home the report will agree with AI's assessment that she went AWOL pure and simple."

Char Jones paced in little circles as her mind started ticking. "Why? Why would she do such a stupid thing?"

Olivia O'Reilly knew that look and was ready with the story. "I believe it's because she wanted Crannog as a lover and he spurned her. She decided the trees loved her so she stayed with them. I heard her mention something about staying behind, but discounted it as grief from leaving the others and having to face certain animosity on the return trip."

Jones looked calmer, more in control now, no more chewing. "Animosity, shit. I told Cedric she was poison! Men and their testosterone."

Olivia slid back into her superior attitude, enough wallowing. "Since you asked, he's still under sedation and Doc estimates he'll stay that way until transfer. The one eye is mashed up bad and most of the sclera is lost, the other is damaged but she says the prognosis is good for that one to recover if the retina doesn't detach. The leg set well and should heal straight."

Char flopped down, clearly weary of these damned Passengers. She fingered a small pill in her pocket. "He's their prize engineer and they put a store and a half on him getting there happy and now look, because of that damn Van Ruin." She drummed her bleeding fingertips on the console. "Doc should have seen this coming. What does she have vid rights for when I don't if not to keep the damned Passengers safe?"

Olivia shrugged on cue. "She's very concerned about his well-being when he comes out of sedation. She says he'll need someone to become familiar with his case and trauma very quickly upon arrival." She felt ill setting Ronnie Sue up like that, but the Doctor had told her unequivocally that she did not want to stay on this tub one more minute than she had to. Olivia knew that she'd stashed some contraband in Dr. Cartier's main supply pod, the full one that was on the Frankie. Wasn't that for Roundabout, though? She knew Doc had a place chosen on a Roundabout pod to transfer the pallets to, all neat and clean. "Yes, she blames herself."

Char leapt up. "Damn right! It is her fault! She can stay over there with him! I'll draw up the court martial and we'll take care of it tomorrow." She smiled broadly at coming to a satisfactory conclusion to this whole sorry mess.

Idly, Olivia nudged. "What about the Captain, what if he doesn't agree?"

"He has informed me that it's my baby, he's retiring when we get home. No stomach for leadership and discipline, you know, I've always said it."

Olivia let a little emotion creep into her character since she and Doc Trogden had spend so much time together. "So Trogden is dishonorably discharged, after decades of demanding service at the camps and here? Char, she's just worn out!"

Char twiddled with her pocket. "Oh, all right. Tell her if she'll resign, I'll grant it effective immediately. That'll leave her pension intact."

O'Reilly nodded perceptibly and waited for the Commander to bale now that the axe had fallen acceptably. Didn't Doc did keep her quietly supplied with her little blue helpers and the occasional beer all this time? She could afford to be magnanimous.

Eagerly, Char headed for the door. "Yes, I'll cut her some slack. Now, however, it is high time for a little relaxation after a hectic day. I will be in my cabin, but don't need me."

chapter 12

Next?

Marta looked around among the scraggly Earth trees in their matrix and the aliens among them, soaking up nutrients and bathing in the artificial light. 'It is the right thing,' she repeated to herself, her new mantra. It tore her heart to see Barto that last time, making sure she was not in the pod. Luckily, Bin-Thaa was wide enough to hide her easily, shielding her from view.

Since then all but TaaTaa lined up along the back wall in an unplanted lane, sleek brown columns, receptors curled inward at the top. TaaTaa indicated it was a good thing, so she figured it must be sleep or travel-dormancy or something akin and he was the watch, maybe something to do with the increased oxygen in the air for her sake. Or maybe he simply wanted to keep her company? She appreciated the company, intended or not.

There were spare coveralls in a supply bundle, there for no other reason than divine intervention as far as she could tell. Whatever the excuse for them, they allowed her to shuck the reeking suit layers as one big exoskeleton, taking great care to pull the mess away from the scab forming from her chip-removal self-surgery. She bathed quickly by swiping wet wipes at key spots, one for her face and neck alone, and happily donned the clean garment. She hadn't spotted any soap while packing, though there was probably an antiseptic scrub in the emergency kit for her mangled shoulder.

As she walked around bladders and over hoses inspecting the systems they'd so carefully put together, she remembered all the hidden monitors and actuators that tall BinThaa and meticulous TaaTaa had pointed out to her; she would never have detected all them alone.

All she had to do was point out the dangerous devices and sensors and they combed the place with their wide spectrum, penetrating sight and found more and more, the sterilizer units shining like novae to them. Level 3 AI qualification certainly came in handy, but really was not much more useful than the hacks she'd learned at college.

Her smile beamed forth with no restrictions or regrets and, with the conspicuous absence of her self-conscious shell, she felt free in her crowded terrarium. What were her human friends thinking now? She had said goodbye and they probably figured she'd sneaked into the pod anyway. Barto probably laughed about her fooling him regardless of her chip telling them all she was among the trees.

She'd been nosy as a nanny goat about that buggy Cedric drove up the last minute, but had refrained from digging into until all the vents clicked without opening and the lenses in her eyes didn't cloud over from a gamma dose. Her suspense lasted until each known device clicked on then off and it continued a while longer until no others actuated. Finally, she felt sure that if the air was still on it would stay on. She would worry about the prodigious amounts of oxygen she'd have to maintain later.

That settled, she could address the tantalizing buggy and its crates in peace. She chose a small box with a lid already pried loose since she had no tools out and it was easy.

With a large bulb cradled her hand, she flashed back to the box she shared with her mother; they were too hungry for tears as she diced the heirloom tulip bulbs and tossed them into the can of boiling water to avert starvation. She realized she had dipped into a dark stream of times past and yanked herself back to reality. This new beginning came replete with the cart goodies, a crate of food packs and fresh apples on top al all that.

She kissed the bulb and cradled it again. She closed her eyes to remember Keukenhof Gardens in May, when garden after garden showcased the gracious Dutch art of extracting amazing beauty from a humble bulb, seeing the riotous yet organized bursts of hues and the myriad of shapes and arrangements, all interspersed with fanciful sculptures and practical art, a welcome memory. She carried the box of bulbs, one special giant for Barto, and ones nearly as large for Alain, Naomi, Thao, TaaTaa, herself and one oddly striated one for Cedric who brought them as if on the wings of good angels.

She set them at the end where there hadn't been enough time to get more trees, near the heat trace but not so close to burn, and where the overhead sloped too low for her Amigos. She harked back to halcyon times and prepared to plant as Mama taught her. 'Talk to the bulb,' she murmured, 'learn how she wants to be placed. Just so.' There, she planted Barto's.

Her peripheral vision caught TaaTaa stroking Alain's bulb. He passed the bulb to lower 'hands' and squeaked at it. He extended a sensory rod above it, as if listening. He turned the bulb counter clockwise and stopped, retrograded a bit, then set it firmly in the sandy dirt. He covered it gently.

Marta wondered, would they grow and blossom? Who could tell? As much as she thought she knew about tulips, she had no idea if the bulbs could survive so many years in a cool, sterile, low ox environment. The changes in gravity as the shuttle met up with the Franklin in a couple weeks, the short time on the interstellar and then again as the shuttle left Frankie for Tembo Topside and then the arrival at Tembo's Ag Domes might confuse them, but that's how life went. Tenembras loomed as a huge unknown for all of them; hot, dusty, what else? The most certain thing she knew at that moment, her comfort and hope, was that TaaTaa and Marta together were planting a beautiful garden.

The End

Made in the USA
Lexington, KY
02 December 2014